See You On The Other Side

I0556502

Willow Salix

DragonCat Press

Welcome to the third book in the Carpe Noctem World, thanks for coming back and continuing to support both my world and the characters that we all love so much. I hope you enjoying reading about them as much as I do translating them to the written page.

As always, my first acknowledgments go to my grandparents, Joan and Albert who always taught me to believe in myself and give everything a try (even if it was just in going for a wee before a long car journey).

Next thanks have to go to my family, who put up with my madness, the times I talk about my characters as if they were real and tel them their entire life stories, and stop me from spontaneously combusting from book related stress.
Special thanks have to go to those in my life that never fail in their support, Linda who edits, reads and corrects my incoherent scribblings and my friends who never complain even when I rant for more than an hour.

I adore you all.

Want more Carpe Noctem? Well don't forget to pop along to my website where you can find short stories, in-depth character bios, explore the places and brush up on your vocabulary.
Find all this and more at www.willowsalix.com

Chapter One

1664

Avery refused to let any more tears fall, he was a man now, one that would have to make his own way in the world, a man that had no one to count on but himself. He tossed the flower down into the grave and turned away from the last earthly remains of his family. His mother and two younger sisters had succumbed to plague, his father to drink, leaving Avery, at the age of 12, all alone in the world.

Not knowing what to do and having very little skills Avery soon found himself homeless, weak from hunger and in desperate need of a miracle. He had tried to find work here and there, doing odd jobs to earn a crust, but most would just yell at him to go away, not wanting the likes of him, a little street urchin, hanging around their property. He survived by eating scraps he found left outside or the odd thing he managed to steal, but it was barely enough to keep a growing boy alive.

He would have died on the streets that winter, as many did, had he not had the good fortune to meet with a man that worked aboard a ship that had recently sailed into port. They were in need of a new cabin boy, the previous one having been a sickly child that died a little way into the journey. Avery was given the chance to prove himself, and that was just what he did.

1672

Avery's ship, the Evening Star, was returning to port, their hold filled with the spoils of their labours. Several Spanish merchant ships had been intercepted and relieved of choice items from their cargo. As their letter of marque decreed, they were returning to share their haul with the authorities. Privateers were given the protection of the crown and government in return for a percentage of the treasures they raided from treasure ships returning to Spain.

They had gained quite a reputation for being one of the best crews working the seas for many years. Their captain insisted that they only attack at night, always going for the element of surprise. He said that the darkness was his friend, that the sun pained him, hurting his eyes, so spending most of his time below decks when it was daylight. Though, his affliction hadn't stopped him from being a very capable and well-respected captain to his crew.

As they always did, rather than sailing straight into port and docking they steered away from port, heading to a small, secluded cove known to but a few. Their purpose there was to relieve themselves of some of their cargo before docking, meaning they had less on board to be split with the authorities. Cheeky perhaps, but they saw it as a necessary evil.

The cove was busy that night, luckily for them as it turned out. Another ship was already there, whose captain was friendly with theirs. It was decided that while part of the haul was taken from the ship and hidden the captains would retire to the Star's main cabin for drinks and to catch up on any news. This was where their luck came in. It became apparent while the captains conversed, that a number of crews had returned to find themselves in trouble, their letters of marque having been revoked while they were at sea.

Fearing that they too might have suffered the same misfortune, Avery's captain, whom always erred on the side of caution, decided that a small number of their party would take one of the small dinghies into port to gather information and basic supplies.

Avery was amongst the few chosen to go, much to his delight, for in that port lived the girl he intended to marry, his sweetheart, the tavern maid, Margaret. He had been without her company for far too long and was practically jumping for joy at the prospect of seeing her again. He couldn't wait to show her the little ring he had been given as his share of one such treasure acquiring expedition and to prove to her that he was worthy of her hand, that he could provide for her a comfortable home and to make a living for their future family.

Under cover of darkness they rowed their little dinghy into port, docking in a secluded spot before splitting up, each with their own job to complete. Avery was charged with purchasing their supply of dried meats needed to see them through a few more weeks at sea if they had to leave. But he believed he had plenty of time, a quick visit to his woman wouldn't cause any harm, surely?

Margaret seemed very happy to see him, throwing herself into his arms as he stepped through the door, plying him with ale and kisses and even bursting into tears when he told her that he was unable to stay. She begged and pleaded with him, pouting when he refused to tell her why he was not staying. Avery couldn't bear her tears, he had always been a bit of a wimp when it came to disappointing a female, he'd never been able to say no to his sisters.

"You don't love me, Avery Callow! If you did you would tell me where you were. Unless you have another love, is that it?"

Desperate to prove his loyalty and love for her, he gave her the ring, asking for her hand in marriage which she readily agreed to, but still she would not let him leave without telling her what was wrong.

"If I am to be your wife, you cannot keep things from me, it's not right. Tell me, I beg of you." She looked up at him, her soft brown eyes swimming with tears, a bosom that heaved just enough to draw his eye and he was lost.

"You're right, my love, what harm can come of telling you?" Avery proceeded to tell her where they were docked, that they suspected they were now seen as the worst kind of crew, Pirates. Leaving her with the promise to return as soon as possible, Avery rushed to complete his task, procuring all the meats he could lay his hands on and carrying it back to the little row boat where the others were already waiting with the unwelcome news they had all been dreading, their marque had indeed been revoked.

They had been back at the Evening Star less than an hour before they were making their way out to sea, the items hastily stored in the ships galley. They had gone maybe two miles when members of the crew spotted a ship trailing them. The warning had barely left their lips when the sound of cannon fire rent the air, the Star shaking violently as the shots hit their target. The tailing ship drew alongside the Star and its crew began to pour over the side, trying to climb aboard. The Star's crew would not go down without a fight, picking off a good number of the invaders as they scaled her sides.

Avery fought as best he could, his opponent seeming vaguely familiar, he recognised his face even if he didn't recall where he had seen him before. It wasn't until their swords struck that he noticed the little ring glinting on the man's pinkie finger, one that he had given to Margaret mere hours before.

At that moment it dawned on Avery where he knew him from, he had seen this man sitting in the corner of the tavern as he entered but had paid him no heed, he only had eyes for Margaret. The realization caused him to falter, it was but a second, but it was long enough. This was to be a fatal mistake.

His crew were gaining the upper hand, fighting back the invading men, but it was too late for Avery. He doubled over as he felt the cold steel of his opponents blade thrust between his ribs.

Coughing and chocking, his left lung refusing to work, his chest cavity filling with blood, Avery collapsed to the floor. His last sight was the laughing face of the man that had killed him, his last thought was of the woman he loved, she who had betrayed him to her new lover, therefore endangering them all.

Chapter Two

Avery stretched his arms back over his head, working the kinks out of his spine. He'd spent the last twenty-four hours -including his death sleep- sitting in this blasted chair beside his bed, in which Amy's sister lay. He had his feet propped up on the bed beside her, his legs stretched out, but other than that he was bolt upright in the armchair, and he was bloody uncomfortable.

Honestly, he thought, first he'd had to spend the night in a cell and then was released only to be told he was now on baby vamp duty, could the week get any worse? Sure, he was happy that everyone was alive and well, and that he was no longer in the frame as a murderer, but really, he needed a break.

He looked over at her again, she looked pale, obviously. But the bite marks that had littered her neck and upper chest were almost gone, fading as her body healed itself. She really was rather beautiful if you liked the plain ones, but they weren't his type. Avery tended to go for the more obvious girls, those that wore make-up, short skirts and weren't shy in their quest for a good time.

His nose wrinkled as he studied her, noting with renewed interest, that she didn't look all that plain any more. Her hair was now loose from the severe bun she favoured and tumbled around the pillow in golden curls almost the exact shade of his own. Her face was relaxed in sleep, the frown lines he'd seen every other time they'd met had smoothed away, leaving her looking younger than before.

Having nothing else to do but wait, he challenged himself to conjure up a few thoughts on how he could keep her looking so relaxed, finding that the experience wasn't as hard as he thought it would be. Maybe he had misjudged her? He looked at her again, taking in her full, inviting lips, the elegant slope of her neck that led down to a chest that could drive a man insane. Where had she been hiding that?

He shifted again in the chair, trying to coax some feeling back into his numb backside. Yes, it certainly helped to have such a pleasant specimen in his bed, but he knew the peace wouldn't last. soon enough she'd be awake and then the real hard work would start. Fledgling Vampires weren't the easiest to look after, constantly needing attention and near constant supervision.

He sighed, guessing he'd have to put the search for his Soul Mate on hold. *But really*, he scolded himself when he realised how bitter he sounded, *what's a little bit longer when he had already waited over 350 years?*

He was jerked from his thoughts by the sound of a low moan. He glanced over at Sapphire, noting that her famous frown lines were back.

Urghh this was the part that he hated, it always hurt like fuck for the fledgling and there was nothing that could be done to ease it, they just had to ride it out.

He watched as her body began to thrash, the Vampire blood mixing with her own, racing through her veins, changing her genetic makeup, changing her. Avery was out of the chair in a flash, diving on top of her writhing body, trying to hold her down, not wanting her to hurt herself.

He pinned her down with his body, holding her arms above her head, but by the gods she was already so strong. He debated on grabbing the bed ties he had in his closet but knew that if he let her go now, she could hurt herself, he had no choice but to hold on for the ride.

He snuggled his body closer to hers, putting more weight down on her pinned wrists, his legs and lower body entangled with hers. She was jerking violently now, and he took a second to think that she was actually turning earlier than was normal, he'd have to look into that at some point, but it was really hard to think with her lush little body rubbing itself against his and he almost immediately lost his train of thought.

Sapphire didn't have a clue where she was, she was just sitting in some kind of limbo, her back against a wall, her knees up under her chin, arms wrapped around her legs, curled up in as small a ball as she could.

She didn't feel right, she'd feel too hot and then, too cold. Her body hurt, ached all over. She raised her head to look around seeing nothing but swirling mist. Well, that sucked.

Then suddenly she didn't have time to think about anything but the fire that flashed through her veins, forcing a scream from her throat, her body dropping to the ground as if a heavy weight pinned her there. She twitched and jerked, her arms feeling like they were being forced back over her head. She had to get free, she had to get away! She went still, gathering her strength, then gave one almighty yank. The weight fell away from her chest, allowing her to sit up, the mist vanishing.

Avery flew back as her spine flexed and she jolted bolt upright. He managed to catch himself on his arms as she opened her eyes and started to scream.

Avery did the first thing that popped into his head, he screamed right back, directly in her face. Which surprisingly shocked her into shutting up. She blinked once, then twice, before shutting her mouth with a snap, yelping in pain as something stabbed her bottom lip.

"Oww, what the hell?" she slurred, trying to speak around her newly pointed canines. Her hand went to her mouth to feel the damage, coming away smeared with blood. Her nose twitched at the scent, but she ignored it, her focus returning to the male that was currently straddling her legs, holding her down.

"Get the hell off me!" she yelled at him, yanking her legs out from under his butt and up to her chest.

Avery couldn't help but smile at the adorably fierce look on her face, her delicate little fangs were peeking out from between her slightly parted lips. He could still smell the lingering scent of her fear, like burning rubber on the air. But she was hiding it well, a fact that rather impressed him. He wasn't ashamed to admit that he had almost shit a brick (not that Vampires possessed that bodily function) when he had woken up with fangs and no heartbeat. Though by the look of things she hadn't noticed...

"I'm dead! I'm dead and I'm stuck in hell with you!" Her hand was nestled right between her breasts- somewhere Avery wouldn't mind his being- desperately feeling for some kind of movement in her chest, a breath, a heartbeat, but he knew she would find neither. Older Vampires learnt how to make their bodies do those things, as a way of blending in with the mortals, but they didn't need to do it to survive and when they needed to conserve some energy those were the first things to go.

"Darlin', calm down." He just wanted to scoop her up into his arms and make everything better again, though he knew that wasn't possible. He could never turn back the clock and fix what that arsehole had broken.

"What happened to me? What did you do to me?" He could hear the panic rising in her voice. But now wasn't the time to discuss what had really happened.

He needed to get her to feed, it would settle her body down and make her feel much better, though it was easier

9

said than done. It wasn't the easiest thing to suggest to a woman as straight-laced as her. He could just hear himself now, *Hey, princess, be a good girl and suck on my wrist, will you? No, I'm not being kinky, you just need to drink my blood.* He rolled his eyes. That would be as bad as when Amy had found them all in the V.I.P area and accused them of being sexual deviants.

Sapphire wasn't sure what was going on, but she wasn't happy about it, she was in a strange bed in a strange room with an even stranger man. She didn't feel right, and was halfway convinced that she'd been drugged, it was the only explanation. Now that Avery had moved off her legs she forced herself to calm down, flopping back against the pillows, covering her eyes with her arm, letting out a deep groan. She just needed to regain her composure, she was obviously in a panic and that was stopping her from feeling her heartbeat, the one that couldn't not be there. It had to be. She felt fear welling up inside her, she had to get away from this madness and the man that always seemed to be around when shit was going south.

Flinging her legs over the side of the bed, ignoring how damned wobbly they felt, she launched herself up and out of the room, tearing down the hallway. But she didn't get far before a sharp pain shot through her abdomen, dropping her to the floor. Holy shit! It felt like the most intense period pain she had ever experienced coupled with what she imagined the weight of a large elephant making himself comfy on her belly, would feel like.

She couldn't think, could only feel, barely registering the racing footsteps behind her. Strong, yet incredibly gentle arms scooped her up, cradling her against a chest that any other time she would have been very pleased to be so up close and personal with. But right now she just wanted to die. Again.

Avery laid her back down on the bed she had woken up in. She tried to take deep breaths but found that the intake of air made her cough, doubling her over as she rolled onto her side. She pulled her legs up to her chest as her stomach began to cramp, feeling like her insides were tying themselves in knots, burning like they were on fire. It was like a mixture of the worst cramps imaginable and a bone deep hunger. She felt like she could devour a Big Mac, large fries, a huge milkshake and maybe a pizza too, along with an entire box of chocolates and still have room for more. She moaned her discomfort, fingers clawing at the sheets as she tried to straighten but couldn't.

Here we go, Avery thought, *she needs to feed*. Her body would be wracked with pain until she drank from someone. He didn't think there was any way she would drink from a Donor even if he had time to call for one and she needed blood from a vein to complete the transformation. Nope, this was all on him.

Letting his own fangs run out he nipped at his wrist, splitting the skin just enough to get a little blood flowing, he moved closer.

Saph's nose twitched, picking up a scent. It was the most delicious thing she had ever smelt, more delicious than a Sunday roast or the sweetest chocolate cake. Her stomach cramped again even as she tried to roll over to get closer to the heavenly smell. Avery wafted his wrist under her nose, watching as her eyes followed his movements.

Saph didn't know what she was thinking or feeling, the world had receded into nothing but that smell, her eyes clouded over a she reached out, reacting on pure instinct. She grabbed at the source of the smell and pulled it closer. Her tongue darted out to lick at his skin and Avery tried to suppress a shiver at the sensation as she lapped at him like a cat would a bowl of cream. He braced himself, knowing what was coming next.

Sapphire's mouth felt weird, like there was a pressure bearing down on her gums, like her mouth suddenly felt over crowded, but she couldn't think about that right now, she ignored the weird feelings as she licked at the delicious

11

liquid that coated her tongue. She needed more, and the substance was almost gone. Without meaning to or even knowing why, she bit down, instantly moaning as more of the decadent sweetness flowed over her tongue and down her throat. Swallowing convulsively, the pain in her stomach easing with each mouthful, she clung tighter, her hands gripping Avery's arm as she fed.

Avery gently stroked her hair, soothing her as well as himself as she fed, her movements going from frantic to lazy sucking as unconsciousness claimed her again. He lay down stretching out beside her, figuring they were both in for a long night, he might as well rest when he could.

Sapphire blinked her eyes open, squinting against the bright light in the room. She wanted to get out of bed and turn it off, but her body felt like it was made of stone, unable to move even if she wanted to. And she didn't, not really, her body felt blissfully pain free after the night she had had, though she didn't recall much of it.

Much like any other sickness bug she had had, her stomach had cramped as it churned, and she had drifted in and out of consciousness. Saph really didn't do ill. She hated being unwell, out of control of her body, in life Saph was always in control and was loath to give that up for anything. Being out of control made her feel uncomfortable, skittish, panicked. Not that she would ever show that to anyone, she was the sensible one, the one in control, the stability of their little family.

She commanded her body to roll over and to her surprise it did as it was told. She snuggled closer to the warm body in the bed with her, closing her eyes again... warm body? Her eyes sprang open like a jack-in-the-box lid as she propelled herself backwards, hands pushing at the brawny chest of the male.

"Your actions lead me to believe that you're no longer happy to see me." The rumbling, sleep filled voice took her by surprise. She looked again as a large, very male hand

12

pushed back the golden hair from his face, revealing Avery's lazy grin, his still sleepy eyes at half-mast.

There was something undeniably sexy about his pose, lying casually on his side, head propped up on his hand, his lion's mane like hair spilling around his face, with a cheeky grin that probably had women's panties dropping like bombs the second he unleashed it on their unsuspecting selves.

But Saph was immune to such things, and yes, she would keep telling herself that over and over until it stuck. She backed away some more, pulling together all her hidden reserves of calm and control. Schooling her face to show nothing but indifference she answered him.

"I have never been happy to see you."

Avery opened his mouth to argue, "I beg to differ, you..." But she cut him off, suddenly angry. She who never broke her calm façade, never lost her temper, was so angry she was spitting like a cobra.

"No, you! You have been there when my sister was in trouble, you were the one that came to my house, you and your freaky friends have practically brainwashed Amy and now I've woken up to find myself in a strange bedroom. So, no, I am not happy to see you and never will be." She was panting, trying to catch her breath by the time she had finished her rant.

Avery just looked as shocked as she was at the words that had flown out of her mouth like bullets, she didn't know where the outburst had come from. She had just felt it and had said it, with no planning, no thinking through, no control. She had the instant urge to say sorry but if her job had taught her anything it was that if you made a decision or said something, you stuck by it, you owned it. Never back down, backing down was to show weakness and she was anything but weak.

Avery had never expected her to have an explosion like that. But in a sick kind of way he liked it. He liked the fire in her eyes, the venom to her words, he found it kinda sexy, but then, he had always been attracted to strong women.

Ones who could stand up for themselves and he sensed that beneath her cool, composed exterior, was a core of steel. And he just bet that that steel was wrapped in passion and fire and feelings that she tried so hard to never show. The naughty part of him that always seemed to be nudging him to push his luck, reared its head again. *Push her*, it urged.

He laid back down flat on the bed, stretching out, his hands clasped behind his head, looking perfectly relaxed. And that annoyed Saph. How dare he be all relaxed and sure of himself when she was freaking out!

She took a few deep breaths, trying to keep calm and she almost succeeded, until he made it worse.

"You were happy to see me when you were sucking on my wrist like I was a buffet."

Saph blinked. She was what?

"I can assure you I would do no such thing," she spluttered, outraged.

"You did, and you loved it," he taunted in a ridiculous sing song voice.

"Why the hell would I do that? I'm not into kink."

Avery debated for a second, not really knowing what to do for the best. Did he tip toe around her and break the news to her slowly and gently, or just blurt it out? He knew from her sisters that she reacted better when she had all the facts, that she appreciated someone being honest and straight forward with her.

Screw it, he was going for it. Keeping his voice calm and cool he answered her question.

"Because you're a Vampire now, like me, and you needed to feed." He screwed his eyes shut, dreading her reaction. Would she burst into tears, yell and scream, or simply go quiet, traumatised by this new information? But once again, she surprised him.

Saph burst out laughing, she couldn't help it, it was just so laughable, of all the things she had guessed he might say, that wasn't one of them. That was something her sister

14

would come out with and actually believe, Tanzanite believed anything, but not her, Sapphire was the sensible one, you couldn't pull the wool over her eyes.

"I'm glad you're finding it so amusing," Avery grumped in a very put-upon voice. "Makes me wonder just why the he l l bothered to stick around all night looking after you, worried that if you woke up on your own and found out, you would be scared. How stupid of me." Feeling extremely pissed off now, he stomped out of the bedroom, slamming the door behind him.

Saph wasn't too sure what had just happened there, how the normally affable Avery could turn so suddenly. But more to the point, why the hell did she care? It wasn't as if she liked the big oaf and really, he didn't deserve her concern when he had just outright lied to her face. All she wanted was the truth, to know what had happened to her, why her body felt like it had been run over by a monster truck one minute, then like she had necked an entire bottle of vitamins washed down by several RedBulls, the next. The only thing that felt vaguely uncomfortable was how hungry she felt, but then, if she had been stricken with some kind of bug as she suspected she had, she probably hadn't eaten in days.

She racked her brains, trying to recall anything of the past few days that could have made her so ill. She didn't remember much past leaving work, late as usual, but lured home by the promise of takeout with her sister. She screwed up her nose in concentration, mentally flipping back through snap shots of memory as they surfaced in her befuddled brain. She recalled a man, one that was familiar and scary, the aura of danger rolled off him in waves. She struggled to picture his face, absently rubbing at her throat, trying again to feel for her elusive pulse. It was then that his face popped into her mind's eye with crystal clarity. The face of a ghost, the face of someone supposed to be dead and buried years ago. Jason.

The minute his name whispered from her lips like magic words, it opened the flood gates, memories assaulting her.

15

She saw it all played out in her memories like a movie trailer, Jason grabbing her, punching her in the face to knock her out, then waking up tied to a chair in an almost pitch-black cellar. She remembered the pain, lots and lots of pain, like searing needles in her skin as he bit her over and over again. She recalled how her body had grown weaker and weaker through loss of blood. She remembered how it had run down from her many wounds, dripping off onto the floor to form a pool around her.

She almost whimpered as she remembered the way he had waved that knife of his around, first slashing at her flesh before he sliced at his own, holding his bleeding wound against her lips, forcing her mouth open so the rank substance filled her mouth, sliding down her throat no matter how much she tried to reject it. She almost gagged thinking about the bitter taste of it. It tasted evil, rotten to the core, she didn't know how she knew what evil tasted like, but she did.

She remembered how it felt to feel her heart judder to a stop in her chest, her breathing to cease, her world to stop.

And now here she was, back again, conscious and aware. Not wanting to believe it but unable to deny the truth any longer, she tentatively slipped a finger into her mouth and ran the pad of her finger along her teeth, feeling the unmistakable sharpness that confirmed what Avery had told her. Unable to comprehend what was happening, her brain going into Danger-Will-Robinson style panic, she opened her mouth and did the only thing she could. She began to scream.

Avery stomped his way around his kitchen, swigging angrily from a bottle of Bud, it wouldn't do anything about his mood, but it made him feel a little more in control just from having something to focus on, the cool liquid sliding down his throat helped to distract his thoughts from the woman in his bedroom. *No*, he told himself firmly, *I won't think about her, she's nothing to me, she won't ever understand our ways or what she is. Screw her.*

He finished off his beer, defiantly tossing the empty bottle into the regular rubbish, ignoring the recycling bin. As soon as he finished the drink he could have kicked himself, he should really have taken some blood to replenish what he d fed Sapphire... and there she was again, right in the forefront of his brain, making herself perfectly at home like a damned squatter.

He was just about to say a very loud 'fuck it' and grab another beer when her scream tore through the silence of the house. He spun round and dashed back down the hall, leaping up the stairs like he had a rocket up his arse, bursting into the bedroom expecting to see her at the very least being tortured by a scary clown making her balloon animals (OK so that was his reason for screaming like a girl but his point still stood) instead he found her curled up in a ball in the middle of his bed, rumpled sheets all around her like a nest, her fingers fisted in her hair as she screamed, a full out, soul deep, emptying the lungs scream that made his throat hurt in sympathy. Without thinking through the wisdom of his decision - going near a hysterical woman had never been on his list of top ten pastimes- he sat down rext to her, pulling her onto his lap.

The second Saph found herself on Avery's lap was the moment she lost it completely, all her anger draining away to be replaced with tears. Racking sobs that shook her whole body as she sniffled and snorted into his shirt. Avery, to his credit, didn't push her away in disgust, but held her tighter, rocking her as he stroked her hair and whispered soothing nonsense into her ear.

She couldn't deal with this, felt too out of control, like her carefully built walls were tumbling down brick by brick, every bit of contrcl she had fought for was slipping through her fingers. She had fangs! She was dead! She was the freak she had always dreaded that she was. How stupid of her to

17

ever think that she could escape the curse of the Summerland Family.

They all had some weirdness about them, something that made them stand out from the crowd and no matter how hard she tried to bury hers, to ignore it, it still popped back up, it just wouldn't stay hidden. And now, now she had something else to make her even more of a weirdo than she was before, damn she must have overtaken Tanzi by now.

There is something very therapeutic about crying, but at some point you have to just stop and deal with it, you can't cry forever, you run out of tears, your nose grows stuffy and you give yourself a headache. Then you have to stop, take a good look at the situation and work out a game plan.

Slowly she sat up, accepting the tissues that Avery silently handed her, dabbing at her eyes.

"Better?" Avery asked.

Sniffing, she nodded, falling silent as she pulled herself together, her hands automatically trying to smooth her hair back into its customary bun, shuddering with horror to find it falling wildly around her shoulders. Without a word Avery leaned across the bed, opened a bedside draw and handed her a brush and a hair band. She studied the brush for a second, spotting a few golden strands tangled in the bristles, knowing it belonged to him. She didn't know what to say, his gesture was so thoughtful, he seemed to constantly be surprising her.

She took a moment to brush the tangles out of her hair and tie it back, feeling a little more in control with each stroke of the brush. When she was done she finally felt calm enough to ask the one question that had been rolling around her head.

"Am I dead?"

Avery had been dreading that question, there was no easy answer. So instead he took her hand in his and held it against his chest.

"Do I feel dead? Do you feel dead?"

Sapphire looked up into his eyes, his sparkling baby blues, like a clear summer sky, and felt his heart beating steadily under her palm, felt the heat of his skin. No. He did not feel dead. And apart from her lack of distinguishable heartbeat, she felt the same as ever, better in fact, apart from that gnawing hunger in her belly that still wouldn't go. Slowly she shook her head.

"No."

He sprawled himself back against the pillows, but didn't force her to go with him, leaving her with enough personal space that she felt it was her own choice to lay beside him.

"Technically, we are undead, but I'm not talking Dracula here, we're not evil. I mean sure you get the odd few bad eggs like you do with anything but on the whole we're just normal people going about our business. We just happen to drink blood to survive, sleep during the day and are allergic to sunlight. No big deal. Our bodies have essentially been frozen at this point in time. We're immortal as long as we don't get staked or our heads cut off, now come on, that's not too bad is it?"

"Yes!" Sapphire was appalled. "What about my sisters? I don't want to outlive them by maybe hundreds of years, they're all I have. I don't want to live without them."

Avery looked slightly uncomfortable, running his fingers through his hair to scratch at the back of his neck.

"Actually, as long as nothing happens to Cassian, Amy will live forever too, she's his Soul Mate."

This was something new. Sapphire barely knew they were dating let alone anything special.

"What's a Soul Mate?" The way Avery had said it, with such reverence and importance that she could practically hear the capitalisation of the words, told her it was something more than a simple term for a loved one.

Avery stretched out further, getting comfy, like he was planning on being there for a long time. Taking the hint, she lay down beside him, careful not to let their bodies touch, she had the feeling that he wouldn't need much encouragement to try to twist things to his advantage.

"A Soul Mate is your perfect partner. Vampires have a belief that there is one person out there that's perfect for you, just one. And not everyone is lucky enough to find theirs. Some search their entire lives for that one."

Sapphire snorted. "Sounds like a lot of wasted effort to me. Why not just date like normal people?"

Avery chuckled. He couldn't help it. He flashed her an indulgent smile, like he was explaining how to go potty to a two year old.

"We do date like normal people, thank you very much. But it's hard. If we date a human, we have maybe ten years with them, tops."

"Why?" The confusion on her face was clear to see.

Avery raised an eyebrow, giving her a look that clearly accused her of not engaging her brain. Saph ignored the look, her body had been through a lot the past few days and she'd taken in a lot of information since she woke, she could be forgiven for not having her Oxford trained brain in gear. Seeing that she was not inclined to think about it or add anything, Avery took pity on her.

"It would look pretty suspicious if one partner aged and the other didn't. Soon we'd end up looking like one of those couples with a thirty year age gap. It's not fun. And even if you can stand that, imagine watching your lover age and die while you stayed the same, unable to help them unless you turned them. And then it wouldn't last, Vampire couples rarely do, we are predators." He paused when she opened her mouth to interject, holding up his hand to silence her, earning himself a glare for his troubles. "In the nicest possible way. We feed, we stalk, we hunt, that's how it's always been, it's part of the Vampire nature. We are used to being the top of the food chain, the strongest, the fastest, the superior being. Now imagine a power couple like that, both of you, even though it's mostly not a conscious thing, fighting to be the top dog in the relationship. It never works.

20

Sure, some manage better than others, last hundreds of years, but even then they usually take breaks of a few decades now and then. With a Soul Mate its different, they are usually human."

Avery watched as Saph pondered this, letting the information swirl around her head. As usual she had some questions. He wondered if there was anything she didn't question. He could practically see the cogs turning in her brain as she processed all the new information, thinking it through.

"If the Soul Mate is human, don't they still die? Wouldn't you have the same problem? And if one was human and the other Vampire, and with all you just said about Vampires being the dominant in the relationship, doesn't the Vampire control and bully their Soul Mate? And how does Amy being Cassian's Soul Mate make any difference?" Thoughts of all her sister had been through were at the forefront of her mind, but ten times worse with the strength and speed of a Vampire behind it. Hell, look at what Jason had done to her and she was just a pawn in his game.

"Soul Mates are special, they complement their Vampire in every way, they soothe the rougher edges of the Vampire's nature. The Vampire bonds with their Soul Mate and the Soul Mate if not already immortal, will then be tied to the Vampire, sharing his or her life force. Basically, the Soul Mate will be as frozen in their body as the Vampire is until the Vampire dies then the Soul Mate dies too. So unless someone stakes Cass or lops his head off, Amy will be around for a long time."

Saph let his words sink in, comforted by the possibility of never losing her beloved sister again.

"But what about Tanzi?" She nibbled nervously on her thumb nail, not even realising she was doing it.

"We hope that she is someone's Mate too, that she lets one of us turn her or she lives out her life to the fullest of its time as is natural." He shrugged, "We can't force her to do anything, but she has options."

21

Saph nodded, forcing herself not to cry again, it was all a bit too much, all seeming to happen at once, none of which she was able to control and that made her nervous. And if that wasn't bad enough the hunger was back.

"I'm hungry," she knew that her voice had taken on a whining note, but she couldn't help it, she just wanted this day, night whatever it was, to be over and to wake up the next morning to find that it had all just been a bad dream.

Avery jumped up from the bed and scooted out the door. In the distance Sapphire heard the muffled ping of a microwave. All too soon he was back, holding out a mug that had a picture of a cartoon Vampire on it, obviously left over from Halloween.

"Drink up," he smiled, handing her the mug.

"What is it, some kind of soup?" she asked as she accepted the mug and took a tentative sip.

"Nope, its B positive," he grinned, tucking his hands into his jeans pockets, rocking back on his heels, neatly avoiding getting splattered as Saph choked on the thick, warm gloop, spraying it back out of her mouth.

"Ewww, what the hell? It tastes like licking a battery. Why would you give me this?"

Avery didn't seem moved by her dramatic outburst.

"Because, sweetcheeks, you're a Vampire now, you need blood to survive. So, you got two choices. You drink from a Donor, which we don't have here right now, or you drink it bottled. I even prepared it for you, warmed it and everything. Now drink up so you can grow big and strong."

Saph glared at him, but she saw the logic in his words. She didn't like the idea of a Donor, biting someone and drinking their blood, it was all just a little too Dracula cliché for her liking. If she was going to be a Vampire, and let's face it, she didn't have a choice in that, then she could at least have a choice in how she decided to live. She would be like a vegetarian, a vegan vamp, she wouldn't bite anyone ever, she would live on this bottled blood and get on with her life as best she could.

22

Decision made she took another, experimental sip. And almost gagged. Damn that tasted like shit. But even that tiny amount had eased the aching knot of hunger in her stomach. Avery was right, she needed this.

Pinching her nose shut, she downed the mug as quickly as possible. It was mind over matter, she forced herself to ignore the thicker texture, the way it seemed to coat her throat as it went down. It was a very unpleasant sensation, and one she was sure would take her a long time to get used to.

Avery watched her drinking with undisguised amusement. He loved how she came across as so unflappable and in control but then out came this drama queen when he least expected it. He guessed that was why they always said, never judge a book by its cover. He took the dirty mug off her and headed for the door.

"Rest, sleep. You need it. Your body is still adjusting to the changes it's going through. I'll see you when you wake." Without waiting for an answer or for her to argue and start questioning him again, he shut the door behind him.

Avery leant back against the closed door, closing his eyes as he took a deep breath. He had the distinct feeling that he was going to have trouble keeping his distance frcm Sapphire. She was growing on him the more time he spent with her. If he wasn't careful the Vampire known for being a hopeless romantic was about to fall again.

Chapter Three

The crime scene tape flapped in the wind, the flashing lights and crackle of radios disturbed what would otherwise have been a quiet time of night. The club's doors had shut more than an hour ago, the last patron having stumbled giggling on their way, either straight home or to ease their sudden urge for greasy food to line their alcohol drenched stomachs.

A stomach churning stench of urine and human waste hung in the air like a fog in the small alleyway, the smell seemed to sink into the pores, clinging to the inside of your lungs. It was a smell that never seemed to leave.

She lay there, her glassy, sightless eyes staring up to heaven, her jeans wet at the crotch, the stain obviously the source of the offending smell. But that wasn't the worst part, that would be the guts that spilled from the large gash in her creamy flesh, spread out like they were on display, which in a way they were, they had been very deliberately arranged that way, neatly and shown off to their full extent.

Her handbag lay beside her and from what the officer poking around inside it could tell, everything that usually inhabited a woman's bag appeared to be there. Purse, phone, mirror, a few items of make-up and a hairbrush.

The police yelled back and forth to one another as they did their best to keep bystanders away from the mouth of the alley, tried to stop them taking pictures on their phones or calling friends to gossip, but no doubt within minutes the news of the body would be all over the local social media pages.

Crime scene photographers were already hard at work, their white overalls standing out in the dimness of the night, the police floodlights trying valiantly to make a dent in the darkness.

Members of the public milled around, patrons that had been in the club and had heard the commotion, the startled screams as the young woman's mutilated body had been discovered, or people that had been making their way home from various other late night bars and restaurants, drawn by a morbid curiosity that seemed so ingrained in humans. They were all chattering excitedly amongst themselves, treating it more like an entertaining spectacle, than the tragedy it was. To them the body laying cooling on the wet ground was not a person, it was a thing and the whole process was their chance to see something they would normally only witness on television. Only one woman seemed bothered by the loss.

Miss Angelica cursed under her breath as she caught sight of the body, that of Miss Layla, one of her girls. This was why she preferred that all bookings went through her or took place at designated feeding spots like Cassian's club. This could have been avoided and was yet another loss, the troubles of last week still not forgotten. The last thing she needed was more danger to her girls, she had only just authorised them to go back out and here was one killed right under her nose.

She pulled out her phone and double-checked her list, though she knew she had made no mistake, Miss Layla wasn't scheduled to meet anyone, so Miss Angelica had no way of knowing whom she had fed before her untimely end. Well, wasn't that just great? She stabbed at the call button, waiting impatiently for someone from the Guild to answer. When the call was eventually picked up she didn't bother saying hello.

"There's been an incident, Miss Layla has been killed... Gutted on the floor as far as I can tell... Yes, the police were here before I arrived. I need a message to go out to all the girls, I want to know where they were, who they were with, who they fed and if anyone saw or spoke to Miss Layla to know whom she was meeting. And I need it yesterday. Also put in a call to the local registered establishments to see if anything suspicious or unusual has happened there." She didn't wait for a confirmation before she ended the call, she knew her orders would be carried out. Slipping the phone back into her pocket she eased closer to the barriers, trying to catch an officer's attention, wanting to gain as much information as possible. She didn't get very far before she was pushed back, all her questions ignored.

DCI Jacobson held the handkerchief over her nose and mouth to prevent herself from inhaling any more of the rank smell the body in front of her was producing. The victim had obviously lost control of her bladder at some point while she was still alive as her jeans were wet at the crotch and had dripped down her legs. Her stomach had been slashed from just under her ribs to almost her pubic bone. The intestines had been pulled out and spread around her, over her head like a macabre skipping rope, her fingers, wrapped around the organs like she was holding them, only added to the effect. When the flesh had been sliced the knife had obviously perforated her bowel, the stench rising from the body, growing more pungent the closer Jacobson leaned. And no one had seen a thing, which wasn't uncommon for London but could seriously hamper their investigation.

Cassian thanked Elena as she brought the drinks to their table. The club had been closed for almost an hour, the staff cleaning up, cashing up the tills and checking the stock for the next night. It had been a long day and he had insisted that Amethyst sit down and relax now that the night was almost at an end, but as usual she had refused unless he did the same. She had probably been wise to suggest it, if he was left to his own devices he would work right up until the sun rose.

He looked at Amy now, barely touching her drink, her eyes unfocused as she stared off into space, lost in her own little world. Unable to stand it he reached out and gently took her hand, shaking her out of her musings.

"She'll be OK, baby, Avery is looking after her. She'll be up and about before you know it, you'll see."

Amy gave him a weak smile in return, but it didn't reach her eyes. He stroked the back of her hand with his thumb, rubbing in light, soothing circles.

"Talk to me."

Amy sighed, taking in a deep breath and letting it out slowly, she had never been one to talk about what was on her mind, Jason had always told her that that was a sign of weakness, that to even have worries was ridiculous, let alone voice them. But he wasn't here, wouldn't ever be again, he finally had no control over her life. But even though she trusted and loved Cassian with all her heart, they had only been together a few weeks and she was still finding it difficult to open up to anyone that wasn't her sisters. Tears welled up in her eyes as she finally vocalised the thoughts that had been circling her head for the last three days.

"It's my fault, Cass," her voice was so low, almost a whisper, that even with his acute hearing he couldn't be sure he'd heard her properly.

"Your fault? Sweetheart, how in the world could it be your fault?"

She gave him a look that let him know she thought he was being rather dense and even that little thing made him smile, showing him just how much stronger she had grown in the past few weeks.

"He wanted me. He didn't want her, she was just a means to an end for him. If it hadn't been for me she wouldn't have been in that position and wouldn't be in this situation now. She wouldn't be turned into something she will hate. It's all my fault. I'm to blame." Tears leaked their way down her cheeks as she looked up at him, needing him to be her anchor. He vowed he wouldn't let her down. He squeezed her hand a little tighter as he spoke.

"Baby, it is in no way, shape or form, your fault. He was crazy. A crazy, cruel arsehole that cared about no one but himself. You could never have predicted what would happen, none of us could, we all thought he was dead. Sapphire will be fine, and she won't be blaming you, you know she won't. As soon as Avery calls we'll head over there and you'll be able to see for yourself."

Amy nodded, swiping at the tears, visibly pulling herself together before his eyes. He was so proud of her and that core of inner strength she always doubted she had, the one that he had sensed from the second he met her.

"I'm just so worried about her, you don't know my sister. She likes to be in control, she likes everything to run on a schedule and to go exactly according to plan. She likes everything her way. She won't cope with this. She'll hate it. She hates anything weird or abnormal. She never used to bring friends home or introduce us to people, she was always too ashamed of us."

Cass sighed, he could see where that would be a problem for one as straight-laced and uptight as Saph.

"She'll learn to adjust, everyone does. And we'll all be there to help her. She has Avery with her, he's good with people, you know that."

Amy opened her mouth to answer but shut it again when Cassian's phone began to ring.

"Is that Avery?" she asked as he looked at the screen.

"No. It's the Guild."

Amy could hear the surprise in his voice, guessing that calls from them were not an everyday occurrence.

Cass answered the phone, a hint of wariness in his voice.

"Cassian Libertas speaking," Cass frowned as he listened to whomever was speaking to him. "A Donor, are you sure? No of course you wouldn't have made a mistake...No we only had Miss Marissa and Mr Richard and they had been authorised by yourselves... Yes, of course, anything at all we'll let you know. Thank you."

Amy couldn't hear the other side of the conversation but what she did hear didn't sound good.

"What's wrong? Cassian?"

"Just a minute, sweetheart." Cass stood, crossing over to Elena at the bar. He had a short, low conversation with her then gestured for Amy to follow as he made his way to his office.

Amy barely had time to get comfortable in one of the guest chairs when Elena came through the door, closely followed by Nikos who was devouring an extra large hotdog.

Cassian wasted no time.

"I just had a call from the Guild. It's not good news. One of their girls was found outside Serenity in town, it appears she was gutted and not in a very pleasant way."

Amy gasped in horror. "Gutted? I'm assuming you don't mean that she had a rather big disappointment?"

Cass shook his head. "I'm afraid not, darling." He turned back to address the rest of the room. "The police are there now so the Guild can't get close enough to clean up the scene themselves, more's the pity. They called to let us know what happened and to ask if we had had any more incidents or trouble tonight. I told them we only had the two Donors authorised by themselves and no one else. That's right isn't it?"

Elena and Nikos nodded in unison, confirming the fact that Cassian had already known.

Cass nodded. "Well, there doesn't seem much else we can do to help but keep our eyes open. Obviously with Serenity being a human establishment the Guild never expected one of their girls to be there. But it does appear that she had been fed from. I need you two to keep your eyes and ears open over the next week at least. Make sure that all Donors are authorised, all feeders are on their best behaviour, don't hesitate to call me if there is even a hint of a problem. Got that?"

"Yes, boss," Nikos answered around a mouthful of pork sausage and bread. Elena simply inclined her head in an affirmative.

"Then you may head home, we're done for the night."

Chapter Four

Sapphire drifted slowly into consciousness, very aware of a heavy weight laying across her middle. Hardly daring to look, knowing exactly what was going on, she turned her head, coming face to face, nose to nose with a grinning Avery, who had apparently invited himself to spoon around her while she slept. The nerve of that man!

She jumped up, batting at his arm when he tried to stop her, suddenly furious. She felt her emotions spike straight into anger and at the back of her mind she registered the fact that this was very unlike her, she didn't let herself get angry, she didn't allow her emotions to rule her, to take over, yet here she was, going from zero to pissed off in a matter of seconds. And it was all his fault. She had never met anyone as infuriating as Avery.

"What do you think you're doing?"

"Snuggling." He smiled a lazy grin at her as he rolled over and stretched like a cat, displaying his sinuous body to its full advantage. Not that she noticed...well, maybe just a little. But she refused to let him distract her.

"You do not just invite yourself in to snuggle whenever you feel like it. It's not right."

"Why not?" To her utter disbelief he actually looked confused, like climbing in behind a complete stranger and spooning up in the most intimate fashion, was a normal, everyday occurrence. And to him, maybe it was. Which was just another thing about them that was so different.

"Because you don't. You just don't. You don't get into bed with someone and wrap yourself around them like a limpet." She heard her voice rising with each syllable, growing more and more annoyed.

"It's my bed," he pointed out in that maddeningly cheerful way that he had. She wondered if anything about him was serious. He struck her as someone that floated through life, treating everything as a joke. Something she could not stand. Life was not like that. Life was serious, life was hard, and it was unfair, she was living proof of that.

She gave up, she bloody gave up. Throwing her arms up in defeat she stalked out of the room, slamming the door behind her.

She stomped her way down a hallway, then thumped down the first set of stairs she came to. She didn't have a clue where she was, though judging by Avery's claim that she had been making use of his bed, it wasn't that much of a leap to assume that she was currently in his house. Great, just great.

She was going through the crisis of a lifetime and was stuck with the most annoying man she had ever met. He was just so damned carefree, something which always got her back up. She didn't know how to react to him, didn't like the way she felt that he was constantly poking fun at her and goading her into a reaction. And damn it, she was playing right into his hands, making it easy on him.

Well no more. She could deal with him, she had worked with far worse people than him over the years and taken each and every one of them down with a few well chosen words. She didn't know why she was letting Avery get under her skin so much, but it was stopping right that second. She doubted that he would have gotten away with half as much if it wasn't for that damned hollow feeling in her stomach, that gnawing hunger that just wouldn't go away. She needed food, real food, not to be fed some rubbish line about being a Vampire, just how stupid did he think she was?

Determined now, she headed in the direction she assumed the kitchen would be, soon finding herself standing in the most uninspiring one she had ever seen. Not a hint of Avery's personality could be seen, which surprised her. To most, the kitchen was the heart of the house, full of cooking smells and odd little bits of clutter that usually accumulated there, and she would have guessed that Avery would have been the same. It was clean, remarkably so, another thing that surprised her, for some reason she had thought he would live like a slob.

Her stomach suddenly growled, reminding her of her food mission urging her on. The fridge was always a good place to start and large as it was she was expecting something good. Her mouth almost watered in anticipation.

She pulled the handle of the monstrosity, peeking inside its cavernous depths to find...nothing. Well, not really. There were a few bottles of coke, half a pint of milk that was rapidly turning into cottage cheese and what looked to be an ancient lemon shriveled up at the back. She didn't even bother to look in the crisper drawers or the freezer.

Fearing more of the same, she gingerly opened one cupboard, finding it stuffed full to bursting with mugs, each seeming to have some kind of slogan or humorous picture on it. Baffled, she opened the next, finding it piled high with glasses, all seeming to have been stolen from pubs or restaurants. She found another cupboard full of different kinds of tea and coffee, but nothing else.

She opened a drawer, expecting to find the usual knives and forks, but coming up with nothing but a disgruntled looking spider and two teaspoons.

Bending down to search the cupboards under the worktop she was very surprised to find it contained a few bags of Doritos, pretzels and various bars of chocolate. This must be his secret stash, how like a man to live on junk food. She had found no pots or pans, hell, not even a plate, so it was blindingly obvious that he never ate at home, or if he did, he lived on take outs.

Not really caring for the reasons why, she reached into the snacks and dragged out a tube of Pringles, popping the top off, she immediately began stuffing them into her mouth, feeling like she hadn't eaten in a month, crunching her way through half a dozen in quick succession, swallowing hard.

It took less than a minute before her stomach rebelled, the crushed chips working their way straight back up. She barely made it to the sink.

Avery stayed stretched out on the bed, his arms propped casually behind his head, the grin still firmly on his face. He didn't know why he enjoyed needling her so much, but he did. She was just so easy to wind up. He heard her make her way downstairs, obviously making as much noise as possible. It made him laugh, she kept proving to him that she wasn't as in control as she liked to pretend.

He heard her rummaging around in the kitchen, not that she would find much in there, he had no use for it other than the odd bag of blood and indulging his hot drink obsession. The only food he had belonged to Nikos who liked to have snacks everywhere he went, a downside to his overly active metabolism.

Avery was debating the wiseness of following her when he heard the sound of violent retching. That made the decision for him. Jumping up, he high-tailed it out the room and down the stairs with a burst of Vampire speed.

He skidded to a halt in the doorway, eyes quickly taking in the situation. Open Pringles on the side, heaving female over the sink. Not good.

He moved up slowly beside her, gently scooping up her hair, holding it back out of the way with one hand as the other gently caressed her back, offering as much comfort as he could. There was nothing else to do but let her finish.

Sapphire had not felt this sick since the one and only time she had gotten completely rat arse drunk when she was 16. Her stomach was cramping worse than ever before, feeling like it was being wrung out by invisible hands, twisting and turning. She heaved and gagged, her spine bowing with each wave of nausea that assaulted her. She had only eaten maybe ten Pringles at the most, surely there was nothing left to bring up?

She almost jumped out of her skin when she felt gentle hands on her back, holding her hair as her stomach continued its purge.

It went on for what felt like hours, but finally the contractions stopped, and she was able to breathe again. Gasping for air she opened her eyes to be greeted by a sight that made her scream out loud. Blood covered the sides of the sink, looking like something had been butchered. She stared in horror at the gore until Avery reached a hand round her and turned on the tap, rinsing it away. He then produced a soft cloth from somewhere about his person. Wetting it under the still running tap, he handed it to her.

She wiped her mouth gratefully, sinking down to the floor, her back against a cupboard door. She felt weak as a kitten, trembling all over, her stomach now feeling as empty as before, wadded up and crumpled like a piece of paper.

She heard the tap turn off followed by Avery squatting down beside her. She hadn't felt this awful in forever.

"Why?" she groaned. "Why did this happen to me?
Avery shrugged.

"Maybe because you didn't listen to me? You aren't human now, Saph, you can't eat people food anymore."

She lifted her head to hit him with the mother of all glares, she never could stand someone that liked to say, 'I told you so,' but she still couldn't bring herself to quite believe that she was so very different and that she would never again be able to enjoy her favourite things.

"What, no food at all? No chocolate, no roast dinners, no ice cream? No nothing?"

Avery nodded a confirmation.

"Then why do you have food here?" she wailed, dropping her head back into her hands. "It's so unfair, you're taunting me with things I cannot have. That's just cruel. You told me Vampires weren't evil, but you most certainly are."

Avery couldn't stop his lips from twitching into a smile that he quickly smothered. She was just so adorable when she was riled up like that, when she was mad and losing control. It made him wonder just how she could be if she truly let go and just enjoyed her new existence. The perks, he felt, far outweighed the bad points, he just had to prove that to her. Which, looking at her stricken face as she lamented the loss of chocolate, wouldn't be an easy thing to do. Luckily for her Avery wasn't one to give up easily. He'd make it his mission to help her embrace her new world. Whether she liked it or not.

"I can assure you that it was not my intention to taunt you with the presence of Pringles. The food belongs to Nikos, he comes over sometimes to watch the odd game or movie with me and he likes to have snacks on hand."

The thought of food made her stomach cramp again and she groaned anew, arms wrapping around her middle.

"Why won't this pain go away?" she knew she was whining and hated it even as tears pricked at her eyes.

Avery draped his arm around her shoulders, pulling her tight against his side. "You're hungry, your body is still recovering from the changes. You need to feed."

Saph had allowed herself to relax against him, sinking into his embrace, accepting the comfort that he offered her, but at his words she sat back up.

"I'm not snacking on you again," she gave him a 'don't even think of arguing with me,' look.

He held his hands up in a defensive, nothing up my sleeves, gesture.

"I wouldn't dream of it."

She narrowed her eyes suspiciously as he scrambled to his feet and opened a cupboard, selecting a tall glass. He then opened the fridge, blocked from view by the door. Sapphire heard the sound of a drawer opening and shutting then an odd popping sound, like when you jabbed a straw into a juice carton, followed by a sluggish glugging sound of pouring liquid. The door slammed shut, the glass appearing before her eyes now filled with a dark red liquid.

"Is... Is that what I think it is?" She shuddered with revulsion. It was one thing embracing her new Vampire life by biting to feed, that was kinda expected, Hollywood having made it almost popular to be one of the undead, but this, this just seemed clinical and if she was honest…icky. "I'm not drinking that stuff again."

Avery waggled the glass in front of her face, the liquid inside sloshing slightly, coating the side of the glass. "Look, num nums."

Sapphire just stared at him. "If you start making choo choo noises I might just have to kill you." She tried to ignore the dancing glass but with each pass under her nose, an enticing smell wafted up, teasing her senses, tempting, cajoling her to take just one sip. Her stomach lurched, cramping even tighter, making up her mind for her. With a sigh of defeat she snatched the glass from his fingers and took a tiny, tentative sip. And spat it straight back out.

"Urghh, that really is disgusting." The liquid felt too thick in her mouth, more like a soup than a drink. And it tasted bland, almost stale but with a metallic aftertaste. Nowhere near as good as it smelt and positively vile compared to the remembered taste of Avery's blood. That had been rich and almost fruity, like a robust aged red wine. "Why does it taste so bad? It wasn't this bad earlier when I drank from you."

"That's because this is basically dead blood, it's not fresh from the vein. It's collected from Donors, just like at a regular blood bank. It's perfectly good and will provide all the nutrients you need, but it tastes like shit unfortunately. Just think of it as a diet drink and keep chugging."

He pushed the glass back to her lips and she tried again but ended up immediately choking, gagging on the thick gloop. She shook her head, pushing it away. "No. I can't do it!"

It was Avery's turn to frown. "Sweetheart, you don't have a lot of options here. You drink the bagged blood, or you feed from me or a Donor, and we don't have time to get you a Donor right now. It's me or the glass."

Avery watched her face as she took in his words. Was it wrong that he secretly wanted nothing more than to have her hot little mouth on his skin, her cute fangs buried in his flesh as she drank from him? His groin tightened at the thought, blood rushing south quicker than he could blink. There was something undeniably arousing about being fed on, he couldn't deny that, but a little thought at the back of his head niggled him, poking and prodding, telling him in no uncertain terms that it was Sapphire herself that was the ultimate turn on.

Sapphire didn't want to rely on Avery for anything else, didn't want to feel like she was beholden to him any more than she already was, yet the thought of drinking the stale, dead blood made her want to cry. She couldn't live on that and she just didn't feel comfortable with the idea of biting someone she didn't know. She didn't like these feelings of uncertainty that she was fighting with, she needed to get back some control, starting with making decisions for herself.

Raising her chin in an act of defiance, knowing that he was probably expecting her to shy away from the thought of feeding from him again. "I want to drink from you. I refuse that gross stuff and if that's my only other viable option, then I choose you."

Avery looked at her, her eyes daring him to deny her, to argue her choice. Instead he simply nodded.

"If that's what you wish, but can we at least get off this cold, hard floor? My arse is going numb. I'm sure we would both find the couch much more comfortable." He stood, holding out his hand to her.

That sounded like a reasonable request, something she herself might have suggested, so she had no problem placing her hand in his and allowing him to haul her to her feet.

Sapphire wasn't sure what she expected Avery's living room to be like, but she had been sure it would have been a damn sight more mancave than it actually was. She had braced herself for girly posters on the walls, big, leather recliners, a large TV and maybe a coffee table strewed with beer cans, DVD covers, dirty magazines and a thousand remote controls. She expected it to be dirty and untidy, but it was neither.

Instead it was, well, nice. Relaxing and normal, somewhere she could see herself being quite comfortable. There was a big squishy sofa complete with puffy cushions and a fluffy red blanket draped over the back.

There was a TV, but it was a reasonable size, the walls held framed photographs of Avery with various people, all from different eras, a time frame that seemed to stretch right back to when photography was probably in its infancy, to modern day. In all of them he looked exactly the same, only his style of clothing changing. His face always sported that big, open grin that she was actually starting to like. Instead of the DVDs and CDs she had predicted she was pleasantly surprised to find a floor to ceiling bookcase that completely covered one long wall, stuffed to the gills with books on all manner of subjects. Who knew, maybe there was hidden depths to this man than she had not been expecting.

Avery dropped down onto the couch, relaxing back into the cushions looking like he had not a care in the world. He casually patted the seat next to him, inviting her to sit down.

Avery wanted so desperately to laugh at Sapphire, though he was pretty sure she would try to make good on her threat to kill him, but she just looked so uncomfortable, perching right on the edge of the seat cushion, putting as much distance between them as possible. He fought the evil urge to make things worse by teasing her, instead he just held out his wrist, waggling it under her nose in much the same way he had done with the glass.

Saph just stared at the wrist that was shoved up in her face. The memories of feeding from Avery earlier were fuzzy at best and she couldn't really remember how she had done it. All she could recall was that hot, sweet blood flowing into her mouth.

"Why the wrist?" she asked, stalling for time as she wracked her brains desperately trying to wind her brain back a few hours. "I mean, why not the neck? That's what they always do in the movies."

Avery withdrew his wrist. "You can have the neck if you want the neck."

She hadn't expected that. Now she had to see it through, the light of challenge in his eyes was too much to ignore.

"I do."

There was that stubborn little up tilt of her chin again. Avery was beginning to recognise the look in her eyes when she had made her mind up about something and he doubted anything could sway her.

He shrugged and leaned towards her, sweeping his hair back over his shoulder, baring his neck to her now hungry gaze.

All Saph could focus on was the pulse beating in his neck. She didn't know how but she could sense the blood

40

flowing through his veins, could almost taste it on her tongue. Had she ever felt this hungry before? Her gums began to ache, feeling hard and sore, the same as they had earlier. She remembered now and sure enough when she ran her tongue tentatively across her teeth her canines were much longer than usual, having once again morphed into fangs. Without knowing she was doing it she leaned closer, letting her instincts guide her.

Avery sat as still as possible, not wanting to scare her off. She was moving with intent now, following her instincts. She nuzzled her lips against his throat, making him bite back a moan. He felt her fangs scrape against his skin but frowned when she paused, obviously unsure or not wanting to make that first bite. Without thinking he gently cupped the back of her neck in his hand, massaging softly with his fingers. He felt her tense for a second before she relaxed. Her lips parted then with a tiny flair of pain, her fangs punctured his skin.

Sapphire couldn't help but moan with pleasure as his blood flowed into her mouth, bathing her tongue. She swallowed quickly, feeling it burn a path down her throat, pooling in her stomach, creating a warm glow similar to a fine whiskey.

"Good girl, you're doing so well," he encouraged. She made a soft purring sound as she drank, a sound that shot straight to his groin.

Sapphire didn't know how to describe what she was feeling. It was like her whole body had come to life, like a low wattage of electricity was running through her veins. Everything seemed sharper now, like the world had suddenly plunged into HD. She could hear a baby crying a few houses down, hear the rumble of next door's television, smell their food cooking. She could hear a cat meowing outside. Things she would have missed ordinarily were now crowding her consciousness. And her body, her skin felt tingly, sensitive where his fingers brushed against the nape of her neck. She couldn't help but shiver as arousal shot through her.

She began to swallow quicker, needing more of the heady flavour of his blood. She moved closer, pressing up against his side but still it wasn't enough. Acting on pure instinct, letting her body make all the decisions, she swung one leg over both of his and slid onto his lap.

Holy shit! Don't panic boy, don't panic. Just keep your hands where they are- currently clutching tightly to the sofa cushion- *and let her finish feeding.* Avery kept up the internal pep talk as she drank, squirming on his lap, managing to sit herself right on top of his now throbbing erection. He could feel the hardness of her nipples through his t-shirt she wore, pressing against his chest. *Don't look, don't look!* he chanted before his eyes disobeyed him and glanced down, taking in the pert little peaks standing to attention. He groaned with frustration as he kept his arms rigidly at his sides.

Sapphire couldn't think, she could only feel. And right now, all she cared about was the sensations assaulting her body. Her belly was full, and she no longer had the sickly feeling in her stomach. She felt her fangs retract and on pure instinct licked the puncture wounds she had left. She felt Avery shiver beneath her, registering the hard length of his own obvious arousal that was currently pressing into her damp, aching parts.

She pulled back to look at him, taking in the handsome face properly for the first time. There was no doubting it, he was gorgeously stunning in a very male way. He had a strong jaw that was lightly sprinkled with stubble. Full lips that were just made for kissing, lips that curved into a devastating grin as she perused his face. His nose was long and straight apart from a slight kink in the middle that showed he must have broken it at some point. But his eyes were the most striking of all. Blue, so blue you could get lost in them, blue as the deepest, clearest ocean, they twinkled with humour most days but now showed only hazy lust as they caught and locked onto her own.

It took scant seconds for her lips to find his, their meeting a thing of beauty. His lips were as soft and succulent as they looked, yielding to hers.

Avery was shocked at her sudden lunge at his mouth, so shocked in fact that he let her control the kiss for a few moments until he recovered his scattered wits. But when he came to his senses, damn did he make up for it.

One hand trailed its way up her back, fingers scraping up her spine, making her shudder in response, to tangle again in the hair at the nape of her neck, holding her head gent y in place much as he had to encourage her to feed, but now he directed their kiss. His other hand wrapped around her waist, pulling her tight against his chest.

Her head was spinning with the sensations of the kiss. She had never had such a strong reaction to simply kissing someone before. Sure, she had had some pretty nice kisses, but this just blew them out of the water. She didn't know if it was the way Avery seemed to dominate her, throwing his whole body into the kiss, his hips lifting to grind his erection into her own happy place. His tongue swept into her mouth, taking over with bossy movements that should have been a complete turn off for her but in reality only succeeded in stoking the already smouldering flames of arousal into a roaring fire.

Her own hands seemed to have a mind of their own, getting in on the action by burrowing their way under his shirt, sweeping across the muscular plains of his chest. He had a light sprinkling of chest hair that tickled her fingers as they danced across his skin, making them shiver in unison.

Her head was spinning, her body feeling so hot she wouldn't be surprised if she spontaneously combusted, burning up into a pile of ash on the sofa. She pulled back, breaking their kiss, dropping her head to his shoulder, panting for breath she didn't really need. She needed to clear her head, to stop kissing him, to gain some control. But Avery had other ideas.

Avery was lost to their kiss, lost to the feeling of her writhing on his lap, the taste of her, the warm, wet depths of her mouth, the feel of their fangs knocking together in their haste to deepen the kiss. And all of a sudden her lips were missing from his. That would never do! Once the lips were gone she might try to remove her luscious self from his lap and then, he was pretty sure he would die. Again.

Quicker than she could track Avery dropped his hands to her hips, holding her firmly as he lifted her and flipped her over onto her back. Her legs automatically wrapped around his waist, tightening as his weight settled on top of her. His lips nuzzled at her neck, kissing a steaming path along the column of her throat, a move guaranteed to reduce her bones to the consistency of jelly.

He kissed his way along her jaw and back to her lips. He didn't kiss her as she expected, not the brutal, hard kisses they had just been indulging in. These were sweet little pecks at her lips, light nibbles and gentle sweeps of his tongue. She couldn't resist him. As much as she wanted to deny it, she wanted him, probably had from the moment she had first laid eyes on him. But he was just so not her type. She went for the steady guys, the normal guys, the ones that slept with their socks on and thought oral sex was for birthdays, Christmas and maybe anniversaries if you were lucky. Somehow, she knew that Avery would be nothing like them. He was wild and free, he had breezed into her organised life and turned it upside down. But damn if she didn't want him.

He yanked her thoughts back to the present with a quick roll of his hips, grinding his hardness just where she needed him, making her moan, arching her hips to meet his.

He chuckled against her lips, repeating the move, loving the way she shuddered under him, loving the way she responded to him. He had been right, there was a little firecracker, a demanding sexual goddess underneath all that straight-laced exterior. He relished the way her fingers dug into his shoulder, holding him in place, not letting go even as her legs tightened, pulling his hips closer as she rubbed against him like a cat in heat.

Saph was lost, totally and utterly lost to the magic that was Avery's body on top of hers. She was shameless in her use of him, grinding against him as she felt the delicious weight of impending orgasm building inside her. She didn't know how they could still be fully clothed, he made her so hot, hotter than she had ever been before.

If he had thought she was beautiful before, in all her polished and primped ice queen glory, the little vixen that had taken her place was simply stunning, cradling his body against her own, her hair a wild mess, lips swollen from his kisses, her eyes bright, her new little fangs peeking out of her mouth. He had never wanted someone so badly in all his years.

She looked so inviting that he just had to give in to the urges of his body and slip one hand up under her top, his fingers quickly finding her breasts as he reclaimed her mouth, his tongue darting out to lap at her overly sensitive fangs.

Sapphire jerked back to reality the second his fingers tweaked at one painfully hard nipple. It wasn't that it felt bad, quite the opposite. It felt amazing, everything did. And that was what focused her lust soaked thoughts. She barely knew him and here she was humping him like a dog on a leg, riding the hard ridge that pressed against his jeans, about to explode in what promised to be a mind-blowing orgasm.

This wasn't her, this wasn't how she acted. She had had too many choices taken away. She'd been turned into more of a freak than she already was, had drunk blood and made out with a sexy man she knew nothing about. She was losing her hard won control.

Freaking out a little she pushed at his chest, surprised at the sudden burst of strength she managed as he flew backwards to the other end of the big couch.

"What the fuck was that for?" he groused as he struggled to calm down. His body was raging at the loss of the warm, apparently willing female that had just a second ago been wrapped around him like a monkey.

"I can't do this," her eyes were wild, skittish as she scrambled off the couch, righting her clothing, trying to smooth her hair with shaking fingers. "I don't want to be like this, I don't want to drink icky blood, I don't want to be stuck here with you, I just want to go home!" Her voice had gained in volume until it was close to hysterical shouting, looking like she was about to burst into tears.

Avery didn't know what to say. He just sat there, his mouth opening and closing like a guppy as he struggled to make words that wouldn't fuck up the situation even more. He didn't even know what had just happened. One minute she had been very happy to have him there, and the next she had gone psycho on him as soon as his hand had slid up to her breasts. *Never touch the tits dude*, he told himself firmly, *just let the woman ride you like a bucking bronco and never, ever touch the girls again*. Damn, even in his mind that just didn't sound right or fair.

"Let me go home!" she screamed at him, obviously unwilling to wait for whatever words his lust addled brain managed to form to placate her. Now she was just pissing him off, he was sitting there was a serious case of blue balls and an erection that could hammer in nails, which she was entirely responsible for, and now she was yelling at him. The woman needed to make up her damned mind. He had been nothing but a perfect gentleman, looking after her and feeding her, he had kept his hands to himself, mostly, and done nothing but join in when she had perched herself in his

46

lap and started attempting to suck his tongue out of his head. Well, he was sick of it.

He was tired and fed up, just as she was. He knew that she didn't really understand just how much he'd taken care of her, but she was still being damned ungrateful. If she wanted to act like that then he could too.

"Fine!" he yelled back, grabbing for the phone on the coffee table and dialling the club's office, praying to whomever was listening that Cassian picked up.

"Cass? Thank the gods. Dude, you have to come and get this mad bitch you call a sister-in-law. She's doing my head in... no, she's fine...yes she's eaten...what am I, her mother? Just come and get her before she screams the place down.... Well, just hurry the hell up."

Avery disconnected and tossed the phone back onto the table, silencing her before she could let out much more than a squeak in protest to him calling her a bitch.

"They'll be here soon, just stay here and wait for them. I need to go feed and fuck someone before my balls explode." And, leaving her in shocked silence he left, slamming the front door behind him.

As soon as the door shut Sapphire collapsed down on the couch, her head in her hands. She had just acted like a spoilt little brat and she knew it. She didn't know why she had freaked out, definitely knew she had been unfair to him, but she hadn't been able to stop her outburst. Now she had nothing to do but wait.

Chapter Five

Avery had never been so annoyed in his life, well he probably had but he just couldn't remember it. He had a habit of storing unpleasant memories in what he called the 'fuck no' box, a box that lived inside his brain, into which he stuffed anything that might screw up his carefully constructed, carefree existence. And that's just how he liked it. He was too old for dealing with shit he didn't want. As he saw it that was one of the advantages to being immortal, not having to do a thing you didn't want to.

But try as he might, he couldn't seem to relegate Sapphire to the fuck no box, she just wouldn't stay put, the second he thought his brain was clear of her, up she would pop again, closely followed by a raging hard on, it was all just too much. He didn't need this, he hadn't asked for this, in doing Cassian a favour he had sentenced himself to what amounted to torture. And that would just not do.

Letting his feet guide him, walking on autopilot Avery made his way to the club, he wasn't scheduled to work that night, but he often found himself there on nights off. *How sad is that?* a little voice in his head piped up, one that he ruthlessly squashed. He didn't have to go there, he chose to. It had everything he needed, his friends worked there, they catered for his kind, what more could a vamp need? He definitely wasn't going there because there was a good chance that Sapphire would be brought there, not at all. And as long as he kept telling himself that, he would be fine.

He nodded to Nikos who was at his usual post, pushing open the door, going through the main entrance for once, not the employees, he was there as a customer after all. The music inside was already pumped up to a level just this side of deafening, the dance floor a mass of writhing bodies, the scent of alcohol and arousal hung heavy in the air. A smile stretched his lips, this was what he needed to forget that harpy back at his house. He spotted one of his favourite Donors loitering all alone at the bar and deciding that he was too much of a gentleman to leave a female all by herself. He moved to join her, his arm slipping around her waist.

Sapphire's head snapped up when a knock sounded on the front door, jumping up she dashed down the hall, flinging open the door, practically throwing herself into her sister's arms, so grateful was she to see them.

She had taken the time to tidy herself up as best she could, finding a brush and some hair ties in the bathroom, no doubt there because of how long Avery kept his hair, down to just under his shoulder blades. She wound her hair up into the best version of a bun she could manage without clips, and had actually smiled when she looked at her reflection, feeling almost like her old self again, her unruly hair wrestled and smoothed into submission. But no matter how in control she looked, the second she saw the sympathy in her sister's eyes, she broke down.

"Thank God you're here…never thought I'd see you again..." She was babbling hysterically, she knew that, but couldn't seem to stop herself, bursting into floods of tears as she allowed herself to be turned and guided back to the couch. Comforting arms encircled her, hands stroked and soothed her frayed nerves and slowly she calmed, taking gulping breaths until she could again talk. She accepted the handkerchief that Cassian, where the hell had he come from, offered her. She wiped her eyes, almost dissolving back into sobs when she saw that the hanky hand come away red with blood, obviously that's how Vampires cried. Because of course she wasn't already freaky enough. Obviously seeing that more tears was a very real possibility, Cass whipped the hanky away and stowed it swiftly in his pocket.

Amethyst shared a quick glance with Cass, who nodded. She turned to Sapphire. "Sweetie, we think it would be best if you came and stayed with us for a little while. We can be there to help you out with anything you might need."

Saph frowned, pulling away. "Why? I don't need anything. I'm fine. I look after myself, I'll be fine on my own, I always am."

Amy shook her head. "Remember what you told me after Jason went to prison? I was a mess but blaming myself, determined to get through it on my own. You said that there was no shame in allowing yourself to rely on other people, to accept help when it was offered. You said it was simply delegating."

Tanzanite, who had been uncharacteristically quiet, now butted in, stating firmly. "Well, now it's time to delegate. Babes, you're going back with them and that's final. You know how much you like to research, to know everything you can about something. Well, where else are you going to learn everything you need to know? To be able to ask questions that are bound to pop up? You'll be less in control if you don't."

Saph narrowed her eyes at her sisters, knowing she had been played, her own logic and habits used against her, but damned if they weren't right. She knew it made sense, she was just rebelling any way she could, needing that sense of being in control. Same as she had done with Avery.

50

Avery, the thought of him actually made her feel bad. He had done his best to help her and she had repaid him by going full out slut on him then pushing him away. Sure, he had been annoying, his too cute attitude mixed with what she would admit was very good looks and his ability to flirt with a wall if he saw fit, nothing ever seemed to be serious with him, but he hadn't deserved that, and he had every right to be angry, she knew that. He really wasn't that bad, she knew that she was probably not giving him a proper chance, but everything about him was just the total opposite to what she was used to, to what she usually noticed and liked in a man. But she was nothing if not honest with herself, she knew her behaviour towards him left a lot to be desired and she owed him an apology, she had basically used him when the urge struck her and that was wrong. She vowed there and then that the very next time she saw him she would say sorry.

"OK, OK I give in. I'll come and stay with you, but only for a few days, that's it. I need to get back to work as soon as I can." The glare she gave them told them firmly that it was not up for discussion, there would be no arguing and they all backed down gracefully.

Sapphire was glad that they didn't try to change her mind or get her to agree to a longer amount of time. She couldn't deal with that right now. She was so happy to see her sisters, thinking that she would never see them again only a few days ago, and she could tell that they felt the same. But she felt hollow inside, she couldn't explain it, didn't know what the feeling was or how to put it into words. She felt like she was missing a limb, like she wasn't all there, wasn't complete in herself. She shook her head to dispel the thoughts, putting it down to just being an after effect of all that had happened to her in the last few days. She and her body had gone through a lot of changes and unfortunately something told her that those changes were far from over.

Obviously noticing the direction of her thoughts her sisters suddenly made a big fuss about having to get back to the club, dragging her up by her arm and hustling her out the door into their waiting car.

Sapphire had only been to the club once before for the opening night, and honestly it hadn't been her thing. She found it too crass, too dark and, definitely too loud. She had never been a fan of the Goth scene, thinking it more the realm of depressed teens that liked death metal, totally not her thing. She much preferred a quiet wine bar or a nice restaurant for an evening out, somewhere that she didn't feel horribly out of place.

Needless to say, she wasn't that impressed when she was ushered not round the back of the club as she had been expecting, but through the front doors. She noticed that Tanzi was watching the door man, a tall, very muscled man that wore an air of 'don't fuck with me' like a perfectly tailored coat. He wasn't classically handsome like Cassian, nor did he have the boyish good looks and that devilish charm that Avery managed to pull off, but there was something about him that was undeniably attractive and Tanzi obviously saw it. The man threw her sister a cheeky wink as they passed, and her sister actually blushed. Sapphire was gob smacked. Nothing made her sister react like that, there was definitely something going on that she hadn't been informed of.

She was about to start asking questions, demanding answers but her attention was snagged the second they entered the club proper. Her suddenly super sensitive nose was assaulted by a wave of scents, different perfumes and aftershaves, perspiration, drinks and other things she couldn't identify, all mixed together to become a full out assault to her nose. And the noise, the noise level was almost unbearable, the music made her head hurt, the sound of a hundred heart beats pounded in her ears. It was too much, all too much. She covered her ears with her hands, desperate for some relief, her eyes darting this way and that searching for the door that led to the offices.

52

She pulled her arm out of her sister's grasp, darting forward, needing so badly to get away, away from the overwhelming onslaught of sights, sounds and smells that were stealing her control. She pushed her way through the gyrating mass of bodies that seemed to close in on her from all sides, caring not a jot for the soft flesh that collided with her elbows as she fought her way through. She made it to the door and freedom, reaching out a hand when the door opened from the other side, expelling a much more relaxed Avery, his arm around a very pretty young woman. Sapphire could do nothing but stare.

Avery hadn't been expecting to see her right on the other side of the door, especially after he had just finished with Miss Melissa. He didn't miss the fact that Miss Melissa was busily straightening her skirt and smoothing her hair, the two raised red bumps on her throat a dead giveaway as to what had been going on. Avery licked at his lips, suddenly self-conscious, though he had no idea why, it wasn't like he had been caught doing anything wrong. But then why did he feel like he had betrayed Sapphire somehow? Convinced that he had seen a flash of hurt in her eyes. His arm dropped away from Melissa's waist as if burnt.

No, he would not feel guilty. She'd pushed him away, she'd treated him like crap, he was allowed to find his fun elsewhere. He forced himself to stand up straighter, arranging his face into an expression that clearly said he didn't give a shit.

Sapphire struggled to pull herself together. For some reason seeing Avery like that, knowing full well what he had been doing, made her feel like warmed up dog shit. Even mussed and looking slightly dazed, the woman he had been with was flawlessly gorgeous, her perky breasts rose up, presented to perfection in the black and red corset she wore, the short tutu style skirt showing off her shapely legs. Her hair was black as night with streaks of red that matched

53

her lipstick, which was currently smudged and in need of repair.

She glanced at Avery who looked for all the world like he hadn't just been almost caught with his pants down. His lips curved into a smirk that she itched to slap off his handsome face. Which just pissed her off even more. She had no reason to want to slap him, no reason to want to rip each strand of hair out of the girl's pretty little head. No reason at all. So then, why was her blood boiling? She had to get away.

Nodding politely she pushed past him, marching down the hall, not knowing or even really caring where she was going as long as it was far away from the annoying Vampire that alternatively got on her last nerve and made her body ache for his touch. Damn, she was messed up.

Avery watched her go, his traitor of a cock raising all by itself as he watched her hips sway seductively as she walked. He bet she didn't even know just how sexy she really was, the way she buttoned herself up so tightly, never a hair out of place if she could help it, always in control. Damn, if he didn't want her right back where she had been earlier, perched on his lap, grinding her sweet arse against his hard dick, her lips on his. His fingers itched to run through her hair, freeing the strands from that tight bun she had once again wound them up into. It made her look severe again, the passionate little fire cracker she had been before was a distant memory. Though, unfortunately for him, not so distant. Try as he might he just couldn't shake her, couldn't stuff her into the fuck no box. His body remembered her all too well and she was all it wanted.

Miss Melissa had offered her throat and other body parts, not unheard of for her, and he had eagerly taken her up on the offer, still worked up from the little make out session on his couch, but as soon as he ran his nose down her throat and inhaled her scent, his erection had wilted like a week old flower. She was gorgeous, her curves the thing of many

54

a man's fantasy, but she felt wrong. She wasn't a golden haired beauty with forest green eyes that made him melt. No matter how much he tried he just couldn't fake an interest in the Donor he had up against the wall. Until he closed his eyes and allowed the visions of exactly what he'd wanted to do to Sapphire if she hadn't have stopped him, to form in his head. Only then could he sink his fangs and his dick into the willing girl and get the job done, hard and fast, no finesse and no messing. But now, now with just a look from Sapphire he was more than ready to take a tumble in a bed, why was life so cruel? His cock, his most loyal and trusted friend was working against him. His dick was broken.

Sapphire just couldn't believe that he was so blatant about it, like he didn't care that he had just done the nasty in what could have been full view of everyone, just hours after leaving her side. What was wrong with him? He was nothing but an animal, one who cared about nothing but where the next feed and fuck came from, that much was obvious. She decided there and then that she wanted no part of it. He would not be getting an apology from her, he could shove it or die waiting for all she cared.

Decision made she waited another minuet until her sisters caught up and led her to the rather spacious apartment above the club where she would be staying with Amethyst and Cassian.

"Oh, come on, baby, let's go back to your place and you can have a little nibble." The Donor was wrapped around his waist like a limpet, normally something that he didn't mind at all, even encouraged. He was well known for being a bit of a ladies man and in some cases, a sure thing and he didn't mind that reputation if anything he was rather proud of it. But now she was just irritating the hell out of him.

Ever since his first love, Margaret, had betrayed him, he had kept himself and his heart separate from women. He couldn't trust them. They could always be hiding an evil, selfish, backstabbing viper underneath their sweet exterior. That was why he tried to never let one in, never see the same one twice if he could help it. He had wavered a little in his convictions over the years, when the loneliness and need for companionship, someone to share things with, grew too much for him. Avery was an affectionate soul, one that was naturally friendly and caring to a fault. So nice, that it often led him into bad situations. Case in point was Miss Jennifer, the Donor's Guild representative for the Edinburgh area, and now werewolf mate. He had a few Vampire girlfriends over the years that he had spent more time with, but on the whole he kept his heart carefully guarded.

He didn't want the Donor that was currently plastered to his side, didn't want someone so blatant and in your face to be draped all over him, practically offering herself up on a platter. He found it too easy, there was no challenge, that and it made him realise that the Donor saw him as nothing special. She was one of the Donors that liked the sexual side of feeding, which was fair enough, Avery himself liked that when he was in the mood, but now she just seemed desperate, like she saw him as nothing but a pair of fangs and a willing dick. And he didn't like that feeling.

For once he wanted someone to look at him like he was special. To choose him first over everyone else, like Logan and Cassian had with their Soul Mates. It was common knowledge that Avery was actively searching for his, fucking everything that moved, waiting for that 'click' of recognition that would give him that one woman that was meant for him alone.

He pulled up with a start, pushing the girl off his lap with an uncharacteristic growl of warning. The girl stared up at him with wide eyes as did three or four regulars that were in the vicinity. Avery never lost his temper, he never got pissed with a female. Looking around, feeling their eyes on him, judging him, he got the hell out of there, muttering dire curses as he pushed through the crowd. What the hell was wrong with him? He was acting like a girl, having feelings and shit that he didn't understand.

"I'm sorry, Miss Cassie," he apologised, seeking to soothe her ruffled feathers. It just wasn't in him to upset a woman. "It's not you, I'm just not in the mood tonight, pet."

"Maybe next time?" She asked hopefully as she looked up at him, her eyelashes fluttering in a way he was sure was meant to be endearing.

"Erm…yeah, sure. Next time," he brushed her off with a noncommittal answer. Fuck, he needed to get out of there.

Hopping over the bar he helped himself to a few bottles of premixed blood and got the hell out of the club, wanting nothing more than to go home, drink himself into oblivion and hopefully wake up in the morning to find his balls back where they should be

Chapter Six

Sapphire pushed the glass away without touching it, the deep red liquid the most unappetising thing she had ever encountered, and she had survived for years on their mother's cooking which largely consisted of shoving a mish-mash of things into the oven for an undetermined amount of time and calling it dinner.

"Sapphie, you have to try and drink it, you heard what Cassian said, this is the most important time of a Vampire's new life, you have to keep feeding to grow stronger, you don't want to be a weakling Vampire, one that's all sickly and pathetic do you?" Amy sure had a way with words.

Sapphire tried really hard to resist the urge to swing out a hand and punch her. It wasn't that she didn't love her sisters to bits, she did, but the last few days had been almost unbearable.

Cassian had given her so much information that her head felt like it was crammed to bursting, history, rules, laws even Vampire etiquette, who knew there was such a thing? And the blood, the constant glasses of blood that they always seemed to be shoving under her nose. Didn't they understand that it tasted like horse shit? Like drinking dead batteries, moldy leaves, school rice pudding, in short bland and unappetising. Sure, it was fine for Cassian, he had her sister to munch on and had been turned in the days before blood banks, way before if what he told her was true. Cassian was a gladiator, from way back in Roman times, Pompeii to be exact. Wasn't that something to blow your brain?

Cassian had said that she could feed from Donors, straight from the vein as she had done with Avery, but that it wasn't something that could be done every day, some days there might not be a Donor available, or you might simply not feel like going out to feed. He said to think of it like going out to eat at a restaurant, or even to a fast food place, nice now and then, as a treat, but you still had to keep food at home to make yourself. She guessed that made sense and he had a good point, not that she was ready to admit that yet.

Saph took a deep breath, trying to stay calm. "I don't want to drink it, I'm really not hungry."

"But you have to," Amy pushed the glass back across the table. "Cassian said-" But Saph cut her off, exploding out of the chair.

"I said I don't want it!"

Amethyst looked up at her younger sister in shock, she had never known Sapphire to even raise her voice, let alone lose her temper, she was always the calm and collected one in the midst of all the drama queens their family had produced.

Sapphire immediately felt guilty for shouting, the look on her sister's face making her regret her actions. "Look, sis, I'm sorry, OK? It's just all getting a bit much, I feel like I'm not even allowed to decide when to eat on my own. And being cooped up here, it's just too much. I need to get out." An idea suddenly struck her as she glanced at the clock, seeing it was a little after ten at night, almost lunch time by Vampire standards. The club would be open, she wouldn't be going far and as it was a Tuesday, it would be relatively quiet. "I'm gonna go down to the club for a bit, I need a break from Vampire 101." She didn't wait to be given permission, just walked right on out the door.

Avery was back where he belonged, where he always felt like himself, behind the bar. He grinned at the two females that were perched on bar stools, watching him with undivided attention as he expertly mixed their drinks, giving them an extra little shake and shuffle routine as he tossed the shaker from one hand to the other. Normally he enjoyed the way customers eyes, both male and female, followed his every movement. And why wouldn't they? He was gorgeous even if he did say so himself. But that evening he was finding the whole sexy bar tender gig to be an enormous effort, taking all his concentration to pull it off.

He whipped the top off with a practiced flourish and decanted their drinks into glasses, adding fruit pieces and a couple of umbrellas, then slid them down to his waiting customers with a wink that was a guaranteed pantie melter.

"There you go ladies, two delicious drinks for the two most delicious looking females in the place," he ran his tongue across his lips, deliberately showing off his fangs, ones that the girls would assume were fake and all part of the club's theme.

The girls basked in his attention, puffing out their chests, showing off their assets to their best advantage, flipping their hair over their shoulders almost simultaneously in what was surely a choreographed move of seduction, their glossy lips pouting to optimum fullness. And any other time he would have taken them up on their very blatant offer, not like he hadn't had the odd threesome in his time, more than the odd one actually, but once again he was left cold. And didn't that just piss him off? That bloody female had ruined him for all others and he hadn't even fucked her. What the hell was wrong with him?

60

"Aww girls, I would love to," he assured them, giving their magnificent breasts a good leer as he continued to lie smoothly. "But we're not allowed to fraternise with our customers. It's against club rules. And you wouldn't want me to lose my job now would you?" He gave them his best pitiful puppy eyes, watching as they melted. Usually he loved the way women reacted to him, how he could almost guarantee their compliance if he worked them the right way, both in and out of bed, but there was no challenge there, it was all automatic flirting with no feelings behind it.

He turned away from them after bestowing on them another of his trademark winks, turning his attention to cleaning up and replacing the bottles he had used back on the shelves. He whistled softly as he worked, wiping down the bottles with a damp cloth, quietly content, that was until the door to the back opened and a luscious scent invaded his nose.

All his blood rushed south, his dick hardening in a rush. He glared down at it in surprise, wondering just why it had decided that now was the time it wanted to wake up and join the party. Grabbing an apron from the side he tied it around his waist then, as discreetly as possible, slid his hand into his pocket and adjusted his aching cock, trapping it under the waistband of his jeans, anchoring it in place before he turned around to greet his new customer, his sexiest grin already in place. A grin that dropped away when he saw exactly who was sitting there.

Sapphire knew it had been a mistake to come down to the club the second she saw who was manning the bar that night. She didn't want to see him, didn't want to have to speak to him again, not right then and not really for the foreseeable future. Yet, her damn pride and stubbornness refused to let her turn tail and run back upstairs to the apartment. She had said she wanted to get out and she damn well would, she wasn't going to let him mess it up for her.

61

Putting on her most casual expression she sat down, waiting for him to take her drink order.

She looked pale, paler than she should be after only being awake for such a short time, and Avery didn't like it. He didn't know why he had such a fierce protective urge when it came to her, but he did. The damned woman was tying him up in knots.

She wasn't looking at him, seeming intent on her task of collecting all the little cardboard beer mats in the vicinity and stacking them into a neat pile. He waited, leaning against the counter in front of her, allowing himself to indulge in filling his nose with her scent. He coughed to get her attention, then waited some more, but she didn't raise her eyes to meet his until he finally gave in and spoke first, deciding that they didn't have to continue their silent stand-off, he could be the bigger man there, forgive and forget. Life, especially theirs, was too long to be dealing in such childish games as ignoring each other.

"What'll it be darlin'?" he asked, nudging her hand aside and rescuing the beer mats, distributing them back along the counter top. Her head jerked up at the sound of his voice and he was shocked to see dark rings under her eyes. Before he could stop himself he asked. "Have you been eating properly?"

Sapphire gave him the full force of her best glare. "Why does everyone keep pushing me to eat? Do you all want me the size of a cow?" She paused for a second and Avery was about to jump in when she continued." No, I haven't eaten, I don't want it, it's disgusting, I'd rather die!"

With that dramatic proclamation she slammed her hand down on the bar top with a resounding thump, then crossed her arms over her chest, a look of defiance on her face. And that was that.

"Sooo, cocktail?" he asked with a shrug.

"You aren't going to argue with me?" she was shocked to say the least and almost forgot that she was supposed to be mad at him.

"Nope." He turned his back on her and began to mix up a cocktail, a house specialty to which he added a good dose of blood. Yes, it was sneaky not to warn her, but he had a feeling it was mostly a case of mind over matter for her. Like she thought that blood would always be disgusting no matter how she drank it, so it automatically put her off. He hoped that if she didn't know what was in it, she would just drink and enjoy, soon she would get used to the taste and actually find it pleasant. And, he told himself, he wasn't really lying to her, she said yes to a cocktail, she just didn't specify what had to go in it.

He poured it into a tall glass over ice and handed it over. Sapphire looked at the deep red drink she had been presented with.

"What's this?"

"That, dear one, is a Vampire's kiss. Go on, give it a taste. It's one of our most popular drinks."

Sapphire picked up the glass, staring at it suspiciously before taking a cauticus sip, rolling it around her mouth like she was tasting wine, before swallowing.

"Good?" He didn't know why he was so bloody eager to please her, to have her like his drink. Apart from the fact that he prided himself on making the best cocktails in London, he found that even though she had been a royal bitch to him, he actually did care about her and her well-being, probably more than he should do. It both disturbed and intrigued him in equal parts.

"Yes, it's actually not that bad." Sapphire had to admit, though rather grudgingly, that it seemed he really did know what he was doing when it came to mixing drinks. The drnk was fruity but with a nice warming kick to it. She happily sucked on the straw suddenly finding that she was very thirsty.

63

Avery watched in silent amusement as she drank the drink down. He held out the shaker, offering her a top up which she accepted after a brief pause.

Avery watched her carefully as she drank, pleased to see the colour coming back to her cheeks, the dark circles disappearing as the blood did its job, repairing the cells in her body, giving her fuel. Noticing another customer in need of a top up, he left her to her drink.

Sapphire sipped the second glass a little slower, letting the warmth it produced pool in her belly, spreading out through her body like central heating, chasing away the lingering cold that she had been feeling since she woke up. Now that she thought about it, her head felt a little clearer too, less like she was about to snap and bite someone's head off, figuratively speaking that is. She felt languid now, relaxed, calm, like she could take on anything. Energy seemed to buzz in her veins, like she had downed six Red Bulls and a couple of pro plus. She was ready to bounce off the walls, feeling like she could take on the world, and win. She slurped the last drops of liquid from the glass and pushed it aside with a contented sigh.

Avery wandered back over, seeing her glass was once again empty.

"Feel better?" he couldn't resist asking.

Sapphire nodded, then deciding that she didn't really have to be rude to keep her distance, plus she was curious, added. "Yes, thank you. What was in it?"

"Vodka, Korbel Champagne, black raspberry liqueur…" Well that didn't sound so bad, she thought. "And a couple of shots of B positive," he finished with a grin that clearly showed he thought himself a genius. Which he kinda was, but she wasn't about to give him the satisfaction.

"A couple of shots of what?" she glared at him but for once she couldn't make someone back down, it was like the man had no fear or sense of self-preservation.

"You needed it, you didn't want to drink it straight, so I helped. You may thank me now." He held his arms out, his

64

head tipped back like he was awaiting a huge round of applause. Saph just stared at him. Let him keep waiting.

Avery opened his eyes again, letting his arms drop back down to his sides. "Well don't you suck," he declared, swiping up the damp cloth he had been cleaning up with and disappearing to the other side of the bar.

Sapphire was actually feeling much better, which pissed her off no end. Why? Because it was that annoying man's doing. All of it was. Well, not the reasons she was a Vampire obviously, but the rest of it was most definitely his fault.

He was the one that had fed her from his wrist, giving her a taste of what feeding could really be like, it was like giving someone the most delicious lobster for their first meal then giving them cheap tinned tuna for every meal after that. Just not cricket. Bagged blood tasted like crap in comparison to Avery's deep, richness and she just couldn't bring herself to drink it. The second it touched her tongue her taste buds recoiled in horror, screaming for mercy. Something she was totally backing them up with.

Now that she was feeling better, able to think more clearly she could understand why everyone had been pushing her to eat. She hadn't realised just how tired and lethargic she had felt until the feeling was gone. She hadn't realised how much it had put her in a bad mood until she felt better. And it was all his doing. That sneaky Vampire had employed some decidedly underhand tactics to get her to drink, but damned if it hadn't worked, she hadn't even tasted the blood in the drink, the fruity flavours concealing it perfectly. She would have drunk a few more if she had the chance. Sure, she could swallow her pride and ask him to mix her another batch, but she didn't think that was wise.

She didn't like the way the need to feed seemed to take away her control. It turned her into what amounted to a cranky teenager with PMS. If she didn't feed she was hungry, grumpy, snapping at everyone, and if she did she almost felt high. Too much energy, her senses on full alert, ready to jump at a moment's notice. She thought back to how she had been that night on Avery's couch, how feeding from his vein had been like Vampire Viagra. Her hormones had rocketed, lust engulfing her until she couldn't think past the need to fuck him senseless, to relieve the ache inside her. And that was something she just couldn't risk again. That was one of the main reasons that she never wanted to feed from a Donor, she didn't want to be humping some random man that she didn't know, like a dog on heat. It just wasn't her. She didn't act like that, she had control for a reason.

Her whole life had been built around her ability to control herself and her abilities. She never shared her gifts with anyone, finding them disturbing. She didn't want to be a freak like the rest of her family. While her mother, sisters and numerous aunties, uncles and family friends had been more than happy to bask in the glow of their collected strangeness, Sapphire had never liked it.

She hated being different. She hated standing out from the crowd. Being picked on for being herself was one of the worst things about life. It made her grateful that her parents had decided to home school their girls until it was time for them to study for and sit their exams, even if they did insist that it was simply a precaution against 'the man' filling their heads with a lot of nonsense. It had allowed Sapphire to hide away from kids her own age, working hard on her control, learning to lock the real her away behind carefully constructed walls inside her, shutting her mind to the other world until she was able to block it all out, it became second nature to her. Then and only then had she felt ready for college and then university.

It was there that she had met Tristian, her one and only love. He was from old money, destined for a glittering career as a solicitor, wanting to build his way up to being a judge or a politician. He was schoolboyishly handsome, his black hair worn slightly long but swept back off his face for maximum affect, his clipped accent making you think of tea with the Queen. She'd made the mistake of bringing him home to meet her family, a mistake she had never repeated again.

They had walked through the door of the old fire station that her parents owned. It was known as a commune of sorts, but her parents insisted that it be called a free home. The doors were always open to any traveller that needed a place to lay their head, people staying for maybe a few days to a few years. They varied from strangers that were travelling, to aunties and uncles that stayed for years.

The girls had gotten their language lessons from foreign back packers, their h story from professors that would stay in town for a conference, religious studies from the wealth of new age travellers that wandered through their doors.

And in the middle of it all were their parents, the aging hippies that never grew out of the 60s. Their mother believed in everything, her way of thinking wasn't 'prove to me it's real,' she lived by 'prove to me it's not real,' she believed in anything until she was given definitive proof that it didn't exist, and even then she was inclined to argue.

Their father was rather like an absent-minded professor that grew his own weed. He was always trying to calm things down when they got a little heated, which let's face it, with four strong willed females in permanent residence and an untold number visiting, arguments were a given. He was a gentle soul, liking to potter around his garden, growing his organic vegetables, tending his chickens and reciting his poetry to whatever would listen, usually his beloved plants.

So of course, when Tristian, whose parents spent their time playing golf or at Ascot, was introduced to her mother whom immediately informed him that he had a 'smudged Aura' and her father quoting Lord Byron, he was rather taken aback. He could have probably dealt with them, the upper class being somewhat used to eccentrics, but he couldn't deal with Tanzi in all her goth glory, sweeping in the door with a cat tucked under one arm, muttering moon chants under her breath. That had been too much. He had left half way through dinner, faking an emergency and the very next day had dumped her, publicly for all to witness, accusing her of being from a freak family and no doubt a freak herself. From that moment on she had tried even harder to keep the stranger side of her family life locked away.

And she had succeeded, yes, she had had lovers, but none of them had really known her, they had never taken the time to scratch below the surface, to look beneath the mask she wore like a shield and see the person she truly was. They didn't seem to care. As long as she looked good on their arms at corporate events, cool, sophisticated with not a hair out of place, then they were happy. The men themselves were always rather dull, ones that wouldn't upset her carefully controlled life, and that was how she liked it. The sex was much of the same, controlled, calm almost mechanically cold.

She glanced over at Avery, her eyes drawn to him like a moth to a flame. He was everything that she didn't want in her life. Fun, carefree, random and spontaneous. He flirted, he laughed, he joked. He had a wildness about him that couldn't be contained, a passion bubbling inside him that she had sipped and now wanted more of. She could barely admit it to herself, but she was parched for another taste of him. Her body craved his touch, recalling how his hands had felt skimming her body that night. The way his lips had mastered hers, his tongue plundering her mouth, making itself at home. And she had liked it, loved it in fact. She had never responded to a man like that.

To her, sex had been to scratch an itch, a purely physical coupling that fulfilled a need and could be mostly forgotten about after. But she just couldn't forget about him. She found herself wanting to respond to his banter, his flirting, to chat and open up. He was worming his way through her defences and it was driving her crazy. Yet another reason that she promised herself she would stay away from him.

Avery could feel her eyes on him, burning into his flesh like a brand, urging him to turn and look at her. He could resist her! He would resist her! He was practically shouting at himself in his head even as his traitorous feet turned him on the spot to face her

"Avery! Darling!" The voice he hadn't heard in over a century flew across the dance floor like a guided missile. Shocked, he looked up, his eyes taking in the female that had just entered the club.

Sapphire looked in amazement at the female that had just walked, no make that strutted, into the club. Her hair was a rich chestnut colour, elegantly wound up into an intricate knot at the back of her head, showing off her slender neck to its best advantage. Her eyes were the dark, dark colour of bitter chocolate, so dark they almost swallowed her pupils. The colours seeming to bleed into each other.

She shrugged off her obviously genuine fur coat, handing it off to the man who accompanied her, without a word, revealing a dress that looked destined for the red carpet but was out of place in such a club. But removing the coat revealed a body that a playboy model would kill for. It was a beautiful hourglass. Not too full hips tapered into a slender waist a man could probably span with his hands, leading up to a chest that was just the right side of too generous, straining at the fabric of her gown. Her bee stung lips pouted, practically begging to be kissed, her nose straight and regal.

Her voice was sultry, practically dripping sexual promises and with each word she spoke her harsh accent, sounding close to Russian, only complimented her bedroom appeal.

Sapphire hated her on sight, something that was reinforced by the possessive way she had commanded Avery's attention and was now draped around him like a vine. She was everything that Saph knew she would never be and that made her want to rip that perfect hair right off her head.

69

"Avery, my love, it has been so long."

"Lili, sweetheart, you look well."

Sapphire might have been imagining it, or just desperately hoping, but it seemed like Avery was actually trying to extract himself from her monkey like grasp. The male with her returned to her side, having deposited her coat somewhere. He said not a word, just stood and glowered.

"Grigory," Avery held out his hand in greeting to the male, who simply nodded, making no move to accept the handshake offered to him.

"Ahh, as pleasant as ever I see," Avery chirped as if he had not just been offended. He extracted himself from the female's grasp and turned desperately towards Sapphire, obviously needing the help. Sighing, she got up and went over to rescue him.

"Sapphire," he cheered, wrapping his arm around her waist, dragging her in close to his side. Sapphire fought the alien urge to sink into him, snuggling close, instead staying stiff and unyielding in his embrace. After a moment he took the hint, dropping his arm but keeping his charming smile fixed in place. "This is Liliya, Liliya, this is Sapphire."

"Pleased to meet you," Saph put on her most professional smile, acting for all the world as if she was happy and relaxed. Liliya it seemed, didn't feel the need to lie even a little for appearances sake.

She leant forward and delicately sniffed at the air just over Sapphire's shoulder, then gave a rather rude snort of distain. "She is but fledgling, mere baby. She is of no matter to me." Liliya gave a vague wave of her hand, as if Sapphire was a servant to be dismissed before slipping her arm through Avery's dragging him away from Sapphire. And he allowed it, he actually allowed the woman to dictate to him like that. Saph was appalled. Not only had she basically been told she was too young and useless to be of any interest or use by someone she had just met, but he had done nothing to correct her. Let him suffer.

70

She watched as Liliya monopolized the conversation and Avery's time, leaving one of the wait staff, a pleasant looking young girl of around twenty, to tend the bar in his absence. Sapphire had been hoping that he would make her another of those drinks but after almost fifteen minutes, she was bored and fed up of waiting for him. Surely she had better things to do than be at his beck and call, waiting around like a lost puppy?

Sapphire pulled out her phone, sending Amethyst a quick text explaining that she wouldn't be coming back to the apartment that night, she was heading home. She needed her own things around her, needed to sleep in her own bed, to feel like her life was still her own, not some horrible nightmare she had yet to wake up from. Everyone had been doing their best to help her and she was grateful for that, but they had also taken over, telling her what to do and when to do it. She was not a child and she abhorred being treated as such. It was not in her genetic make up to take orders from anyone.

Grabbing her bag she headed for the back exit, located just beyond the stock room, it led out to the other side of the road, nearer to their house which was only a ten minute walk from the club itself, something that had attracted Amethyst to the job of day manager in the first place.

Avery saw Sapphire pick up her bag and prepare to leave. He had made sure that Liliya kept away from Sapphire after her rude comments, not wanting them to clash more than they already had. He had been trying unsuccessfully to get away from her for the last ten minutes but with no luck. He didn't want Sapphire to leave. Time to get firm.

"Lili, sweetheart, it's been lovely to see you again, we must catch up more at another time, but I'm supposed to be working," ignoring her protests and the way she clung to his arm, her nails digging in like talons, he extracted his arm from her vice like grip and followed Sapphire out to the store rooms. He called out to her, trying to get her to stop but the stubborn female ignored him. Quickening his pace to catch her up he reached out an arm, hauling her to a stop.

"What's wrong, why did you leave?"

Sapphire had tried to ignore him, she really had, not wanting to get into another argument with him. He was nothing to do with her, it didn't matter to her what he did or with whom, be it the slutty girl he emerged from the back with or this new trollop that had claimed him as her own. None of it mattered to her, not one ounce of it. Or so she kept telling herself, begging her brain to remember that little fact before she opened her mouth.

"I left because I had no reason to stay. You were more than busy, as you seem to be every time I bump into you. It's high time I went home and got on with my life, not hang around here like a shadow."

"I wasn't busy…" Avery started to protest but she steamrollered right over him.

"Of course you were! You always seem to be busy with some female or another, it appears to be your goal in life to never be without the willing arms of a woman."

"I wasn't with her…" he tried again, wanting her to listen to him so he could explain that they actually meant nothing to him, he might even have gone as far as to tell her that after their impromptu sofa make out session, she was the only woman he was thinking about, period. But she was too angry now to stop. She was finding it harder and harder to control her emotions lately, to rein in her words and keep an even temper, all things she used to be well known for.

"Oh please!" her arms flew up into the air in a gesture of pure frustration before coming down to settle on her hips, propped there school teacher style. "You cannot tell me that you didn't screw that little chickie the other night and you cannot expect me to believe that you and that glamour puss out there haven't hooked up a time or two also."

He opened his mouth to protest again but gave up. She was right, he couldn't very well deny it. But it wasn't in his nature to let someone get the last word and be pissed at him without him having a chance to defend himself.

"Alright! Yes, OK? So, I fucked that Donor the other night. And why shouldn't I? I'm free and single. And until I meet my Soul Mate, I'm staying that way. And yes, Lili and I had a thing a few years ago, sometime last century, but again, not my Soul Mate. So, I think you'll find that I am doing nothing wrong. So maybe you should hurry up and take your prissy arse back home where it belongs and get out of my face. Stop trying to make me feel bad about something you have no rights to even comment on." And with that last verbal arrow that hit her right between the ribs and straight into the heart, he turned on his heel and stomped down to the basement, leaving her standing alone in the corridor.

Avery didn't know how she managed to do that to him, to get under his skin and make him lose his cool so effectively. She might be all cool control and unflappable poise, but he prided himself on being the most laid-back Vampire in the history of blood suckers, he never let anything get to him, only truly caring about a select few people, his friends, who meant the world to him. When you were a Vampire of any considerable age it was almost unheard of to have any blood relations left, friends became your surrogate family. Avery would fight to the bitter end for those he counted as close.

Sapphire wanted to yell after him, wanted to scream at him that it was her business, that she had every right to be jealous, because that's what her real problem was. She wanted to demand that he came back and kissed her, took her as he did the others, but she didn't. She wanted to chase after him and demand to know what was so wrong with her that he had stopped trying. That, even after their kiss, he didn't want her any more. She had grown used to his flirting, his taking care of her and now that he had stopped, she realised just how much she missed it.

73

She had to pull herself together. She had never acted in such a way over a man before and she wasn't prepared to start now. What she needed to do was go home, have a nice hot bath, curl up in bed and read until the sun came up, forgetting all about Avery and his wandering pants syndrome. Forcing herself not to even glance in the direction he had gone she pushed open the back door, letting herself out into the walled courtyard that served as a loading bay.

Chapter Seven

Sapphire didn't notice it at first. It was subtle, just barely there. Like a tickling at the edge of her subconscious. But the second she took notice of it, it was like she had awakened her senses. The scent slammed into her nose, almost taking away what little air she had left in her lungs. It was vile. The metallic tang of blood, mixed with the stench of open drains. Human waste, with a sickly sweet, yet, somewhat sour undertone she couldn't place.

She twisted her head this way and that, sniffing at the air like a blood hound, attempting to locate the source of the smell. It was then that she noticed the woman.

She had short blond hair that was spiked up from her head. Her clothes were black and tight, her leggings shiny and seemingly spray painted onto her body, her t-shirt slashed and torn in places. Saph could only see her from behind but she looked vaguely familiar. She was sure she had seen her before.

The mystery woman was standing just outside of the loading bay, beyond the double gates. Gates that Sapphire was sure would normally have been closed. There was a single wooden gate in one of the side walls that employees used when coming or going, which she herself had planned on using.

"Hey, you!" Sapphire called out, using her firm, authoritative voice. "What are you doing back here? This is a private yard."

But the woman gave no reaction. She either didn't hear or was simply choosing to ignore the question. Either way she was pissing Sapphire off. If there was one thing she hated it was being ignored.

"Hey! I'm talking to you," Sapphire stomped over, ready to get her attention no matter what. As she got closer Saph noticed the woman appeared to be standing over something on the ground, looking down at it in obvious fascination, though to Sapphire it appeared to be a pile of rubbish bags set out for collection.

"Can you hear me?" Saph questioned as she got closer, not wanting to startle someone she didn't know. The scent was getting stronger the closer she got to the woman. The air was thick with it, the stench seeming to fill the air.

Sapphire couldn't help but cover her nose and mouth with her cupped hand, fighting down the urge to gag. It was like the smell was coating her insides with every breath she took, the sweetness at odds with the foulness of human waste. She was profoundly grateful that she didn't actually have to breathe.

The woman turned just as Sapphire was sure her body was about to forcefully evacuate the drinks she'd just enjoyed. Sapphire's eyes locked on her face, finally recognising her as one of the females that had been wandering the bar, acting almost as a walking buffet for any Vampire present. Donors, Amethyst had called them.

Sapphire opened her mouth, about to ask her again what she was doing hanging around out back, when the woman's eyes flickered down again towards the ground. Sapphire's eyes followed, almost unable to take in and make sense of exactly what she was seeing.

76

The woman's shirt was torn right down the middle, the sides flapping open. And whatever had done it hadn't stopped there. The woman's stomach and chest was in tatters, her insides on the outside, guts and intestines spilling out. She looked like something out of a horror movie. How was she standing? How was that even possible?

"Ohmigod," Saph yelped. "Holy shit, sit down. You need help!" She flapped her hands uselessly, not quite knowing what to do, she didn't want to touch the woman from fear of doing more damage, but she couldn't do nothing. "I'll fetch help," she stated in what she hoped was a calm, controlled voice. "You're going to be OK."

The female still looked sadly down at the ground, refusing to meet Sapphire's eyes, but she slowly raised a hand, pointing at where she was looking.

"We don't have time to bother with rubbish..." Sapphire started to say, until she actually looked down and saw what the woman was pointing to.

There lay her body. She was curled on her side and at first Sapphire assumed it was due to her trying to protect herself, that was until she looked closer. Her insides were cradled in one hand, as you would hold a baby to your body while sleeping, her other hand was up close to her face and when she leaned closer, she could see that her thumb was in her mouth, giving her a distinctly childlike pose.

She was clearly dead though she actually looked peaceful. Her eyes were closed as if she were sleeping, her features relaxed in death, yet the splashes of blood on her pale skin marred that image.

Sapphire looked back up at the female standing over her own dead body, knowing that it could only mean one thing. The ghosts were back. It was all too much for her and without even knowing she was doing it, she let out a blood curdling scream of pure horror.

Avery was keeping himself busy behind the bar, not wanting to keep thinking about what had just happened with Sapphire. All they seemed to be able to do was argue. He swore he could hear her in his head screaming, no doubt directed at him for some wrongdoing that she had dreamt up, it wasn't like he could actually do anything wrong, he was perfect. She just, like all women, couldn't make up her mind what she wanted. She was driving him mad. He shook his head, trying to dislodge her from his thoughts as he turned and began stacking clean glasses under the counter.

It took him a few seconds to realise that the screaming he heard, though faint, wasn't actually in his head at all. As soon as he acknowledged it he felt overwhelming fear and disgust that he was pretty sure didn't belong to him. He looked down at the glass in his hand for a second, trying to focus, when he heard the scream again. Without thought the glass slipped from his fingers, smashing to the ground as he vaulted over the bar top and raced outside the way Sapphire had left.

As soon as he threw open the fire exit he smelt it. The unmistakable stench of death clung to the air. Blood, and a lot of it, had been spilt and recently too. He didn't allow himself to breathe deeper as he caught the smell of excrement along with the acidic tang of urine.

He didn't let that put him off as he spotted Sapphire leaning against a far wall, as if that was the only thing holding her up. She let out another ear-piercing scream as he reached for her, gathering her into his arms. She struggled violently against his grip, pointing madly at something he couldn't see. She was obviously in shock and extreme fear.

She was standing beside the body of a young girl, maybe at most 25 years old. He recognised her as a Donor, one that he had partaken in a few times. He struggled to remember her name. He always found female names the hardest to remember, mostly because he heard so many while working the bar. He would often empty his pockets at the end of the night and find at least six separate scraps of paper, each bearing the name and number of some female (and a few men) that he had caught the eye of during the course of a shift.

He didn't know what to do for the best, Sapphire was obviously about to have some kind of break-down. Deciding he couldn't do anything for the dead woman on the floor at that moment he scooped Saph up, cradling her against his chest, turning to take her back inside.

"No, I can't leave her!" Sapphire wailed, thrashing in his arms so violently that he struggled to not drop her, she was certainly gaining her Vampire strength.

"It's alright, darling, you can leave her, there's nothing we can do for her now," he tried to soothe her, to placate her as he took another step.

"But she's right there!" Sapphire argued, pointing over his shoulder. He glanced back but saw nothing of interest. Frustrated, she pushed at his chest, kicking her legs until he gave in and put her down.

"I know, but you can't do anything to help now!"

Sapphire suddenly looked up at him, all big, tear filled eyes. "What's her name?"

Avery blinked. Her name? Why did she need to know the name of a dead woman? He wracked his brains trying to remember, but they all passed in and out of the club at different times, Donors' faces and names tended to blend together after a while. It wasn't that he wanted to think of them as simply a food source, they were human beings after all, but you did have to afford yourself a certain amount of distance. He pictured her face, the one before she died, not the blood splattered mess he had just seen and finally, blessedly, it came to him. Cassie.

He tried to urge Sapphire forwards, wanting to get her back inside, away from the horror show that was laying on the cold ground, but she was having none of it.

79

"Cassie," he finally answered. He hadn't wanted to, didn't want her to associate the dead body on the floor as a person, didn't want to give her a name and see her as real. It would be easier on her if she didn't. But she was nothing if not stubborn.

She pushed him aside, going back around him towards the body.

"Cassie? Cassie, can you hear me?" She waved her arms at the air, as if trying to get something's attention. He just stood and watched, dumbfounded.

Sapphire was getting so annoyed with that pushy man. Who did he think he was just swooping in and picking her up like that? Didn't he see Cassie standing right there, needing help, looking so lost? It broke Saph's heart to see it. She had to help her.

"Cassie?" she tried again, raising her voice and this time the girl seemed to hear, turning her head slightly away from staring at her own mutilated corpse. And didn't that just top the list of weird things to think to yourself? Sapphire ignored that one.

"Sapphire?" Avery's voice tried to break through her concentration, but she ignored him, utterly focused on the girl.

"Cassie, stop looking at it, look at me. Me, right here." She pushed as much command into her tone that she could manage, and it seemed to work.

She heard Avery jog away, the distant sound of the back door being thrown open, his yells as he called out for Cassian and Amy. But she ignored it all. The girl deserved her full focus.

The girl turned fully to look at her, once again her insides on display for all that cared to look. Which Sapphire didn't, she kept her eyes fixed rigidly on the girl's own.

"Cassie, it'll be alright." *Lying, I'm lying to a ghost. Is that something I can go to hell for?* The thoughts bounced

80

around her brain like rubber balls, making no real sense, random and disjointed. She shook her head, trying to focus.

"Cassie, can you tell me what happened? Who did this?' She didn't hold out much hope of the ghost being helpful, but it was worth a shot.

She knew that Cassie had heard her, saw it in her eyes as she looked down at the body again, then at herself, as if only just that second registering that she was looking down on herself. Her image flickered, her mouth opening in a silent scream of denial before she winked out of sight.

"Cassie?" Sapphire looked all around, but in her heart she already knew it was wasted time. "Are you still here?" She asked even though she knew she was gone. Suddenly saddened, hoping beyond anything that the young girl had moved on to a better place, she turned back to Avery.

He was standing there, looking so on edge, like a skittish cat, that she almost wanted to laugh.

Avery looked all around, like he was expecting a headless horseman to pop out at any second.

"So…erm…what was that all about then?" He ran his fingers through his hair, obviously trying to look casual but failing.

"She was standing right there? You really didn't see her?"

"No, pet, there was no one there." He looked at her with utter sympathy, which just pissed her off. How dare he judge her and her mental state? He knew nothing about her or her life before he came barrelling into it. She was done letting people belittle her, judge her, make her feel bad for being herself and having a gift.

"I'm not crazy, I'm a medium!" she yelled at him, shocking even herself, but proud of the fact that she had said it, owning what she was, yet still scared of the ramifications.

She wrapped her arms around her body in an attempt to stop the shaking that had started. She didn't tell people about her gift, certainly didn't voice it out loud and now here

81

she was, blurting it out and exposing herself for the freak that she was. But now that she had spoken the words, she couldn't seem to stop.

"I see them, I hear them, the dead, I always have. But not that strongly, not like just then. She was so clear, like she was right there. I didn't notice at first, not until she turned around..." she trailed off, unable to get the image of the woman out of her head.

"A medium," he whispered, quite dazed. A true medium, they were rare. Not the kind that blagged their way through a reading or pretended to give messages from the other side, but a true, genuine medium, with the ability to not just see the dead but communicate with them, they were like gold dust sprinkled rocking horse shit.

"Yes, a medium." She felt defensive now. "What of it?"

He shook his head, amused by the fierce look on her face.

"Nothing, it just makes you more special than you already were."

Her head canted to the side as she watched him, looking for a sign that he was lying, that he was secretly freaked out by her revelation. But she didn't see any of that in his expression. All she saw was something she wasn't used to seeing in relation to her, something that looked rather like awe and amazement. But she had to be wrong. She was a freak, one that people avoided at all costs when they learnt of her gifts. She had suffered enough at school to know that. But Avery didn't seem to see it that way.

She took a step towards him.

"You don't seem to mind. Why is that? And what do you mean, more special?"

He looked scared, like he didn't know what to say or do, his face registering panic. Panic that instantly morphed into profound relief when Cassian, closely followed by Amy, burst out into the courtyard to join them.

"What's happened? What's wrong?" Cass was all business. Clearly glad of the distraction, Avery led the way over to the body.

"Amy, sweetheart, stay back," Avery warned. "Take your sister and go inside." Amy didn't argue, just grabbed her sister by the arm and tugged her inside.

Cassian bent down beside the body, closing his eyes briefly to say a short prayer.

"She's a Donor," Avery offered helpfully. He wasn't a stranger to death but the sheer brutality of this one was affecting him. It was something about the way she had been seemingly arranged that way, to look as innocent and childlike as possible.

"I know," Cassian replied, shaking his head sadly. "Miss Cassie, I believe her name is. I shall have to inform the Guild. They won't be happy, another girl killed in less than a week. I'm beginning to think this place is cursed."

He pulled out his phone as he spoke, dialing and putting it to his ear, delivering the bad news while Avery waited impatiently. He was anxious to check on Sapphire, not liking the way that she had been so distressed, not that he could blame her. He heard Cassian say goodbye and hang up the phone. Not wanting to make a big deal out of it but knowing that his friend would need to know, he strove to keep his tone casual as he made his announcement.

"Sapphire said that she saw the victim's ghost." He pretended to fiddle with his own phone, not wanting to look at either Cassian or the poor girl on the floor. "So, what did the Guild say?"

Cassian blinked, not knowing what to say or which to answer first. He eventually went with the easiest. "They are sending a crew for clean-up and to investigate, obviously we won't be calling the police." He slipped his phone back into his pocket, watching Avery. His friend seemed tense, on edge, which really wasn't like him. Something must really be eating him up.

"Look, I know you don't really like Sapphire, but I don't think this is something she would lie about, if she says she saw the deceased, then I believe that she did. So, thank you for staying with her, but we can look after her from here."

"No!" Avery almost growled, his voice edged with steel.

Cassian was surprised at Avery's tone, that wasn't like him either.

"No?" Cass's head tipped to the side as he studied his friend.

Avery knew he had reacted strongly and that it wasn't his usual way. He took a deep breath, trying to calm the ridiculous flair of panic that had erupted inside him at the thought of Sapphire being taken away from him again, to deal with all this on her own. He wouldn't have it.

"No," he kept his voice as calm and steady as he could. "I'm not leaving her with you on her own. She's scared and vulnerable right now, I want to make sure she's alright."

"Of course she'll be alright, why wouldn't she be? Amy is with her." Cassian was thoroughly confused and that didn't happen often, he decided he didn't like the feeling at all. He took a wild stab at a guess. "You like her, don't you?"

Avery was sure that if he could blush he would be as red as a tomato right that second. How the hell did he know? He could try to deny it, but his friend obviously knew him better than he thought.

"Yeah, so what if I do? She's a nice girl." He shrugged, trying to sound casual. He didn't succeed. "I just want to make sure she's OK, you know? That's all. She's only just turned, and it was scary for her, finding the body like this. And the ghost. That can't be easy." He paused, his brain finally catching up and processing what he was saying. "You know, now that I think on it, she didn't seem that surprised. She was shocked about finding the body yes, but the ghost, she was actually rather matter of fact about that, even said she was a medium. I think this is something she's always been able to do. Did Amy not tell you anything about it?"

84

Cassian shook his head, processing this new information.

"No, it's as much news to me as it is to you. Amy and I have spoken at length about her family, especially now that Saph has turned. I'm sure that if Amy knew she would have told me."

"Well, something is going on here and I intend to find out the second the Guild get here and we're free to go find the girls."

Cassian nodded his agreement, his Soul Mate's sister definitely had hidden depths.

Chapter Eight

Amy sat with her arm around her sister, silently offering comfort. She had tried to get her to talk but Saph had remained tight lipped, refusing to talk, just staring with wide eyes towards the door they had come back through, like she knew that the body was still out there. To be honest that thought gave Amethyst the creeps too.

Sapphire couldn't move, she couldn't think. Couldn't believe what had happened out there. She felt cold, so dreadfully cold, chilled right down to her bones. Normally she always talked things out with her sisters, wouldn't keep anything from them, but now, she just couldn't deal with Amethyst's unwelcome chatter. She knew that her sister was trying to help, to keep her mind off things, but she didn't want to talk, she just wanted to be left alone to try to make some kind of sense of the thoughts pinging around in her brain.

She felt oddly alone even though she had her sister with her, one of the most important people in her life, but right that second it wasn't enough. She could feel the old panic building up inside her, the knowledge that they were back after all these years. Years of her trying and for the most part, succeeding in suppressing her weird talent. You know what they say, use it or lose it, and she had been praying that she would lose it. She thought it had worked, the voices had gone quiet, she had stopped hearing whispers in her ear about people around her, she had stopped seeing horrifically pale faces, battered bodies and hollow eyes. She had shut it all out, out of sight, out of mind, and it had worked. It had been more than five years since she had seen or heard anything. But it seemed her unwanted turning had undone all her good work. Another thing to hate about being a Vampire.

She didn't know what she would do if they started visiting as regularly as they used to, if she started seeing them while shopping or at work. She didn't want people to look at her like she was crazy and talking to herself. She just wanted to be normal. Her mind chose that moment to pipe up with an unhelpful little note, *Avery didn't look at you like you were crazy, he believed you.* She hadn't really allowed herself to dwell on it that much, but the little voice was right, he had. Avery always treated her like she was normal. She found herself actually wishing that he was there. And didn't that just piss her off all over again?

Avery and Cassian watched the Guild officers as they raked over the back yard and the alley beyond, with a fine tooth comb, looking for any tiny thing that was a possible clue that might shed some light on who was responsible for the mess that had been made of the young girl. Someone had obviously taken great pleasure in her murder and that would not go unpunished. They would catch the culprit eventually, they could count on that.

Miss Angelica made her way over and they stood up straighter in anticipation of getting this unpleasantness over and done with, so they could get back inside to the girls. They nodded their heads in greeting, trying to ignore the clean-up crew that had now arrived busying themselves with zipping the poor girl into a plain body bag and loading her into the back of a waiting van. Avery couldn't help but feel sorry for her all over again. Vampires didn't have funeral rights as such, some chose to greet the dawn or end their long lives at the sharp point of a stake, but as they very rarely ever left a body behind for someone to find, they didn't go into the whole ceremony the same way the humans did. But he felt for the girl's family. They wouldn't have a body to bury, they wouldn't know what had happened to her, she would simply become one of the many girls that vanished without a trace. And for some reason this bothered him so much more than it normally would have, maybe it was seeing how close Amethyst, Sapphire and Tanzanite were, seeing the devastation on Amy's face when she thought she might have lost her sister.

"Did you two see anything?" Miss Angelica's demanding voice snapping him out of his musings. They both shook their heads without the slightest hesitation.

"Our newest turnee happened across the poor girl when she was heading home. It obviously scared her and upon hearing her screams, I ran out after her to see what was wrong." Avery kept the details truthful but sparse at first, wanting to judge the situation before he revealed what Sapphire might want to keep a secret.

The Vampires had a good relationship with the Donors Guild, one that they didn't want to jeopardize. It was a mutually beneficial partnership, the Donors craved the bite of the Vampire, almost like a junkie after their next fix, and the Vampires liked having a meal on tap. It meant that they didn't have to skulk in the shadows and hide what they were from their feeding partners. It was nice sometimes to just feed and not worry. It meant that they could call up and arrange for a Donor to come to their home or to come to a club like Carpe Noctem or Night Walkers and socialise while securing an evening meal. It worked for them all, as it had for hundreds of years, and no one wanted to mess that up. Cassian was determined to cooperate with the Guild as much as possible, having already given one of the team the key to his office and permission to take the CCTV footage for viewing.

Miss Angelica's tone softened at the mention of Sapphire. "How is she doing? You didn't call for a Donor. We had kept a female on standby for the last few days, we didn't think she would want to feed from a male after what that monster did to her."

Avery was pathetically grateful that Vampires lacked the bodily functions to blush, as the memory of Sapphire's delicate little fangs buried in his throat made things south of his body suddenly stand to attention. He rubbed at his hair in what he hoped was a casual gesture to draw her attention before he gave her one of his patented, dazzling smiles.

"She's doing well, as good as can be expected given the circumstances of her turning. Thank you for asking."

Miss Angelica nodded in understanding. "Obviously, I understand that all of this," she waved a hand towards the area of bloodied pavement that her team were busily cleaning, "must have come as a big shock to her, especially after all she's recently been through herself. But, I'm afraid we must talk to her. The council is ready to get involved if we can't come up with some information as to why it seems to be our Donors that are being targeted. There's been a report of other bodies found the same way in other cities, even a few others scattered in France and Germany over the last few years. They are worried that it's the same killer and I'm inclined to agree with them."

One of the clean-up crew called out to let them know that they were finished and would be moving out. Miss Angelica held up a hand in acknowledgement and waved them off.

"We've done all we can here for tonight. Go check on your newbie but warn her that we will be back tomorrow to talk to her. Any information she can give us will be a help at this point, no matter how insignificant she believes it may be."

"We'll do that," Cassian assured her, speaking for the first time. Avery had seen him watching the cleaners with an eagle eye. This was his place of business and in the few short weeks they had been open it had already had its fair share of scandals, he didn't need anything else damaging its reputation. Much as it sadden him to have lost a Donor in such bad circumstances, he was determined that his establishment wouldn't be blamed.

They said their collective goodbyes, Miss Angelica arranging to come to them a few hours after sundown the next evening.

"Well, mate, that didn't go too badly," Avery attempted a casual tone, but Cassian wasn't fooled.

"I know you're worried about Saph, I can see it in your eyes. I won't let anyone upset her, that's a promise. But I'm not looking forward to telling her that she has to talk to the Guild tomorrow. She's already been rather resistant to getting further into our lifestyle than she already is."

Avery nodded, he couldn't help but agree, a happy Vampire she was not.

Amethyst's head snapped up the second the men entered the room. Her eyes lighting up to see her Soul Mate, looking profoundly grateful to no longer be alone with her sister.

"How did it go? What happened?" her words come out in a rush as she left her seat and met the boys halfway, slipping her arms around Cassian's middle, tipping her head back for a kiss, an offer Cass eagerly accepted.

Avery rolled his eyes at their obvious display of affection, coming over to take the seat that Amy had vacated.

"You doing alright?" he asked Sapphire.

The sound of Avery's voice, soft and almost intimate, broke into her thoughts and she gave her head a little shake to clear it, blinking to focus on his question. She managed to dredge up a wane smile and nodded. "I'm OK. What happened out there?"

Amy and Cassian joined them as Avery answered her.

"The Guild has cleaned up and removed the body. They didn't find anything of importance out there, so they need to talk to you tomorrow.'

"Me?" Sapphire looked panicked all over again, something the others couldn't help but notice. "Why? What did you tell them?" her tone had grown accusatory.

"Nothing!" Avery defended himself. "Just that you found the poor girl, which you did. I had to tell them that, they wanted to watch our CCTV and have taken the memory cards with them. We can't hide the fact that you were out there first."

Sapphire crossed her arms, hugging herself as if she was suddenly freezing cold. She seemed to shrink down into herself and Avery wanted nothing more than to pull her onto his lap and hold her, but she would probably hit him if he tried.

"I don't see what more I can tell them. I don't know anything. I found the girl and I screamed and then you came. Why can't you just talk to them instead? I haven't had any contact with her, I didn't even know her."

Avery gaped at her, his mouth hanging open for a second before he spoke. "You did talk to her though. You saw her out there. You saw her spirit. You could help more than you know. You just have to tell them everything."

Sapphire jerked in her chair like she'd just received an electric shock. Her voice when she finally spoke came out as a harsh hiss, her face a mask of anger. "Don't ever talk about that, don't tell anyone. I didn't see anything, my mind was obviously playing tricks on me, shock or something." She stood abruptly. "I'm tired. I'm going to bed."

She turned on her heel and marched stiffly out of the room and up to Cassian and Amy's apartment above, obviously forgetting her previous desire to go home.

Amy appeared shocked at her sister's outburst. "Avery, I'm so sorry, that was so rude of her, she's never normally like that. She never loses her cool. I don't know what's gotten into her."

Avery waved away her concern. "It's alright, love. She didn't mean it. She's just upset. But why is she suddenly saying that she didn't see anything out there?"

Amethyst sighed deeply, looking troubled. She glanced up the stairs in the direction her sister had gone, then lowered her voice, as if parting with a great secret.

"She used to be very open with us about her abilities. Our mother always said that everyone is born with the ability to contact the spirit world and to be aware of it but most of us lose that ability as we get older and start believing in less and less. Sapphire had always had imaginary friends and was always talking to someone invisible to us, ever since she could form words. But it was only as she got older that our mum realised that, upon asking her questions, she was actually conversing with deceased family members and friends. Mum would show her photo albums full of old pictures and Saph would know everyone there. We always encouraged her to be open about it. I guess that was our mistake. We were so proud of her and our family that we never stopped to consider what the outside world would think." Amethyst snuggled into Cassian as she talked, instinctively seeking comfort from her Soul Mate.

"When Saph was about fifteen some girls from school found out. I'm afraid they weren't very nice about it. They called her a freak and teased her about it so much that Saph soon refused to go to school. Eventually our parents moved her to a new one. But she was never the same after that. She became quiet and withdrawn, and she never spoke about the spirits again. We asked her once and she just said that they had gone." Amethyst shrugged as she finished. "Mum guessed that she turned her back on her powers and shut them out. She hasn't mentioned it in ten or more years."

Avery listened to his friend, feeling so sorry for the young girl that Sapphire had been, to have her wondrous gift ridiculed and to be picked on for it, he couldn't imagine how she must have felt. He could understand why she wouldn't want to talk about it now that she had had time to compose herself, the shock of finding the dead Donor obviously wearing off. He could understand completely why she would shut herself off from the spirit world, effectively giving up on her abilities, locking them away within her mind, letting them fade away. But what he couldn't understand was why she was using them again now.

"Cass, do you think the turning could have awoken her powers again? Enhanced them somehow so that her mental shields just aren't strong enough to keep them contained?"

Cassian thought about this for a few moments, turning the idea over in his mind, before he slowly nodded. "It's entirely possible, in fact I believe it's a very good theory. But, Ave, we need to get her to open up to it more. We need to get her to embrace them again and trust that she isn't a scared teenager any more, she's a strong woman in her own right. She can't hide from them anymore. If what we think is true, then the more she struggles and fights against them, the harder they will push back. She won't have any peace until she accepts it. And it would really help if she could tell the Guild what she saw, maybe even try to contact the spirit again and get some answers that way. Someone needs to talk to her.'

The men both looked at Amethyst, silently volunteering her. But she had other ideas.

"Oh no, don't you dare look at me. Tanzi and I tried for years to get her to be true to herself and to not hide away, but she never listened, she'd just shut down on us. The more we tried the more she withdrew, wrapping herself up in that self-confident, capable shell that she erected around herself. You guys are on your own."

Avery knew it was coming before Cassian even said it, but there it was.

"Mate, you're up."

93

Like a condemned man walking to the gallows, Avery got up and followed after the pissed off female that dominated his every waking thought.

Chapter Nine

Avery knocked on the closed door, lightly at first, then harder when he received no answer. She had only been gone for maybe ten minutes, there was no way she was asleep in that short space of time, even if she hadn't done what every Vampire did and slept a full day, waking up only a few hours before.

He knocked again, a full on bang of his knuckles against the wood. It remained stubbornly shut and she remained just as stubbornly silent. He was being ignored. Avery hated being ignored. It was one of the very few things that he simply could not stand.

"Sapphire, sweetheart," he wheedled. "Open the door, honey, so we can talk." He waited, his superior hearing picking up the subtle rustling of bed sheets as she shifted on the bed. And damn, if the image of her in bed didn't pop right into his head. Again, his traitor of a dick swelled in his pants, becoming unbelievably uncomfortable in a matter of seconds. He took a moment to adjust himself, trying to relieve some of the pressure before he hammered on the door again.

"Open the door. We have to talk about this." But again, he was ignored.

He wasn't prepared to stand there like a lemon all night banging on the door, he'd tried being nice, now he had to be tougher.

"Listen to me, I know you can hear me, even if you didn't have Vampire hearing, you'd have to be deaf not to. You can't run from this, Sapphire. I thought you were stronger than that," he paused and listened but still heard nothing. She must have been lying stiff as a board in there. "I understand that you may have had negative reactions from people in the past, but I promise you, upon my word, that no one will ever treat you that way again. You have a wonderful gift that can help so many if only you would embrace it and accept it. Be proud of it, don't hide it."

Again there was no answer, though he knew she heard him, he'd caught her sharp intake of breath.

He sighed, banging his forehead against the closed door in defeat.

"OK, you win, I'm not going to stand here talking to a door all night. But I will say one thing before I leave. This won't go away. The Guild are coming tomorrow. And if being a Vampire has triggered your powers again, they will only get more intense the longer you try to deny them. They are a part of you. Deal with it."

He turned to go, stopping to throw one more parting comment.

"You won't get rid of me. I'll be back tomorrow for when the Guild get here." There was nothing else he could do if she didn't want to talk to him. He wasn't about to destroy the fragile trust she had in him by forcing his way into the room. She would talk to him when she was ready. If there was one thing he had realised about Sapphire, it was that she could be as stubborn as a mule when she wanted to be.

Avery forced himself to walk away, much as he wanted to set up camp outside her door and wait for her, pouncing on her the second she appeared, he knew that that would drive her further away from him.

Cassian and Amethyst met him at the front door, raising an eyebrow in silent question. Avery shook his head, no he hadn't managed to talk to her.

Sapphire heard when he left, letting out a sigh of relief. Why did he have to push her so much? Why couldn't he just leave her alone? Always interfering in her life. Like earlier when he had tricked her into drinking bottled blood. OK, so it hadn't tasted bad when he mixed things with it and it had made her feel so much better, but that wasn't the point.

Everything in her life felt like it was running away from her, like she was losing all control, all her choices were being taken away and she hated that. She needed her control, she needed to be in charge of her own life. She wasn't about to let the actions of one monster destroy her life as he had done to her sister. She and Tanzanite had been the ones to help pick up the pieces of their sister's shattered confidence, her trust and her happiness. Though, she had to admit, Amy hadn't really started living again until she met Cassian, she had simply been existing until then.

She heard a new, more tentative knock on the door, knowing that it was her sister, but again she stayed silent. She knew that they wouldn't really believe that she was asleep, the only time she actually felt tired was when the sun came up and she sank into a dreamless sleep, she had no choice in it. It was yet another thing she had no control over. It was something that her body now did without her say so. She had always been able to survive on very little sleep, staying up for days working if she had to, now she simply passed out with the dawn and woke when the sun went down.

She didn't want to talk to anyone, didn't they get that? Couldn't they respect that? Just accept that she was her own person and could make her own decisions? She didn't want to start seeing spirits again. Didn't think she ever would, if she was a hundred percent honest. She occasionally caught the odd flicker out of the corner of her eye, but she had always been able to ignore them, telling herself that it was a trick of the light. But tonight, with that girl, she had seemed so solid, so there, that at first Sapphire hadn't been sure what she was seeing. Her powers were back, and they appeared to be stronger than ever.

She didn't want to admit, even to herself, that Avery could be right. That her unwanted turning had somehow broken through all her defences to reawaken the one thing she had tried so hard to bury.

She gave herself a mental smack upside the head, telling herself firmly to grow up and deal. She hated to admit that Avery was right in many things that he had said, not that she would ever tell him that and inflate his ego even more. She was trying to run away and hide, something she knew would get her nowhere. She knew that the spirits never truly went away, they were always there, lurking in the background, ready for any weakness from her.

Now that she was being honest with herself, she could admit that they had been around far more than she had allowed herself to believe. That when she was tired or stressed they appeared more, the voices in her head were louder. She knew in her heart of hearts that it was something she did have to deal with, to stand up to. It would never go away, it was a part of who she was. She had just never wanted it. She didn't have a choice now, fate, it seemed, had forced her hand. The Guild was coming and there was nothing she could do about it.

She had to trust, something that was very hard for her, that Avery told the truth, and that no one would treat her badly, no one would think she was a freak. She was in a different world now, one where everyone was a freak in their own special way. She might be able to be herself with no fear of ridicule, it was a novel idea. One that she didn't want to look at too closely. When you trusted and believed in people, those people tended to let you down.

Cassian and Amethyst hadn't seen Sapphire again after she locked herself in her room, nor in the few hours since nightfall. So, when Miss Angelica, a male from the Guild who introduced himself as Roger and another female, a Vampire by the name of Vanessa, who represented the Council, knocked on the door, Cass was pretty sure that he would be buying a new bedroom door before the night was over.

The Guild might have agreed to try the softly softly approach, but he knew the council never would. No matter how delicate and sweet Vanessa appeared to be, he knew that she had to be very, very old to have risen in the ranks to the position of council representative. Old and most likely tough. She would break the door down without batting an eyelid.

So, he was rather grateful when Avery appeared in the hallway, following the visitors into the lounge. He left Amy to show them to their seats while he made his way over to talk quietly to Avery.

"Did she come out at all last night?" Avery asked as soon as Cassian reached him.

"Nope, and she hasn't appeared this morning either. Amy tried last night to get her to answer but she ignored her."

"Much the same as she did to me," Avery agreed. "Want me to try again?"

Cassian didn't get a chance to answer. Sapphire breezed into the room, her hair neatly put back in a perfect chignon, her immaculate suit pressed. She radiated an air of self-confidence and control. Anyone that didn't know her, or wasn't looking that closely, would have been easily fooled into thinking she was perfectly at ease with her surroundings. Avery however, was not fooled for a second. He saw the tight set of her jaw, the slight lines of worry around her eyes, the subtle shaking of her hands. She was giving a stellar performance, but he worried that she might crack at any moment.

Miss Angelica, Roger and Vanessa each stood in turn, introducing themselves and thanking her for her time. She dutifully shook hands with each in turn before taking a seat in an armchair. Avery didn't wait to be asked, he simply sat on the arm of the chair she was perched in and relaxed, ignoring the little squinty eyed glare that Sapphire levelled his way.

Obviously eager to start, Roger leant forward in his chair, the overhead lights reflected off of his slicked back, too shiny hair. He looked smarmy and Avery instantly took a disliking to him.

"So, Miss Summerland, is it? Or can I call you Sapphire?" He bestowed upon her a charming grin obviously meant to put her at ease. Avery was secretly pleased when it didn't seem to work. Sapphire remained stiff and composed, sitting up straight in her chair.

"Sapphire is fine," she answered in a crisp, curt voice.

Undeterred, Roger kept his tone friendly.

"Could you talk us through the events of last night? In your own words, take your time. Remember that no detail is too small or insignificant no matter what you might think."

Sapphire nodded, acknowledging his words before she spoke. She kept her voice even, loud enough for all to hear her but not too loud as to be shouting. She spoke in an almost toneless voice, like she was delivering a sales pitch to a client. But Avery could tell that the apparent lack of emotion was anything but. She was holding herself together as best she knew how but taking as much control as she could.

"I have been staying here with my sister and Cassian since my turning," she began. Avery noticed that she failed to mention the fact that he had been the one to nurse her through the first three difficult days. That pissed him off, but he kept his mouth shut, biting back the retort that was on the tip of his tongue. He would talk to her about that later, it was not something he would let go.

"I was growing tired of being in their apartment all the time, I wanted my own things around me, a change of clothes, to sleep in my own bed. I stopped into the club for a drink before I left to walk home. We only live a few streets over; the walk takes barely ten minutes. I left through the staff entrance, I didn't want to have to make my way through the crowds outside." She gave them all the pertinent information but also managed to answer their unspoken question as to why she had been out there. Avery was proud of her, she was doing well so far.

"I had barely gone a few feet when I saw her laying there, on the ground. I took a closer look, I don't really know why. And then, I guess I began screaming. It was just such a shock for me. I'm not used to seeing things like that. The next thing I knew Avery was there with me and he took charge."

Roger nodded, as he had the whole way through her statement. Vanessa had stayed silent, while Miss Angelica made notes.

"Did you see anyone else out there?"

Sapphire had to pause before she answered, technically she had seen someone out there other than the dead body, it just happened to be the spirit that had recently vacated it. She didn't know what to say, didn't know how to proceed. She knew that they would most likely have some kind of Vampire superpower that let them know she was lying, so what choice did she have?

Avery knew exactly why she had paused, why she was struggling to form an answer. Cassian and Amethyst were keeping to themselves, their mouths firmly shut. He didn't want to be accused of leading her or forcing her to tell her secret, but he wanted her to know it was OK. Gently, he laid his hand on her shoulder, giving it a squeeze, letting her know with gesture rather than word, that he was right there and wouldn't be going anywhere. He felt her shoulders stiffen for a moment before they relaxed, and she finally spoke. Hesitantly at first, he could tell that she didn't feel comfortable talking about her gift out loud, bracing herself for ridicule and name calling. But she bravely continued.

"Yes, sort of."

"Sort of?" Roger prompted, glancing quickly at Vanessa before he leant forward once again in his chair, eagerly awaiting the details.

"I saw her, the Donor."

"You saw her before she was killed? Did you see it happen? You just said that you saw the body first," Vanessa spoke for the first time, her upper class, cultured English accent was a treat to the ears.

Sapphire shook her head. "No, I didn't see anything but her. She was already dead when I got out there. But I saw her. At first, I thought someone had snuck back there and was trying to cause trouble. She was just standing there. I called out to her, but she didn't answer. She didn't look at me until later."

Avery could tell that the other Vampires were finding it difficult to make sense of what Sapphire was trying to tell them. For once she wasn't her usual clear and concise self. He could tell that she was skirting the issue, not wanting to say the actual words. So, he helped in his usual, forthright, blunt way.

"Saph sees ghosts, spirits. She's saying that she saw the poor girl's spirit before she saw the body."

Sapphire could have killed Avery at that moment, if he wasn't technically already dead. She braced herself for the laughter, the jeering jokes at her expense. But much to her surprise, they didn't come.

"Could you communicate with her? Could you talk to her now? Is that how your gift works?" Vanessa wasted no time in getting to the point.

Sapphire was taken aback by the question. "Well, yes, I mean I could try, if she's still there and hasn't moved on."

Roger looked eager, like the cat that had just had a canary lunch.

"Would you try for us now? Would you come with us to see?"

She didn't know why, but she turned to Avery, looking at him. Her sister stood across the room from her, but it was him, sitting next to her, his hand solid and comforting on her shoulder, that she wanted the support from. He nodded.

"If you feel comfortable with that, darling. Then it might be a good idea to try. It could certainly help a great deal."

Saph nodded, understanding what he meant. It was a case of use it or lose it. She had tried the losing it part and that hadn't worked out too well for her, now she had no choice but to use it.

"Excellent," Roger crowed, standing immediately. "No time like the present. Let us go now."

Sapphire felt like a bit of an idiot, standing in the loading bay, surrounded by Vampires and Guild members as she called out to a ghost. She had been trying for almost ten minutes without so much as a flicker. They were about to give up when Miss Angelica piped up, breaking her silence for the first time.

"I knew Cassie, maybe if I tried?"

She looked to Roger, who inclined his head, giving her permission.

Miss Angelica moved closer to the spot where the body had been found, as if physical distance would help, then she called out in a surprisingly soft voice.

"Cassie? Cassandra, are you here?"

They all waited with barely concealed impatience as she called twice more, their gazes shifting between Miss Angelica and Sapphire.

Sapphire felt like she was on display, a performing monkey that wasn't doing its trick. She wanted to shout at them all to just go away and leave her alone. That it must have been a fluke, she didn't really see ghosts. Deny deny deny.

She started to turn away, not wanting to look at that spot any longer. Yes, the blood itself, the physical evidence that a girl had lost her life there, was now gone, but details were burned into her brain. She couldn't help but picture it as she stood there. The image of how she had seen Cassie, standing all alone, bloody and torn, staring down at her own broken body came unbidden into her mind. And along with it, came Cassie.

She shimmered into form slowly at first, like a stirring of dust motes in the air, they swirled and danced on the light breeze, growing bigger and bigger, more and more, all condensing down into one image, forming into the spirit of Cassie Ford. She looked exactly the same as she had when Sapphire had seen her the night before, just like the victim of a brutal murder. Her hair still clung wetly to one side of her head, covered in blood. Her insides still spilt out of the gash in her abdomen, trailing down like a macabre apron.

"She's here," Sapphire whispered. She didn't want to speak too loudly, as if it would break the spell, send Cassie back to wherever it was she had come from.

"She is?" Miss Angelica looked around as if she too would be able to see the girl.

"Make sure that you tell us everything she says," Roger reminded her. He had told her repeatedly during the walk down the stairs that it was of upmost importance that she repeat everything the spirit said exactly as she said it.

Sapphire pointed to where the spirit now stood, her other hand reaching out blindly for Avery's. He took it without a moment's hesitation, giving it a reassuring squeeze as he linked their fingers.

"Ask her if she knows what happened to her," Roger commanded, all hint of charm gone from his voice. He was a man that expected things to be done when he asked.

"Cassie, can you hear me?" Sapphire asked. The spirit looked over for the first time, her eyes meeting Sapphire's. Slowly, she nodded.

104

"Can you talk? Will you try for me?" Sapphire gently asked. She didn't want to push the spirit, they didn't always have the ability and she didn't want to cause her to leave.

Sapphire saw the ghost's mouth open, moving as if she was talking but no sound came out, not at first. But the more Sapphire strained to hear her, really opened up to her gift, the louder and clearer her words became.

"Can you hear me?" the ghost pleaded to be heard and Sapphire was so grateful to be able to reassure her that, yes, she could.

"What happened to me?" the ghost asked. Sapphire didn't know if she should tell her, but then, they were out there to talk to the girl and see if she could give them any information. "Am I dead?"

Sapphire nodded slowly. "Yes, I'm sorry, but you are. Someone killed you." She didn't feel the need to translate that to the people standing around watching her with avid fascination, it was obvious what had been asked.

Sapphire expected the poor girl to start to cry, to become upset. What she didn't see coming was the level of pissed off that Cassie reached.

"That motherfucker killed me? What a wanker!"

Sapphire choked on a laugh.

"What did she say?" Roger asked.

"She called him a motherfucker and a wanker," she supplied.

"So it was a man?" Vanessa homed in on the important information.

Sapphire turned back to the still ranting ghost. "Can you remember much about last night? Other than it was a man?"

Cassie screwed up her nose like she was concentrating, then her face cleared, replaced by a look of sheer determination.

"Yes, I remember everything. I came to the club around my usual time. There wasn't much action going on, so I had a quick drink with another girl and decided to call it a night and move on somewhere else. He," she pointed at Avery, "used to be a sure thing, but since he went all noble and turned me down the other night, I hadn't been with anyone else."

Avery looked uncomfortable as Sapphire repeated all that Cassie had said to the eager audience.

"Hey, Avery," Cassie called. "Sorry, baby, looks like you missed out on the chance to tap this." She gave a booty wiggle that Sapphire assumed was supposed to show him what he was missing. Saph wished she had missed it, the action caused her hanging guts to do a strange worm like dance, though they appeared to have withdrawn back into her stomach somewhat and now that she looked closer, the blood that stained her shirt and hair seemed to have faded. It should have been hard to tell in the dark, but it seemed that enhanced night vision was another perk of her new Vampirism. She guessed that it made sense for a night predator to have a sight advantage.

"I'm sorry, no one else can hear you. That's why I'm repeating everything you say."

"What did she say?" Roger demanded.

"She said that Avery missed out on his chance to 'tap this'," she looked over at Avery as she said it, finding quiet amusement in the shocked look on his face. "And then she wiggled her butt. I think I like her."

"I don't care about how easy Avery is or isn't, what else does she remember?" Vanessa gave an impatient shake of her head. "Make her continue."

The older Vampires tone made Sapphire's hackles rise. She snapped back, unable to hold her tongue.

"She isn't a thing to command. I can't make her continue. I can ask her, but she's just found out she's dead. Have a little compassion."

Avery immediately stepped in front of Sapphire, unsure what Vanessa would do in retaliation to Sapphire's rudeness. But to his surprise the older Vampire smiled.

"You have spunk, young one. I like that. Of course, you are right, please ask her to continue."

106

Sapphire gave a curt nod of acceptance and turned back to the spirit who was beginning to look impatient.

"What happened after you decided to leave?"

"Oh, remembered I still exist have you?"

Great, Sapphire thought, *an uppity ghost.*

"Of course I know you exist," she soothed, not wanting the ghost to vanish in a snit fit. "And we want to help you, we want to find out what happened to you and catch the guy that did this."

"Will that bring me back to life?" Snippy ghost asked. Her image appeared more solid now, the blood having faded even more. It seemed the more that Cassie felt like herself the more normal she projected herself as.

"Ugh... no. I'm sorry, it won't. But he will be punished. I'm sorry about what happened to you, so sorry. But he won't be allowed to get away with this. He will be punished. I promise you that."

Cassie seemed to ponder on this for a moment before she made up her mind and spoke again. "OK, so Avery got all noble and I decided to go. I got my coat and decided to slip out the back."

She paused so that Sapphire could repeat it all to the others.

"Why did she go out the back door?" Miss Angelica asked her first question.

"Seems to be a trend at the moment," Avery muttered pointedly under his breath earning himself a squinty eyed glare from Saph.

Ignoring Avery, Sapphire turned back to Cassie.

"Why did you go out the back door?"

Now it was the ghosts turn to glare at Avery. "After he turned me down in front of everyone I didn't want people to see me leaving so early without having had a bite," she paused to let Sapphire repeat her words. "So, I went out the back. I stopped to light a cigarette. I was supposed to be quitting, my mother kept telling me it would kill me. Guess she was wrong there huh?" She gave a bitter laugh.

"Anyway, I was fighting with my lighter, it was sparking but wouldn't light. I was about to give up and take it as a sign that I wasn't supposed to be smoking when someone behind me offered me a light. I couldn't see him very well, it was so dark, and he stayed in the shadows mostly, but he had a nice voice. So, I leant in and let him light my cigarette. I didn't stand a chance. As I leant in he grabbed me and the next thing I knew his fangs were in my throat."

"So it was a Vampire?" Vanessa confirmed after Sapphire repeated the next part of the story. She was about to ask Cassie, but the ghost was obviously on a roll.

"He began to feed from me. I started to struggle, but then, well, it began to feel really good, you know how it is when you're fed from."

Sapphire didn't, but she knew how good it felt to feed from Avery and immediately her mind began to wonder just how much better it would be to be fed from. Avery had certainly seemed to enjoy it. As if he could sense the smutty direction her thoughts had taken Avery gave her a secret smile, one she studiously ignored, quickly repeating what the ghost had said so she could continue.

"So I just let it happen. I'd been feeling bad, like no one wanted me anymore. But he fed for a long time, much longer than he should have. I went from feeling kinda blissed out, like being a little drunk, to full out woozy. I tried to push him away and tell him to stop but he wouldn't listen. I punched at him, hitting at his shoulders and chest but he was too strong, way too strong, and big. I tried to fight it, but the blackness, it took over. I felt each pull of his mouth on my neck, it started to hurt but I couldn't stop him. I couldn't see anything anymore, it was so dark. And then I guess I passed out. The next thing I remember is just standing here, seeing you and my body."

Sapphire filled the others in on everything that Cassie had told her. She questioned her further on a few details, but it appeared that she really had told them all she knew. The Guild had all the information that they needed and took their leave. Sapphire couldn't help but feel slightly used, though at least they had believed her.

"Thank you, Cassie, for helping us. I promise you that we will catch the one that did this to you, and they will punish him, he won't get away with this. I wish you well on your journey to the next world."

She expected Cassie to fade away, but she didn't, she continued to stand there, arms crossed over her chest. Sapphire was glad to note that all her insides seemed to back where they belong, the horrible slash that marred her stomach and torso had gone and the clothes seemed to have repaired to their former glory. Her face had that stubborn look back on it.

"You're trying to send me off to some angelic afterlife, aren't you? Well I won't go. I'm not going anywhere until that monster is found and I see them lop off his head. Stake that arsehole right through the heart. That will teach him to kill me. Oh no, I'm staying right here until I get to look that dick in the eye. You're stuck with me."

Avery slipped his arm around Sapphire's waist, giving her a squeeze. "Has she gone?"

Saph snorted in response. "As if. It seems that she is determined to stay until we catch her killer."

Avery blinked. "So, we have ourselves a ghost?"

Sapphire pulled a face that clearly said, 'what can we do about it?'.

"I think we need a drink."

"I don't want a drink. I just want to go home. I assume I'm allowed to go now the Guild have left?" she said it in a challenging tone that he dared not argue with.

"Of course. I'll walk you there."

"I don't actually know how to leave this place yet, but I will, don't think I won't. I'll be back to haunt you both until you find that murderer," Cassie threw that parting shot before she blinked out, vanishing into the shadows.

"Now she's gone. But she'll be back." Sapphire turned back to face him. "Look, I don't need you to walk me home, but as I have the feeling that you won't take no for answer. Get moving. I want my own bed."

"OK," he agreed, gesturing for her to lead the way.

Chapter Ten

"You're very quiet," Avery remarked as casually as he could, not wanting to spook her into clamming up on him as she usually did. "You OK? I know tonight was a big deal for you, but you did very well."

Sapphire had been silent the entire time they had been walking and now that they neared her home, she realised that she wasn't feeling the sense of relief and peace she had expected. Nothing was the same for her any more, even her own home didn't feel right.

"No, I'm not OK. I don't think I ever will be again," she answered him in a quiet voice. She was beginning to feel like she was losing herself completely, slowly but surely, bit by bit. She found herself wanting to confide in the one person that had been there for her from the very start of this nightmare of a life she had woken up in.

"Of course it will, darling. We'll find the bastard that killed Cassie and that other girl and then things will calm down."

She shook her head, he just didn't get it, he had been a Vampire for years, obviously liked his life like that, he didn't get that, for her, this was the worst thing ever.

"I almost wish that he hadn't turned me, that he had simply killed me when he had the chance. He's ruined my life. Nothing will ever be alright again. Don't you get that? He turned me into an even bigger freak than I already was, and now, because of him, the ghosts are back, and they will never leave me alone. I'll never get away from them now, never. They will continue to follow me and talk to me and drive me crazy." Her voice was rising into panic with each word, her control slipping further and further away from her, something that she hated.

Avery didn't know what to say or do for the best. He had the feeling that no matter what he told her, she wouldn't believe him. She was stuck in the mindset that being a Vampire was the worst thing that could ever have happened to her, even worse than losing her life completely. Still he had to try.

"You can't really believe that, sweetheart, it's not that bad. Nothing is worse than dying. Your sisters would be lost without you."

Tears began to track down her cheeks as she looked up at him, her expression one of utter helplessness. She looked so lost that he reached out and pulled her into his arms.

Sapphire was shocked into silence for a moment, finding herself smushed up against his chest. She held herself stiffly in his embrace, trying to pull herself together, not wanting to lean on him, not wanting to break down and show even more weakness. This wasn't her, she wasn't like this, this pathetic, weepy thing. Another thing that her turning had fucked up.

"Baby, you can talk to me. It's not good to keep everything locked up inside, you need to let it out sometime." He felt her take a shuddering breath before her arms slipped slowly around his waist as she burrowed into his arms. He barely heard her at first, she spoke so quietly.

"It's fucked up everything. Everything that I've worked so hard for is gone. I've lost my job, my control, the ability to eat and enjoy food, and now, the one thing I always hated about myself is back and worse than ever. I've lost all say in my own life. I can't control anything. I'm going to spend the rest of what is apparently a very long life, alone in the dark, drinking blood from people and sulking. I don't want to live that way, Avery, I can't cope with that. I need to think, to work, to organise things and take control, it keeps me sane, it keeps me grounded and normal. But I'll never be normal again, will I? Never!"

Avery couldn't help it, he laughed. He couldn't believe that that was what she really thought. That she'd have to hide out in a crypt somewhere and have no life. She didn't have a clue. Which for someone like Sapphire, who was used to knowing everything about what she was doing and facing, he guessed that that would be rather unsettling.

He laughed at her, he actually had the cheek to laugh at her when she had just opened up to him, spoke her fears to him. How bloody dare he! She smacked at his arm as she pulled away from him, needing to not feel his body pressed against hers.

"Why are you laughing at me?" She demanded, her face fierce, prodding at his chest with her index finger, emphasising each shouted question. "Do you think it's funny that I've basically lost my life and everything in it? Is that amusing to you?"

Avery fought to keep his face straight as he harmlessly batted her poking finger away, she was so funny when she got mad like that, like a little spitting cobra, all attack and venom.

"It's not you that I m laughing at, darling, I promise you, it's more the situation."

113

"You're laughing at the situation? The fact that I've lost my life as I know it and found dead girl, that's amusing you? What is wrong with you?" She was so mad she was only just stopping herself from punching him in his smug mouth. She turned away in disgust, stomping up the path to her house, wanting to get away from him, and fast.

Avery grabbed her hand as she turned to go, towing her back.

"I don't find that funny, at all. What I'm finding funny is the fact that you're so clueless. I keep forgetting that you really know nothing of our world, the world that you are now part of. Well, I'm going to show you that life doesn't end when you become a Vampire, it begins. Come on," he started to drag her back down the street, much to her confusion, until they got to the main high street where he stuck his hand out, hailing a taxi and bundling her in.

"I'm going to show you my world."

Sitting at the table inside a dingy little cellar of a pub was not how Sapphire had envisioned spending the rest of the night. She had wanted to go home and have a hot bath and wallow in self-pity, but damn it, Avery never let her get away with that.

"I still don't get why we're here," she groused, her arms folded defiantly as Avery ordered them two house specials.

"Because you need to realise that as much as you want to look on the bleak side of things for the rest of your days, I can't allow that."

"And bringing me here to this dingy flea pit is the answer?" She didn't sound convinced.

"Yep," he grinned unashamedly, a slightly crooked smile that showed off his even white teeth to perfection, emphasising his full lips. Lips that she could recall all too well. "Now, while we're waiting, tell me calmly exactly what's wrong and how you feel."

114

"I don't want to," she retorted stubbornly, sounding much like a petulant child, even to her own ears. She didn't want to be thinking about his lips and how much she would enjoy sampling them again. She needed to keep her head around him, not be thinking about sliding onto his lap in front of everyone and attempting to suck his tongue out of his mouth. She squirmed in her seat at the thought of how good he had felt pressed up against her chest, recalling the hard length that had grown against her arse as he proceeded to show her what she had been missing all her years of kissing the boring men she met at work. They had been like a luke warm puddle compared to his boiling, hot passion.

Avery shrugged, attempting to keep his tone casual even as his acute sense of smell caught the cloying scent of her arousal. He would have given his right arm to know what she was thinking about right then, because all he could think about was throwing her down on the table and having his wicked way with her. He cleared his throat, trying to dispel the thoughts as he proceeded to goad her. "I didn't peg you for a coward but if you want to hide away and sulk, that's your choice. No skin off my nose, pet."

"I'm not a coward. I just don't want to talk. I would if I wanted to."

"Of course you would," sarcasm dripped from his tongue.

"I would!" She didn't know how he did it, but he always managed to get her so riled up so quickly. She hated anyone to think that she was scared, she had never backed down from anyone and she wasn't about to start now.

"Prove it," he challenged as their drinks arrived. He took a casual sip and quirked one golden eyebrow at her in question. "Talk to me."

If there was one thing that Sapphire could never resist it was a challenge, she couldn't stand the idea of someone getting the upper hand over her, hated the idea that someone, even someone like Avery, would think her too scared to admit to how she as feeling. She would prove him wrong.

"I don't like feeling this way. I thought it would just take some getting used to, but I'm not, I'm still feeling like it, every day."

"Like what?" he nudged her drink over but didn't say anything else, he didn't want her to close down again now that he had tricked her into talking. Trying to get her to discuss things was like trying to get blood out of a stone at times, but he was learning the best ways to handle her.

"Like I'm constantly hungry, my stomach feels hollow and empty the whole time, like permanent cramps. And I'm so thirsty, I must have drunk about four pints of water the other night, and it did nothing. I didn't even need to pee it out, which is just weird. Cassian keeps trying to get me to drink that shitty bagged blood, but it tastes like crap. It's like having a diet milkshake when I want a steak."

"It's not always that bad, you'll get used to it. Your body is still getting used to the changes it's undergone and is probably using up blood faster than normal to compensate. You just need to drink more. I know that you don't like the taste so why not use a Donor?"

Sapphire shook her head vehemently "No thanks, Ewww, just no."

"You fed from me OK," he pointed out, rather smugly she thought.

"That was different!" she protested. "I didn't really know what I was doing then, I was acting on instinct because I was so hungry. I don't want to keep being hungry all the time, I don't want to be a Vampire, I don't want my stupid gift to start dictating my life again."

Avery knew that he wouldn't change her mind, even if he did point out that she had, in fact, been in her right mind when she had chosen to feed from him the second time, that wasn't how she worked, she had to discover things for herself and alter her own way of thinking in her own time. She didn't see that she was a fascinating creature, or just how special she was.

116

All Vampires developed gifts over time, but she had had hers all her life, and the talent was a rare one. He was desperate to know more but asking her straight out never worked, she clammed up as soon as she was pushed. He was learning to tread softly around her, not so much tricking her into his way of thinking but nudging her in the right direction.

"Your gift can't be that bad, I'd love to have that ability."

"No, you wouldn't," she chuckled bitterly, as if the idea amused her on some level. "I first found out about it the day of my grandmother's funeral. It was decided that I was too young to go. I stayed behind with one of the people staying with us. I don't remember who it was. I was sulking, so I wasn't paying much attention."

"You? Sulking? Never!" Avery joked, earning himself a squinty eyes glare.

"Do you want to hear this or not?"

"I do," he mimed zipping his lips shut and throwing away the key.

"I guess that's one way to shut you up," she muttered under her breath as she took an experimental sip of her drink while Avery feigned being heartbroken. It wasn't bad, and she took another longer swallow before continuing.

"I was in my bedroom, feeling very sad. I remember that so clearly. I'd been hearing everyone around me talking about the funeral being a chance to say goodbye to her and I wasn't there. I felt like I had missed out on the chance, like she might think I didn't care because I didn't say goodbye with everyone else. I was lying on my bed crying, when my grandmother walked in to comfort me. I didn't understand at first, I knew that she wasn't supposed to be there, but I wasn't scared. Not of my own Nan."

Avery's eyes had grown wide as he listened. He could picture it so clearly in his mind, this beautiful, golden haired little girl, with her big blue eyes, crying all by herself, feeling like she was missing out and then being faced with the ghost of her dead grandmother in her room. Any normal child would have been scared out of their wits, but not Sapphire, she was strong even then, something he admired so much about her.

"After that Nan was a regular visitor to me. I'd asked my sisters about it, but they never saw her. Just me. After that I began to see other people as well. I didn't really know what they were at the time, to me they were just scary people that came to me and no one else. Strange people in my room, or following me around at the shops. I would see live people walking around with dead people following them."

She didn't want to look up at him, to see the look on his face, she needed to just keep talking, not get distracted by the squareness of his chin or how much she would like to nibble on his Adam's apple.

"It became more obvious as I got older that no one else saw them. My sisters and my parents had always believed me and encouraged me to be proud of my abilities. But they always warned me that people outside of our special house and family wouldn't understand and might be mean to me about it. I never understood that at first, I'd never been picked on, not more than generally happens between siblings." She twirled her fingertip in her drink, sucking it clean as she talked.

"We were home schooled you see, so I'd had no real experience with other children. It wasn't until I started going to school for the last two years of senior school, to sit my exams, that I began to socialise with people outside of our house. I made friends with a girl named Alison. I was enamoured with her, totally in awe of her. She was everything that I wasn't. Her parents had normal, boring jobs, she was allowed to dye her hair and use real beauty products, not ones made by her mother and her hippy friends in exchange for bed and food for a few nights."

Sapphire took a long gulp of her drink, not wanting to look at Avery, whom she knew was watching her intently, paying full attention. Even now she wasn't used to people looking at her, she didn't like being the centre of attention.

118

Avery watched the emotions play across her face as she talked. He could tell that it was difficult for her to let herself talk about something that was a painful memory for her. He knew that he was somewhat guilty of tricking her into telling him, but he also knew that if she really hadn't wanted to talk, she wouldn't have. She liked to pretend that she didn't need anyone, that she didn't want to share, but he knew better. She needed someone she could trust and confide in, someone that wouldn't let her down and treat her badly. He was determined to be that person for her.

She didn't know why she let Avery talk her into things, why he had the ability to wheedle out of her all her deep, dark secrets. But he did. And she found, much to her surprise, that once she started talking to him, she didn't want to stop. For once she genuinely felt that she didn't need to hide herself, she could be honest, and he wouldn't judge her, he wouldn't think she was a freak. But old habits die hard, and she still felt uncomfortable talking about the past. She fiddled with the beer mat that her drink had sat on, shredding it slowly between her fingers.

"I wanted Alison to like me, so I told her my secret, thinking, hoping I guess, that she would be impressed. She wasn't, she didn't believe me and immediately told other people at school about it. Not in a nice way either. I hadn't realised before, but Alison was a terrible bully. She was very good at making herself seem like a nice person, someone that had lots of friends that you would want to hang with. But she wasn't, not really. She would encourage her friends to tease others, she would point out things about people and tell secrets, gossiping about people." Sapphire made a face to show her disgust that people could act like that.

"She started a hate campaign against me. I couldn't walk anywhere in the school without people making ghost noises at me, throwing screwed up balls of paper and yelling 'ghost'. They called me a liar, an attention seeker, that I was a freak like my freaky family. Tanzanite and Amethyst had gone to that school too, but Amy had been quiet at school and had managed to get through with barely anyone noticing her. Tanzi was the exact opposite, she had practically taken over, challenging everyone and usually winning, she earned the respect of people there, but she was a few years above Alison and her cronies. I tried so hard to be normal, I told people that I had been joking, but that didn't help. I tried so hard, I convinced myself that if I didn't see the ghosts again, then all my troubles would be over. I started ignoring them, I pushed them away if I saw them, told myself they weren't real, and slowly, they began to leave, and I didn't see them again, not properly. I always knew they were there, but I believed that if I didn't react to them they would leave me alone."

She sighed, sipping again, her drink almost gone. "But the damage had been done. In the end, my parents had me transferred to another school and I never told anyone again."

She had turned the beer mat into confetti that she was sifting through, still not looking at him. Avery could tell that there was more to her story than she had told him, and he waited patiently for her to continue.

They sat in silence for a few minutes just sipping their drinks until finally Sapphire cleared her throat.

"I tried to forget all about it, but that sort of thing sticks in your mind, you know? But still, I thought I had moved on, not seeing them anymore was freeing in a way, I didn't have to worry about being seen talking to myself in the street or watching something no one else could see. I knuckled down and did very well in my exams, good enough to get into university. That's where I met Tristian."

Avery's ears pricked up at the sound of a male he'd never heard of before. This male was obviously an important part of her life and for some reason this really bothered him. It was irrational, but he didn't want anyone else being important to her, he wanted it to be him. He wanted to be the one she thought about and wanted.

"I didn't know anyone there, I was there on a scholarship, working in a café to earn enough to live on, while he was fully funded by his parents. He was so smooth and sophisticated. Everything that I wanted in a man."

Avery held in the growl that rumbled in his chest, he didn't want her to know just how much he hated hearing that he was nothing like the type of man she wanted. He didn't like it at all. He was used to being God's gift to women folk, was proud of his good looks and easy way with the ladies. To hear that he wasn t perfect was actually a below the belt blow to his ego that he didn't appreciate.

Sapphire didn't seem to notice, lost in her own memories as she continued, the words spilling from her lips without hesitation now that she had started. She hadn't intended to tell him about Tristiar, but something about Avery made her want to open up and share with him. She didn't want to hide any more.

"I didn't think he would ever be interested in someone like me, but he was. He flattered me, was a real gentleman. Everything about him was polished and smart. He was courteous and seemed to respect me and my intellectual pursuits. He was my first boyfriend and honestly, I thought the sun shined out of his behind. He could do no wrong in my eyes. I thought of him as perfect. Everything I had ever wanted, the whole package. We became an item and eventually I felt comfortable enough, trusted him enough, believed that he loved me enough, to take him home for Sunday dinner. It was the biggest mistake I could have ever made."

"Why?" Avery spoke for the first time in what felt like forever. "Your sisters are wonderful women and I'm sure that your parents are amazing too."

"They were, we were devastated when they passed, almost one after the other, death is never easy for those left behind." Sapphire smiled a little smile, one that spoke of sadness and loss. "I suppose everyone will soon think I'm dead too, won't they? Cassian said I'll have to find a way of disappearing soon," she tried to sound casual, like it was no big deal, but Avery heard the hurt in her voice, something that bothered him way more than it should have. He didn't like to care about a woman this much but found it almost impossible to hold himself back from her. He wanted her, more than he had ever wanted any other woman. That in itself was disturbing, he loved women of all shapes and sizes, he prided himself on being an equal opportunities lover, but an uncomfortable little voice at the back of his head told him that he was now ruined for any other woman. There was only one that held his interest now.

"We haven't told them anything yet. They don't need to know immediately, and what they know is up to you." He didn't want to push her into talking but his curiosity over this perfect Tristian was so piqued he had to know what the idiot had done to fall from her good graces. "So, you took him home for Sunday lunch, and then what happened?"

"I took him home, wanting him to meet my family and love them as much as I did. I was wrong. He hated them, Avery. He barely touched his food, not liking the vegetarian dishes my mum had prepared, he spoke down to my dad and treated my sisters with pure contempt."

Sapphire looked angry just talking about it and Avery realised that she was still very hurt by it.

"They were on their best behaviour, but they still weren't good enough for him. I don't believe anyone would be, he thought himself above everyone else, I didn't notice that until after. Tanzi offered him a tarot reading, Mum told him his aura was off and Dad tried to get him to pee in a bottle to add to his beloved compost heap. They were all quirky, but lovely to him. They didn't deserve his scorn. He walked out as soon as he could and was very cool towards me."

Avery reached out to take her hand when she paused again, he could tell that she was uncomfortable telling him what happened next. He stroked his thumb back and forth across the back of her hand, trying to soothe her.

122

"You don't have to tell me anything else, sweetheart, the show should be starting in a few minutes. Let's just enjoy the rest of our night, yeah?"

Sapphire smiled, a genuine smile. He really was such a darling when he wasn't being a man whore that got on her last nerve. He was trying to reassure her, she appreciated that more that she could say. She squeezed his hand back the feel of his thumb still caressing her skin helped relax her. She was embarrassed about what happened next, how desperate she had been to keep the man she thought she had loved, but she knew that Avery wouldn't judge her for it.

"No, thank you, but I want to finish. I want you to hear it all. It's important to me that you understand me a bit better and know that I wasn't always this control freak, straight-laced thing that I am now."

"I happen to think you're perfect as you are, very sexy too," he gave her a lascivious wink. "But if you feel you want to explain, that's fine. I'm listening. I'll always listen to you."

"I do." Sapphire finished off the last of her drink and Avery signalled the bartender for another. "I followed him home. I know it was stupid of me, I should have just let him go, he had been rude to my family, but I couldn't stand the idea of losing him. I thought I loved him and was desperate to keep him. I'd been putting him off, in regard to sex."

She knew that she would have blushed if she was still capable of it, instead she avoided his eyes, feeling embarrassed all over again.

"I was a virgin, as I said, I'd never had a boyfriend before. Tanzi had always been the wild one, the one full of confidence, the one that the boys flocked around. But I was the shy one. I had this romantic notion of waiting for someone that I loved. And I thought that I loved Tristian. So, I offered myself to him that night. I guess I was trying to make up for how my family were, even though I loved them, I understood that they weren't everyone's cup of tea, but he really made me feel like I should be ashamed of them and apologise for them."

123

Avery knew where this was going, he just had a feeling and already, before she had finished her story he knew that he wanted nothing more than hunt this Tristian fellow down and beat him to a pulp.

"I slept with him that night. It wasn't anything special, not like it should have been. He wasn't very gentle, and he didn't take his time with me, he thought more about himself if I'm honest and he insisted that I went home after. He said that his housemates wouldn't like me being there. The next morning I felt very pleased with myself, feeling like I was finally a real woman, with a man I loved and that I thought loved me. I was so wrong."

The bartender chose that moment to bring their drinks over and she took a grateful gulp, Dutch courage and all that. Avery still held her hand gently in his and that gave her the silent support she needed to continue.

"I knew something was wrong the second I got onto campus. People were whispering behind their hands, laughing as I walked by. It was exactly the same as it had been at school, I knew it was all aimed at me. I heard one whisper about a "freak house" and a "Witch" and I knew they were talking about my family. And the only person that knew about them was Tristian. I went straight to his class and waited outside for him. I confronted him when he came out, wanting to know what he had been saying about me and why. He was cruel, so cold and uncaring when he finally emerged. I won't bore you with the actual details but apparently I was the subject of a bet between him and his cohorts. They had a bet each term about who could 'pull'…" Sapphire made quotation marks with her fingers, "...the saddest virgin. Obviously, that was me. He had dated me with the intention of bedding me and dumping me. Having my family to gossip about was just a sweet bonus. He broke my trust and my heart in one go. I didn't think I would ever live it down but eventually someone else fucked up worse than me and I was left in peace to finish my studies and get the hell out of there. There have been a few others after

124

him, but it's never been serious, and it's always been on my terms, nice, safe, admittedly boring men that I am in control with. And I like it that way."

She didn't know why she felt the need to add that last comment, in a way she hoped that it would make Avery back off and rethink whatever attraction he thought he had for her. It would be safer for her that way, less chance of getting her heart broken again. Because she knew, in her heart of hearts, that she could easily fall for Avery, way too easily. In fact, she might be more than half way there already.

"Fucking arsehole," Avery growled in a low, dangerous voice that she had never heard him make before. "I can't believe he could treat you that way." An evil smile broke out on his face. "Just out of curiosity, what was this guy's last name and where did he live? I think he might be due a visit from the not so friendly local Vampire."

Sapphire actually burst out laughing, surprising herself. She hadn't thought that she would ever be able to laugh about Tristian, but there she was, with sweet Avery, laughing. Something inside her, some tight knot of tension in the pit of her stomach that she hadn't even realised was there, suddenly eased. She felt lighter than she had in a long time, even though she was facing life as a Vampire. All of a sudden it didn't seem so bad.

The lights around them dimmed then, and the spotlight above the small stage in the corner came on, illuminating a microphone and a lone bar stool.

"Show's about to start," Avery sounded pleased. "Sit back, sip your drink and enjoy. I promise you that after this, you'll change your view on life as a Vampire." Avery was absolutely horrified by what she had told him. He was fighting the urge to track down the loser that had taken her virginity so callously and throw her aside as soon as he had dipped his wick.

But he was beginning to understand her better. He now got exactly why she acted the way she did. Why she seemed so prissy and stuck up, as if she held herself apart from everyone around her. Why she never let herself go and just relax. She was scared. Scared that she would see ghosts again, scared that she would trust, scared that she would make the wrong decision and be made a fool of again. He understood why she buttoned herself up so tight and made sure she kept hold of her rigid control. It was her way of coping.

He would bet all of the considerable amount of money in his possession that she had never once as an adult, let herself go and had fun. He doubted she had ever gotten drunk, let her hair down, figuratively and literally, he was sure that he would develop a massive headache if he wore his hair scraped back that tight. Well, he was determined, he made a vow there and then, that he would make sure she had the most fun of her life with him.

He promised that she would change her mind about Vampires and their lives. Well it had to be one hell of a show. Sapphire sat up a little straighter, reaching again for her drink. This she had to see.

Chapter Eleven

Two hours later and Sapphire's hands were sore from clapping, her voice hoarse from cheering and laughing. Avery had taken her to what had turned out to be a Vampire variety club.

They had sipped their drinks which turned out to be yet another blood mixed cocktail, though she found it impossible to be mad at Avery for not telling her. They had been delicious and even though she still had the gnawing, empty ache in her stomach her throat was less parched, and she had been able to stomach the taste quite well. She didn't think she would ever be able to drink 'from the source' as Avery told her feeding from a human was called, or be swigging from a cold bottle of O, but she was sure that if she picked up some liquid flavourings she would be able to mix up something that might be palatable.

The show itself had been brilliant fun, just as he had promised. It transpired that the club held open mics every night they didn't have a live band performing.

They had comedians that told topical jokes about the trials and tribulations of being a Vampire, including one particularly funny joke about a Vampire bat and a light bulb that still had her giggling when she thought about it.

One particular female singer had the most hauntingly beautiful voice Saph had ever heard, she sang a song in a language that Sapphire didn't understand but assumed it was from the singer's homeland.

They enjoyed a Vampire ballet dancer and a magician along with a few more singers, a guitarist and a petite little Asian Vampire that played the violin beautifully.

While the acts themselves had each been wonderful in their own way, it was the Vampire Drag Queen that was acting as compère, that had made it so good. Sapphire was now a fan for life and couldn't wait to tell her sisters.

Avery had watched her more than he had watched the show, little secret sideways glances as often as he had dared at first and then by the end, openly staring at her. She was more beautiful than ever right then. He could tell she had enjoyed the acts, fighting to hold in her laughter at first with demure little giggles or just a smile that she tried to hide behind her hand while he was doubled over with laughter, letting out huge belly laughs at certain risqué jokes.

She had finally lightened up and by the end was calling out with the rest of the audience at the magician and clapping along with the guitarist. She looked relaxed and happy and that in turn lightened her eyes, her smile less forced and stiff, a genuine grin that he vowed to see every single day.

It amazed Sapphire that they had performers like that and she said as much to Avery.

"Why would you think that we wouldn't have our own performances?" Avery was genuinely curious.

"Because they are Vampires," she said it like it was the most obvious thing in the world.

"Yes, they are," Avery explained patiently. "But that doesn't mean they lost themselves." For such an obviously smart woman Sapphire looked so adorably confused by it all that he couldn't resist leaning across the table and planting a kiss on the tip of her nose. "Think on this. Apart from the sleeping pattern and the new diet, do you still feel like yourself?"

She opened her mouth to answer but he stopped her. "I mean, do you still think about other people, do you still think about work, did you enjoy this show? Just because you are a Vampire doesn't mean you have change. You don't lose your creativity when you become a Vampire. You don't lose your love of words or of song or the urge to dance. They continue to perform and create. Some are even famous, you wouldn't know it, but when you have these big stars that suddenly meet with a tragic accident while still young, its likely one of us. We wait a few decades then come back as someone else. That's why you occasionally get photos that pop up of new stars that look like ones from fifty years ago."

Sapphire was absolutely dumfounded.

"Vampire's still have jobs?"

Avery actually laughed. "Of course we do, I work don't I? What about the bartender here? We all work. Money doesn't grow on trees, you know."

Sapphire actually felt kind of stupid, something she hated.

"I guess I just assumed that you were all rich or had old money, you know, years to make your fortune."

"Yes, we do. But we have to start somewhere. And the baby vamps like yourself, that were normal people, they need money too."

A thought struck her like a bolt between the eyes.

"You mean I could go back to work? That would be possible?"

Avery shrugged. "Of course it would. We'd have to glamour your boss into letting you work nights, maybe make it so that you dealt with foreign clients in different time zones, but there's no reason why that wouldn't work. That's why I said you didn't have to tell your friends and colleagues yet, you can still visit them, just at night. And you can petition to the council for them to be allowed to be let in on the secret, if you can guarantee that they won't tell anyone. They might not say yes, but it's worth a shot."

Sapphire could feel tears prickling her eyes again, this time with relief and hope.

"So, I don't have to give up my life?"

Avery laughed again. "Of course not. Who told you that you did?"

"No one, I guess I don't know that much about Vampires other than what I've read in a few books and seen in the movies. I guess I just assumed it would be like them. With the Vampire withdrawing from society, skulking in the shadows sucking on the necks of unsuspecting victims."

"Ah, well you know what they say about people that assume," he teased with a grin before he added, completely straight-faced. "You do have to live in a crypt though, no going home for you."

Sapphire was horrified, her happiness leaking away with his words.

"What? Are you serious?"

Avery snorted out a laugh. "Of course not, you're just too easy to tease, pet."

Sapphire didn't know whether to be mad at him or to laugh with him. She settled on bashing him on the arm with her fist, she doubted that it would stop him, but it made her feel a little better.

"Ouch," he laughed, rubbing at his arm. "You're getting stronger, pet, watch who you punch." He was still grinning at her, loving their easy banter.

She didn't know what the hell to make of him, and that made her wary. He infuriated her and made her laugh in equal parts. She just couldn't seem to keep her footing with him. She was really starting to warm to him though, more than she wanted to admit. She had always noticed that he was a handsome man, you would have to be blind not to, but now she was realising that he wasn't just a nice package on the outside, he was lovely on the inside too.

She had been trying to stop herself from thinking of him in that way, reminding herself frequently that he had had more women than she could possibly guess, was well known as a bit of a player. But the longer she spent with him, the more she got to know him, the more she found that, for all her inner pep talks and practiced control, she just wasn't strong enough to resist him. She wasn't strong enough to stay away.

She kept having visions of kissing him again, kept remembering the way his lips had felt on hers, his taste, the feel of his silky hair sliding through her fingers, how his body had moved against hers. She wanted it again in the most desperate way.

She just didn't know if she could handle it. She knew that he would turn her carefully ordered mind and heart upside down even more than t already was, she couldn't cope with that. She couldn't cope with being rejected again, and it was blatantly obvious to her that he would get bored with her, sooner rather than later. He was probably only taking care of her as a favour to Cassian and her sister. Hell, he probably only kissed her back because he was male, and she was there, availab e and at the time, willing.

The thought sobered her, dousing her roaring libido almost instantly. No, she wouldn't allow herself to get close to anyone again, her life was hard enough as it was, the adjustments she was having to make were already too much to get her head round. She needed to protect herself, she needed to tougher up and not let him in any further than he already was.

Avery didn't know what he had done wrong, but it must have been something truly despicable, like maybe kicking a puppy he didn't know existed, because he was getting an icy blast from Sapphire that was obviously arctic in origin. One minute they had been talking happily, having what he thought was a fun night, and the next the shutters descended, effectively locking him out. Her expression closed off, her body language warning him not to get too close. He didn't understand it. He now had more of an insight into her mind and how her past had shaped how she coped with things, but he hadn't done anything to her. He was all for the softly softly catchy monkey approach, but he wasn't prepared to keep letting her blow so hot and cold with him, he needed to get firm with her.

He was about to ask her just what the fuck was up with her now as he was getting pretty fed up with her PMS like mood swings, when he heard his name being called from across the bar. Liliya.

Liliya looked around the dusty bar with barely concealed distaste. She couldn't believe she had had to follow her love to a disgusting place like this. But if he did insist on taking that little bitch out, she was glad that he seemed to have made very little effort. She was sure that he had only done it out of duty to his friends. Her Avery was loyal like that, generous to a fault. It was her duty to rescue him from his self-imposed baby vamp sitting.

She shrugged off her fur wrap, tossing it carelessly to Grigory, who caught it effortlessly, he was good for some things at least. She was aware that every pair of eyes in the place were watching her, not that she expected anything less, she was beautiful, no doubt they had never seen one such as her. She gave her hips a little extra swing as she glided over to the small, way too intimate in her opinion, table that her Avery shared with the little blonde wench.

"Avery, my precious, you shame yourself being in a bar such as this," she fought not to make a face as Grigory pulled out a chair for her that she was sure hadn't been cleaned in years. She gingerly sat, hoping that it would not leave a mark on her cream dress.

"I don't see it as shaming myself, actually, but if you dislike it so much, why, pray tell, are you here?" Avery

132

wasn't fooled for a moment with her apparently coincidental appearance in the same bar he was in with Sapphire. He really hoped that Liliya didn't decide to make things difficult as was her speciality.

Liliya laughed, a tinkling sound like fairy bells that instantly got on Sapphire's nerves, placing her hand on Avery's arm and stroking in a subtly suggestive way that made Sapphire want to punch her.

Unless Avery was very much mistaken, and to be fair, there was a possibility that it would happen occasionally, Sapphire was glaring at Liliya in a very unpleasant way, one might even call it jealousy. It seemed that his little baby vamp couldn't make up her mind what she wanted. Judging by her history with men she was running scared again. Well, he'd let her come back to him in her own time, he was prepared to wait, but it wouldn't hurt to give her a little incentive to stand up for herself. Avery plastered his most charming grin on his face and turned it on Liliya, prepared to flirt his arse off.

Sapphire wanted to smack Liliya's skank hand with its red tipped claws away, and claim Avery as her own, but she didn't dare move. Her mind was made up that Avery wasn't good for her, maybe it would be easier if Liliya kept him occupied, diverting his attention and allowing her to slip away.

She took her time, slowly finishing her drink, trying not to listen to Liliya as she twittered on about all the wonderful things she had seen and done since they had last been together. Avery was returning her attention with interest, his megawatt smile turned in her direction. Sapphire put her empty glass down, muttering her apologies as she excused herself to go to the bathroom, not that she needed to go, she hadn't since she had woken up dead, but they didn't seem to notice that she was gone.

She risked a look back as she stood by the door, but Avery hadn't looked her way, didn't even seem to register that she had left.

"Well screw you," she snarled as she flung open the door. "I'm going to find my own entertainment." She let the door slam shut behind her, refusing to look back again.

Avery tracked Sapphire by scent alone, she had the subtlest fragrance of lilac that he loved. He noted that she hadn't even gone to the bathroom to freshen her make-up, as he had assumed. No, Elvis had left the building.

He didn't want her to go off on her own and immediately felt guilty for his childish behaviour with regards to Liliya, he had thought that Sapphire would get mad and then make some move to win him back, that's what he would have done, but she hadn't, instead she had lied and left.

If she was mad and he would bet his last pound that she was, then she could be dangerous. Anger and hunger often went hand in hand and she hadn't been feeding as often as she needed to. He had brought her there and it was his duty to look after her.

He made his excuses and quickly followed her, she had drunk his blood so in that he had a small connection to her and he used this to his full advantage, taking off down the road after his little runaway.

Liliya couldn't believe that he had brushed her off, again. What was wrong with him? She consoled herself with the fact that he obviously took his babysitting duties very seriously, going after the spoilt little brat. He had flirted with her, returned her affections in equal measure. He still wanted her. She just knew it.

Chapter Twelve

Sapphire stomped along the road, going at quite a fast pace, walking as Tanzi would say 'with the power of pissed off'. She was just so angry at Avery and that little tart he had been fawning over. She had not felt this level of anger in years, had never allowed herself to. In her mind anger served no purpose, it stripped you of your control and made you weak, susceptible to suggestion. But she just couldn't shake the trembling of her hands, the grinding of her teeth, the images and thoughts that buzzed around her head like flies.

"Who the hell does he think he is?" she raged, not expecting an answer but needing to rant even if it was just to herself.

She was feeling hungrier and hungrier the more annoyed she got, but her mind was too far gone to register that fact. All she felt was the hollow feeling in her stomach that demanded nourishment.

"What's wrong with me? Why do I fail at everything in life that isn't boring? I didn't have the guts to stand up for myself and my gift and I'm too much of a wimpy Vampire to bite someone." Her stomach chose that moment to growl in agreement, her fangs making her gums ache. "I just need to get over it. I'm not going to rely on Avery or anyone else ever again. I can bite someone; how hard could it be? I fed from that bed hopping Casanova, so I'm sure I can feed from a normal human. I just have to man up and do it."

Inner pep talk delivered, and her mind made up she stopped and looked around, looking for the perfect first victim. *Too fatty,* she decided as an overweight man waddled past, *I doubt his blood would be very healthy to eat.*

A pretty female walking her dog was next to come under her hungry scrutiny but the thought of getting that up close and personal with a female just wasn't in Saph's plan. She waited, leaning against a wall, casually looking at her phone as if she had not a care in the world. Yet her insides were churning, cramps building until she could barely stand it.

Why did she have to be so picky, so in control all the time? Cut yourself some slack, she told herself, trying to relax, *you just want to make sure you're eating right, if you're going to look after yourself and not need anyone, you need to do it properly. No one would eat a plate of bacon fat would they? No, healthy is key.*

Avery could feel her emotions coming off her in waves now that he had tuned into her, a potent mixture of anger, jealousy and hunger. He jogged after her, following their blood bond. She pulsed like a rage filled beacon in the night, the fire in her veins calling to him, leading him closer.

He knew that he really shouldn't be feeling so smug about the fact that she was jealous and that she was angry he had ignored her, but he did. He wasn't used to people turning him down, wasn't used to females not falling into his arms or his bed whenever he wanted them. It was a new feeling to him too, one that left him confused and out of sorts, his confidence in himself shaken. But knowing that she did feel something for him was enough to make it worth all the effort.

Sapphire's head spun with the delicious scents that surrounded her on all sides, pressing in on her like a blanket, flooding her senses. Like all of her favourite foods mixed into one, roast beef, apple pie, hot coffee, melted chocolate, chicken curry. All the things that she could no longer have but that she still craved almost constantly. It just succeeded in making her feel even hungrier. She heard the steady drum of what sounded like hundreds of heartbeats, a percussion of life all around her, the swishing, pumping whoosh of blood in their veins. Their individual scents teasing her nostrils, making her hungrier than she had ever been before in her life. She was famished, feeling like she hadn't eaten in a year, her stomach a balled up, shriveled nut in her belly.

She found she was able to hone in on one particular human and focus all her senses on him. He looked to keep himself in good shape, something made all the more obvious as he came towards her. The shoulders of his jacket filled out nicely, it hung loosely to reveal a t-shirt that stretched over a well-defined chest that narrowed to the hips. She just bet that if he turned around his jeans would cup a pert backside that would fit perfectly in her hands. He would be a good first meal from the human side of the menu.

She could smell his cologne, a nice fresh fragrance that she approved of, though it couldn't hide the manly hint of musk that rode his skin. She was surprised to find she could tell that he had eaten some kind of spicy food not long ago. She wondered if that spice would transfer to his blood, she had always been a fan of a hot curry or Thai dish. Her mouth watered at the memory of some of her favourite foods, she couldn't resist any longer.

As her chosen meal walked past her, her arm shot out, faster than she had ever thought she could move, and dragged him into her embrace. The man spluttered in shock, obviously not expecting to find himself in her hungry clutches. He began to yell, demanding to know what she was doing and commanding her to let him go, all of which she ignored. Food shouldn't talk.

She was so hungry now, her mind focused entirely on the blood she could hear pumping through his veins, she focused her gaze on his throat, seeing his carotid tick away just below the skin. She moaned out loud, imagining just how good he would taste, his red cells coating her tongue, easing her parched throat, relieving her of the knotting hunger.

She leaned in, breathing in his scent, taking it deep into her lungs as she ran the tip of her nose down the length of his throat. He struggled, clearly wanting to get away, though she held him steady in a vice like grip. She felt her fangs descend, punching out of her gums, razor sharp and, wickedly deadly. She opened her mouth, ready and more than willing to bite. She had ceased to see him as a person, as a scared human, now he was nothing but a warm, walking blood bag.

Her fingers gripped the hair at the back of his head, angling him closer, anchoring him as she used her own body to pin him to the wall.

To anyone looking they must just look like a passionate couple locked in a clinch, oblivious to the world around them, but Avery knew what was really happening. He couldn't let it happen, couldn't let her feed out in the open like that, not only was it against their rules to feed from non-donors or romantic relations, it was dangerous and forbidden to feed in public, that was why they had bars such as Carpe Noctem and Night Walkers.

He reached out a hand and yanked her unceremoniously away from her meal, ignoring her indignant squeal of displeasure and shock. He pushed her behind him, holding her there with one arm as he focused on her would be dinner. He pushed power into his eyes, catching and holding the man's gaze as he spoke calmly and clearly.

"Nothing happened. You have never seen this female before in your life. You left the restaurant where you ate with your friends and you went straight home. Go now, and when you get home, go straight to bed. You will sleep for a full eight hours and wake up feeling refreshed and remembering nothing of what has happened here."

The man nodded his head, his eyes glazed over, slightly unfocused as he listened. When Avery looked away, releasing him from the hypnotic power of his eyes, the man walked off, obviously following Avery's instructions to the letter.

"What the hell do you think you are doing?" Sapphire demanded to know, hammering her fist against his shoulder, forcing him to turn around to face her.

Avery was clearly furious with her and it was her first instinct to back down, to shy away in the face of his anger, but she forced herself to stand firm. She was a Vampire now, she refused to be corralled into behaving in a way that others thought she should. She was her own person, even more so now than before. She had realised that night, watching all the performers at the club, that she had her whole, now very long, life in front of her and it was about time she began to make the most of it, actually living rather than existing as she had been doing all her life.

"I could ask you the same thing," he hollered back at her, his face just inches from her own, his eyes seeming to glow with an inner light she hadn't seen before. His own fangs had run out, looking wickedly sharp and dangerous. Though strangely enough, she wasn't scared of him.

"How stupid are you?" he continued to shout. "You don't leave on your own and you certainly don't pick someone off the street."

She couldn't believe that he was yelling at her. He was the one that had treated her like she was invisible as soon as the Russian doll, Liliya had twitched her hips his way and he was the one that had now barged in and disrupted her meal. She wouldn't stand for him shouting and blaming her.

"Just leave me alone, you don't want me, I'm nothing to you. If I want to pick someone up on the street then I will. You have no claim or control over me. So why don't you just fuck off and leave me the hell alone?"

She turned her back on him, determined to hunt down another meal and then go home, as she had been planning earlier before he dragged her out.

"Oh no you don't!" Avery was having none of it. He was sick of her uppity, self-righteous act and he refused to put up with it any more. He had no claim over her? He would see about that. He was going to wedge himself so deep between her thighs she would feel him there for a month, and then he was going to make her promise never to go off like that again. He was going to tame his little prissy vamp with her hoity toity ways. He was going to show her just how a pirate took what he wanted.

Giving her no choice he wrapped his arms around her waist, spun her round and lifted her up, dumping her over his shoulder. Then he gave her butt a short, sharp smack in warning.

"Behave, woman, and don't you even dare try to argue. I'm taking you home and I'm going to show you exactly how it's done," he ignored her wiggling, her flailing arms and kicking legs, simply holding her tighter in place as he took off to his home.

One moment Sapphire was yelling at Avery, venting her anger right in his stupid handsome face and then next she was slung over his shoulder like a sack of potatoes, screaming at the indignity of it all.

She would not let this go unpunished! She screamed and yelled the whole time, attempting to kick him in the nuts, which he foiled easily by hoisting her up a little further so that her head dropped towards the ground, causing her to scream in fright and grab on to his waist. He used the distraction to lock his arm around her legs, effectively

140

pinning her in place. She was beaten but it didn't mean she would go quietly.

Chapter Thirteen

Avery ignored her shrieking, continuing to walk and talk calmly now that he had diverted disaster.

"You should stop wiggling, you're only going to hurt yourself you know." He gave her butt another affectionate swipe, letting his hand linger for a moment too long, stroking over the firm, round cheek.

"You have no right to treat me like this!" she screamed back at him as he walked up the steps to his front door.

"And you have no right to think you are above our laws and can just bite some random human in the street. What were you thinking?"

She paused in her wiggling as his words broke through her rage haze.

"Are we not allowed to do that?"

"No!" he yelled back, losing his calm all over again. "We only drink from registered Donors, other Vampires or beings that know about us, with permission of course, or bagged blood. We don't just go for takeout!"

She tried to lift her head to look at him, bracing her hands on his waist and levering herself up in a strange version of push up. She desperately wanted him to receive the full force of her glare.

"Well, I'm sorry if I didn't know that. No one tells me anything. Everyone is pushing me to learn to drink and one time I decided to do it, its bloody wrong too! I'm sorry, I was hungry and pissed off, all I wanted to do was drink that hot guy and forget you. But I didn't get to and it's all your fault. Now put me the fuck down!"

Now she was just annoying him. He had been trying so hard not to imagine her fangs in the throat of someone else, tried not to see the way he would have reacted to her bite, how she would have reacted to his blood. He had refused to think about it the whole time he was carrying her home, her delectable arse just inches from his face, so fucking tempting that he had to stop himself from taking her right there and then. And now she was shoving in his face the fact that the man she had chosen was hot. And that just set his blood boiling, she was his damn it, and he was done messing around. It was time to show her who was boss.

Avery unlocked his front door and walked in, kicking the door shut behind him. As soon as the door was closed he swung her down from his shoulder and back onto her feet.

He used his body to back her up against the wall, getting up in her face, his words firm, leaving no room for argument.

"You will not feed from an uninitiated human, you won't even feed for a Doner. If you want to feed you will come to me, do you understand me? No one else, only me."

He didn't give her time to register what he was doing. He grabbed the back of her neck in a tight, yet still gentle hold, pulling her head into his neck, his body caging her in, giving her no room to move away or pull back.

"Feed," he growled. "Do it now. If you're so hungry that you have to pick up some guy off the street, feed dammit!"

He was fuming with her. Never had he wanted so badly to shut someone up. She was driving him mad with her ever changing moods, blowing hot and cold with him, encouraging him one minute and pushing him away the next. He didn't know how to deal with that, didn't know how to keep treading carefully around her when all he wanted to do was force her into admitting exactly what she was feeling for him. She obviously didn't trust him, something that hurt him on a level he didn't even know he had. He wanted her to believe in him, to want him as much as he wanted her. He knew that she had feelings for him, but it was almost like she wouldn't allow herself to give in to them, was punishing herself and him by holding herself back and refusing to be with him, while at the same time getting mad at him for talking to another female. She was a walking contradiction that made his head hurt.

Sapphire tried to extract herself from his grip, but he was just too strong, he wasn't hurting her, she doubted that he ever would, but she knew that she would never get away unless he let her. She turned her head away from the tempting expanse of his throat, trying so hard not to remember the taste of his blood and how good it felt when she had fed from him. She had been in shock then, desperate and only just turned, she hadn't really been in the right mindset to fully understand and enjoy the experience. She knew that if she had a taste now, she would never want anyone else. She couldn't let that happen, she wouldn't let him take control from her.

"No, I don't want to. You aren't the boss of me." She ignored how childish she sounded right then.

"When was the last time you just enjoyed something without worrying about the consequences? When was the last time you just enjoyed? Just listened to your body's wants and needs?" he leant in to whisper in her ear, his tongue flickering out to lap at her lobe, sucking it into his mouth, biting softly before releasing it. He felt the way her body shuddered in response. She wasn't as immune to him as she liked to pretend, she wasn't anywhere near as cold as the icy exterior she portrayed. He bet that under all that stiff, buttoned up attitude was a dirty little minx just waiting to be set free. And he was just the man for the job.

Avery's body pushed so close to hers was doing strange things to her control. It was stripping away her layers of defence way too fast for her to rebuild them. Her body was responding to him in the most elemental of ways, clamouring for him to touch her some more, to do all the things that were promised in his words and actions.

She wanted to take him up on his blatant offer, she wanted so badly to sink her fangs into his neck as he in turn sank into her with the delicious hard length that was pressed against her stomach. She wanted to let go and enjoy for once in her life. But she was scared. Too scared of being out of control, too scared that she wasn't strong enough to deal with the emotional baggage that might drag up.

She was so close to giving in, so close to being freed from the self-imposed restraints she forced on herself. She just needed to trust in someone other than herself.

"When was the last time you had a truly hot kiss? A toe curling, spine bending, body shivering kiss that you never wanted to end?" He kissed his way down from her ear to her throat, nipping softly at her skin, hearing her sharp intake of breath, and stifled moan of arousal.

She wanted to tell him that it was with him, that the only time a kiss had truly moved her, made her feel anything at all, had been with him. She wanted to dive in and experience it all, to be wild and free. She just didn't know how.

"I bet you've never had a good, hard, dirty fucking," his hand slipped down her side, finger tips caressing lightly, making her shudder, leaning in for a more satisfying touch. "You said yourself, boring men, lights off, missionary and no tongues. Baby, you've been missing out." His lips worked their way to hers, light little pecks that just left her craving more.

They hovered over hers, a hair's breadth away, not touching, though she desperately wanted them to. Her body was on fire, a raging inferno that pooled low in her stomach.

She grew wetter by the second, her body feeling so sensitive that the right touch would make her explode. She wanted it so badly, needed it more than she could stand.

"I can give you everything you desire. Everything your body craves. Everything you need," he whispered as the tip of his tongue slid against the seam of her lips. They parted for him, a soundless little gasp that told him she was so close to giving up her hardened control. "Let go, baby, I'm right here." His lips closed the distance between them, shattering the last thread of her control.

She wrapped her arms around his shoulders, dragging him closer, needing to lose herself in him, needing to forget everything in the past and embrace her new life. To stop worrying about judgement and enjoy. She knew he was right, she needed him. She wanted him.

He felt the second her control crumbled to dust, when her resistance was lost. Her body sagged into his, going soft and pliant, willing and warm. That's how he wanted her to be, free and uncaring to how she thought she should be. He wanted her to let the wildness inside her out.

He ran his hands down to her thighs, lifting her legs, grunting his approval into her mouth when she instinctively wrapped her legs around his waist, fitting their lower bodies together like they were made for each other, the perfect fit.

Her fingers tangled in his hair, directing the kiss with renewed confidence, her insecurities flying out the window. She could feel his passion as if it were her own, knew without a doubt that he spoke the truth. And that was better than any amount of promises.

She was hot, hotter than he had ever imagined. When she let herself trust, let herself be guided into letting go, she opened to him in the best way, blooming into the most beautiful of flowers.

He broke the kiss, pulling back to look at her, pleased to see that she looked every bit as affected by their kiss as he was. Her lips were swollen and damp, her hair mussed, tendrils escaping from the severe bun that she favoured.

Without thinking he tugged at the pins, shaking out the glossy waves until they fell around her shoulders.

"Last chance to back out, baby," he warned her. "I don't think I can force myself to stop again."

Her fangs were aching with need, her body wet and willing and he was trying to stop? He had broken through her barriers and now thought to protect her delicate sensibilities? She didn't want tender right now, she wanted what he had promised her, the hard, hot fucking that she had always dreamed about. Lonely nights in her bed with nothing but a romance novel for company and her battery-operated friend, fantasising about a dashing prince, a knight in shining armour, a roguish pirate that would sweep her off her feet and have his wicked way with her. She wanted it so badly she could scream.

She licked at his exposed throat, feeling his body shiver in response. For once she was going to let herself be free, to not worry about being right or wrong, of weighing up the pros and cons. Needing to not think anymore, needing to lose herself in Avery, she let her instincts guide her. Without answering, she let her actions speak for her, sinking her fangs deep into his flesh.

Avery's body jerked with a sudden jolt of pleasure as her fangs breached his skin. She fed like a pro, natural instinct riding her. Her fangs slid in clean and smooth, her tongue massaging the skin as she sucked, encouraging the flow of blood into her mouth. It was like she had a direct link to his cock, which pulsed in his too tight jeans, demanding its own share of the attention.

He didn't ask permission, he couldn't speak, couldn't form words, his brain had short circuited somewhere between her fangs sliding home and her luscious little body undulating against his as she rode the bulge in his pants, moaning almost constantly.

He fumbled between their joined bodies, her skirt already rucked up around her waist where her legs were locked around him. He burrowed his fingers down lower and pushed aside her panties, pleasantly surprised to find that they were what appeared to be a small, lacy thong. He had expected some kind of Bridget Jones granny pants nightmare, not this sexy little number. It seemed that his girl had hidden depths, just as he had suspected all along.

He ran his fingertip gently down her soft folds, feeling the welcoming dampness, the proof of her arousal. She didn't push him away, instead she bucked closer and, encouraged, he slid an experimental finger inside her, finding her dripping wet and more than ready.

He yanked at his zipper, dragging it down and his dick sprang free, bobbing as it pulsed, eager for its own share of the attention. He palmed it, stroking firmly a few times before teasing the head against her swollen clit, loving the way she responded.

Sapphire had never been so aroused in her life. She felt like she would explode if he didn't get inside her soon. His blood was coursing through her veins, finally eradicating the hollow, hungry feeling she had had for so long. She felt sated in one way but was now starving in another. She needed him, just as he had promised. She wiggled against him, her back still pinned against the hall wall, not that she cared, she had lost track of their surroundings the second their lips had joined.

Avery felt his tip slip down, sliding just inside her entrance and he almost came right there and then. She sucked strongly on his neck, still happily feeding and he had no intention of stopping her any time soon. Unable to hold out any longer he slid forward, burying himself to the hilt in one smooth move.

Her whole body tensed as he entered her, stretching her to just this side of too full, she was sure that if she hadn't been so very ready it would have hurt. He paused inside her, his chest heaving as he sought to keep control, allowing her body time to adjust to his invasion. She appreciated the gesture, but she was growing more desperate by the second, she wanted him to move. She bucked her hips impatiently drawing back, then using her legs to yank him back in.

Holy shit, she felt good, so hot and tight. Nothing had ever felt so right, and he doubted it ever would again. They fit together perfectly. *Hold back, man,* he chanted desperately in his head, all too aware that she probably hadn't had sex in a long time and even if she had, her boring humans would pale in comparison, he didn't want to hurt her. But she obviously had other ideas.

Her tight sheath squeezed him like a fist as she moved her hips backwards. He couldn't help but moan with pleasure at the feeling. He felt her legs tighten around his waist, her heels digging into his arse as she flexed, yanking him forward. His cock slammed in hard and fast, lodging deep inside her, stealing his breath and the last of his control.

He jerked backwards pausing for a second, just to enjoy the feeling of her squirming on his dick before he surged back in. His hands slid under the hem of her blouse, finding their way to her breasts. He pulled down the cups, freeing them. He eagerly cupped them finding them to be a generous handful that she kept hidden in her dowdy work suits. Her nipples pebbled against his palm and he couldn't resist giving them a little tweak, grinning when he felt her purr against his throat. Her sucking had slowed from desperate hungry gulps to lazy swallows as she savoured his taste.

He settled into a pounding rhythm, his fingers squeezing and kneading her breast as he kissed his way up and down her neck, nuzzling with his nose, loving the way she responded to him. Her body moved against his like liquid, fluid and graceful, heightening each thrust with a draw on his throat. With each thrust he moved closer to completion, feeling his balls draw up tight as his orgasm built. Not knowing how much longer he'd be able to hold back he eased one hand back down between their bodies, seeking her clit with his thumb.

She jerked in his arms as he found it slick with her juices and began to circle it firmly with just enough pressure to hurtle her towards her own finish. Little whimpering cries escaped her, muffled against his throat as she writhed against his hand, burying his cock deeper.

She was so close, about to tumble over the edge, she just needed a little more. She sucked in another mouthful of his blood, she just couldn't get enough of it, it was like mulled wine, spicy and warm, it slid down her throat like melted chocolate and pooled in her stomach, warming her from the inside, making her tingle all over.

He felt her inner muscles gripping him tight, rippling around his shaft, milking his cock, demanding his orgasm. He sped up the circling of his thumb, rubbing hard and fast as his body took over. He pounded between her legs, enjoying every little noise of pleasure she made. He kissed at her skin, nipping her throat gently, surprised when she leant closer, elongating her neck in a blatant offer.

Did he dare? Her having his blood had been a necessity to ease her through her turning, creating a bond between them that would never be broken, he would be able to find her no matter where she was. Could she handle the same from him? She moaned her impatience, her own fangs sliding free, her tongue lapping at his skin to seal the punctures, making the decision for him.

"Just fucking do it," her voice was husky with desire and possibly the sexiest thing he had ever heard. "Bite me." He heard the command in her voice and was powerless to do anything but obey.

When he bit his fangs struck fast and deep, the pin prick flash of pain that made her gasp faded quickly, replaced by bone deep pleasure that shoved her over the edge. She came wetly around his cock, her muscles gripping tightly as his thumb danced on her clit. Pleasure zoomed up her spine, stealing her breath as she cried out, whimpering his name over and over like a prayer.

Her body moved with his, twitching and bouncing unable to get enough, her orgasm seeming never ending. She felt the second he joined her. He stilled his thrusting, going shock still as his body trembled and shook, his mouth leaving her throat as his head tipped back, his groan deep and powerful. On instinct she tightened her pussy around him and tipped her hips forward, drawing him in deeper.

Something snapped inside him as he clutched her tighter, his fingers gripping her thighs as he hoisted her further up the wall, his hips pistoning forward to slam inside her again and again, his cock pulsing with his seed, marking her with each cool lash. Their lips mashed together in a desperate kiss, teeth nipping, tongues dueling for control as their orgasms built to their peak.

After what felt like forever they slowed, their kisses losing the desperate edge, changing to something gentler, more tender, their bodies re axing into each other. Her body was shivering in his embrace as she cuddled against his chest, their kiss languid as it wound down. Avery pulled back to look at her, searching her face for any sign that she might now be pissed off with him, it had happened before. He'd seen first-hand the way her moods could suddenly change, and he would rather bask in the afterglow of fantastic sex for a while longer if he had the choice.

Sapphire could feel him watching her and though she barely had the energy to move she lifted her head to give him a small smile. He was right there to greet her, his lips spreading into a lazy grin in response. His eyes gazing at her, as if seeing right down into the very heart of her being. She felt strangely naked and vulnerable right then, open to him, unable to hide and she had to fight down the urge to freak out and begin worrying about what would happen next. She forced herself to relax back into him, resting her head on his shoulder.

He had a distinct feeling of dread come over him as her eyes lifted to meet his, one that vanished as soon as he saw the small smile she gave him. It was then that he felt it, he was as sure as he was of his own name. It was a bone deep knowledge that just felt so right he wondered how he had ever been without her. It was like something inside him just clicked into place, something that had been lost, now found. Some of the aching loneliness he had tried so hard to bury deep inside him eased. He knew what Topaz had talked about all those months ago when she had mated with Logan, the surety in her voice. He felt the same. He had waited for this moment all of his long life and now that it had happened, he knew he'd never want another. Sapphire was his Soul Mate.

Chapter Fourteen

Sapphire could barely think straight, her mind swimming with the echoes of their time together. He was still buried inside her, her body still wrapped around his and he was showing no sign of moving. She didn't really know what to do about it. Her previous partners had never wanted to cuddle, let alone hold her for an extended amount of time without moving. The more that she thought about it the more uncomfortable with her exposed state she became.

Avery was in awe of her. She was nothing like he had imagined his Soul Mate would be. He had always envisioned someone more like himself, a free spirit that was always game for a laugh, that had zero inhibitions and would keep him on his toes.

He had no idea why he was attracted to her so much. Sure, he had always thought she was pretty, beautiful actually, now that he looked at her again, her hair free and hanging down, framing her face. But now that they had been together, now that he had felt the depths of her passion, the way she reacted to him, he knew that the fates had picked well for him. She would be the perfect complement to his wild side, would rein him in from his more stupid impulses while she could let herself go with him, she could relax and enjoy without fear of judgement.

He could help her to explore the world around her, to step out of her comfort zone by knowing that he would always be there to catch her if she fell.

But now he had to get her to believe him. To believe in them. To take a leap of faith and trust that they were destined to be together and that her future was with him. That shouldn't be too big a challenge, should it? Well, he was never one to shy away from a difficult task. He would just pretend that nothing had changed, take the softly softly approach and pretend that it had just been a casual hook up. That should put her at ease. He'd work on her, gradually winning her around until she couldn't imagine her life without him. Yep, that was a sound plan.

Sapphire squirmed, now feeling rather like a bug pinned to a board. She needed some space, some room to think, her lack of control bothered her, she needed to analyse all that had happened and have it make sense in her head again. Too much had happened too fast and she didn't know what to make of it.

She couldn't quite believe that, one, she had just done that, in the hall way of a near stranger's house and, two, that she had enjoyed it so damned much. It was like nothing she had ever experienced before. She had never done anything anywhere but in a bed and had never expected to want to, let alone enjoy it and be wondering just what else Avery could do to her body.

He was changing her and that was scaring the shit of her. She had never been so wanton before. Even during sex she had always kept her composure, always thought of it as a pleasant pastime but didn't really see the big deal. Tanzi would wax lyrical about how she had had 'the best sex ever' and Saph would smile and nod with her, but inside she really had no clue what they were talking about.

She had read so many things in her romance books that she had never experienced but had always wondered about, always picturing herself with the dashing hero of the book, but now when she thought about it, all she pictured was Avery. With his puffy pirate shirts and skin tight trousers, his too long hair and his over the top personality. And that shocked her to the core.

She was falling for the idiot. She had all these thoughts and feelings buzzing around in her head that she didn't understand and wasn't comfortable with. She was attracted to someone that she shouldn't have even looked at twice. Someone that had made her body come alive with his touch, his skilled fingers bringing her so much pleasure. She cringed to think where he had learned those skills and just how much practice he had.

Unbidden she thought of the women she knew about, obviously Liliya and he had dated before, the Donor she had caught him screwing in the hall. She pulled up short as the memory invaded her mind. He had fucked her the same way he had fucked the Donor. She had thought she was special, that he had been with her because he wanted her, not because she was yet another notch on his belt. She was suddenly so angry she could spit.

She couldn't deal with this right now. Now that she had fed, the hunger gone for once, she buzzed with energy, felt like she could run a few marathons and climb a mountain or two. She was restless, wanting to walk, run, dance, move, anything that got rid of her nervous energy, the rage that was now rolling through her.

She pulled away from him as best she could, trying to get him to move. He stepped back when she pushed at his shoulders and dropped her legs down to the ground, effectively forcing him to put her down and let her go. She felt his cock slide out of her, a curiously intimate thing that left her feeling empty and alone. She felt how damp she was, felt his seed starting to leak out as she righted her clothes, and retied her hair in silence.

Avery wasn't sure what had just happened and how he had managed to go from bliss to miss in such a short time without even opening his notoriously big mouth. One minute he had his girl in his arms and the next she was pulling away. He didn't get it. He silently tucked his softened dick in to his pants and zipped up before he dared to speak.

"Is something wrong?" he asked gently, half afraid of the answer.

"No," she answered curtly. "Why would it be? I was just under the impression that when you fucked a girl in a hallway you wanted to be done with her as quickly as possible to move on to the next one. I was just saving you the trouble of kicking me out."

She bent and grabbed her bag, feeling the twinge in her neck as the skin pulled, a reminder of where his fangs had been. Somehow that just made her angrier.

Avery pulled up short at her words, suddenly realising what she was referring to. He deeply regretted the fact that he had slept with the Donor, let alone the fact that she caught him just after. But there was nothing he could do about it now.

"I was never going to kick you out, I never would."

"Well, now you don't have to wait until morning. Thanks for the fuck, it was fun, but I'm going home now."

Sapphire was out the door before he could utter a word in his defence, walking away at a quick pace.

Avery stared after her, unable to quite believe what had just happened. He threw his hands up in despair, slamming the door behind her.

"Gahh," he screamed in frustration, his fist connecting with the wall. "I will..." punch, "never understand..." punch, "women!"

Sapphire didn't notice Cassie standing silently on the kerb side watching her as she left his house, she was too intent on getting home, needing to finally be somewhere that she could relax and be in control again.

156

Chapter Fifteen

Tanzanite snuggled in deeper under his arm, resting her head on his muscular chest, her eyes glued on the TV screen as they ate their way through a huge bowl full of popcorn, two bags of chips and a large bottle of pop, all while accompanied by the sounds of six stupid teenagers slowly being hunted down and murdered by a deranged killer. Just your usual Wednesday night in.

She reached for another handful of the popcorn, shifting to get comfier. She had gotten used to having Nikos around and found that she missed him when he wasn't there on the nights he had to work or deal with pack business, especially now that one of her sisters had moved out and the other hadn't been home in over a week. Nikos in turn loved the peace and quiet of her place, he'd shared a huge house with his family and pack mates, something that he'd grown rapidly tired of, and had recently gotten his own place.

Nikos tightened his arms around her, pulling her in closer, dragging her onto his lap, his head dipping to steal a kiss when they heard the sound of a key in the lock. They sprang apart instantly, Tanzi diving to the other side of the couch, the popcorn bowl between them as a barrier, their eyes firmly fixed on the screen as Sapphire came stomping into the room.

Sapphire's walk home had not cleared her mind in the slightest. The second she was in the door she began ranting, yanking her shoes off as she headed down the hall.

"Avery is such an arsehole. I swear I could have staked him tonight, you know, if I actually had a stake. I don't know what I ever saw in him, or why I believed him, all men are the same!" She threw her jacket over the banister and grabbed a can of diet coke from the fridge, needing something to wash the taste of Avery's blood out of her mouth. She didn't want any reminder of what had happened, how easily she fell for his lines, his practiced seduction techniques, she really must have been desperate. She slammed the kitchen door shut and followed the sound of screaming coming from the TV, knowing her sister must be watching another of her slasher flicks.

She pulled up short when she noticed the Shifter sitting on the couch with her sister. She looked from one to the other.

"Am I interrupting something?

"No, no," Tanzi grabbed the remote and muted the TV. "We were just watching a film. No big."

Nikos stood up, sensing that Sapphire needed to talk and most likely wouldn't while he was there.

"Oh no, please don't go. I'm sorry, I didn't mean to ruin your film night."

Nikos shook his head. "It's no problem, I am obviously a man and therefore scum of the earth right now," he gave her a wink to soften his words. "So I shall take my leave. But before I do, just one thing. Avery might seem like a dick sometimes, but he is a good man, cut him a little slack huh?"

Sapphire crossed her arms in a pout. "He's a man whore of epic proportions. How do I cut him slack for that?"

158

Nikos blinked as Tanzi howled with laughter, he had never heard the usually calm and composed Sapphire raise her voice, let alone swear and use terms like 'man whore' in a sentence.

"Well, yes, OK, I can't deny it, he's shared the love. But that's only because he's been looking for his Soul Mate for years. He's never kept it a secret that he's an old romantic at heart and is looking for that special someone. What did he do this time, sleep with someone and leave you to tell them that he wasn't there when they came looking for seconds? He's done that to me a few times…" he trailed off when he saw the look on Sapphire's face. "Oh, don't look like that babe. He never promises them more. Hell, he hasn't even taken them home, he never does. Someone would have to be pretty special to see the inner sanctum." He could tell that he really wasn't helping. Best to leave the talking to her sister. "Yeah… I'm just gonna go now before you two start planning ways to emasculate the entire male species with nothing but a rusty teaspoon."

Tanzi could barely see through tears, she was laughing so much, watching poor Nikos splutter his way through his speech, digging himself further and further into a hole of which he would never get out of.

"Wimp," she yelled after him as he made his escape as if demons were on his tail.

Sapphire took his vacated seat as the door slammed shut behind him.

"Why was he here?" Since when do you two hang out?"

"To watch a movie, Cassian sent him to watch me one time and we discovered we both have the same taste in movies. Since you find them boring and Amethyst is scared of them, I invited him round to watch a few, it's nice to have company. I didn't think you would be home tonight or I wouldn't have asked him."

Tanzi sounded far too casual and for the first time Sapphire realised that both she and Amethyst had been neglecting their big sister. She was always there for them

159

but while they had had stuff going on they hadn't thought about her, just assumed that she would be happily going about her day as she usually did, Tanzi wasn't one to let things bother her or get her down for long.

"I'm sorry I wasn't home." She'd never felt so bad.

Tanzi snorted. "Yeah, because you weren't busy enough getting kidnapped and recovering were you? It's fine. It's not a big deal. Now shut up about me and tell me why Avery is an arsehole."

Sapphire could tell that her sister didn't want to talk, anything that made her out to be weak was not allowed. Tanzi prided herself on being the tough cookie of the family, the big sister that sorted out everyone else's messes. There was no way she would get any more information out of Tanzi unless she wanted to talk, it was like trying to push a boulder uphill wearing 6" stilettos.

"Spit it out, sissy. You stomped in here angrier than the time I borrowed your shoes and broke the heel in the drain cover. What happened?"

"I still haven't forgiven you for that," Sapphire grumbled with a sigh. "It's nothing. He just annoyed me that's all, forget it. I just need to chill out in the bath with a good book and forget about him." She took a sip of coke, swilling it delicately around her mouth briefly before swallowing it.

Tanzi wasn't convinced.

"Don't lie to me, missy. I know you better than that, what did he do to you? Do I have to go on a murderous rampage?"

Now that the wind had gone from her sails and she was beginning to calm down, Sapphire really did want nothing more than to just have a bath and pretend that it had never happened. She felt like a real idiot to have fallen for him even the tiniest bit and to have allowed that to happen, the last thing she wanted was to talk about it and have someone else know how stupid she had been. Of all the people she could have picked to scratch an itch with, to

160

break her out of her comfort zone, Avery was the worst possible candidate.

"Really, it's fine. It's nothing. He was just acting like a bit of an arsehole tonight, nothing more than usual. I guess I'm just tired and a bit highly strung right now, usually it wouldn't have bothered me. Just got on my nerves tonight, that's all. I just need to rest."

Tanzanite wasn't fooled for a second by her sisters casual glossing over of the facts. It wasn't like her to get so annoyed, coming in practically spitting feathers over someone acting like a bit of an arse. She took that sort of thing with a pinch of salt, letting it sail over her head as if it was nothing, people like that weren't worth her time.

But Tanzi knew that Avery was the one that had nursed and guided Sapphire through her turning and the first few days after that, that had to have obviously been a traumatic time for her sister. Sapphire was allergic to anything weird and unusual, it would be hell for her to wake up and find herself completely changed.

For the umpteenth time Tanzi wished that she could have been there for her more than she was, but the others had warned her that it was too dangerous for her to be there when her sister woke up, there was nothing she could have done to help. Nikos had promised her that as they sat watching endless movies, his attempt to distract her from her worrying.

Finally, Tanzi nodded her understanding. This was her first time home after her turning and everything had changed in her life, of course Sapphire just wanted to slip back into her normal routine and find that things were still exactly the same as they had always been.

"Go and have your bath then, sis, I'm going to finish this popcorn and the movie before bed."

Sapphire was grateful for the reprieve, she knew that her sister hadn't completely bought her story but knew her well enough to know when she really wanted to be left alone. Giving her sister a quick hug, just for being awesome,

Sapphire grabbed her can and took it with her to the bathroom.

Avery lay alone in his bed, still trying to wrap his brain around just what had happened. One minute they had been basking in their shared afterglow and the next the woman had morphed back into her screaming harpy persona and yelled at him before walking out of the door.

He understood that she had been upset with him somehow, had mentioned the female he had fucked a few days before. But surely she knew that that had meant nothing to him? Hadn't he made her feel special, shown her that she was different from the Donors that he picked up?

He let the thoughts percolate in his head and slowly he realised that maybe he hadn't. Not enough for her anyway. She had obviously hated seeing him with someone else, and he had played up to Liliya in front of her. Now that he thought about it, he really hadn't thought his plans through. He wasn't used to having to work to get a female he desired. Maybe that was one of the things that had really attracted him to Sapphire.

He promised himself that he would be on his best behaviour from now on, well, as good as he could be. She had to fall for him as he was, not as he pretended to be. He'd always believed that Soul Mates were connected for a reason, he had complete faith that she would come around, he just had to bide his time. And if he managed to make her a little jealous along the way to push her in the right direction, so be it, it had certainly had a favourable outcome earlier.

He settled back against the pillows, his body aroused and aching with need, wishing that he had his woman beside him. He knew now without a shadow of a doubt that she was the one for him, he just had to make her see it. He knew that she doubted him, but in truth he believed that she doubted herself more. All of her turns in attitude seemed to spring from her thinking too much. Of her living in the past

162

and holding onto her hurt from past experiences. She was much better when she wasn't thinking, only feeling. Maybe what he needed to do was keep her so aroused and sated that she didn't have time to think. He smiled to himself, yes that was a good plan.

Chapter Sixteen

From the memoirs of Liliya Khilkov

I was born the daughter of the most noble of families, the Khikov's, proud descendants of Prince Vladimir Svyatoslavich. We enjoyed many servants, lavish parties, our riches allowing us to live a good life. I had many admirers, many suitors that sought my hand in marriage. Attention from men was nothing new to me, I accepted it with graceful dignity, as was right and proper.

But all men, they paled in comparison to Yury. He was everything I was seeking in a husband, strong and handsome, the most eligible bachelor to grace our family functions. I loved him upon first sight.

He was attentive in his courtship of me, doing as was proper, asking permission of my father to spend time with me.

I did not notice at first, the fact that he only courted me during the night time hours, though when I did question the fact, he assured me that he toiled long hours to keep me in gifts and furs as I so deserved. I fell deeper and deeper in

164

love with my handsome Yury, our happiness untainted until father intervened.

There had been talk of a marriage being arranged for me and I could not stand the idea, I wanted no one but my Yury, no one else held my heart.

Upon hearing father's plans, Yury appeared distraught, unable to control his heartache at the loss of my company. He told me that it would be too hard for him to see me wed another and that he must leave.

I cried, such heart-rending sobs, begging him to take me with him, convincing him that we belonged together. He had reservations, fearing I would be saddened without my family but I assured him that he was all I needed. Eventually he relented and agreed to take me with him.

We left that evening at dusk, travelling by carriage many miles, throughout most of the night. We settled in a boarding house for the few hours left before dawn, our horses were tired, and I found myself in need of food and sleep.

That was the first night I shared a bed with Yury, giving him my maidenhood and my promise of utter devotion. I vowed never to be parted from him, begged him to keep me with him forever. He promised that he would and bent to kiss my neck.

I woke up three nights later as a Vampire, his undead bride, together forever.

But, as they say, not all things are meant to be. We were happy for many years, Yury schooling me in the ways of my new life, bringing me humans to make my meal, always stopping me before I took too much. Yury was an attentive sire at first, showering me with attention and love but slowly his affections began to wane, much to my sadness.

I awoke one evening from my death sleep to find myself alone for the very first time in my life. My father had always taken good care of me and after him, my sire. I am not proud to say that I knew nothing of tending to myself. I knew not how to hunt and stalk my prey, I knew nothing of the stealthiness that Vampires employ to find their food. I suffered greatly. I had no coin with which to purchase lodgings, so was forced to spend my daylight hours cowering like a peasant in a hay loft, sharing space with rats and other such vermin. My clothing grew dirty, my hair and body unkempt as I spend more and more nights alone.

I grew hungrier and hungrier, wasting away to practically nothing before the hunger grew too much to bear. I had waited, believing naively I now see, for Yury to recover his senses and come back to me. But alas he did not.

I dared to venture out that night in search of sustenance and eventually came across a young woman of around fourteen years of age, walking alone. I didn't pause to think about it, I simply pounced, dragging her into the shadow of a nearby church building.

I sank my fangs into her neck, feeling the blissful relief of her blood coating my tongue. My parched throat easing with each draw, the terrible gnawing hunger in the pit of my stomach lessened with each mouthful I took. Yury had always been the one to control my feedings, monitoring my meals heartbeat and timing my drinking to prevent harm. But he was not with me then and I found that the more I drank, the more desperate I became. My hunger rose like a monster, obliterating any sense of self I had retained.

I did not return to myself until the poor soul was drained dry of every drop of her blood. I felt her life slip away, felt her pulse cease, her heart stop pumping, growing still as she took her last breath, and the monster inside me, the one that resides in us all, rejoiced in her death.

I had not meant to, but I found that I now craved that rush of power taking a life gave me. I confess that I was indeed reckless in my pursuit of humans to feed from. I lost count of the lives I took in those dark days I was first left to fend for myself.

One night, one special night, I left my makeshift shelter to feed, waiting as long as I could stand for the perfect person. Yet, my usual preference of a young girl or a boy first discovering his manhood, failed to materialise. I grew desperate and suffered a lack of judgement that would end up changing my life for the better.

Unfortunately news of my victims had begun to spread, and people were wary of venturing out of their houses after dark, fearing they too would lose their lives. I saw a male in his late thirties come strolling by as if he had not a care in the world. He was handsome in his own way, and strong, much taller and broader than Yury had been. He carried himself with an air of confidence that I appreciated. But I was still hungry and against my limited judgement in my blood lust state, I attacked him as I had so many others.

But unlike the others the male did not go down easily, he appeared to find my fangs more alluring than something to be feared. He fought well but after the initial struggle I managed to overpower him with my superior Vampire strength. I sank my fangs into his throat but rather than screaming as so many others had, he allowed me to feed as I wished, going limp and placid in my embrace. And then he spoke.

He asked that I turn him, make him as I was. He tired of his life in the villages, tired of manual labour that would get him nowhere. He desired adventure and a companion that would never leave him like his beloved late wife had done. He promised that he would protect me, treat me as I deserved, feed me as was my due, he vowed that he would take care of me. And I rejoiced in his words, quickly agreeing.

Thankfully Yury had informed me of the process by which my change had happened and I was able to replicate it successfully, my new Vampire companion, Grigory rose three days later, just as he had promised.

Liliya put down her custom made fountain pen, carefully blotting the pages of the diary she had been writing in. She had decided that it would be in her best interests to document her life. She wished to share every part of herself with her Soul Mate, good and bad, she wanted him to know all there was to know about the woman he would be tied to the for the rest of his immortal life.

He may not have recognised her yet, he may not have opened himself up to the truth of the situation all those years ago when they had first been together, but she had. She had known even then that they were destined to be together. But she knew that he hadn't been ready to settle down, that he was too much of a free spirit, needing to sow his wild oats a little longer. She had been patient, she had given him the space and time he had required, but now he was ready, and so was she, ready to claim that which was hers.

She slipped the book back into its spot in her dressing table drawer, picking up her brush to run it through her already smooth hair. The action calmed her. She was still beyond angry that Avery had blown her off the night before to run out after that little nobody of a fledgling. She had almost lost her cool completely in front of everyone in that godforsaken little hole that he had seemed so comfortable in. She didn't understand the appeal and doubted that she ever would. She had had to have Grigory run her a steaming bubble bath to rid herself of the dirt she had been sure was clinging to her.

She checked her already flawless makeup, slicking on yet another coat of lip gloss, giving her already plump lips an extra dose of pout, she blew herself a kiss in the mirror as she jumped up and pulled on her coat. She looked up to see the dark shape of her companion standing silently in the doorway, watching her as he always did. Always faithfully by her side.

"Grigory, it is time for us to leave."

She danced her way out into the hallway, a happy little spring in her step. Her plan was coming together nicely, soon she would have Avery all to herself.

She had obviously been there all night, left almost hidden behind the dumpster, her innards spread out around her as had the others before her.

Cassie stood over the body of Mellissa, her friend and fellow Donor. She had never felt such anger before, which sucked now that she couldn't actually do anything about it.

"He's done it again," she whispered to herself, rage filling her being with power, the dumpster lid suddenly flinging itself backwards to smack into the wall with a resounding bang, no doubt alerting the people within the Donors Guild office that the killer had struck again and deposited a present right in their back yard.

"I have to find Sapphire," Cassie winked out of existence just as the sounds of running feet drew closer.

Chapter Seventeen

Sapphire awoke from her death sleep to see Cassie standing over her, staring down at her with a look of fascination on her face. Sapphire screamed her head off in a completely undignified way, yelling and scrambling away to fall on the floor in a heap of blankets.

"I've never seen a Vampire sleeping," Cassie commented as she proceeded to float halfway through the bed, standing in the middle of it to bend over and look down at Sapphire. "It's weird. I kept calling you to wake up, but you wouldn't, not until the sun set anyway. You looked dead, really dead, not like me dead. I still look good. You looked all waxy and pale, like a corpse. Wasn't nice girl, wasn't nice."

Sapphire untangled her legs from the sheets and scrambled to her feet, rubbing her sore arse where it had met the floor in such a brutal manner.

"What are you doing here?" she asked the ghost, calming down now that she was back on her feet.

"I saw another one."

"Another what?" Saph was thoroughly confused having only just woken up.

Cassie rolled her eyes like she was dealing with a first class simpleton. Which, Saph had to admit, she was feeling like quite frequently in the week since she had woken up as a Vampire. She was feeling completely out of her depth in a world she knew nothing about.

"Another victim," Cassie reiterated slowly. "He's killed again."

"Holy shit! Another Donor?"

Cassie nodded. "Mellissa, nice girl, took care of her little sister a lot while her mum was at work. She just graduated college, only did feedings at the weekend, part time, not full time like me, just enough to pay her bills."

Sapphire felt tears well up in her eyes. "That's so sad. I'm so sorry you had to see her like that."

Cassie shrugged, brushing it off. "I thought I would come and warn you because I'm assuming that the Guild and the Council will want you to try and do your little ghost whisperer bit again and try to talk to her."

This hadn't occurred to Sapphire until Cassie mentioned it. The possibility of seeing another ghost wasn't something she had wanted to think about, let alone do. And this time she wouldn't have Avery with her for support. She squared her shoulders, mentally chastising herself for thinking she needed that oaf to do anything, she had survived without him for long enough and would get through this too.

"Did you see her there?" Saph had to ask. "I don't know if you spirits can hang out together or anything like that, so I didn't mean to be insulting when I asked that."

Cassie appeared to think about it for a moment. "No, she wasn't there. But she could have been somewhere else. It's strange, it's like we're all on different planes of existence now. Like there is the light and the spirit realm where I was supposed to go. I saw the light but then I saw you standing there, saw my body and I refused to go, I wanted to help." Cassie wandered out of the bed and made her way over to

171

the dresser top, appearing to concentrate as she tried to pick up a lipstick, her ghostly fingers just sliding straight through it.

"Then there are other earthbounds, like me, I can see them walking around, but most seem to ignore me. I've tried to talk to them, but they seem lost in their own world. Maybe the movies were on to something when they say that we have unfinished business, I certainly feel unfinished, I refuse to go anywhere until that pig is caught, maybe they can only do things related to their life. I don't know." She growled at the lipstick, appearing to give up and move on to a pen lid, poking at it with her finger tip.

Sapphire just listened, letting her speak, knowing that she was getting a rare glimpse into how ghosts saw things, she didn't want to risk pissing Cassie off and the ghost getting into a snit and shutting up.

"And as for humans, you lot don't notice me at all. It's weird, like you're all behind glass or something, like frosted glass that I can see through, but you're slightly blurry and the words are a little muffled. Only you I can see and hear clearly. Or people that I seem to have a strong connection to. Like my parents, I can see them."

She poked one last time at the pen lid, watching as her fingers slid right through it, not looking at Sapphire as she continued to speak. "They miss me, they keep saying that they hope that I've moved on. Someone that works for the police and also the Guild, went to them, told them that there had been an accident and that I'd been hit by a car, a hit and run. That I was found dead at the scene, no witnesses. They have to wait for the Guild to release my body until they can hold my funeral and then they aren't allowed to see me. My mum just kept crying and saying that she hopes they catch whoever did this to me."

Finally, Cassie looked up at Sapphire. "We'll catch him, won't we?"

Sapphire didn't really know what to say, she wanted to reassure the girl that they would indeed find the one that had so brutally murdered her. She recalled saying to Avery that it would have been better if Jason had just killed her. But now that she saw what Cassie was going through, she was grateful that her sisters weren't having to deal with her death and she wasn't stuck as a ghost.

"Of course we will," she finally said. "I will never give up on you. I will find out all I can and help the Guild in anything they ask. That I promise."

Cassie nodded as if not trusting herself to speak, crystalline tears forming in the corners of her eyes. Apparently, ghosts could indeed cry. Saph wanted to comfort her, wanted to say something, anything to make it better, but Cassie winked out of existence as suddenly as she appeared.

Sapphire rushed to get dressed, hurrying through a quick shower, expecting the call any minute now. They didn't disappoint. She heard the phone ring somewhere downstairs and Tanzi pick it up, talk for a minute or two before calling up the stairs.

"Sis, you're wanted."

Sapphire stood in the courtyard at the back of the Guild house. It was situated in a large, late Victorian house that looked perfectly normal from the outside, as if maybe a big family lived there, but inside it was the epitome of minimalist office chic.

The body had been removed, for which she was pathetically grateful. She didn't want to make herself look like a weakling in front of all these people, and there were a lot.

Miss Angelica had arrived to personally escort her to Guild house, explaining on the way that they had all been in their offices, ready to start the morning's work when they heard a loud bang outside and, worrying that it was kids or someone causing trouble, they had rushed out there and found the poor Donor's body. It was cold, like it had been there for a long time. They guessed that it must have been

173

sometime between four and five that morning, while it was still dark. It wasn't a large window of time, just the hour between them going home and sunrise, if it was indeed a Vampire that was doing the killings.

Now Sapphire was standing there, in the cold, feeling like a prize monkey that was expected to perform. She looked all around, but saw nothing. She had tried calling out to the Donor, Miss Mellissa, but she got nothing in return. She didn't have that tingling up her spine awareness that she usually got around spirits.

"Anything yet?" Roger asked, looking rather impatient as he leant against a wall, checking his watch every two minutes.

Sapphire had been trying for half an hour, moving around the courtyard in an attempt to pick up on any energies that might have been left. She had tried everything she could think of but had gotten a big, fat zero.

"I'm sorry, I don't think she's still here. I think she has moved on."

"Nothing at all?"

Sapphire shook her head. "No, I'm sorry."

"But you're a medium," his tone was rather disgruntled, as if she had somehow lied to him, playing him for a fool. "Can't you summon it or something?"

She forced herself to keep calm as she answered.

"Yes, I am, but that doesn't mean I can magic up a spirit. They don't always answer, like making a phone call, sometimes the person just isn't on the other end. Plus, I never trained, I actually don't know that much about spirits, I wouldn't know how to summon one if I wanted to."

Roger looked very put out by the news but made a valiant effort to hide it, instead thanking her for trying and promising that they would keep her informed of any new news they had, instructing Miss Angelica to take her home after promising she would be hearing from them soon.

174

Chapter Eighteen

Sapphire had tried to avoid going back to Carpe Noctem that night, begging Tanzi to stay in with her, even promising to watch one of her sister's awful horror movies. But Tanzi had told her quite firmly and with the unerring honesty of a sibling… "I don't want to be chilling on the couch one minute and the next have my sister deciding I'd make a good chew toy, you're going to get some blood into you that I don't have to bleed for."

Saph knew that she was right, knew what she said made sense. She didn't want to suddenly get hungry and flip out at her sister and if what Avery told her was true, and even though he was a womanising cad she didn't believe he would lie to her, she wasn't allowed to feed from some random human from the street, that was only allowed from Donors. She had no choice but to go to the club and face the music.

Walking into the bar, all Sapphire hoped for was the chance to have a quiet drink with her sisters and that they would be served by someone other than Avery, honestly did the guy never have a night off? It was like he never went home, he was always there. All the better to pick up women, Saph snarked to herself as she pushed open the door.

What she didn't want to see was Liliya leaning over the bar, her pert arse displayed to perfection in her skin tight, almost indecently short, dress. She had captured Avery's attention like a snake with a rat, holding him captive. Her constant shadow, Grigory she thought Avery had called him, was keeping his distance, sitting by himself at a small table, nursing what she assumed was some version of the house specials.

An almost instantaneous burst of jealousy flared through her as she watched the way Liliya pouted and smoldered in Avery's direction, apparently basking in the glow of his attention. Nice to know I'm so easily replaced, Sapphire thought to herself. She wanted so much to march over and rip each perfect strand of hair out of her perfect head. She indulged herself in the visuals for a moment or two before forcing herself to turn away and pay attention to her sisters.

Tanzi was not as oblivious as she liked to lead people to believe but even she would have had to be blind not to notice the tension that stretched between her sister and the blonde Vampire, Avery. She had known that Sapphire had blown her off the night before, refusing to give any real reason as to why she was so annoyed with Avery and now that she saw the narrow eyed squinty glare that Saph was levelling at the pretty brunette that was all over Avery like a rash, she could pretty much piece together the rest.

Her sister and the Vampire had obviously indulged in a little bump and grind action together and it had fallen apart after. She knew that her sister had little to no experience with real men and had a habit of running scared, so she in no way thought that her sister was innocent in the whole thing, but she was also not ashamed to admit that she was eyeing up the pretty boy's chest for a good staking if he hurt her sister.

176

Liliya was so happy she felt she would burst. He loved her, he really, truly, loved her. She knew it as sure as she knew her own name. He really had just been looking out for that fledgling as a favour, she was sure of it. After all, why would he want someone like that when he could have her? Liliya was perfect for him, she had known it the first time they were together, and she knew it now.

Unable to wait any longer she took full advantage of Avery leaning in to talk to her, turning her head so that their lips met. She wasted no time in threading her fingers through his hair, locking his head in place as she parted his lips with her tongue.

To say that he was shocked was an understatement, Avery had never thought that Liliya would be so forward. He had tried to gently discourage her, but she clearly hadn't gotten the hint. It took him a few seconds to really register exactly what was going on and then another half a minute to manage to discreetly untangle her claw like fingers from his hair without scalping himself. He didn't want to push her away and embarrass her in front of the people that were in the club, but he also didn't want her overly glossed lips on his.

By the time he succeeded in extracting himself from her limpet like grasp he was just in time to see Sapphire stride up to the one male Donor in the club and take his hand, leading him to one of the private feeding rooms.

"So, drinks, girls?" Amethyst asked, breaking the silence that had descended over the table. Tanzi eagerly agreed but Sapphire was a little slower with her order.

Sapphire refused to look over at the bar and see the snog fest that was going on over there. She wanted to go home. But she had promised her sister that she would feed and that was exactly what she was going to do. She recalled Avery's growled words to her the night before, declaring that she wasn't allowed to feed from anyone but him. Her inner rebel that she hadn't even known existed, suddenly stood up and took notice, making its opinion to that order perfectly clear.

"Actually," Sapphire announced to Amethyst, making sure that her voice was loud enough to be heard. "I want a Donor, is one available?"

Amethyst couldn't have been more shocked if her sister had suddenly stripped down to her underwear and danced the can-can on the bar top. She silently nodded, not trusting herself to speak, instead simply pointing across the room to a nice looking, bespectacled man of around 20. He looked like he had just stepped off the cover of nerd monthly. For her first feeding that wasn't going to involve sex, she could do a lot worse. Her mind made up, Sapphire headed over to talk to him.

Avery tried to ignore the fact that Sapphire and the Donor had vanished almost ten minutes ago. It shouldn't take that long for a simple feeding. His imagination was running riot with all the possibilities of other things that could be taking up their time.

Liliya was preening like the cat that ate the canary, clearly feeling pleased with herself. He had told her that he wasn't allowed to fraternize with customers, as she technically was, especially while he was working. She had bought that excuse and was, for now, content to keep her hands to herself.

She was talking to him, keeping up an almost constant chatter that he had no hope of even registering the gist of. His head swam with visions of Sapphire and the Donor, imagining her reacting to the young human the way she had to him. He imagined her blood lust turning to physical lust as she fed, and it was all he could do to force himself to stay behind the bar.

"Avery, are you listening to me?" Liliya demanded of him, waving her hand in front of his face.

He cringed, having been caught out not paying the slightest bit of attention. "Yeah, sure. That sounds great, love," he fudged hoping that he had answered correctly.

He is so obviously enamoured with me, Liliya praised herself, *distracted by my beauty that he cannot pay attention*. Their kiss has obviously meant as much to him as it had to her, so eager was he to agree to come home with her after the bar closed.

"We shall wait until bar close and walk together, it will be romantic no?"

Her words finally registered in his jealousy muddled brain. "Sorry, what?" he asked, somewhat confused. What the fuck had he agreed to?

"We will walk together so I can see your house, yes?"

"No," he shook his head, finally understanding. "No, I'm sorry, that's not going to happen, I don't take anyone to my house."

A flash of anger crossed her perfect features, lasting but a second before she smiled again. "Then we shall go to mine, yes?"

Urghh, he wanted so much to thump his head against the wall, maybe he'd succeed in knocking himself out or doing some permanent damage. She just wasn't getting it. He couldn't deal with this right now, not when he was trying so hard not to launch himself across the room and drag Sapphire away from that human.

"No," he told her firmly. "I won't be going home with you either, we're over Liliya, we had fun a long time ago, but we won't be again." His ears pricked up as he heard a familiar giggle over the thumping music. He couldn't stand it any longer.

"I'm sorry, I just have to…" he didn't bother finishing his sentence. This had gone on far too long. He knew that he had promised himself that he'd give her space and let her make up her own mind, but he hadn't realised just how torturous it would be for him. He was done playing the gentleman.

179

He hopped his arse right over the bar top, ignoring Liliya's indignant squawks of horror that he had dared to turn her down. He cut his way quickly through their busy Thursday night crowd, all gearing up in preparation for a full on Friday and made his way to the curtained off V.I.P area. He didn't bother to pause and find out what was going on, just flung back the curtain.

Sapphire loved Jefferson. She had explained that she was nervous, that it was her first time feeding from someone that wasn't a Vampire. He had been so sweet, telling her that he was happy to just chat and get to know each other so that it would make her feel more comfortable. Something she had readily agreed on. It turned out he was doing the same accounting course that she had done at Oxford. She had mentioned the firm she worked for, one of the most prestigious in the city, and had promised that if what Avery said was true, when she returned to work, she would see what she could do about an internship for him.

They talked about the university, which tutors were still there and about campus parties and other wild things that still happened there. He had put her at ease so much that when he suggested trying to feed she was more than willing to try. She was hungry and even just sitting next to him, he smelt delicious, making her mouth water. She wasn't sure how to go about it, leaning in just felt so awkward and he was too big to cuddle up to her. With Avery it had seemed to happen naturally with none of this awkwardness.

She felt stupid, flapping about not knowing what to do. She felt that she should instinctively know how it worked, it shouldn't feel this awkward. A little voice at the back of her mind chirped up unhelpfully that it hadn't felt this way with Avery. She shot the voice down in flames, Avery didn't want her, and she had to move on.

"How do they usually do this?" she asked Jefferson, he seemed to understand that she was very new to this and didn't judge.

"Normally the females just sit on my lap, it's comfier and gives easy access," he said it without even a hint of a leeringly suggestive grin that Avery would have given her, Jeff was all business, weirdly enough she found that she missed it.

"Really?" she wasn't convinced but allowed herself to sit rather gingerly on his lap. "Like this?"

He nodded, canting his head to the side, displaying the length of his neck to its full advantage. She watched the vein pulse there for a second or two, working up the courage to bite. She slowly licked at his skin, letting instinct take over as she placed her hand on his shoulder and leant in, ready to feed on her first human. She felt Jefferson tense below her, knowing that it was more in anticipation then fear. She opened her mouth, letting her fangs run out, just as the curtain near them was yanked open.

Avery was profoundly grateful that they hadn't yet begun to feed, he wasn't sure he would have been able to control himself if they had. As it was, his anger flared up to see his woman perched on the lap of some other guy. It didn't even enter his mind just how she might have felt to see him being kissed by Liliya. All he knew was that it had to stop. Right now.

"What the hell do you think you are doing?" he demanded, grabbing her by the hand and yanking her off the offending male's lap. "I told you that if you needed to feed, you come to me."

Sapphire couldn't believe he had the audacity to shove his way in and start to order her around when his lips were still stained by that sirens lipstick. She was getting so tired of it, so tired of his attitude, acting like he owned her, like she was something special when he'd made it quite clear that she wasn't. He was pissing her off on so many levels she couldn't even begin to yell them all at him. She couldn't deal with it now. Her hunger had been awakened by the close proximity to Jeff's vein and yet again she had been denied by Avery. She needed to get out of there before she exploded. She took a deep breath, collecting herself before she spoke, pulling on all her years of holding back.

"You seemed a little busy to even be bothered by what I was doing. And I thank you to keep your nose out of my business, the same as I do yours," she kept her voice low and steady, firm, showing she meant what she said.

"You are my business," he argued. "And I don't want you with anyone else."

Her eyes narrowed as she looked at him. "And I don't care what you want." She turned her back on him. "I'm sorry, Jefferson, I seem to have lost my appetite, another time perhaps." Not waiting to hear his answer she marched through the curtain and past her sisters.

"Saph, wait, what's wrong?" Amy called out, abandoning her drink to chase after her.

"Nothing, I'm going home, that's all. You stay here with Tanzi," she left the club as quickly as she could, ignoring Nikos as he called out from his spot on the door.

"I'll get her some bottles to go, it appears she hasn't fed," Amethyst commented as the male Donor left the VIP area with a furious Avery on his heels. "You can take them home with you for her."

Tanzanite nodded her agreement. She was getting more and more worried about this situation with her sister and Avery, it seemed to be getting out of hand.

Avery was stalking Jefferson across the room like a pissed off tiger, ready to pounce on him and warn the little idiot never to go near Sapphire again, when Tanzi appeared in front of him, her hand on his chest stopping him in his tracks. He looked at her. She glared at him. If looks could kill he'd have dropped down dead...again.

"What the fuck is wrong with you?"

He attempted innocence. "Whatever do you mean, beautiful?" She wasn't fooled, he could tell.

"My sister, what did you do to her? What is this…" she waved her hand back and forth between Avery's chest and Jefferson's hastily retreating back.

"Nothing, she just shouldn't be feeding from him, that's all." He shrugged as if it was the most normal thing to say, ever.

Tanzi snorted, the most unlady like noise. "Pffft, what bullshit is this, Vampire?" she poked at his chest, and suddenly he realised where Sapphire got it from. "The only reason you wouldn't want her to drink from someone else is if she was your Soul Mate and that-" she interrupted herself mid rant, catching sight of his face. "Dear gods, is that it? I'm right aren't I?"

Avery was caught, he had two choices, and as far as he could see, neither of them were good. He could run away, he was Vampire fast, she would never catch him, or he could tell her the truth and enlist her help. He went with door number two.

He grabbed her by the arm and dragged her over to the VIP area, not wanting anyone else to hear or see them talk.

"Yes, OK, yes. She's my Soul Mate. And she's being a pain in the arse about it."

Tanzi barked out a laugh. "Well, of course she is, she's a Summerland, we're pain in the arses about everything. It's in the job description."

Avery groaned, closing his eyes as his head dropped forward in defeat.

"You have to help me. I can't win with her, she's hot one minute and cold the next. Just when I think I've gotten somewhere with her she suddenly turns into this screaming banshee and rips me a new arsehole before leaving me a whimpering wreck on the floor as she struts that sexy arse of hers out the door."

Tanzi sat down, patting the seat beside her. Now that she knew the reason Avery was acting like a world class dick, she felt sorry for him. Her sister was hard work when she got something into her head, and it looked like she was determined she wouldn't like Avery back. Something needed to be done.

"OK, normally I wouldn't tattle on my own flesh and blood like this, but I actually think you'll be good for her. She needs to loosen up a bit, have a bit of fun and stop taking life so seriously. She's always been that way, a very serious thing, even as a child. She was the youngest but acted more mature than me and Ames put together. She doesn't find it easy to give up control and just let things happen. She needs to feel secure."

Avery nodded along, listening carefully like Tanzi was presenting him with the secrets of the universe.

"So, how do I win her round? How do I make her realise that I'm the best thing ever and she wants me?" he sighed, raking his fingers through his hair. "It wasn't supposed to be this hard. She was supposed to feel it when I did, she was supposed to know that I was her Soul Mate, want me as much as I want her and we were supposed to have lots more hot sex."

"Ewww."

Avery couldn't help but smirk. "Sorry."

"No, you aren't. Dude, that's my sister you are talking about porking, that's just not right."

He cracked up laughing, he couldn't help it. Her language and terminology were almost as bad as his. He had been accused of picking up the worst of modern slang and mixing it with his old style English, but she took things to the next level. Once he regained the ability to speak he asked again.

"Come on, Tanz, help a guy out. What can I do to get her to trust me? Every time I think I've managed she throws a curve ball at me."

"She doesn't trust easily. You just have to let her rant it out, because she's trying to push you away. She's trying to prove to herself in this warped way that she has, that you would have always left her, she just made you do it before she got truly hurt. If she lets people in, they will hurt her. Or at least that's what she thinks, and to be fair, she hasn't

184

been wrong. She's had shit and so has Amy. I think I'm the only one that hasn't had some great heartbreak."

Avery nodded, taking mental notes. "But I've tried to gain her trust."

"Yeah, and from what I've seen, you've left when she's pushed you and taken up residence with the first Russian slut you could find." Tanzi raised an eyebrow, daring him to argue.

Avery couldn't look her in the eye, she was right, and he felt terrible about it. He had just been playing, flirting a little to make Sapphire jealous. He hadn't meant to hurt her.

"I didn't mean anything by it. I just thought that maybe if she could see me with someone else she would realise how much she wanted me and would stop resisting. I just wanted her to admit to her own feelings."

Tanzi rolled her eyes, patting him sympathetically on the arm. "You poor, dumb, little man."

"Hey!" he protested but she carried on regardless.

"You can't play that sort of game once you leave school. It's just not the adult way. She won't understand that's what you were doing, she would have simply thought you didn't want her. And, dude, you do have a bit of a reputation, she probably thought you saw her as nothing but a quick screw.'

"I'd never see her as that, she's my Soul Mate!" He looked truly horrified at the idea.

"I know," she soothed. "But she doesn't. If she pushes you away, back off, give her a little space, just to calm down, then get back in there. Show her that nothing she does will keep you away, you have to keep showing her that you want her, keep showing her that she is special to you. She'll resist, but she's worth it. You have to show her that you're in it for the long haul. No more women. Chat to them yes, flirt, sure, but no more touching. Show her that she is all you want."

"So, basically ignore all her pissing and shouting and keep showering her with attention?"

Tanzi nodded.

185

"That will work? I'm not used to chasing after women, they are always the ones that chase me."

Tanzi made a face that looked like she had just smelt a particularly ripe fart. "Yeah, maybe don't say that to her. And don't tell her about the Soul Mate thing yet, that might scare her off. Just date her like a normal person, I mean, Vampire. Just keep at it, she'll come around. Now, I'm going to go home, take her some blood and help her calm down. Leave her alone for tonight. Give it a fresh try tomorrow evening."

Avery thanked her for her help, feeling more positive than he had in days. He should have talked to her sister in the first place. Then he might have gotten more of an idea what was going on inside his woman's head.

Tanzi never thought she would see her little sister in a sulk, but that was what greeted her when she returned home from talking to Avery. Sapphire was curled up on the couch, in her pyjamas, huddled under a blanket, with a half drunk bottle of wine beside her, and she was staring mournfully into a bag of M&M's that she could no longer eat.

"Even chocolate isn't the answer anymore," she wailed pitifully as she spotted Tanzi in the doorway. "I have drunk so much wine and I still feel thirsty, nothing seems to help!"

Tanzi didn't say a word, just took away the offending chocolate and produced two ready mixed bottles of bloody margarita.

"Try this," she offered, popping the cap and wafting the bottle under her sister's nose.

Sapphire grabbed at it and immediately took a bit mouthful, sighing with relief as she swallowed. "I don't know why I can't seem to drink it without it being mixed with something, but I can't seem to get my head around the idea of drinking blood. I wish I could, the effects are worth it."

Tanzi waited until Sapphire had drained the first bottle and started on the second before she breached the subject at hand.

"So, what's up with you and Avery?" she asked, as casually as possible as she munched the confiscated chocolates.

Sapphire almost choked on her drink, wiping her mouth with the back of her hand, looking at her sister through suspiciously narrowed eyes.

"Nothing is up with us. He just seems to think that because he helped me with my turning he has the right to tell me what to do and with whom, which he does not. Nothing more."

Tanzi knew better.

"Don't bullshit me girl, I know you better than that."

Sapphire knew that she was never going to get away with lying to her sister, Tanzi and Amy always knew when the others weren't being completely honest, it was a sister thing. Sapphire's best hope was to down play it.

"OK, so we might have had sex and kissed a bit, but only once. I had fed and it has a certain effect on me," she paused and rolled her eyes when Tanzi scooted over on the couch. "Very funny. Anyway, he was there to take the edge off as they say. It didn t mean anything to him, I was just another in a long string of women to him, nothing more. So, there is nothing really to tell. I made a mistake, it's done with now and I'm trying to move on." She sipped her drink and fiddled with the TV remote, flicking through the channels but not really seeing what was on.

"But what if it did mean something more to him?" Tanzi asked gently.

Sapphire closed her eyes briefly, as if praying for strength. "It didn't. He does that sort of thing all the time. Now that's the last I want to hear of the matter, either watch this film with me or I'll go to bed, it's been a long night and I just want to relax and forget about that man. Is that OK with you?"

Sapphire knew she was being bitchy in tone and word, she didn't mean to be, it just seemed to come out when she was faced with thinking about what had happened between her and the Vampire world's answer to Casanova.

Tanzi knew when she had been beaten, holding her hands up in mock surrender, she gestured to the TV as they both quietened down to watch, but her mind was anything but quiet, skidding over the almost unbelievable fact that her baby sister had sex with someone that didn't carry a briefcase, a lunch packed by his mother and sport a pocket protector. Things really were changing.

With a scream that rattled the windows, Liliya picked up the handheld antique mirror from her dressing table and launched it across the room, taking great pleasure in watching it smash against the wall, its glass raining down into hundreds of tiny pieces. The matching brush and comb went next, snapped between her fingers as if the solid silver handles were nothing but a tooth pick. Gifts from Avery that she couldn't stand to look at right then.

She looked over at the broken items, finding their destruction to have done little to calm the anger inside her.

She was screaming again, the desperate, rage filled sound almost made Grigory's ears bleed. He hated to see his beloved mistress like this, hated to see her so sad over someone that he felt didn't deserve her. She was beautiful and wished so desperately to be loved. He just wished that she would look at him in that way. Unable to do anything to soothe her, he simply stood and watched.

Still screaming she swiped her arm along the dressing table top, bottles of perfume smashed, along with various other potions and powders, cosmetics of every kind, all crashing to the floor to mix together in a messy puddle. She panted heavily, the blood she had recently drank giving her body the energy it needed to power every bodily function mortals had. It forced her heart to beat to circulate the blood around her body, forced her lungs to work, dragging in air to oxygenate the blood that was already getting to work on

188

fixing the damage her cells had sustained during the night. A Vampire's body couldn't regenerate more than it had at the time of death, although they could regrow limbs, fix broken body parts that they lost after, but it took a lot of blood to give them the energy to do it.

Grigory watched as she stomped her way through the mess to the bookshelf, grabbing a book at random she began to rip out page after page in big handfuls, determined to do as much destructive damage as possible. The pages fluttered around her like confetti as she worked her way through all the books, her movements slowly going from frantic madness to weary resignation. When she finally stopped she looked around with wide eyes at the mess she had made, the sticky footsteps she had tracked through the mess from her dresser. She looked down at the broken mirror, bending to pick it up, big, fat tears landing on its shattered face.

Her feet were cut and bleeding from the perfume bottles she had laid waste to. Without asking permission, he picked his way through the minefield and scooped her up in his arms, cradling her gently as one would a baby, holding her as she collapsed into floods of tears, sobbing into his chest.

He vowed right there and then that he would do anything to make his mistress happy, anything.

Chapter Nineteen

Nikos had been surprised to see Sapphire go storming out of the club so soon after arriving, but being unable to leave his post at the door he had sent a quick text to Tanzi to check on the situation and they had arranged to meet up for breakfast once Sapphire had settled for the day. So, the last thing he had thought he would be greeted with when he arrived was a locked front door. Normally Tanzi left it open for him.

He knocked on the door, feeling slightly out of place standing forgotten on the doorstep so early on a Friday morning like an abandoned bottle of milk. Maybe he was too early and Tanzi wasn't yet awake. She wasn't the most bright eyed and bushy tailed person he had ever met. He himself hadn't even been to bed yet, he had stopped off on the way to grab himself a snack after work, nothing fancy, just a large pizza, a helping of wings and two orders of wedges. He had settled himself on a bench in the park to enjoy and watch the sunrise. But now he was feeling peckish again and wanted his promised breakfast.

He banged on the door with his closed fist, making a pathetic whimpering sound that he hoped would tug on her heartstrings. No dice. He bent down and stuck his fingers through the letter box, lifting the flap to peer inside the house. Instantly his nose began to twitch, as he squinted through the small gap, spotting smoke coming from the kitchen. Poor Tanzi must be trying to cook again, no doubt she had her headphones on and couldn't hear him.

He was about to pull out his phone and call her, when the smoke increased, spilling out in a noxious cloud accompanied by flames that leaped out of the kitchen and into the hall. This was no cooking accident.

Jumping to his feet he set his shoulder to the door, using his Shifter strength, it took but one small bash for the door to fly open. The air from outside rushed in, fanning the flames, feeding them. He ignored them, his first instinct to protect, instead he rushed up the stairs, needing to find the girls.

The smoke stung his sensitive nose, dulling his senses as he tried to block out the rancid smell and focus on what he was doing.

He went to Tanzi first, the smoke beginning to fill the lower level and creep its way up the stairs. He found her fast asleep in her bed, the covers having been kicked off her during the night, she lay there in all her naked glory. He groaned loudly, dropping his chin to his chest briefly. "Denied, so denied!" he whined under his breath as he grabbed underwear, leggings and a t-shirt from her wash basket, she never bothered to put her clothes away, stating that her favourite stuff was always in rotation so it took less time to just wash, dry and wear.

He shook at her shoulder, as gently as possible but firmly.

"Tanzi, come on, baby, wake up. You have to wake up."

191

The smoke was curling in under the door now and he knew they didn't have long.

Tanzi took her time waking up but when she did she didn't expect to find Nikos tugging at her leg in an attempt to dress her. She snatched her foot back indignantly.

"Why are you trying to put clothes on me? That's not how we usually work."

He sighed with relief that she was awake, tossing the pile of clothes onto her chest, hitting her in the face with her own knickers.

"Do you mind?" she groused, never liking to be woken after so few hours sleep, her sister had wanted to stay up all night talking, damned Vampire.

"Just get dressed and don't argue woman, the kitchen is on fire and I'm pretty sure it's spreading fast. We have to get Sapphire out."

Tanzi blinked, taking a second to let his words register in her sleep fuddled brain before she glanced to the door, spotting the intruding smoke winding its way under and into the room. That gave her the kick up the arse she needed. Yelping, she leapt out of bed, pulling on clothes as quickly as she could.

"We need blankets," Nikos instructed, "And lots of them." He snatched up the duvet from her bed and flung open the door. Smoke billowed in after him, making them both cough. Tanzi felt the searing heat on the floorboards as she followed after him, but she pushed it out of her mind as best she could, directing him to Sapphire's room down the hall.

Her sister was curled up in bed, fully into her death sleep. Nikos wasted no time in getting to work, something Tanzi was pathetically grateful for, she wouldn't have had a clue what to do and would probably have just laid there, in her bed, petrified. He raced to Sapphire's closet and pulled out two of the scarves she always wore for work. He wrapped one around his own face and quickly gestured for Tanzi to do the same as he moved Sapphire into the centre of the bed. He then proceeded to wrap her up firmly in

Tanzi's duvet, then her own, making her into a sleeping Vampire burrito. He added another blanket for good measure, checking that none of her skin was exposed.

Lifting the precious bundle into his arms, he carried her like a baby out to the hall.

"Go first," he gestured to Tanzi. "And hurry, hold on to the banister, the smoke is thick down there. Just close your eyes and run, OK? Don't look back for me, I'll be there, just get out. I left the front door open, hopefully the neighbours have noticed and called the fire service."

Tanzi had barely had time to think in the time since he had woken her up, her only thought was that of her sister. But now she was looking down into what looked like the bowels of hell itself, she was suddenly too scared to move. The flames were heating the air, making it stifling hot, painting the cream walls a dancing orange red.

She shook her head, backing up away from the top of the stairs, plastering herself against the wall, her chest heaving as she tried to draw breath, though all that managed to do was suck the smoke into her lungs quicker, causing her to double over in a fit of hacking coughs. "I… I can't do it," she gasped as she tried to stop coughing, her hands on her knees where she was doubled over. "I can't, Nik."

He wished desperately that he could pick her up and make it all better for her, that he could offer her some kind of comfort, but he had his arms full with her sister.

"Baby, listen to me," he tried to soothe her, trying not to emphasis the urgency of the situation in his tone. He could feel the floor getting hotter under his feet, the heat sinking through even the thick soles of his trainers. He ducked down as best he could with his unyielding bundle, trying to catch her eyes behind the heavy fall of her hair.

"You have to listen to me, Tanz, focus on me, listen to my voice. Be brave for me, baby, I know you can do it. It's just a few steps. Trust me, I won't let anything happen to you." She was still shaking her head, her eyes wide as saucers as they flickered over his face. "You have to do this,

193

I will be right behind you with Saph." He noticed that at the mention of her Sapphire, her eyes left his face and darted to the blanket bundle in his arms, her beloved sister. He knew then that he had her.

"Come on, Tanz, she needs you, darling. Trust me, just close your eyes and run down the stairs, don't look back. OK, baby? I'll be right behind you I promise. I won't leave you. Just go!" On impulse he ducked his head and gave her a quick kiss. "GO!"

She went. She trusted him more than anyone else that wasn't family. All their nights spent together watching movies, spending time together, she had grown so fond of the dishy wolf that had been her constant support throughout the ordeal with her sisters. She trusted him. She knew that if he promised to be behind her and look after her sister, he would.

She did as he bid, closing her eyes tight, her heart pounding in her chest, seemingly bouncing off her rib cage, it beat so hard. She could barely catch her breath but what she managed to suck in she held in her lungs and ran. Her hand clutched the banister in a death grip as she used it to guide herself down the stairs. The wood beneath her feet seemed to dip and sag, feeling uneven, like the heat had warped it and for all she knew it had. She stumbled once, twice, three times before she hit the hall floor running.

She heard Nikos's steps pounding behind her, following just as he had promised. Lungs burning with a mixture of lack of air and smoke she darted through the flames that by now had almost consumed the hallway. She aimed for the front door, stumbling gratefully into the fresh air, collapsing against the railings, sucking in great lungfulls of air.

She heard the sound of buckling wood, the ceasing of his footsteps and then his sharp yelp of shock that made her heart stutter to a stop for a second.

"Nikos!" she yelled. Where was he? Why wasn't he out there with her?

"Nikos!" she screamed again, her throat hoarse from the smoke, making her double over coughing again as her lungs burnt. Time seemed to stand still, leaving her frozen on the spot, wanting to run back in and help him but knowing he wouldn't want that.

"We're OK," he finally yelled back after what seemed like forever. She heard him cursing loudly and the sounds of a struggle. She tried to peer through the thick smoke and flames but saw nothing but black. She heard more wood splintering and then his footsteps started again, sure and strong. The sweetest sound she had ever heard.

Nikos burst out two seconds later, his big chest heaving with the strain of holding his breath and running.

"What happened?" she gasped, so pleased to see him out there in the sunlight with her.

"Stairs collapsed out from under me." He wanted badly to do as she was, double over in the hope of relieving the tightness in his chest, to drag some blessed air into his lungs, but he couldn't stop to recover himself. Not yet. "My keys, in my pocket, get them," he wheezed, his voice sounding harsh, strained even to his own ears.

Dragging herself upright, still hacking every time she tried to take a deep breath, Tanzi stirred herself, digging her hand into his back pocket to locate the keys to his car. Once she had them she looked at him questioningly.

"Open the boot, we have to get her out of the sunlight." Tanzi sprang into action, amazed and humbled that he had dealt with all that, saved her life, encouraged her to get out, stayed calm and still his first thought was that of her sister and keeping her safe. Tanzi was ashamed to admit she hadn't even thought of that herself. She wasn't used to dealing with Vampires no matter how open she was and how much she knew about them.

They heard the wail of sirens in the distance as she popped open the trunk of the car and helped him arrange her sister in there as gently as possible, even though she

195

was in her death sleep and wouldn't feel a thing. After making sure the blankets still covered her, they shut the lid down tight, just in time before the fire truck turned into the road, followed by an ambulance.

They stepped away from the car, not wanting to draw attention to it and the precious cargo in the trunk and turned back to the now rapidly burning house. The flames had spread to the upstairs, and even as they watched the curtains in the front bedroom, Amy's room, caught on fire.

Tanzi heard the crackling roar of the fire as it devoured anything in its path like a rampaging monster. The heat was intense, pouring out of the house, toasting her skin, leaving it feeling red and itchy. She wanted to rub at it but forced herself not to.

Nikos backed her up out of the way as the fire truck pulled in near his car. He kept his arms around her, rubbing his hands along her arms. Even though the fire was enough to heat the air around them she was still covered in goose bumps, shivering in shock as they watched the firemen leap out and immediately set to work, unrolling hoses and tugging on breathing apparatus.

"Anyone left in there?" the question was shouted at them but Tanzi barely heard it, let alone registered the meaning of the words. Nikos answered for them.

"No, we were the only ones home. My girl here was asleep in bed, I just got off a night shift and came by for breakfast. The door was locked, I knocked then looked inside, that was when I saw the smoke coming from the kitchen. I busted in the door and ran up to wake her before it got too bad. Both the other girls that live here are with their boyfriends." He stuck to the facts as best he could, he didn't know who might have seen him arrive and the last thing he wanted was awkward questions and attention.

The officer nodded and began to shout instructions to his team, leaving them to the mercy of the ambulance crew. Nikos insisted that he was fine but submitted to a quick check up they insisted on before he could get free. Tanzi

196

wasn't as resilient as he so it was a relief when she was deemed to be suffering a little from smoke inhalation but was otherwise, none the worse for wear.

It took almost an hour to subdue and eventually extinguish the fire, in which time it had gutted the house. That which it hadn't consumed was damaged beyond repair by the smoke and water. The walls dripped with dirty, sooty water, the carpets sodden from what they could see from the front steps, they had been banned from going in any further. The front door was boarded up along with the windows and eventually they were allowed to leave.

Nikos had been growing more and more concerned, Tanzi was freezing in her thin clothes, even huddled in the blanket the kind paramedics had given her. In the end he had made her get into the back of his car, crawling in with her to hold her as they watched.

She was too quiet for his liking, the shock of it having hit around midday, her body sagging into his as the tears came. He held her while she sobbed, wondering just what had happened, what would have happened if he had been any later or for that matter, earlier and they had already left the house, leaving Sapphire alone.

As soon as the fire service cleared them to go, promising they would do a full investigation into the cause, he had sat Tanzi in the passenger seat and gotten her straight to the nearest drive through. He ordered her a big veggie burger, fries and a large chocolate milkshake, knowing that she had to eat.

At first she only took tiny nibbles, but pretty soon, to his relief, her hunger took over and she devoured the burger, reaching over to steal one of his mozzarella sticks from the box he had perched on the dash, though he had already chomped his way through two large burgers, fries and a coke. Satisfied that she would be OK he dealt with his next priority, Sapphire.

Chapter Twenty

Avery had been feeling bad all night, feeling like a complete dick with how he had used Liliya to make Sapphire jealous. He hadn't meant for things to go as far as they had, and after his talk with Tanzi he realised that he really had gone about things the wrong way. Sapphire wasn't like him, she wasn't a man that would take on anyone that dared to go near his woman. She wasn't one to take what she wanted and damn the consequences and from what Tanzi had said, she had little experience with men that hadn't been a nice work place dalliance with someone that fit the perfect man ideal she had held onto for so long.

He knew he had pushed her too much, knew that he should have had more patience with her. He was just not used to thinking about a woman in that way and not used to them turning him down. He knew that he needed to prove to her that he was trustworthy. He had waited long enough. As soon as he woke he hurriedly got dressed. He wouldn't waste another second letting her know how he felt.

Avery gaped at the blackened shell that was Sapphire's house. He had known true terror only once before in his life and this beat that. He didn't care that the door was nailed shut, he kicked it open with one swift, well placed kick. Running up the stairs he searched the bedrooms, the acrid stench of smoke seeming to coat the inside of his nostrils right down into his lungs. His eyes actually watered as the smell assaulted him.

The downstairs was a burnt out shell, totally gutted. The upstairs wasn't much better. The front bedroom had taken the brunt of the flames before they had been put out.

He was almost too afraid to look in the other bedrooms having found nothing in the first one. The blankets were missing from the second bedroom, and finally in the third, it was much the same. The walls were blackened with smoke, everything soaked as if the fire fighters had doused the entire house.

He found the rest of the house equally as empty. He didn't know whether he should be relieved that he hadn't found her, or scared as to why. Had she been in the house when it had burned? The walls were cold now, the whole house boarded up, chilled to its bones. It had obviously happened earlier in the day, during the daylight hours.

Had the fire fighters found her and assumed her dead, which she technically was in her death sleep? Had she burnt in the fire, burnt in the sunlight, had she been taken to the morgue? Endless possibilities and questions swirled in his brain as he pulled out his phone, dialing Tanzi.

On the first ring he heard a phone ringing in the second bedroom he had looked in. He shut off the call in frustration. The fact that her phone was here meant that she had obviously been home when the fire had raged. Was she OK? Had she been hurt? In desperation he called Cassiar, knowing that whatever was going on, he would know about it.

Cass picked up on the third ring, sounding calm and not in any way distraught, Avery took that as a good thing.

199

"What the hell happened?" he demanded to know.

Sapphire was getting rather fed up with waking to find herself somewhere she hadn't expected to be. She blinked as she sat up and looked around, it took her a few moments to work out that she was in the room she had previously occupied when she stayed with Amy and Cass. But she had no clue how she came to be there.

She stretched, feeling the muscles in her back pop and unkink as she moved. She held the stretch for a moment or two before flopping back down onto the mattress.

As she could hear people talking in the living room, she couldn't very well stay in bed all evening, plus she was hungry. Her throat felt dry and weirdly, tasted vaguely of charcoal, like when you stood too near to a BBQ, or took a bite of a burnt sausage.

She was still dressed as she had been when she went to sleep that night but when she moved she caught the unmistakable wiff of smoke clinging to her clothes, her hair and her skin. She didn't know what the hell was going on but she didn't like it and she wanted answers.

She swung her legs out of bed, not caring that she was in her night clothes, they had obviously seen them before if they took her out of her own bed and into this one, though even the thought of it seemed too weird to think about.

She burst into the living room, demanding to know just what they thought they were playing at. Her sisters were there, with Cassian and Nikos. Cass was in his favourite armchair, Amy perched happily on his lap. Nikos and Tanzanite were on the couch. They looked close, even though they weren't cozied up like Amy was to Cass, yet, she could almost see a bond between them. And they looked like shit. Their clothes were blackened with smoke and soot and Tanzi looked like she was about to fall asleep at any minute, dark circles under her eyes that were a stark

200

contrast to her too pale skin. She looked like she had been to hell and back.

"You two OK?" Saph asked, now more concerned about her sister than herself and her apparently magical bed hopping abilities.

Tanzi nodded silently, not trusting herself to speak. Now Sapphire was awake, oblivious to everything that had happened, they had to tell her, and that made it all the more real. The fact that, if not for Nikos's impeccable timing, they might have both died in their beds, was not lost on her. The thought made her feel cold, chilled to her bones. She hadn't been able to warm up all day, but now fresh shivers wracked her body as Nikos wrapped his arms around her, pulling her close as he explained what had happened.

Sapphire was in shock, that's all it could be. She could hear everything that Nikos and Cassian were saying but it was like she was listening to them from the end of a very long tunnel, their words drifting in and out of focus as she struggled to make sense of what they were saying.

All their things, gone, their home, destroyed. She couldn't take it in. Everything in her life had changed dramatically in the past week and the one thing she had been clinging to, the one thing that had been stable and familiar, was their home, filled with her orderly, comforting things. She felt in control there, like she knew where she stood, she was on an even keel there, not in the world she knew nothing about and that was so very very strange. There she was just Sapphire again, not the new turnee that had been attacked and killed by her sister's mad ex-boyfriend.

She didn't know what she was going to do now, she had no clothes, no home, nothing that was hers. She felt lost, bereft and she didn't know how she was going to cope. She tried to think about something else, but then all that popped in as they kept talking was the fact that she could have died, again, permanently this time. She could have burnt in her bed and there was nothing she could have done to save herself. Even the fire service could have killed her by bringing her outside. She could have been shipped to the morgue and autopsied.

She sat down in a chair with a thunk, not sure what to think or feel. It all felt abstract, like it was happening to someone else, not them. But then, the whole week or so since she had woken as a Vampire had seemed so out there crazy she still wasn't entirely convinced that it wasn't a bad dream and she would wake up soon in her own bed, her heart beating and daylight streaming in through the window.

There was no logic to this new world she had found herself in, no rhyme or reason for the things that happened. She found herself floundering in a sea of uncertainty, able to see land but not get to it, reaching out, touching with the very tips of her fingers, desperate to catch and cling to something solid when seemingly the last remains of her old life had literally gone up in smoke.

And then he came, like an angel from the darkness, he burst through the front door without even bothering to knock. Strong arms wrapped around her, dragging her out of her chair and up against a hard chest, holding her close. His hand supported the back of her head, his fingers tangled in her hair as he held her as if afraid she would vanish if he let up for even one second.

They stood there, the world around them seeming to melt away and for the first time since she woke up she felt like she could breathe, the hard lump in her throat eased and she no longer felt like she was falling apart. There was just something about him that made everything seem like it would be OK, like he could achieve anything he set his mind to. He might drive her nuts but in that moment, that one perfect moment she truly felt like everything would be alright, that she would be alright, she could make it through. She wasn't alone.

"I thought I'd lost you," he whispered against her hair, so low she barely heard him, but his words warmed her down to her toes, his tone belaying the very genuine fear he had obviously felt. He might have been a dick the night before, but none of that seemed to matter now, she couldn't seem to drag up the energy to be angry anymore. Staring death in the face, again, gave her a new perspective. She was alive in as many ways as it counted, and she had been given a second chance at life. A chance to do all the things she had been afraid of doing before. Taking life by the balls and giving it a vigorous shake up that it so desperately needed. She had been hiding away for too long, hiding away in her house with her sisters, convincing herself that she needed to be the one constantly in control, to never do anything spontaneous. Sure, her past had affected her, but she couldn't let it screw up her future too, and that was what she had been doing. She had been living in the past, too scared to take a leap of faith. She had to learn to trust again, had to believe that people could be good and genuine, and in her heart of hearts she knew Avery was one of them. She had messed him around as much as he had her. Well, no more.

Before she could think herself out of her new, determined course of action, she pulled her head back and kissed him. A full out, no holding back kiss that had everyone in the room gasping with shock, having never seen her act that way. Everyone but Avery. He moaned in response, his tongue nudging at her lips, immediately demanding entry. She parted them for him and he took full advantage, his tongue sweeping in like it owned the place, getting bossy with her own. It was a hot, desperate, life affirming kiss that ignited a flame of lust in the pit of her stomach that swept outwards at the speed of light to engulf her body.

Sapphire was pretty sure they would have started stripping each other there and then, Avery's hand had snuck its way up under the hem of her nightshirt to stroke the underside of her breast, the best he could manage with her chest squashed so close against his. They heard the very distinct sound of someone insistently clearing their throat, and pulled reluctantly apart.

"Wanna get a room guys?" Nikos asked, staring pointedly at Avery's crotch, the very distinct bulge showing just how into this he really was.

Sapphire immediately pulled back, embarrassment crashing in to wipe out the feelings of arousal as affectively as a bucket of cold water. What was she doing? This wasn't her, making out like horny teenagers in someone else's living room. The absurdity of it. She tried to pull back and regain her composure but he held firm to her hand. He sat down in the chair she had previously occupied and then firmly pulled her down into his lap. He refused to let her distance herself from him again, to pull back physically or emotionally. He was beginning to recognise the signs with her and was ready to fight for what he wanted. And what he wanted was her.

Sapphire was shocked to find herself suddenly perched on his lap, his still impressively hard erection digging into her arse every time she moved even so much as a muscle. She kept deadly still, not wanting to encourage him. Not that he seemed to need any help, Avery never seemed to get embarrassed by being caught in public necking with a female. The thought made her stiffen against him as her brain threw up images of him getting lippy with Liliya. Yeah, she was still pissed about that. Avery, Nikos and Cassian were busily discussing the fire but she tuned it out, not wanting to hear all the terrible details.

Amethyst was quietly crying as Cassian held her, stroking her back in a comforting fashion, while Tanzanite sat silent. That was probably the scariest part of it all, that something had actually affected her sister that much that it had silenced her. Usually Tanzi was the loud one, the one with an opinion on everything, the one that made everything better with her easy going humour and her big heart. Now she looked like a shell of herself, curled up against the big chest of the Shifter, her body seeming so small compared to normal, or maybe that was just because she was so quiet.

Normally she dominated a room, now she was huddled up, her knees drawn up to her chest, her beautiful hair laying lank and dirty around her shoulders. Yet still Nikos held her, his fingers playing absently with a strand of her hair like it was the most natural thing in the world.

Again, Sapphire wondered just when they had gotten that close and why she hadn't noticed. She was usually the observant one, the one that noticed every little detail of everything. Suddenly she felt bad, really bad. She had been so selfish. Concerned more about how her life had changed and what she had lost, than what the people around her were dealing with too. Her sisters had had to deal with the fact that they had almost lost her, seen her dead body before she had awoken. They had had to make sense of everything that had happened just as much as she had. And while Amethyst had Cassian to explain it all to her, Tanzi hadn't had that luxury. Amy had been there when she had just woken, Avery had looked after her and nursed her through the turn, they had known what was going on with her. Tanzi hadn't, she had been stuck at home, just waiting for news. But at least it seemed that she had had Nikos to help.

I have to start thinking of others, she told herself firmly. *I need to make up my mind what I want and stick to it.* She knew it wouldn't be easy, but she had no choice. This was her life now and she had to make the best of it. She wasn't a quitter.

Avery wished he knew what was going on in his woman's head. He would give all of his considerable fortune to be able to peek inside and know what she was thinking, feeling and how she was about to react. Her moods were so mercurial, changing like the weather, that he could barely keep up. Once again, he wished desperately that they shared the mating bond that Cassian and Amy had, Cass never had to guess, he would feel any strong emotions from his love.

The conversation rolled on around her while she sat on Avery's lap, a million thoughts and feelings rushing around her head, too distracted to really listen to what the others were saying. But even she was dragged back to the present by the unusually soft voice of Tanzi.

"What are we going to do? We have no home, no clothes, nothing."

Nikos immediately piped up, reassuring her. "You can stay with me," at the same time Amy stated, "You'll stay here with us obviously." Tanzi opened her mouth to answer but Avery butted in with his own opinion. "Saph is staying with me, I won't take no for an answer."

That pissed her off and she jumped up off his lap, wrenching her hand from his when he reached for her. "No. Enough of people making decisions for me!"

Avery wanted to argue, but he saw the way Tanzi seemed to slump back into her shell and the tender way Nikos held her. It wasn't the time for arguments. He wanted to get manly with her, do it the old fashioned way and simply pick her up, toss her over his shoulder and take her where he wanted her, but these modern women didn't seem to appreciate that line of domination. He took a deep breath before he nodded, swallowing his pride.

"You're right, we haven't asked you. So, I'm doing it now. I'd very much like you to stay with me." He looked at her with puppy dog eyes. "Please."

It was the please that did it, that had her nodding her agreement when she really felt she should say no. But try as she might she couldn't bring herself to refuse. Though she had to know one thing before she did.

"What about Liliya?" she asked in a small voice, suddenly nervous and unsure if she actually wanted to know the answer.

"What about her?" he looked genuinely confused.

"Will she be there too?"

Avery stepped back, shaking his head like she was the single most frustrating thing on the face of the earth, which to be fair, she probably was.

"Woman, you'll be the death of me. Liliya means nothing to me. And I'm sorry if I made you think that she did." He took her hands in his, squeezing them tight, uncaring to the fact that they were surrounded by people that would probably tease him mercilessly for being so soppy.

"I want you. No one else. And if you would stop pulling away from me and letting the past colour your judgment of me now, I'd prove it."

She opened her mouth, obviously about to protest but he stopped her with a gentle finger pressed to her lips.

"I know, baby, I know I didn't help by acting the way I did, but that's only because you were so cold to me all of a sudden. I'm sorry that I went about things the wrong way, sorry that I tried to make you jealous and to fight for me rather than simple fighting for you, proving to you that I was serious. And I am. I promise you with all that I am, that you are all I want."

She hadn't expected him to be that upfront, that honest and it had shocked her. She was used to him being the teasing, joking bartender that floated his way through life with not a care in the world. But for him to lay it on the line like that, to open up his heart, for that's what he had done, there was no question of her not believing him.

"I'm sorry too," she whispered as she looked up at him. "I'm sorry that I treated you that way, that I expected you to be the same as the others. I should have known you wouldn't be and have trusted you."

Avery laughed, so happy to hear her words. "I didn't really give you a reason to. But I promise you, here and now, that that will never happen again. I can't promise I won't flirt with anyone, that's just me, I doubt I could ever talk to a female without checking out her chest, but that's all it is, flirting. No one could compare to you, I'll never want anyone but you ever again. You're mine, baby and I'm never letting you go."

Sapphire wanted to cry, but with happiness this time. He was saying the words that she had wanted and needed to hear for what felt like forever.

"Just kiss her already and take her home, someone has to open the damned club and I'm guessing it's us tonight," Cassian piped up, interrupting the moment. But Avery didn't mind, he'd effectively just been given the night off to woo his woman and he wasn't about to turn that down.

"I hear ya, boss man." He snapped to attention and grabbed Saph around the waist, sweeping her back in true swashbuckling hero style, planting a big kiss on her lips before straightening and releasing her. "We're out of here."

Chapter Twenty-One

Avery barely gave them time to get through the front door before he had scooped her up in his arms and high tailed it to his bedroom. He didn't want to give her a chance to begin over thinking things, to start convincing herself that his intentions weren't true or honourable, to think that he didn't really want her.

He was determined to show her, there and then, just how much she affected him, just how much he wanted her, determined to wipe out any negative thoughts that might stubbornly linger in her head with regards to his feelings and their future. He didn't want to scare her off by telling her straight away that they were Soul Mates, that might be too much, too soon for her. She was sometimes like a scared kitten, you had to do the softly softly approach and let her get used to one thing before you piled on another. So now the plan was simply to fuck her brains out until she had no energy left to think. *Good plan, my man*, he congratulated himself with a mental pat on the back as he tossed her down on the bed.

Sapphire bounced in place on the mattress, unable to hold in the giggle of delight that bubbled up. For the first time in forever she felt light and carefree. She allowed herself to remember the way he had made love to her against the hall wall, because she now fully believed him when he said that was what it had been, not just sex, but making love, and her body heated in anticipation, feeling dampness flood between her legs. How did he do that? How did just the thought of him make her react like that? She'd never had such a strong reaction to a male before, hell, she'd never had that kind of reaction, period.

Avery wasted no time in yanking off his clothes, tossing them aside, uncaring as to where they went, he threw himself down on the bed beside her, as excited as a bouncing puppy. "Strip," he demanded, his eyes roaming as much of her body as he could see. "Hurry, woman."

She wanted to argue, to tell him where he could stuff his orders, but in truth she was as eager to get naked and down to business as he was. She yearned to feel his skin against hers, to stroke and touch him, to trace each muscle with her fingers and possibly her tongue. She had never done oral sex before but for him she would try.

She slowly sat up, her fingers going to the hem of her nightshirt, hesitating. It felt weird, they had had sex before, but he had never seen her fully naked and now she was starting to doubt herself. Were her breasts too small, her hips too wide, her stomach and butt too round? Cellulite had taken up permanent residence on her thighs and a few too many late nights eating at her desk had rounded her in all the wrong places. She had hoped that being turned would have had some kind of magical effect on her body, making her grow a few inches and lose more than a few pounds, and she was ashamed to admit that she had looked in a mirror the second she was able to. TV and literature had a lot to answer for.

Avery saw her hesitate and he didn't like it, he had told her to get naked damn it and he wanted her naked now, right this second, no waiting. And she was being too slow, much too slow. He would do the gentlemanly thing and help, he was nice like that. He took over the removing of her shirt, brushing her hands aside to grip the hem and pull it over her head and off with a flourish that would do a magician proud. He even threw in a 'tada' as he tossed the material over his shoulder. She couldn't help but laugh. Sex for her had always been a rather serious affair, carefully folded clothes, missionary position, lights off and pot luck on if she came or not, which was mostly not.

Avery went straight for her chest, his hands smoothing over her creamy soft skin, cupping her delectable breasts. He made a happy humming noise in the back of his throat as, unable to resist the lure of such gorgeous flesh, he dipped his head, flicking the tip of one pretty nipple with his tongue, smiling to feel how it instantly hardened. It obviously liked the attention and he was happy to indulge it.

Sapphire hadn't been expecting him to just get to work so quickly, the sudden burst of pleasure that shot through her like a lightning bolt actually made her jump. Her head dropped back in response as she struggled to hold in her moan of appreciation. She had never felt comfortable being vocal with love making, not that she ever really had much to shout about in the past, but she knew with him, it would be different.

Avery cupped the soft mound of flesh in the palm of his hand, gently kneading with his fingers, plumping it up until he could suck the whole cherry bud into his mouth, working his tongue all around in tight circles, loving the way she arched closer. He loved her little moans, but he hated the way she stifled them, kept herself quiet. He lifted his head, looking her straight in the eyes.

"Baby, stop it."

Sapphire stiffened, wondering just what she had done wrong. Typical, the one time she was with someone that she really really liked she did something wrong straight away that she wasn't even aware of doing! That sucked! She braced herself for the words she was dreading, something along the lines of 'what the hell are you doing you freak? Get out of my house!'

Avery leaned back in, beginning to kiss a path up the length of her neck to her ear, pleased to feel her relax slightly. "Stop hiding from me. Don't stay quiet, don't hold in those sweet moans of yours. I love hearing them, it means I'm doing it right. I want to hear more. I want to hear you asking for what you want. Relax, let go."

Sapphire shuddered at his words, the sound of his voice in her ear, the feel of his lips on her skin. Could she really do it? Could she actually form the words to ask for what she wanted? Could she actually bring herself to moan out loud and not be embarrassed?

"I'll try," she whispered back, not trusting herself to say more.

"That's all I ask, that you try. That we both try our hardest to make this work between us, because we're worth it. You know we are." He tucked a finger under her chin and tipped her head up so he could catch her eyes, forcing her to look at him, to see the truth in his eyes. He held his breath as he waited for her answer and almost sighed with relief when she nodded.

He dipped his head, capturing her lips in a bruising kiss. Gone was any pretence of softness as passion exploded through them once again, effectively wiping out any lingering doubts she had in herself. She was in a new life now and she was determined to enjoy it, the old Sapphire stifled her moans and lay still, showing as much enthusiasm as a dead fish. The new Sapphire was strong, independent and would enjoy the fuck out of this, life was too long for bad sex.

Avery felt the shift in her, felt it the moment that she relaxed completely and let herself trust in him and damn, if that didn't just make him hard as a fucking rock. This time it would be all about her, he would show her just how good it could be between them if she only let it.

He gently laid her back down against his pillows, turning his attention back to what he was sure were the most perfect breasts in the history of the world. He braced himself on his elbows, leaving his hands free to cup each delectable mound, his mouth lowering to her left one. He lapped gently at the underside of her breast, slowly working his way in towards the middle where he knew it was the most sensitive. His fingers mimicked his actions on her right breast, tracing gently in circles with his finger tip, delighting in the shudder that travelled through her body.

He circled with his tongue, teasing her, going so close to her sensitive peak, then backing off, or letting just the tip of his tongue sweep briefly over her, but not enough to give her any satisfaction. He wanted her desperate for him, he wanted her wild and writhing and begging for his touch. And by fuck he was going to get it.

Sapphire wanted to smack him and tell him to get on with it. Her nipples were harder than ever before, harder even than when you dived out of a hot shower in the middle of winter, and they were desperate for attention. Yet, the infuriating man kept edging closer and closer, winding her up and up, only to move away again. Her nipples were aching with need and even though she boldly tunnelled her fingers into the thick waves of his hair and tried to direct him to where she needed his attentions, he refused to be led. Then he lifted his head.

"Talk to me, baby, tell me what you want, tell me what to do," his tongue wandered from her left breast across the heaving expanse of her chest to the other side, just to begin the delicious torture all over again.

Talk to him? She didn't even know what to say. What did she want? More of everything he was doing would be an awesome start. She had obviously paused too long and received a nip of his teeth on her flesh which succeeded in jolting her out of her musings. Damn, that felt good and unable to stop herself she let out a lusty moan.

Avery's ears pricked up at that positive affirmation that was her sweet moans. He risked another little nip and pinched the other nipple with his fingers. And hell, she almost shot off the bed, her back arching as she tried to get closer, her legs dropping open further in invitation. His little Soul Mate had a wild streak that he couldn't wait to explore. He knew she wanted more, the way she squirmed and made a little pleading noise in the back of her throat. But he wanted to hear her voice, he wanted to hear her say it. That was a barrier that he was determined to break. He loved to hear a woman demand and instruct him, there was nothing sexier.

"Tell me you want more," he wheedled, pushing her with just the barest hint of a lick to her straining little nipple.

Gahh he was the most frustrating man she had ever met in her life, why couldn't he be like the others and just dive on in and get on with it? Why did he have to be so giving? So determined that she would get what she wanted? Yes, she knew that she sounded like the most irrational female in the world right now and probably damned ungrateful too, but she was just so far out of her comfort zone she could barely see it, comfort zone was a dot on the horizon right now. Oh, but she ached, she wanted more so badly, needed more. And she knew that if she wanted it, she would have to concede to him, just a little. She licked her suddenly dry lips and tried to speak, the words sticking in her throat, emitting a croak that sounded like something that Kermit would utter

214

Clearing her throat, she tried again, her voice barely breaking a whisper.

"More. I want more."

Avery knew that if he didn't have supernatural hearing he would have missed those precious words, and was tempted to be a little more evil and pretend that he hadn't heard them, but he couldn't bring himself to be that cruel to her, she was trying to do as he had asked and he couldn't find t in himself to refuse her.

"Since you asked so nicely," he crooned as his tongue swept lazily around one hardened peak, making her gasp and her back arch off the bed in response. His cock was aching like fuck, he didn't think he had ever been this hard, this desperate to sink inside a female. But he was determined to restrain himself for the moment. He wanted to wring at least one orgasm out of her before he took his own pleasure.

He let his tongue begin its downward journey, wandering its way down her ribs, stopping to take in the scenery with a little nibble here and there, a nip or a scrape of his fangs against her silky soft skin.

He wasn't, was he? Sapphire tensed with anticipation as her brain derailed at the thought of that skilled tongue of his working its magic where she was aching the most. She squirmed with each sweeping brush of his tongue as he took his time, teasing around her belly button then just brushing over her pelvic bone. She thought he would continue on to her now dripping pussy but instead he pulled back, bending her leg at the knee and beginning to kiss along her inner thigh, nipping with those very sexy fangs of his.

The anticipation was killing her, visions swimming in her head of just how amazing it was going to feel. He was barely a whisker's width away from her throbbing clit, she felt the cool exhalation of his breath tickling the fine, curly hairs that covered her sex…and he stopped, moving away again. She couldn't hold in the scream of frustration.

"Avery!"

He blinked up at her, all innocent Vampire, like he'd done nothing wrong, he hadn't just teased her and denied her, oh no, not he.

"What's wrong, darling, you can tell me. What do you want?"

She almost decked him, her fist curling up ready to launch a flying death punch. He knew what she wanted but he was still wanting her to say it. Annoying man! Fine, she told herself, if he wanted her vocal, she could be vocal, she would tell him exactly what she wanted, hell she would demand.

"I…" OK this might have been harder than she thought, "I want you to do what you were going to do."

Avery quirked an eyebrow. "Maybe I was just going to keep kissing your delectable thighs and then go to sleep."

She narrowed her eyes at him. "You wouldn't!"

"Oh, but I would," he smiled cheerfully. "Unless you tell me what else you want me to do."

He had her there, the bastard. But still she hesitated, that was until he gave her thigh a nip that was just hard enough to startle her into shouting.

"Lick me, I want you to lick me, dammit."

He smiled a wicked smile that had her groaning before he even touched her. But God, how he touched her. He used his thumbs to spread her apart and started with a long, slow lick from low down, skimming her entrance and then up to circle her clit, making her jump with the sudden pleasure. She moaned low in her throat, the sensation was so decadent, pure pleasure, just for her. She had never experienced it before, her previous partners never one to venture to that territory with anything other than their dicks.

His tongue lapped at her like he was devouring an ice-cream, long strokes up and down, using the flat of his tongue, making her writhe on the bed. Every now and then he would circle over her clit, paying it special attention before closing his lips around it and sucking it into his mouth

216

briefly, making her breath catch in her throat, her hips jerk up to follow, then he would release her and she'd flop back down to the bed like a puppet with its strings cut. His tongue would then do a little flickering thing, like butterfly kisses across her clit, and that, that felt amazing as fuck, every time he did that she felt her clit swell, growing more tingly and sensitive.

And then he stopped, just as her hips were rolling in rhythm with his tongue, shamelessly grinding herself against his mouth for maximum pleasure. She knew what he wanted this time, what he was waiting for.

"More," she demanded. "Do that some more," and just like magic, that torturous tongue returned to her wet flesh. He moved his hands, using the finger and thumb of one hand to keep her parted for his tongue, while the other moved down between her legs to dance his fingertips around her entrance. She felt her muscles clench in anticipation of penetration and she wasn't disappointed. One finger slipped slowly and gently inside her, easing in easily, so wet was she. His finger crooked up and to her surprise, brushed along her inner wall. She had no clue what he was doing, until his finger hit a certain spot that had her gasping, seeing stars. And damn him, as soon as he felt her reaction, he stopped, removing his finger, his tongue barely touching her flesh, going whisper soft.

"More," she gasped.

"More what?"

"More fingers, please!" she was wound up so tight, feeling like she was about to burst if he didn't continue with what he had been doing.

"Such a good girl," he praised as his finger returned, this time with a buddy, sliding smoothly inside, stretching just a little.

Sapphire could barely think from the sensations riding her, the steady thrust of his fingers catching that sweet spot he'd found, over and over, was like something out of a dream, it felt so good. She kept thinking that she was about to explode, her body tensing in anticipation and then relaxing on a sigh when she didn't quite make it. She needed just that little bit more, making her groan with frustration. She waited for him to ask her again what she wanted, but this time he didn't, he just kept up the slow, even thrusts of his fingers, winding her higher and higher.

"Lick me again," she panted, writhing on the bed in desperation. "Make me come."

Avery smiled against her thigh, doing as she bid, diving back in with tongue and fingers, he lapped hard at her clit, feeling her inner walls clamp down on his fingers as her breathing became desperate gasps. He closed his lips around her clit and sucked hard, scraping just a little with one fang, rewarded with her scream of pleasure as she bucked against his hand, her fingers burrowing into his hair, nails digging into his scalp and fuck did that turn him on. He lifted his head, gently sliding his fingers out of her, using their slickness to work her clit, keeping her orgasm going as he shifted, positioning himself between her legs, thrusting in, forcing his way through tightly clenching muscles to seat himself deep with a pleasured groan.

Sapphire had never felt anything as amazing as what she felt now. The combination of his tongue and fingers sent her screaming over the edge of pleasure. She thrust her hips, riding his hand, almost mindless, unable to think past the sensations flooding her body, nothing could feel better....then he slipped inside her and she screamed again, her hands clutching at his shoulders as he lifted her legs and wrapped them around his waist, bracing his arms either side of her body, he drew back almost all of the way, her walls fluttering, clenching, seeking to hold him inside. She felt his body tremble with the effort of going slow, felt the flex of his hips as he stroked forwards, angled to hit just the right spot that his fingers had previously grown so intimate with.

When she felt him pull back again, rasping against that sensitive spot she tensed, waiting for that exquisite forward thrust. Gahh, he was taking too long, she didn't want slow. Acting on instinct she squeezed her legs around his middle, trying to urge him into a faster pace. But the stubborn, obstinate, annoying male, simply froze and refused to move, making it very obvious what he wanted her to do.

"Fuck me," she demanded. "Hard and fast!" She dug her nails into his shoulder and squeezed with her legs again. That was all the encouragement he needed. He curled his hips forward with a snap, driving all that hardness back inside, their flesh slapping together, making her gasp at the sudden rush of pleasure.

"Oh, fuck," she shuddered, clutching at his shoulders, then letting her hands run down the length of his back to cup his arse, feeling the flex of the tight muscles there.

He set a pace that was exactly what she needed, hard, fast and deep. She felt his hands run down the outside of her thighs, gripping and lifting to drape her legs over his shoulders. He bent her legs back just a little and when he thrust back in, she cried out with pleasure. The angle of this new position tilted her hips in the most perfect way so that when his pelvis hit her mound he gave a swivel of his hips that ground against her clit perfectly.

She quickly felt that now familiar growing weight of orgasm building inside her, a buzzing warmth in her belly that spread outwards, tingling at the base of her spine, sending little sparks of sensation shooting through her. Her clit pulsed and strained with each grinding caress. The way the tip of his cock rasped against that spot inside was almost too much, yet she never wanted it to stop. She felt her whole body tensing, felt the skin tightening on her bones like a mild pins and needles. Her breath was coming in ragged pants, her nails scoring his skin as her hips bounced with him, waiting for that one perfect stroke... the pleasure detonated like a bomb blast, shaking her with its intensity, making her scream his name before she latched on to his lips, kissing him desperately as she rode the waves of pleasure that rolled through her.

She felt his rhythm falter, growing more rapid and intense as his tongue fought for control of hers, bossing it around. She felt him suddenly go still, felt his body stiffen, his head thrown back with a moan as the first lash of his seed exploded from him, his hips jerking, stuttering, before he dropped her legs and collapsed on top of her.

They were both panting, bodies shuddering sporadically as she wrapped her arms around his body, her thighs open to create a cradle for his hips. His hair tickled her bare skin as she stroked a hand up and down his spine, enjoying the way he shivered at her touch, giving a little laughing moan as she shifted slightly, her inner walls still clamped around his cock, making his shaft twitch inside her.

His lips nuzzled at her neck, kissing the skin there lovingly before he pulled back to look at her. She didn't want to admit what she actually saw in that look, the soft, almost tender way that his eyes gazed in to hers. For the first time she actually felt like she had made a connection with someone, that they had been with her, not because she was easy, or a conquest, another notch on their bed post, or the safe option, but because he truly saw her for who she was and he wasn't seeking to change her. That in itself meant the world to her. Then he opened his mouth and went and ruined the whole moment.

"There, I knew I could get you to let your wild side out, and if I do say so myself, that was some damn good sex." His smug, self satisfied, very male, smile made her want to punch him in the nose. But she had to admit, he had a point. Asking for what she wanted, being demanding, letting herself go and allowing herself to actually enjoy it, had been a very good experience, one that yes, she found she was eager to repeat. She couldn't blame him for being a little smug, he had certainly fucked her just as hard as she had wanted and given her two amazing orgasms. But one thing he said stuck out, making her instantly feel uneasy.

"Is that all this was to you, just sex?"

The tone in her voice made Avery instantly regret opening his mouth, he didn't even know how to answer for the best. He opened and shut his mouth a few times, then sighed, opting to just say the truth and hope that it really was the best way to be with a female. Apart from when she asks you if the dress makes her look fat, then whatever you do, deny deny deny.

"It's never just sex with us, baby, never has been and never will be. You're mine, now that I have you, I'm not letting you go." He watched her eyes flicker over his face, studying his expression, weighing his sincerity until she nodded. He let out a sigh of relief as he rolled gently off of her and settled at her side, pulling her into his arms.

Chapter Twenty-Two

From the memoirs of Liliya Khikov.

From the moment that Grigory awoke he was strong, he possessed the self-control that many new turns, myself included, did not. He found it easy to stop feeding before it was too late. I envied him that. He was true to his word, looking after me as he promised he would per the terms of our bargain. He allowed me to feed from him on the nights that we did not procure a human, he made sure that I had a comfortable shelter for the daylight hours and saw to it that I was always well protected.

He suggested that we travel and I was all for that, I had always wished to see the world. Grigory was a good companion, having grown up amongst the lower classes himself, he found it easier to converse with the owners of inns or coach men that assisted us on our journeys. I had little patience for it, preferring to simply glamour those that sought to argue with me or refuse me the things I desired. Grigory insisted that there was no need for such measures, that simply stating your request in a polite manner was sufficient, and he always seemed to arrange things to my liking.

Grigory seemed to have endless patience with me, I found that, since I had been turned, it was not just a case of blood lust that I had to contend with but physical lust also. I had many beautiful male lovers, but I knew that they were not my Soul Mate, if so they could not have treated me so badly, Grigory held me as I wept for every one of them. Each was more piggish than the last, only seeming to want me for my looks. And none compared to Yury. My heart still ached with that loss, I was now convinced that some tragedy had befallen him and he had met the final death. Though that, it transpired, was fanciful thinking on my part.

One night, some eighty or so years after I had sired Grigory, we found ourselves in a little theatre in Vienna. We were comfortably ensconced in our box, listening to the most delightful opera when movement in the box across from ours caught my eye. I did not need the provided opera glasses to glance across and see something that broke my heart into a million pieces.

Yury was in the box with a female. A Vampire such as we were. I could tell that from the fangs she had buried in his throat as she squirmed on his lap, bouncing in place. A disgusting spectacle that no woman of breeding would be caught dead in. I couldn't help but watch in morbid fascination as her movements grew faster, jerkier as they apparently reached their climax. It was then that I caught a glimpse of her face as her spine bowed and she threw her head back in ecstasy. Majya, the tavern girl that was well known for parting her legs when her customers parted with their money. It was then that it made sense to me. Yury had vanished to be with her. Had turned her and left me, for her. A commoner. I was so enraged I could not sit there a moment longer. I leapt up and ran for the curtained back of the box, ready to confront them. But, as always, my ever loyal Grigory stopped me from making what could have been a mistake. He took me away, helped nurse me through the pain of such a discovery. My constant, always by my side. We decided to get away, travelling to America. Which was where I met you my love, my Soul Mate.

Liliya made her way into the club with the ever present Grigory by her side, her eyes immediately searching out Avery, who was, as usual, behind the bar, shaking a cocktail maker for a group of females that were all leaning over the bar gazing adoringly at him, their low cut tops affording him a good view of their assets. And she didn't like that. With a huff she made her way over, she would show them just who he belonged to.

Sapphire sipped her drink, one of Avery's specials, meaning he'd snuck a shot of blood in for her. It really was the only way she could stomach drinking blood like that. Not that she was thirsty, at all, she had fed from Avery before they had left the house, meaning that he was a little late for his shift. It seemed that feeding always led to something else with him, this time he had attacked her after her shower, not that she was complaining.

It had been a very strange experience, to wake up wrapped in his arms, in a bed that yet again, wasn't her own. But it had also been nice. She felt safe and content for the first time in what felt like forever, feeling like her life was finally beginning to come together again, to settle down into something she could see herself actually liking. Finally, she was beginning to see a good future ahead of her rather than the one she had been robbed of. Things really did happen for a reason and as she allowed herself the simple pleasure of snuggling closer to the man that had been so patient with her, placing a little kiss on his chest, she couldn't help but smile.

And she was still smiling now as she watched the way that all the females swarmed around her man, and yes, that's what he was, hers. He had promised her that he didn't want anyone but her, that he was hers, and she found herself believing him. She noticed a change in his behaviour. Sure, he was still flirting with the females, giving them attention, but she caught the way that his gaze kept flitting back to her and when he gave her a wink and blew her a flamboyant kiss, she couldn't help but let her own silly side out, blowing him a small kiss back. Baby steps, but he seemed to appreciate it. All in all, she was feeling rather happy, that was until she saw Liliya enter and make a beeline for the bar.

She half rose to her feet before she forced herself to sit back down, Avery could handle her. She didn't want to be seen as the jealous girlfriend, especially since they were still such a new thing, their relationship in the earliest stages. She settled back into the padded booth she was in, flicking another page of her magazine, she pretended to read, though her eyes kept a very close watch on the older female.

Avery humoured the females, who were regulars to the Goth clubs of the area. They were the type that kept their clubs in business, the ones that believed in Vampires and constantly threw themselves at the staff. The staff never gave a hint that they were real Vampires, simply playing up to the stereotype, even going as far as to carry fake fangs in their pockets to 'prove' that they weren't real. That allowed them to 'pop fang' without the worry of hiding from the mortals. The females all held on to the dream that Vampires were real and that one day they would be chosen as their lover or be turned. They were the ones that Vampires always avoided getting involved with, that was why they had registered Donors.

Avery liked the girls, always chatted with them and found them to be fun company, the fact that they all wore some variation of either standard sexy Goth dress or some corseted version of biker chick, leather and studs being their decoration of choice, only helped to sweeten the appeal. But tonight he found that it was a chore to even pay attention to their chatter, his mind firmly on Sapphire. His Soul Mate, and how he loved thinking that. Sure, he hadn't broken that news to her, she was as skittish as a bunny still, but he had nothing if not time, and she was more than worth it.

He had noticed her reaction to Liliya's presence and was secretly pleased that she sought to stake her claim on him, feeling slightly disappointed when she sat back down, but at the same time, pleased by her trust in him. He vowed, yet again, that he wouldn't let her down.

Liliya strode over to the giggling gaggle of simpering females that were drooling over her Soul Mate. She couldn't blame him, he was just being himself, working the crowd to get them to buy more drinks. But she couldn't bear to watch it a moment longer. One of the girls grew bolder, beckoning him over as if she wished to order another drink and couldn't be heard over the music, she took advantage as he leaned in and planted her lips on his. Liliya saw red and reached out, not noticing that Avery himself had broken the kiss and was gently but insistently, pushing the girl back to her own side of the bar. Liliya shoved the girl aside with little regard to hurting her, not caring that using her strength on humans was forbidden.

Anger was bubbling inside her and all she could think about was getting her and her cronies, away from her Soul Mate. The girl went sprawling as the bar stool she was perched on toppled over, sending her crashing to the floor the side of her head smacking into the edge of the bar. Almost instantly the scent of human blood filled the air, all the Vampires in the place stirring to look in their direction, their nostrils flaring as they inhaled the intoxicating smell.

"What the hell do you think you're doing?" Avery demanded as one of the servers ran up to help the fallen girl and to usher away her friends to be glamoured into forgetting what they had seen. But Liliya ignored him, slapping aside the server, her hands closing around the upper arms of the bleeding human female, lifting her off the floor and hoisting her a good foot into the air. Liliya brought the girls face down close to hers, allowing her fangs to descend, snarling at the now terrified girl.

"Never touch him," she growled low. "He is mine. Do you understand what I am saying?"

The girl managed to nod an affirmative, stammering a sorry before Nikos rushed in from the front door, drawn by the noise. He grabbed the girl from the enraged Liliya, scooping her up in his arms, taking her away to be patched up and glamoured, just as Avery rounded on her, his own voice taking on a quiet fury.

"That is not right, Liliya, not at all. You cannot treat our patrons like that, not for any reason, especially not that. I am not yours."

Liliya's eyes grew wide as he spoke, her whole demeanour changing, she seemed to shrink in on herself, becoming the sweet female he had known before, but now he wasn't fooled.

"Oh, come now, my love, let us not be hasty. I apologise for my rash actions, it is unlike me. I simply reacted as any female would at seeing someone touch her Soul Mate." Liliya reached out a hand to caress his arm but he brushed her away.

"Soul Mate," he scoffed. "I'm not your Soul Mate," he reached out to take her arm, to set her back from him but she latched on, clinging desperately.

227

"Do not talk like this, you are confused, my love. Do not cast me aside."

Sapphire had seen and heard enough. She tossed aside the magazine she had been pretending to read, anger at the females actions and words boiling in her veins, red hot fury pounding in her head. She stomped over, placed a hand on the annoying harpy's shoulder and forcefully spun her around, shoving her away from Avery.

"What on earth do you think you are doing?" Liliya stuttered, glaring at Sapphire, her sweetness forgotten.

"Getting you away from MY man," Sapphire retorted, sliding a proprietary arm around his waist, partly to mark her territory and partly just to rile the bitch. Oh, she knew it was wrong but she couldn't help it.

"Your man?" Liliya tossed her head back with a snort. "A common fledgling such as you? I think not, you are but dreaming, little one," she waved a dismissive hand as if to brush her aside. "Kindly step away and let me claim that which is mine."

Sapphire raised an eyebrow at this, refusing to budge even an inch.

"No," she stated it calmly, not raising her voice in the slightest.

Liliya's eyes bled to red, the sign of a very pissed off Vampire, as she shot Sapphire a look that should have killed her on sight.

"No?" She repeated. "You dare to tell me no? Avery has no need for a whore like you or the bleeder feeders he has been giving his body to, I am back now and so you can-" she was cut off as Sapphire's fist smashed into her nose, sending her flying backwards.

Saph looked down at her hand in shock, unable to believe that she had actually done it. One second she had been listening to the vile things spilling from her mouth and the next her arm had raised almost of its own accord and buried itself in the bitch's face. And she couldn't say that

228

she was sorry, she wasn't anywhere near done. She stepped closer, towering over Liliya to give her a piece of her mind.

"You," she enunciated far more calmly and clearly than she felt she should be able to, "are a grade A bitch. You are delusional and a pathetic, desperate, idiot that is clinging to the past. He is not yours and he never will be again, he is mine. So get that through your thick head and leave us the fuck alone."

Grigory rushed over from one of the private feeding rooms, blood still staining his lips, just in time to hear the tail end of Sapphire's rant, noticing how Liliya had struggled to her feet, her fangs bared in a vicious looking snarl. Moving quickly, he grabbed Liliya before she could launch herself at Sapphire, holding her at arm's length as she hissed and spat like a house cat, arms flailing as she screamed obscenities.

"Oh, shut up," Avery tossed over his shoulder as he turned Sapphire away from her, putting himself between the females. Liliya, obviously realising that she had lost the battle promptly burst into tears, burying her face in her companion's chest.

Avery couldn't believe his eyes as he watched his female stand up for herself in that manner. He hadn't thought she had it in her, his usually calm and composed Soul Mate looked like a wildcat as she pushed back her hair, which he had insisted she leave down for the night, her chin raised in a gesture of defiance, daring the other to come at her again. Fuck, she was beautiful.

"You, are so hot," he growled, pulling her into his arms with a lascivious grin, Liliya firmly forgotten as Cassian pounded across the dance floor, yelling orders.

"You made her cry," Grigory growled. "No one is allowed to make her cry." He started forwards as if to go after Sapphire but Cassian stepped in front of him, along with a recently returned Nikos, stopping him in his tracks.

"Get her the fuck out of here," Cassian bellowed at Grigory as the man gave up on his planned attack of Avery and Sapphire when faced with the other two men, instead he turned, scooping a still sobbing Liliya into his arms.

"Take her away and do not let her back, you're both banned. Get out!"

Grigory wasted no time in removing Liliya but Sapphire barely noticed. Her attention was riveted on Avery as his lips captured hers in a kiss that made her blood heat in a different way. The anger drained away, quickly replaced with full blown lust. She could think of nothing more than getting him somewhere private as quickly as possible. That was until a familiar voice piped up.

"That's him!"

Sapphire extracted herself from Avery's embrace and turned to look at Cassie, the ghost standing in the middle of the dance floor, looking towards the door that was swinging shut behind Grigory and his now silent mistress.

"That's who?" Sapphire asked, half afraid she already knew the answer.

"That's the man that killed me!"

Chapter Twenty-Three

Shocked was an understatement, it didn't even cover the multitude of thoughts swimming through the collective heads as Sapphire relayed Cassie's words to the assembled group.

Nikos sprang into action along with Cassian as they raced out of the door, following along behind Grigory and Liliya. They couldn't have gained more than a minute head start, that is if they were on foot.

Avery wrapped his arms around Saph, offering her silent comfort as she listened to the ghost describe again, in detail, exactly what had happened to her and what she remembered.

"Cassie says that he was the one that offered her the light for her cigarette and then began to feed from her, she remembers it clearly now that she has seen his face again. Sometimes the trauma of dying can have that effect on them, they don't recall details or faces until something triggers it, but she's absolutely positive that he is the one."

Avery nodded. "Which means that it's not that big a leap to assume that he is the one that's responsible for the killings of those other poor girls."

Sapphire couldn't help but agree, it was the only logical explanation, which meant that while Grigory was out there, other female Donors were in danger, she hoped and prayed that Nikos and Cassian caught up with them and stopped him before it was too late.

Avery called the Donors Guild while Sapphire had a steadying drink with Amethyst, who had ventured downstairs not long after the fight had been stopped by Cassian. Saph didn't know exactly what had been said during the, very brief, phone call between Avery and the Guild, but her Vampire wasn't looking very happy.

"What's wrong?" she asked, putting down her drink as she turned to face him.

He shook his head, as if he couldn't form words as he raked his fingers roughly through his hair, dropping down to cover his face with his hands, muffling the growl of annoyance and frustration he let out, before turning away and bringing his fists down onto the bar top with a bang so loud it made her jump even though she was expecting it.

"Talk to me, damn it," she demanded, grabbing his arm, and using it to pull him back round to face her.

"There is another girl missing," his voice was low, devastated at what he was reporting, the look in his eyes betraying just how hopeless he felt. "We had him right here and he got away. He got away, Saph. Not more than five minutes ago a group of females were attacked. Three got away, but one didn't. The girls called the police. The Guild heard it from one of the vamps that are on the local force. Difference this time is, it's not a Donor."

She bit her lip in an effort not to allow the tears that had gathered in her eyes to fall. No one needed her breaking down right now. They had to think positively, had to look at things as best they could and believe that there was hope.

"Maybe Cassian and Nikos caught up with them," she suggested. "Maybe they weren't the ones that attacked those girls..." she trailed off when she saw her sister sadly shaking her head.

"They lost them almost as soon as they left the club, they were just a little too late, they had too much of a head start. Nikos even shifted to try and catch their trail but there were just too many scents around for him to distinguish. I'm sorry." Amethyst showed them the text that she had just received. "They are going to check the apartment they were staying in, but I doubt they will find anything, they will know that we suspect them and will most likely have made their escape."

Sapphire slumped down on the closest available bar stool, needing the support on her suddenly wobbly legs.

"There's another missing?" the quiet question caught Saph's attention and she turned to look over at Cassie, who didn't seem to notice (or maybe she just didn't care) that she was standing in the middle of the bar top, her legs invisible through the wood, her torso seemingly floating above it.

Sapphire opened her mouth to reply but Cassie winked out of existence, going wherever it was that ghosts went when they were upset.

Saph knew there was no point calling her back, she wouldn't be heard.

Cassie was so annoyed, there wasn't even words to describe the wave of pissed off that she was currently surfing. If her feet were solid you could have bet they would be stomping along the ground hard enough to rattle windows. But as it was she could do nothing much to express the hopelessness she currently felt. Being a ghost sucked. Seriously.

Not only had she died, but now another girl was next on the list, maybe her life had already ended, maybe they were looking for someone that had a good chance of already being a ghost...Cassie blinked, the magnitude of that last thought hitting home. Maybe, just maybe, Cassie could find her if she was dead already.

Surely there had to be some kind of ghost wide web, a way for them to interact with each other, there had to be. You heard all sorts of stories about spirits meeting up with their loved ones once they too, passed over. There had to be a way that they did that, someone to make that shit happen. Didn't there?

Cassie sat her non-substantial arse down on the nearest surface she found, not caring that it happened to be a fence and that she must look pretty damned strange to be perched there with a wrought iron spike sticking out through her chest.

"Think, Cass, think," she instructed herself, like that would kick start her brain. "How do other ghosts do this stuff? Do they just instantly know it? Did I miss the memo? Why don't we have a damned handbook like in 'Beetlejuice'? That would be seriously handy." She swung her legs like a child sitting on a too high chair, wracking her brains for some knowledge that she was sure should have been popped in there when she was ghostified.

"If people can meet up with their loved ones as soon as they pop their clogs and shuffle off the mortal coil, why can't I? I mean, they know who they want to see but it can't be that hard..." For the second time in too short a time, she trailed off as realisation hit her upside her see through head They knew who they wanted to see? God, she was dumb as a brick sometimes. Now that she thought about it, it made perfect sense. When she wanted to see Sapphire, the thought was there in her head and when she thought about talking to her, all of a sudden, there she was, magically transported through ghost time and space, to the only one that could see her. It was because she knew who she wanted to see. That's what was different now. Cassie didn't know who she was searching for.

She jumped to her feet, ignoring the way her spirit seemed to hold on, very briefly, to the iron railing, letting her feel a slight resistance as she pulled away. Ewww, now that was all kinds of weird and hadn't happened to her before, but this wasn't the time to ponder it, her brain could only cope with so much at one go and she was about to hit short circuit overload. Sticky chests would have to wait for another day.

She closed her eyes, though why she thought that would make a difference, she didn't know, and pictured the building that housed the Donor's Guild. She saw it clearly in her mind and wished herself there, there was no other way to explain it, and when she opened her eyes again, there she was, exactly where she had wanted to be. She slipped inside, locked front doors being no barrier to her now, and went in search of something that might lead her to the missing girl.

It took Cassian and Nikos less than a minute to break into the apartment that was leased to a Miss L Khikov. Cass was surprised that she still used her old family name, but then again, knowing just how snobbish Liliya was, and how influential, and not to mention rich, her family had been, there was no way she would give up that title.

The rooms themselves were spotless, looking almost like it they had never been occupied. The only signs that someone had was the clothing in the wardrobes, the vast array of beauty products that littered the bathroom sink and the cloying scent of Liliya's perfume that clung to the air in a thick smog.

They were too late. They knew as well as anyone that Vampires that old were never without a bolt hole, a secret place that they could run to should the need arise. Yes, the days of superstitious villagers were gone, but now the constant threat of exposure from CCTV cameras and the like, was just as dangerous. There was no way that they would return to this place now. There was nothing to be done but return to the club to break the bad news.

Chapter Twenty-Four

Sapphire blinked open her eyes, once again waking the instant that the sun went down. She had always been an early riser when she was human and it appeared that as a Vampire, she was no exception. She marveled for a moment on the fact that she could awaken from what Amethyst called the 'death sleep' -the time when a Vampire's body shut down completely during the daylight hours, reverting back to a corpse like state essentially how their body would look if they were truly dead– and feel wide awake and alert. Amy had explained it as being almost like the magic that animated them drained away with the sunlight and that the spark of life inside them, went out, only to reignite with the coming of the night.

It was all very strange to Sapphire who had never been into the supernatural, and yes, she knew how weird that was since she was the one that saw and talked to ghosts, but she had spent so much time trying to ignore that side of her and to put on the guise of normalcy, that she had worried anything otherworldly would just encourage that side of her to come out more and more, and that she didn't want. So she had ignored all Tanzi's talk of the stories she had heard, the next myth she was chasing, and had kept her feet firmly on the ground in the here and now. Unfortunately, her new here and now had her dealing with it in the most real way.

She gently pushed Avery's arm away from where it was draped across her stomach. He was still sound asleep, something she found highly amusing. She always woke up feeling completely refreshed, not even a hint of grogginess like she used to have when she was human, no matter how early she went to bed or how much sleep she got, but Avery seemed to be a typical male. He was the laziest person she knew, taking a good hour more than her to rouse himself from his day coma.

She looked over at him, smiling at the way he stayed curled on his side, his arm stretched out on the mattress where she had slipped out of his embrace. The first time she had woken to find him wrapped around her like a clinging vine she'd had to fight the urge to run away, having never slept a full night with a male. Yet now, she hated to admit it to herself, but she liked it, she liked the way he kept hold of her all night, keeping her close like she was something precious that he couldn't bear to be parted from. She knew that sounded ridiculous and way too romantic to actually be the truth, but that little voice at the back of her head couldn't help but wish that it was.

She pulled on a dressing gown and made her way to the kitchen to heat up some blood. She still hated the taste, but Avery suggested she try to drink it through a straw so that it didn't hit her tongue, and that way she could imagine it was

238

a thick milkshake. She still didn't want to, preferring to feed from Avery, but she knew that she couldn't rely on him forever, and so she was determined to try her best to learn how to drink down the rotten stuff.

She braced herself and took a sip and again, made a face, like licking dead batteries, that almost metallic taste that hit the back of your throat no matter what she did. It was gross. She put the glass back down and stood back, taking a deep breath and really trying not to throw up, not that she thought she could, not having anything in her stomach that was solid, but it was like her body remembered the sensation from when it was alive and was determined to evacuate the offending substance

She couldn't do it, couldn't keep having Avery rescue her from her Vampire inadequacies, surely she could do the same sort of thing that he did for her, flavour it with something, mix it with another flavour that would disguise it a bit. She wrenched open the cupboards and began to rummage through the contents, not really expecting to find much seeing as Avery didn't actually eat, though she hoped the fact that Nikos was there so often would yield some positive results.

She was wrong. There was nothing in the cupboard except ketchup, soy sauce and some mustard. Old Mother Hubbard had more than they did.

She picked up the ketchup and the mustard, deciding the soy sauce would be just too much. Dare she? Dare she actually mix her own drink? *Those who dare, win*, her mother's voice echoed in her head and with that in mind she upended the ketchup bottle into the glass of blood, giving it a generous squirt and then, taking a spoon, she scooped out a heaped teaspoon of mustard and dropped that in too. She gave it a vigorous stir, making a face at the way it seemed to halfheartedly bubble. It was thick and gelatinous and not in a good way, with clumps of ketchup floating on the top like little ducks in a pond. She picked it up and gave it an experimental sniff. It had a definite tomatoey, spicy undertone that blood should never have, but her parents would smack her if they knew she was thinking of wasting something she had poured and then doctored, so, holding her nose, she tipped her head back and sucked down a big mouthful.

Immediately she gagged but forced it down, swallowing the foul liquid before she could spew it back out. There, down. She pushed the glass aside, suddenly no longer hungry. The experimenting was so over for the day. She would get Avery to teach her how to make drinks as he did, then get the ingredients in so she didn't have this problem again.

Chapter Twenty-Five

From the memoirs of Liliya Khikov.

I loved you from the moment I first laid eyes on you, when our gazes met across the room. Ragtime music had never seemed so sultry, so moving, so sexy, as it did at that moment. The way your body moved to the tempo was nothing short of perfection. But I didn't like the look of the female you were dancing with, the way her body twinned around yours. I knew then that you were mine, we were meant to be together, our souls were meant to merge, we were made for each other, we were Soul Mates. You just didn't know it yet.

I made my way over, cutting in, giving you my most beautiful smile, the smile that men always loved. It made them wish to protect me, something which I was always happy to encourage, and it made them realise what a sweet, honest, loving person I truly am.

I saw the way your eyes lit up when you saw me for the first time, and when we danced, our bodies moved so perfectly together, we knew instantly that sex between us would be nothing short of explosive. We danced and moved together in sync, in harmony with each other and when our lips met for the first time, we both felt the meeting of souls.

We wasted no time in finding a room for the night, taking our time to explore each other's bodies, to get to know each other in the most primal way. I knew, as sure as the sun would rise in the sky, that we were destined.

And then you left me. I understood my love, I understood. I know you better than you know yourself, you weren't ready to settle down, you weren't ready to be with just one woman, but you would be, you would.

And so I waited, found you over and over, sometimes we would have a magical night, and others I had to watch as you took another female to your bed, had to watch as you cheated on me, betrayed our bond. But I didn't blame you too much, my love, I didn't. Because I knew that you didn't understand our relationship as I did. I knew, I believed, that one day, you would understand and come to me. To be home in my arms as you are meant to be.

There were many things that Avery would have loved to see when he awoke from the blissed out stupor that only really good sex can produce, some of the things his incredible active imagination could conjure included Sapphire laying beside him in bed, all naked, warm and willing or waiting for him in the shower like a delectable treat. What he had not expected was to find her camped out in his kitchen with her slightly deranged sister, bottles and jars spread around them, littering every surface, empty blood bags scattered around the general area of the kitchen bin as if they had simply been tossed aside, which he guessed they probably had, and his Soul Mate, the saviour of his long and lonely existence, cackling with crazy glee in the middle of the chaos like a mad scientist.

He cleared his throat, hiding his smile when they both jumped guiltily, like children caught doing wrong. He raised one eyebrow in silent question.

"Erm…we, Tanzi, well that's is... I…" Sapphire stuttered to a stop, looking adorably flustered and embarrassed. Something her sister seemed to know nothing about.

"She couldn't stomach the blood as it was, she tried to mix it with ketchup and mustard, like some dodgy undead hotdog, and almost made herself sick. Then she called me for reinforcements. And here we are," Tanzi informed him, her hands going to her hips, firmly planted, her expression daring him to laugh as his eyes took in the war zone formerly known as his kitchen.

"Did it not go too well?" he questioned gently, noting that Saph looked a little green around the gills, something he wasn't used to seeing from a Vampire. She shook her head, finally finding her voice.

"How do you make it look so easy? You just seem to throw in a little of this and a splash of that and voila, a delicious drink. We got pig swill."

"Well, for one thing I don't mix soy sauce, mustard, milk and strawberry jam. That's a big no no."

Sapphire nodded seriously, like she was listening to a lecture of utmost importance, Tanzi just looked bored as she fished a bag of vegan jelly babies out of her bag and popped one into her mouth.

"I told her to wait," she supplied unhelpfully as she chewed. "But she was determined to feed herself without relying on you."

He would never understand females as long as he lived, which was a bloody long time. Sure, he could flirt with them, seduce them and befriend them, but understanding what

243

went on within the dark recesses of their multi layered minds? Not a fucking chance.

"Why would waiting for me be relying on me? All you had to do was ask and I would have shown you what mixes well together so that you would be able to make your own after that. There's no shame in a little instruction, think of it as watching a cookery show, you can't expect to be able to make something perfect without first getting the recipe."

Sapphire wanted badly to argue with him, to save face a little. She knew that she had acted like an idiot but the self-reliant streak in her would never truly die down, she also knew that if she was truly prepared to try to make it work with Avery, and she had to be honest with herself, she badly wanted to. Even if she couldn't admit it to herself, the thought in the back of her mind, that knowledge that she was already falling in love with him, was there and she didn't want to be responsible for their failure. She would have to try and accept his help as a true partnership and squelch her more defensive tendencies.

She nodded, earning her a hug, Avery obviously knowing how much it cost her to argue that out in her head and not let it slip from her mouth.

"How about we go to the club and take advantage of Cassian's bar, since you two seem to have burned your way through all the blood in the house?"

He couldn't hold in his laughter any longer when both girls heaved a sigh of relief and ran for the front door, leaving the kitchen bomb site behind. Making a mental note to bribe one of the club cleaners to stop by and deal with the mess, he followed them out of the door.

244

Chapter Twenty-Six

The club was buzzing with Guild representatives when they got there, Cassian has wisely closed the club for the night, giving it over to the Guild to hold a meeting there before they opened the doors to the assembled Donors that waited for news.

Avery pulled the girls over to the bar, wanting to distract them from the rumble of conversation that came from the Guild's tables. He knew that Sapphire was worried, saw it in the shadows in her eyes whenever the missing girl was mentioned, it had been three days and they all knew that the odds of her being found alive were roughly in the region of zero. They were essertially looking for a dead girl.

And he knew that Sapphire blamed herself. She was under the misguided impression that if she hadn't confronted Liliya, hadn't goaded her as she did, then the girl would still be safe.

He had tried his hardest to get her to understand that Grigory was not sane, that he didn't think in black and white like they did, he didn't think logically, there was no way they could have known that he would take another girl so soon, or at all really. Logic said that he would lay low now that he knew they were aware of his extracurricular activities, but again, logic seemed to have no part in his life. There was no way that it was Sapphire's fault, but still she felt like she had failed somehow. Like she was betraying Cassie by not protecting her fellow Donors. Obviously, the self-blame was pure bullshit, but she was such a sensitive soul under the tough exterior she showed to the world, that he knew she would never truly believe him.

So he saw it as his duty to take her mind off the nasty business, at least for a little while. He focused on teaching her how to mix his famous cocktails, mostly fruit based, some laced with alcohol. The alcohol was purely for taste reasons as it barely affected them, their bodies seeing it as a harmful substance that it sought to heal as soon as it entered their stomachs. The only way they could experience the buzz of being drunk was to feed from an inebriated Donor.

It was something he himself had indulged in more times than he cared to remember. Avery the party animal, Avery the seducer of women, the fun loving guy that was always game for a laugh. He hid his loneliness behind his bright smile and sunny disposition. But now, now he truly meant it when he smiled, because he was no longer alone, never again would he be lonely, would he hate the lack of connection he felt after another random coupling with a willing female.

His wild days were now well and truly behind him, and as he smiled over at his female, watching the way she giggled with her sisters as they added random splashes of the fruit juices he assured them would not curdle the blood as some of their experiments had earlier, naming their concoctions with the most bizarre names he had ever heard, he had never felt more content in his life.

Sapphire slurped down the last of her cocktail, one they had named 'up and at em,' it contained blood (obviously)two shots of strong espresso coffee and chocolate syrup, a drink that Avery assured her would more than make up for the fact she hadn't had her morning mocha since she had turned. She could already feel her body perking up, the lethargy that seemed to come from not feeding, a bone deep weariness, a heaviness in the limbs, that all faded away as the blood soaked in to her parched system, revving up her organs in double quick time, making her feel almost like a vamperic version of Popeye, suck down the chow and bam, flood of strength that made you feel like you could take on the world.

It was strange just how much a shot of blood could affect her. She had found that while she bounced awake from her death sleep feeling like she could take on the world -or at the very least, the January Sales- that quickly wore off once her body woke up fully and the blood began to flow.

Avery had explained this, saying that the blood rushed around the body, seeking out and repairing any damage that may have occurred during the night, most of the time there was very little to do unless the Vampire had been gravely injured, but as she was a new turn her cells were still fighting each other. That would apparently settle down within the next few months, but until then she would still need more blood than usual, making her feel like a new born baby in need of regular four hour feeds.

She had noticed that her senses began to dull the longer she went without feeding, kinda like when you were tired and dozing on the couch, images seemed to blur a little at the edges, sounds seemed a little muffled and she had the worst urge to nap. And that wasn't good. Vampires as a species, relied on their instincts being as sharp as a tack, either because they needed to hunt down food or because there was always the danger of someone deciding that it was the perfect time to hunt them down.

It wasn't as important as it had been, say two hundred years ago -or so Avery said in one of their impromptu history lessons, she found that now she was a Vampire she wanted to know everything there was about them- these days they didn't have to worry too much about hunting down food, since it was delivered straight to their door from blood banks or they could hire a Donor. But they did have to be careful not to go too long between feedings or they might jump someone in the street and that wouldn't be good. And now, since most of the world wasn't as superstitious as they used to be, mobs of angry villagers weren't something they needed to keep their eyes open for.

Now that she felt more human -no pun intended- she began to take note of the conversations going on around them, the serious murmurs from the Guild's tables, the light giggling coming from Tanzi and Amy as they sipped their none blood laced cocktails where they sat a little way down the bar. She picked out the sound of Nikos speaking quietly into his phone from his place on the door. Avery and Cassian were chatting lightly in that manly way that boys tended to do, with the odd bellow of laughter and slap on the back. She suspected they were talking about her, but, found that she didn't care to raise an objection to that, which was testament to just how far she had come in the past few weeks. Then, almost as an undertone, she heard her name being called.

Her head snapped up as she looked around, trying to find where the sound was coming from, her eyes darting wildly, but she saw nothing. Just heard that whisper calling to her over and over again. She couldn't ignore it, now that she heard it, it was like the ticking of a clock in a quiet room, the scratching of a mouse, the snuffling of a sleeping dog, something that was firmly in the background, that you could miss if you weren't aware of it, but once you were, there it was, pricking at your conscious like the poking of an insistent child. She had to find out where it was coming from. She looked at the others, but no one else seemed to hear it.

She got slowly to her feet and took a few steps forward, her ears cocked for any little sound. Maybe she had imagined it, maybe it was some weird Vampire thing that happened during the dark moon period on a Thursday when Mercury was retrograde, or some other such nonsense. She had almost convinced herself that she actually hadn't heard a thing, that her tired and overwhelmed mind had simply conjured the noise as a way of distracting her from the truth of what was happening the thing that none of them wanted to admit, that they were out of ideas and ways to save the poor girl, that and the fear that she wasn't going to be the last one.

She shook her head and edged back to her stool, starting to sit, when she heard it again. Louder this time, more insistent. Her butt paused mid descent and she sighed, knowing now that she couldn't just ignore it. Straightening back into a stand, she listened, hearing it again, and this time she was able to pin point the sound as coming from just beyond the main floor.

She hurried over, not wanting whomever was calling her to leave before she found out what they wanted. She flung open the door that led to the back hall and peeked inside. The hall stretched practically the length of the club building, offices dotting one side, while direction signs, rules and regulations dotted the other. She glanced from side to side, trying to guess which way to go, the voice having now grown silent. To the right was the door which hid the stairs to Cassian and Amethyst's apartment and to the left was the doors to the stockroom, cellar, loading bay and the back entrance.

She doubted that anyone would be beyond the door that led to the upstairs, the door was always kept locked just in case any customers went wandering. She had a key, all important people did, but she was pretty sure some mysterious calling voice wouldn't have the required importance to have earned entrance.

Left it was. She went slowly, not being so stupid that she would rush in like a fool. In any horror movie there was always some ditzy female that followed an unidentified sound and was immediately killed because she tripped over something while not watching where she was going, or she ran straight into the killer. And since they actually did have a killer running around on the loose, caution was needed.

As she reached the door she paused and on a whim, grabbed the fire extinguisher off the wall, unhooking the nozzle. OK, so it wasn't the most deadly weapon in the world but it might be enough to startle someone enough to buy her the time she needed, should she have to make a run for it.

Holding the weapon in one hand, keeping it tight against her body, hose nozzle pointed out, ready to fire, she turned the door handle and pushed open the door. She peeked her head into the first stock room that they used to keep the bar items they ran out of the quickest -bottles of beer, various juices and a few bottles of their most popular spirits- which they always needed easy access to when busy.

The room, no more than a small cupboard really, was empty, which was exactly as she had suspected. It would have been way too easy for whomever was trying to get her attention to just be standing there, ready to spit out whatever, no doubt unhelpful, thing they wished to tell her and then to just toddle off so she could go back to her sisters and the Vampire that she was almost certainly halfway in love with. Nope. Way too easy.

She took the few steps it took to cross the room and opened the next door that led down some steps to the main stock area and loading bay.

This was not the place to be if you were worried about someone killing you, really it wasn't. Too many hiding places. Boxes were piled up here and there, crates full of bottles, both full and ones waiting to be recycled, boxes of snacks and glasses, along with housekeeping essentials like industrial sized packs of toilet rolls, cleaners, extra chair cushions, a spare set of curtains for the VIP areas, coat hangers for the cloak room and numerous other sundry items that a bar would need. In short it was a hide and seekers paradise.

Sapphire paused in the doorway, extinguisher raised in the most threatening way she could manage, which to be fair, wasn't that threatening really, ready to either spray or smack anyone that dared jump out at her. A quick look around showed her that the place appeared to be empty, though she wasn't discounting the possibility of someone hiding out ready to bash her brains in.

The voice was now silent, which was just typically her luck. Not really knowing what else to do, she weighed up the pros and cons of calling out to whomever was there. Really what other choice did she have? She cleared her throat, suddenly finding her mouth drier than a desert, and croaked out.

"Hello? Is there anyone here? Did you want me?"

Nothing. She tried again, louder this time.

"Hello?"

Nothing. Now she was pissed off.

"OK, that's it! You dragged me down here and now don't want to talk. Well fine, I'm going. I'm not prepared to stand around here all night when I could be with my family." She turned on her heel, now of the mind that if anyone wanted to kill her they would have done it already.

"Sapphire!"

She froze, the voice clearer now, louder, and slowly turned back around.

Cassie stood there with another female, this one looking almost as bad as Cassie had when they had found her body. She was bloodied and dirty, her insides on the outside, trailing down after her like the macabre train of a dress, the skin of her abdomen sliced clean through, skin peeled back from her ribs like they did in an autopsy. She

251

was looking down at her draped intestines with a sad tilt to her head.

"Hello," Sapphire greeted. What else could she do? She knew from experience that some ghosts needed you to treat them as normally as you could, it helped keep them calm. Though obviously that was more for the ghosts that didn't yet realise that they were dead, and there was no chance of that with this one.

The new girl raised her head at the sound of Sapphire's voice, as if it broke her from the spell of her contemplation. The straggly, blood soaked, hair hung limply around her face, fell back as she looked up, and for the first time Saph saw her face. She hadn't wanted to see it, but in her heart of hearts she had known that she would. It was the young girl that had been getting a little too close to Avery the night that Liliya had been there, the one that the crazy bitch had attacked. They hadn't known her name, had just known that a girl had been snatched from the street. But Sapphire had had her suspicions.

Cassie spoke up. "This is Gemma. I found her."

Sapphire nodded her acknowledgement of this information as she spoke softly to the girl.

"Gemma. Can you hear me?"

The girl blinked, once, twice and then a third time before she nodded.

"Can you tell me what happened to you?"

This time the girl shook her head almost desperately, fear evident in her eyes, in the tight, pinched nature of her mouth. She was terrified even in death because of the treatment she had endured at the hands of Grigory.

"Do you know where they took you?"

Again, the girl shook her head, her movements jerky, panicked. Sapphire watched as her image began to flicker, fading the more anxious she grew, but there was no help for it, they needed information and she had to try her hardest to get it.

252

"Is there anything you can tell me about them? Anything at all? Think Gemma, think!"

She flickered again, buzzing in and out until with an anguished cry she popped out of sight completely.

Cassie sighed, her hands on her hips. "Newbies."

Sapphire shook her head, fixing her with a look that bordered on a glare. "She was scared, she didn't understand. You were just as bad as I recall."

Cassie opened her mouth to retort but Sapphire simply arched an eyebrow, daring her to argue the truth of her statement and Cassie slumped in defeat.

"OK, I'll try be nicer to her. I do understand, I do. It's just frustrating, I don't want him to hurt anyone else. This isn't right!"

Sapphire nodded her agreement, dropping down to sit on one of the many crates that were piled up here and there. "I know. I want to stop Grigory as much as you do. But we can't find him. We have no leads as to where he went, where he took Gemma, or who he will pick next. The only things you all seemed to have in common was the fact you were all Donors, except Gemma, she wasn't. That makes her different and throws the pattern into disarray. If we had no clues when he stuck to his M.O, now that he's broken that pattern, we're even less informed than we were before. I really don't know what to do next."

She propped her elbows on her knees, dropping her head into her hands, sighing deeply, feeling a sense of utter uselessness settle on her shoulders. She wanted so badly to help but there was only so much she could do. Her skills laid in ghosts and even then, they weren't that honed. Years of denying her gifts had left them rusty and even though they were apparently enhanced by her vampirism, she still couldn't work miracles.

Cassie paced, she found that easier than sitting, because then she had to waste so much energy and concentration in simply staying in the position her body would have taken on its perch, focusing hard on not falling

253

through the damned object, that she couldn't think of anything else.

So, she paced, back and forth, back and forth across the length of the stock room, wracking her brains for something she could do.

Think Cassie, think, she chanted to herself as she stomped her way across the floor.

The ghost was annoying her, much as Sapphire liked Cassie, her pacing was just weird, seeing someone walking back and forth in front of you, yet hearing no footsteps was disconcerting and putting her off as she tried to wrestle her brain into gear. Just as she was about to give up, call it quits and yell for Avery, she had a thought.

"Cassie?"

The ghost, blessedly, stopped her pacing and turned to look at her.

"Yeah?"

"How did you find Gemma?"

Cassie shrugged. "I don't know, I just thought about her and there I suddenly was, right there in front of her. She was hanging around outside The George, you know, the pub on the high street? I think she lived near there or something. She didn't know how she got there, so it stands to reason that she spent a lot of time there if she ended up outside it."

Sapphire digested this new information, the thoughts tumbling around in her head, speaking out loud as she thought.

"So, you just thought of her and poof, you were there?"

"Yep. That's pretty much how this ghost thing works."

"So, can you do that with other things, not just people?"

Cassie looked confused. "What do you mean?"

"I mean, say if you were thinking of the London Eye, or Big Ben, would you suddenly appear there?"

The ghost's expression changed to one of contemplation. "I don't know. Maybe."

Sapphire wanted to smack her, in the nicest way possible, but she still wanted to smack her for being so damned slow on the uptake. Yet she managed to keep her voice calm, Cassie had a habit of getting a little sniffy when she felt she was being picked on.

"Do you think you can try?"

Cassie seemed to think about this too, before she nodded again. Her face screwed up in a look of pure concentration, that or ghosts got constipation just like the rest of us. And then suddenly she vanished.

She was back less than a minute later, bouncing with excitement.

"I did it, I went straight to that big wheel and I didn't end up in the water." She stopped her bouncing and looked over at where Sapphire still sat. "Why did I need to do that?"

"Because now that you've seen what Gemma looks like, you can try thinking about her body and seeing if you can end up there." Really, Sapphire was surprised she didn't have to whip out the hand puppets to explain it all. Brain of Britain Cassie wasn't.

"Ohhhh." There it was, it had finally dawned on her. "Right, I can try to do that. And if it happens, I'll try to find out just where the hell it is." She vanished once again.

Cassie was gone for a lot longer the second time, long enough for Saph to get impatient with waiting and start to tidy the stock room, finding that her new Vampire strength made it a much easier task.

"I did it!"

Sapphire jumped in shock, dropping the box of pork scratchings she was trying to balance on top of a tower of coke cans, the box clonking her on the head as it bounced to the floor. Luckily it was light and didn't hurt.

"You did it?" Saph rubbed her head anyway, almost an automatic reaction.

"Yes! It only took me three tries and I found her body. I then worked my way out of the house and got an address, then I came straight back. He's there, the man that killed me. He was there, with that little mouthy bitch. You know, the one that touched your man."

"Liliya, yes, I know the one. She's there too? Then we have to go catch them, now!"

Sapphire started to run to the door, fully intending to race wherever it was that they were hauled up and confront them. Then she stopped. What would Avery think?

What if she got hurt and Avery didn't know? She was so used to doing her own thing without consulting anyone. She was her own person. And she would still be her own person now that she was with Avery, in fact, he would make her a better person. He made her feel confident, desirable, like she could do anything she wanted to and succeed. He helped her when she needed it, he encouraged her, and he believed in her. He was her partner now, in her life, and there was no one else she would want.

And as her partner, he should be with her. She had to stop and tell him.

"I'll be right back, stay here," she yelled over her shoulder to Cassie as she raced back up the stairs to the bar.

Chapter Twenty-Seven

Avery was sure that females didn't need to take that long in the bathroom, surely they didn't. Sapphire had been gone for ages and he was beginning to worry. He couldn't help but be scared when it came to her, she had a bit of a habit of running out on him whenever their relationship seemed to be heading in a new direction. Though he thought she had been happy, that they were actually getting somewhere. Maybe he had been wrong.

"No," he said out loud, startling a sweet, timid looking female Vampire as she made her way across to the bar with her glass, obviously intending to secure a refill, but at his yell she hurriedly slammed her glass down on the bar top and scuttled back to her co-workers.

Without stopping to say he was sorry, he jumped up, heading to the door that led to the back just as Sapphire burst through it.

As Sapphire skidded through the door into the main bar she paused and took in the atmosphere of pure despondency. The Guild members were still quietly talking amongst themselves, Cass had Amy perched on his lap as they whispered to each other, heads bowed together in such an intimate way it was clear that they were in their own little world and oblivious to that which was going on around them.

And then there was Tanzi, she had managed to vanish again, and since Nikos was also missing in action, Saph surmised that they were obviously taking a little alone time. There was definitely something interesting going on between the two of them, even if they refused to admit it.

Saph couldn't help but smile as Avery appeared the second she entered, almost like he was tuned in to her on a level that went beyond normal. But weirdly enough, even though her mind should have been screaming out for her to run, get away before he sought to control her by keeping an eye on everything she did, she didn't get that feeling from Avery, instead all she felt was a warm glow of rightness, and that was actually nice to experience.

She beckoned him to follow her, ducking back out, deciding there and then that she didn't want to disturb the others until she was sure they had a good reason to. Everyone was so tense and, while they seemed to be in a bit of a lull, she was loath to do anything to ruin this temporary reprieve of peace.

Avery, to his credit, didn't waste a second, he didn't question, he just followed her out of the door into the hallway beyond.

"What's up, baby? Where did you disappear to? I thought you might have fallen in the toilet or something."

Sapphire tried very hard to ignore the little thrill that skittered through her at the ease in which he spoke such an endearment, especially one that was aimed at her, along with his little joke. Cute as he was, they didn't have time for fun.

"I heard someone calling me-"

"And you followed without me? Are you crazy? You could have been hurt!"

Ahhh, the rantings of the dominant, male Vampire. Sapphire ignored him. She had known he would be like that, and surprisingly it didn't annoy her, it didn't make her want to prove that she didn't need his permission to do anything, in fact she found it rather sweet. He had obviously broken her. But now wasn't the time to make a fuss about it. So, she continued as if he hadn't spoken. Which she had found was mostly the best way to deal with him.

"I found Cassie, with the missing girl. Her name is Gemma, and she's the girl that Liliya attacked. Unfortunately, this proves that she's dead."

Avery slumped, his head dropping into his hands at this news, and Sapphire knew that he was blaming himself for it, even though he had had no way of knowing at the time that Grigory was the murderer and that he would seek revenge for his spurned mistress.

"There's nothing we can do for her now, but Cassie says she managed to find the address of where they are hauled up. Now, I can't be sure how accurate she is, ghosts can sometimes make mistakes, especially when they are as new as she is. So, I don't think we should bother the others with it, I think we should go and check it out." She silenced his protests with a finger to his lips. "Nothing dangerous, no heroics, just go and see if they are there, and if they are, call for back up. No rushing in to try and save the day. OK? I won't get hurt, I promise."

He appeared to debate this for a few seconds before he nodded.

"Where is this place?"

Sapphire shrugged helplessly. "I don't know. Cassie said she can give us a door number, maybe a street name, but otherwise she doesn't know."

"No problem, love. We can no doubt look it up online and find a map, they can't have gotten that far out. Knowing

Liliya, she never gives up on something she wants, and unfortunately, she seems to have set her sights on me. Grigory won't ever tell her no, so my betting is that that are barely out of the city center."

Sapphire led the way back down to the stock room where Cassie was impatiently waiting, her insubstantial foot tapping soundlessly against the hard, concrete floor.

"About time, what took you so long?"

Sapphire ignored the surly tone and instead asked for the address, one that neither she nor Avery recognized but once Avery had pulled out his phone and plotted it in to an online map, they saw that he had indeed been right. It was maybe ten miles away at most, and they wasted no time in jumping in his car and, following the directions, headed out after the murderer.

Chapter Twenty-Eight

The house, for that's what it turned out to be, no matter how much Sapphire had been imagining a castle straight out of Dracula, was one of those non-descript terrace houses, late Victorian, that were so often found in and around London. Its neighbours on either side were in darkness, which wasn't surprising seeing as it was almost 2am on a relatively quiet street, but the house they were looking for, and Sapphire checked twice hoping there had been some mistake, was nothing like the others on the street.

Boards covered its windows and the glass part of the front door, preventing them from peeking in to assess what might be going on inside and checking for any possible danger. The front garden was so overgrown, the grass almost at waist height, looking for all the world like a mini field. The paint on the front door was chipped and peeling, a sad looking green that may have been bright once but was now reminiscent of pond scum.

"There's no way we can tell if they are even in there with the place locked up like this. We have to go in." Sapphire didn't need to look at her love to know that he was shaking his head vehemently. She turned and saw that she had predicted right. "We don't have a choice. We can't get the Guild down here without proof. What if Cassie is wrong and while they are out here something else happens and another girl gets hurt or worse?"

Avery knew that what she said made sense, but he still didn't have to like it. He had the He-man like urge to protect her at all costs, seriously, he was fighting the urge to scoop her up and run back down the path with her, down to the end of the street where they had left the car, toss her inside -moving quickly before she realised what he was doing- and lock her in. And by the narrowed, squinty eyed glare she was giving him, she knew exactly what he was thinking.

He sighed.

"OK, we'll go in. But you have to promise me that you'll stick right by me and not go running off on your own. Promise?"

Sapphire nodded. To tell the truth the gloomy looking house didn't look very inviting and she didn't really want to be alone in it, sticking by Avery would have been what she'd have chosen to do anyway. The heroine in the movies always managed to get herself killed because she ran off on her own into danger.

After checking the latch on the front door and the security of the boards that covered the windows, finding them all to be still held firmly in place, Avery led the way around to the back of the house, checking for any possible entrance point. They tried the back door, finding that the lock didn't just turn when they quietly tugged on the handle, but that it had been broken inside its chamber, spinning uselessly. The door swung open surprisingly quietly and Avery slipped inside, holding Sapphire back with an upraised hand until he had checked out every corner of the room.

They had walked in to a kitchen, one that was filthy, the cupboard doors either hanging off or missing, broken crockery still lay in the sink, an old kettle sat on the dirty, food encrusted worktop, its lid flipped up as if inviting you to fill its belly and plug it in, yet it too was in a disgusting state.

The kitchen door, which seemed to lead to a hallway, was open and they quietly made their way through, checking in a room that contained a toilet and sink, that seemed to have been made from an under stairs cupboard. Victorian houses rarely had indoor plumbing as standard, so most conversions had bathrooms squeezed in wherever they could.

They reached the end of the hall which either led to the outside world through the boarded up front door, to the left into what they assumed was a sitting room and to the right, the start of a staircase that led up to the first floor, this being a two storey town house, and from the quick look they had taken outside, the attic appeared to have been converted too, the skylights in the pitched roof a giveaway.

"Stay here," Avery instructed as his foot hit the bottom stair, ready to check out the upstairs. They had listened carefully for any signs of movement within the building but heard nothing. Their sense of smell was severely handicapped by the mold that crept up the walls here and there, along with the smell of stagnant water from the kitchen sink and the toilet under the stairs. Really the place was a mess. It was obvious that people had taken to squatting in the house now and then over what must have been a few years that it had been unoccupied.

Sapphire waited impatiently for Avery to finish his recon mission in the upper part of the house, her back to the front door preventing anyone from sneaking up on her, again with the horror movie lessons. She never got why the scardy cats Shaggy and Scooby always wanted to go last, making their braver friends go first to check things out, knowing her luck something would grab her from behind while the others were distracted. Nope, she would choose to go in the middle, it was safer.

There was something about the house that she didn't like, that she couldn't put her finger on and she couldn't wait to get out of there. Sapphire wrapped her arms around her chest, hugging herself as a sudden chill breeze made her shiver

"Cassie?" she whispered but couldn't see the ghost. Avery came back down the stairs, shaking his head at her silent question, no sign of them.

"Well this was a bust," Sapphire groused, rubbing her still cold arms. "Cassie must have been wrong."

"I wasn't wrong," the disembodied voice piped up before Cassie's head popped up from the floor beneath their feet, which was just fucking weird in itself. Sapphire leapt back with a yelp of shock, equal parts freaked out and scared of stepping on her friend's head.

"What the fuck?" she hissed, her fingers digging into Avery's arm where she had grabbed him for support.

But Cassie must have been taking lessons in how to be as creepy as possible. She followed her sudden appearance with an ominous declaration of, "Down here," before she sank back through the floor.

Sapphire glanced over at Avery, who was staring at her in puzzlement, his fingers gently releasing his arm from the death grip she had on his flesh.

"Cassie," she said by way of explanation. "Does this place have a basement?"

They found the basement door just off the kitchen, one they had mistaken for a pantry. They found a light switch on the side of the wall close to the door which, surprisingly, worked, a bare bulb hanging from the ceiling flaring into life. Avery stopped in front of her, preventing her from moving down the stairs without him, but he allowed her to peek over his shoulder as both their eyes scanned the area for any signs of Grigory or Liliya.

The whole dingy room looked like something out of a movie. A work bench of some kind stretched the length of one wall, rusted tools littering its surface, others mounted to the wall above the bench. It had obviously been a family home at some point if the pile of abandoned garden toys in the corner was any clue. There was also the remains of family life evident in the form of a pile of sagging, damp boxes that displayed the names of a few people with the accompanying 'kitchen', 'linings', 'winter wardrobe' and 'pictures'. What looked like a sofa was covered in a sheet, along with a double mattress and a single leaning against a wall. What was obviously a couple of dismantled beds lay near them, a dining table with its chairs stacked on top of it and a chest of draws the final piece of furniture. It made her feel bad that these things that had probably once been so precious were now forgotten, left behind.

A sickening smell was assaulting her senses, seeming to stick in the back of her nose, an almost sweet smell, one that reminded her of the time they forgot a half pack of bacon in the back of the fridge, the meat had been slimy and rancid when they had finally thrown it away.

Everything was covered in a thick layer of dust, dust that floated on the air, clogging up her throat and settling on her tongue as she cautiously explored. The smell was stronger now that they were starting to move a little way down the stairs, seeming fouler when mixed with the musty scent of the mold that crept up the walls in the corners.

The basement itself was small, not that much to see beyond what she had already noticed. The workbench, the furniture, the boxes of belongings and garden items. A dismantled slide and swing set was dumped in one corner, laid out next to one of those little clam shell paddling pool/sand pit combos, a kid's bike leant against the swing set, rusted and paint chipped, looking forlorn without an owner.

265

They made their way down the surprisingly steep stairs, Sapphire following along behind Avery as close as she could get without clinging to his back like a monkey. She was scared, she would admit it, but she knew that she had to pull herself together and deal. She paused, letting Avery continue on his own while she looked all around again, eyes scanning both the ceiling and the floor below them, just in case they had missed something.

And she was right, they had. There, crumpled up in a ball to the side of the stairs, tucked away in a darkened corner was no doubt the source of the horrible smell. Gemma. Or at least, the poor girl's mangled corpse, tossed away like meaningless rubbish. She pointed it out to Avery as she continued down the steps, ignoring his questioning look.

Sapphire knew that there was nothing they could do to help her, knew beyond a shadow of a doubt that the girl was long past saving, she would have known that even without having met the poor girl's spirit. Yet, she still found herself searching through the stacked boxes, opening the one that apparently contained linings, she extracted a nice pink sheet. Ignoring Avery's questioning look, she carefully draped it over the girl, tucking her in with infinite care the likes of which she hadn't experienced in her last hours on the mortal plane. She felt they owed her dignity and care.

There was something infinitely sad about the basement, as there was the whole house. The left behind items, telling of a happy family, years ago, but now the house was abandoned, left to rot, nothing but a shell that people used for their own advantage. It made her want to cry, left her imagining what could have made them leave behind such precious things.

She almost jumped out of her skin when a hand gently touched her shoulder, startling her out of her morbid musings.

"I need to call the Guild to come and collect her body and to post people here in case they come back," Avery said quietly, his hands resting lightly on her shoulders, massaging just a tiny bit, seeking to give her comfort.

"My phone has no signal, I need to go back upstairs. You coming?"

Sapphire nodded, not wanting to be left alone down there with a dead body. Sure, she was a Vampire now, but that didn't suddenly make her in to a ghoul.

They carefully climbed the stairs, breathing freely for the first time in what felt like forever, the air, while certainly not fresh by any means, thankfully lacked the stench of the basement.

Avery gave her quick kiss and stepped out in to the hall, his phone already in his hand but judging by his muttered oath, he still had no signal. He slowly walked the length of the hall, his arm in the air as he slowly waving his phone back and forth, trying to catch a signal as he took a couple of steps up the main staircase.

A noise from behind her, like the creaking of a door, startled her, her head whipping around, but not quick enough. She heard Cassie's cry of warning to herself and Avery -who obviously wouldn't hear her- but couldn't reply as a hand clamped itself over her mouth, her scream muffled by the big palm.

She heard Cassie's yell, followed by Avery's bellow of rage as he raced back down the stairs. The hand on her mouth eased only to be replaced by strong arms banding around her waist, pinning her back against a large, firm torso.

She saw Avery race down the hall towards them when she was thrust aside. She fell heavily against a wall, her head cracking against the kitchen door frame. Pain bloomed hot and fierce in the back of her skull, blackness winking in front of her eyes as her body grew heavy, unconsciousness claiming her.

Avery heard the noise the second he was out of range to actually do anything to help, like that bastard Grigory had waited for the perfect moment, which of course he no doubt had. He turned and ran back down the stairs, hating the fear in her eyes as she struggled to get free.

Before he could get to her, to help her, Grigory moved, tossing her aside like she was a rag doll, and sprang at him, catching him around the waist in a crude rugby tackle.

Both Vampires went down. Avery was unable to check on Sapphire to make sure she was alright, instead having to concentrate on fighting off the big brute that sat astride him, his big fist upraised. Avery managed to get his arms up quick enough to block the first punch but the second caught him in the side of the head, making his ears ring from the force of the blow.

He heard Sapphire stir and took advantage of Grigory turning his head a little to watch her. He moved fast, bucking his hips up in an effort to knock his attacker off balance. Grigory tipped sideways just enough that Avery could turn on to his side, sending the other man sprawling onto his back.

Avery was on him like butter on toast, raining punches on every bit of flesh he could reach, stunning Grigory with his ferocity. His worry for Sapphire and anger that someone had hurt her gave him a boost of adrenaline and rage that was no match for the larger man. Avery dug his fingers into the man's hair, getting a firm grip and using it to lift his head, slamming it down against the floor over and over until the man's struggles ceased and he fell back limply.

Avery wasted no time in jumping up, panting with exertion, to check on his girl.

There was something awful about waking up with a head that felt like elephants with hobnail boots were tap dancing in your brain, it was worse than a hangover from hell. And she didn't know how it happened. Since becoming a Vampire she hadn't woken with even so much as a twinge behind her eyes, not like when she was human and her irregular sleep patterns had often led to stress induced headaches.

She reached out a hand, automatically searching for the body of Avery, thinking she would tuck herself back into his arms and maybe try to sleep a little longer. But instead of her fingers encountering soft bed sheets and sleepy male, she felt hard, cold floor. That had her opening her eyes immediately.

Blinking, she looked around, finding herself sprawled out on the kitchen floor. The cracked lino she was laying on was filthy, gritty dirt stuck to her hand where she had reached out. Now that she was moving her neck she realised that the pain wasn't coming from the inside of her head so much as it was the back. The back of her skull felt tender, bruised and very sore to lie on. Distantly, she heard a loud grunting and banging coming from the hall but she could barely focus, concentrating on not succumbing to the inviting darkness that hovered at the edges of her vision.

She forced herself up into a sitting position, the dingy room spinning around her as her body tried to deal with suddenly being somewhat vertical. She gingerly touched the back of her head, her fingers coming away sticky and stained with blood. Well, that explained why she had the stonking headache to end all headaches.

She closed her eyes and waited, trying to breathe through the dizziness that engulfed her. Her stomach was churning, making her feel like she was about to throw up, the same hollow gnawing that she got when she was hungry and first turned.

She felt her head again, finding that the blood felt more tacky now and the bump wasn't as tender, yay for Vampire healing. She rolled over on to her knees and hauled herself to her feet, taking her first real look towards the source of all the noise.

"Fuck, I should have stayed unconscious."

Avery was beating the ever loving shit out of Grigory, the man barely able to move as her Vampire's fists flew, almost a blur as they landed with sickening thuds.

She rolled over on to her knees and reached up, grabbing as firm a hold as she could on the dirty worktop, ignoring the thoughts of the thousands of germs that were right that second clinging to her hand, using it to haul herself to her feet.

"Saph, baby, are you alright? Let me look." Avery was already at her side, having left Grigory on the floor. He turned her around, making her lean her head down so he could examine it, his fingers gentle as they pushed her hair aside and tenderly probed the cut, most likely from the edge of the door frame.

"It's already closing, you'll be fine. But you will need to feed. Here," he shoved his wrist under her nose, waving it enticingly. The scent of his skin chased away the lingering stench of decay that was even now floating up from the basement below them. She felt her fangs drop as she leant in, her lips kissing lightly at his skin.

"Avery!" The squealing shriek of his name came suddenly, making them both jerk around, just in time for Avery to catch Liliya as she threw herself into his arms, managing as she did, to knock into Sapphire enough that it caused her to stumble back a few steps before she could regain her already wobbly balance.

Tears streaked down the woman's face, her words coming in heaving sobs as she clung to Avery like a limpet.

"Oh...Oh...I was so scared. Grigory...he has gone mad. Mad, I say!"

Avery just stood there, looking stunned for a second, his gaze flitting between Sapphire and the hysterical female that was glued to his chest. He shrugged, not knowing what to do, before he wrapped his arms around her and awkwardly patted her back.

"Shhh Lili, it's alright now. We're here."

270

"He… he killed those women, and I could not stop him. I thought he would hurt me if I tried. I didn't know what to do. I thought I would die here, until you came, my love."

Sapphire tried not to let a sudden spurt of jealousy affect her, Avery had no choice but to try and comfort her, it was what any decent person would do, and Avery had a big heart, there was no way he could be cold to an upset female. *It doesn't mean anything*, she told herself firmly even as Liliya sobbed even harder, pressing herself as close to Avery as she could, her heaving breasts squashed so tight to his chest you would be hard pushed to slide a piece of paper between them.

"I knew it," Liliya sniffled, burying her face in against the curve where his neck met his shoulder. "I knew you would come for me. I knew that you loved me and were just bewitched by that thing."

Sapphire raised an eyebrow at that, taking a step forward, ready to smack the bitch if Avery didn't say something. Avery, being the clever man that he was, didn't particularly want to get in the middle of a girl fight and wisely extracted himself from Liliya's grasp.

"Liliya, I don't love you. I didn't come to save you, I didn't even know you were in trouble."

Liliya blinked, looking for all the world like a confused little girl.

"What you mean, you didn't know?" she dabbed at her still streaming eyes with the hem of her dress. "Of course you did, you felt it."

Avery shook his head. "No, Liliya, I didn't, there would be no way that I could feel it."

She snorted, a very unladylike noise and made a sound like steam escaping from a pan. "Pffft, of course you did. Through our bond, no?"

"No."

"But we are Soul Mates, you and I. We are in love, we belong together."

"No, I love Sapphire, she is my Soul Mate, not you."

271

Now it was Sapphire's turn to blink in shock, her voice low. "You love me?"

Avery turned to look at her, opening his mouth to reply but Liliya beat him to it.

"Bah," she batted at Sapphire with her hand like you would an annoying fly. "He is confused. What he talks about, it is not love. It is but the affection he feels as your adoptive sire. That is all. Nothing more. We, we are in love."

She wound herself around Avery like a vine, her fingers straying to play with the ends of his hair, but he quickly shrugged her off.

"No. Woman, listen to me. I'm not wrong. We are not Soul Mates. I don't love you." He grasped her arms firmly as he set her away from him, trying to get some distance.

"You are a very beautiful female, very special, but you aren't for me. Your Soul Mate is out there somewhere, you just have to find him. But it's not me."

Sapphire knew that Avery was trying to be as nice as he could to Liliya, trying to let her down gently, but Sapphire didn't buy her act as she started crying again, her head in her hands.

"Oh, come now, honey, don't start to cry again." He took a step towards her but Liliya turned to avoid his hand, her eyes flashing with anger, her tears forgotten.

"She has bewitched you, can you not see this? She and that Witch sister of hers must have placed some kind of hex on you. It is making you say such horrible things to me."

Avery glanced at Sapphire in question. "Tanzi is a Witch?"

Sapphire shrugged. "Among her better qualities, yes. Problem?"

He grinned. "Nope."

Liliya, not liking that her little announcement hadn't achieved the desired effect, she stamped her foot, regaining their attention.

"Do you not care that her ugly sister is a Witch? That they have cursed you to not be with me, your true Soul Mate? Do you not care?"

Her eyes glowed red as she ranted, her accent growing more pronounced with every word until she was screaming in his face.

"You will love me!"

Sapphire was the first to notice the dark shape looming in the hall behind Liliya, watching it make its slightly unsteady way towards them.

"Liliya, Avery!" Sapphire shouted, pointing behind them in warning.

"Liliya, come here, quick! Run!" Avery reached out a hand for her, trying to grab her even as he pushed Sapphire behind him for protection.

Liliya turned, as if in slow motion, her eyes growing wide as she watched the shape of Grigory come closer.

"Move your arse!" Sapphire yelled, trying to move around Avery, her eyes searching the kitchen for anything they could use as a weapon, but he pushed her back again, refusing to let her put herself in any more danger.

Liliya pressed herself back against the door frame as Grigory came close, which allowed him to step around her and enter the kitchen. Then she stepped up beside him, her arms going around his waist as she cuddled in to his side.

"What the fuck, Liliya?" To say Avery was stunned would be an understatement. "Get away from him before he hurts you like he did the others."

Liliya laughed, the sound like the tinkling of teacups, sweet and mocking.

"My pet would never hurt me, in fact, he wouldn't hurt a fly unless he was protecting me."

"Tell that to the girls he killed," Sapphire snorted, her voice hard as she tried once again to push her way past Avery to look Liliya in the eye, but Avery's arm was firm as he held her back.

273

"You still try to protect that little bitch," Liliya sneered. "It is pathetic." She slammed her fist down on the kitchen counter, breaking it in half with the force of her temper.

"Why do I have to do these things to keep my loves? Why? Why can I not just keep the ones I love without having to fight for it?" She snapped her fingers, a quick hand gesture but one that Grigory obviously knew. Without warning he lashed out, his fist catching Avery in the chin with an uppercut that lifted him off his feet and sent him sprawling to the floor. He then grabbed Sapphire, who began kicking and screaming, hauling her bodily to the basement door and dragging her down the stairs.

Liliya scurried after him, setting up one of the abandoned dining chairs in the middle of the floor. Grigory dropped Sapphire in it, holding her in place while Liliya secured her with a length of rope that had been left coiled up on the work bench.

As Grigory went to fetch Avery, Liliya couldn't resist crowing in Sapphire's face, her tone that which you would speak to a disobedient child.

"You may kid yourself that he loves you, little one. But I can assure you that he does not. He is man, he knows not his own mind. They are all but simple creatures, ruled by their dicks, are they not?"

She spoke conspiratorially, like she was imparting a great secret and her voice set Sapphire's teeth on edge.

Liliya turned sharply as Grigory carried an unconscious Avery down the stairs and tossed him on the floor.

"Pet! Be careful with him, will you?" she chided gently as she extracted a wicked looking knife from her pocket and handed it to Grigory, nodding her head in Sapphire's direction.

Chapter Twenty-Nine

Avery awoke to a soft hand stroking his hair. He shifted, eyes still closed, feeling his head pillowed on what appeared to be a lap. His jaw hurt but it was nothing he couldn't live with now that he had his Sapphire with him. Sluggishly, he turned his head, nuzzling his cheek against the hand. And froze. The scent invading his nose was not that of his beloved.

He shot upright, eyes pinging open, going wide in horror as he took in the sight of Sapphire, tied to a chair, the blade of a knife pressed against her delicate throat. He heard her swallow with fear as he pulled away from Liliya, tossing a glare over his shoulder.

"I'm OK," Sapphire managed to squeeze out before the blade was pushed tighter against her skin, a tiny rivulet of blood trickling its way down her pale neck, making him growl with anger. No one treated his female that way.

Liliya got gracefully to her feet, stretching like a cat, obviously trying to draw attention to her bountiful breasts that strained the low cut top she wore.

"Avery, darling, forget the infant, she is of no concern."

"She is to me," he growled, only holding back because of the obvious threat to his female, his rage barely contained.

Liliya either couldn't take a hint or simply chose to ignore it, instead slinking over to wrap her arms around Avery's neck, holding him back when he tensed to pull away.

"One move and Grigory will cut her weak little throat and then you shall lose your new plaything, just as you did your others."

That got his attention.

"My others?"

She gave the girlish laugh again, mocking in its sweetness, oozing innocence. "Of course, the other whores that you took to your bed." She tapped him on the nose as if he were a naughty school boy.

"You thought I didn't know about them, but I did. Liliya knows everything." She walked her fingers up his chest then span away, twirling on the spot as if dancing to music only she could hear.

"But no matter, I took care of them. They deserved to die, do you not see? They touched that which was mine." She paused in her spinning, her eyes locking on to Avery's as the full meaning of her words struck home.

"You were not to know, it is not your fault, my love. You are but a man, ruled by your cock," she gestured to the area in question with a dismissive wave of her hand. "But they should have known better, no woman should touch another's male. It is not done. But they were simply whores, of no consequence, either selling their bodies or their blood, it is all the same. Pitiful. They were not worthy of you, or your attentions. Same with that thing." Her finger pointed accusingly in Sapphire's direction.

She's mad, Avery thought, *off her rocker, completely bats in the fucking belfry, nuts.*

"They had to go, do you not see that? Please see that." A note of worry had crept in to her voice as she laid her small hands gently against Avery's chest, looking up at him imploringly.

Sapphire felt Grigory's hold slacken on the knife that he held to her throat, the blade no longer digging into her tender flesh, but she wasn't stupid enough to make any sudden movements. She had to wait it out. Liliya was clearly insane and no doubt Grigory was the same way. Though, there was something about him that made her wonder.

As they listened to Liliya talk about the whores, Sapphire was sure that she felt Grigory shift uncomfortably, something that was noticed by Liliya when his disgust grew more pronounced the more she talked.

"Yes, my pet. I am aware of your thoughts on the issue, but they left me with no choice. You understand this, no? They were interfering with my happiness, you wish me to be happy do you not, my sweet, Grigory?" Her voice was wheedling, enticing him to agree with her, a hint of a pout in her tone showing that she wouldn't be happy with any answer that didn't agree with her.

"Yes, mistress," he intoned dully. Liliya narrowed her eyes but this was apparently satisfactory because she turned back to Avery.

Sapphire watched carefully-her stomach cramping even worse than it ever had before, which she tried to ignore, no doubt her body working through the blood she had drank earlier, soaking it up to repair the damage that had been done to her head when Grigory had tossed her-wondering what Avery would do next, how he would take this new knowledge. She braced herself for his explosion, for him to get mad, anger to pour from him. What she didn't brace herself for was the lance of pain that shot through her heart at his next words.

"You're right, Liliya. They shouldn't have touched your man, you did what you had to do, what was within your right to do."

Liliya's eyes grew wide as he continued, saying the words that she longed to hear.

"They were nothing but a dalliance, a time filler, nothing more. Same as you are right about Sapphire, I do believe my judgement was simply clouded by the emotion between a sire and his young. I mistook that for love. I was wrong. It is you I love. You I want to be with."

Avery's heart physically hurt as he heard Sapphire's sharp intake of breath, the little sob of distress that slipped from her lips, but he forced himself to keep looking away, to keep staring into the eyes of the demented, evil, twisted bitch that clung to him.

His brain had been whirling the whole time she was talking, piecing together the information that slowly trickled out of her as she pranced and giggled, ranted and raved in equal measure. And he could think of no other way to protect Sapphire than to agree with what Liliya said. To make her think that he had changed his mind and that Sapphire now meant nothing to him.

"Avery, what are you doing?" Sapphire's soft question almost killed him, he couldn't look up, couldn't look at her and see the evidence of the tears he heard choking her throat. He couldn't say the words that he would never, ever mean, if he was looking at the one he loved more than anything else in this world. He forced the words out, words that almost stuck in his throat, such terrible lies that hurt him to speak, yet he did it, for her.

"I'm doing what I should have done weeks ago, claimed my Soul Mate." He wrapped his arms around Liliya, praying that her little squeak of joy would be the last thing she ever had to be happy about. He swore revenge, swore by all that he held dear, that he would find a way to stop her, that he would find a way win back his Sapphire, to prove to her that it was her and her alone that held his heart in her hands. He swore this as his lips swooped down and captured Liliya's in a deep kiss that stole her breath.

He pulled back, smiling down at the deceptively small and innocent looking female that he held so tightly, resisting the urge to squeeze and crush her bones or worse. He needed to protect Sapphire.

Feeling physically sick he held back his disgust as he bent and nuzzled her neck with his nose, allowed his fangs to slip out and trace the length of her throat.

"I want you," he whispered as seductively as possible, pulling on all his years of charming the female population. "Now."

He felt her shudder of pleasure and had to stop himself from dropping her on her arse there and then, of pushing her away as forcefully as possible.

"What about her?" Liliya crooned in his ear.

Avery shrugged. "What about her? Let her go, she won't say anything if she knows what's good for her. You can't kill her, too many people would notice and they would never stop until they found you. I can't risk your safety like that, my love." He cringed as he said the words, forcing a callous coolness into his voice that he hoped they would believe.

Liliya obviously didn't care about anything but Avery, about having him and keeping him, anyone that she saw as a problem or a contender for his affections had to go, and now that Avery was telling her he wanted her, that was all she could focus on.

In her warped mind she believed that people in love didn't lie to each other, and that she and Avery were very much in love. If Avery was telling her that he loved her and wanted her, then it must be true and that was all that mattered to her. But she was also wary of pushing things too far and pissing him off so she quickly agreed.

"Yes, yes, my love, whatever you say, whatever you think is best." She called over her shoulder. "Grigory, when we are away from here, release her. She no longer matters to us."

Avery held his breath as the great brute lowered the knife from Sapphire's throat and moved away.

Liliya turned with a flouncing toss of her hair, holding out her hand for Avery's.

"Come now, let us leave."

Avery placed his hand in hers, tugging her back into his arms, letting her bury her face in against his neck, his chin resting on top of her head. He was such a glutton for punishment, but he couldn't leave like this, he couldn't leave Sapphire with her thinking that he might not want her. He just couldn't. Risking everything he lifted his head, looking at her for the first time, her beautiful tear stained face shone back at him like a beacon of hope in the darkest of nights and he mouthed three little words. I love you.

Sapphire tried to hold herself together, tried to tell herself that this was all part of some plan of Avery's, but really, who was she kidding? Men never really wanted her, she was never good enough. She would forever be the one that was good enough to sleep with but not good enough to keep, she was disposable. And now, the one person that she had let worm their way in to her heart, the one person that she had trusted, had hurt her in the worst possible way.

Seeing Avery kiss another was like a sucker punch to the gut, it drove the air from her lungs, it made her chest hurt in an actual, physical way, she felt her heart stutter, like it was shattering into a million pieces. She couldn't watch, looking away but not managing to block out the happy little noises that Liliya was cooing, the sounds of their kiss seeming to burrow their way into her brain.

She barely registered what happened next, tempted to actually bounce forward onto the blade that Grigory still held to her throat, that was until the blade was no longer there. She risked a look up and saw Avery watching her, her breath caught, her heart giving a rousing little cheer as she saw his lips move. She mouthed the words back, knowing then that the doubting voice in her head had been wrong, Avery loved her, he truly did mean everything he had said. And somehow, she had to have faith that things would work out, they were destined to be together.

"Mistress," the deep voice startled them all, but Liliya was the first to recover.

"Yes, my pet?"

Grigory opened his arms and without hesitation Liliya extracted herself from Avery's embrace and skipped over to him.

Grigory held her tight to his chest.

"I will always love you, mistress. From the moment I first saw you, I was in awe of you, and I wanted nothing more than to protect you and make you happy. Are you happy now, mistress, truly happy?"

Liliya lifted her head, looking up at her only Vampire turn, her constant companion, the one that had been there for her no matter what, and she smiled. A big, wide smile.

"Yes, my pet, I am. I always get what I want."

They hardly heard the whispered words, could barely track his movements, he moved so fast.

"Not this time."

His arm lifted, and surged down, the sharpened wooden handle from some kind of garden tool plunged deep in through her back to protrude out of her chest.

Liliya's faced registered the shock that both Sapphire and Avery felt as her body began to shudder.

"I couldn't let you hurt anyone else. They are in love." He stroked the hair back from her face, looking deep into her startled eyes as they went from accusing to lifeless. "I'll see you on the other side, my love."

Grigory held her. He held her cradled on his lap as her legs gave way. He held her, stroking the hair back from her face as the light faded from her eyes. He continued to hold her as her body began to turn grey, skin flaking away from her bones as she disintegrated down in to dust, leaving Grigory cradling nothing but a pile of bones inside her clothes.

Chapter Thirty

Avery wanted to say that he stood and watched, giving Liliya the dignity in death that she deserved, but he didn't. The second he saw that stake come down, the second that he knew that Grigory had turned on his mistress, his only thought was to get to Sapphire.

He ripped the ropes apart with his bare hands, his fear for her safety over the last few minutes, along with his need to hold her in his arms again and prove to her that he loved her, dictating his actions. He never wanted to see that pain and doubt in her eyes again for as long as they lived. If they got out of there alive he wouldn't take no for an answer, he was claiming her, bonding with her and keeping her by his side until the end of time.

Sapphire melted into her Vampire's embrace, sliding her arms around his middle, needing to feel close to him, needing him to be her anchor as she tried to make sense of just what had taken place.

Avery kissed the top of her head, holding her close as he watched Grigory hold Liliya like she was the most precious thing in his world. It was obvious that he had loved her, probably loved her from the moment she had turned him. Avery felt so very sorry for him, he couldn't imagine loving someone that much that he had stayed with her, for hundreds of years, watching as she fell in love with others over and over again, and still not be able to live without her. He imagined choosing to plunge a stake into Sapphire's heart, to stop her if she had become a monster like Liliya had, but he just couldn't.

He felt Sapphire pull away from him and he fought the urge to yank her back, not wanting to let go, but he knew he had to, they were far from out of danger.

"Grigory?" Sapphire spoke softly, in a soothing tone that one would use to calm a skittish horse.

The bigger man looked up slowly, his eyes wet with tears as he took in the sight of them together. And he smiled.

"As it should be," he nodded as he gently laid Liliya's remains on the floor and got slowly to his feet, arms raised as if to prove he was unarmed and making no sudden movements.

"I am sorry," he said, and the remorse in his voice was all too real. "I am sorry that I allowed her to continue her ways for so many years."

"You weren't to know," Sapphire soothed, unable to ignore her need to make him feel better.

But Grigory shook his head.

"You are too kind, a kind, kind lady that did not deserve to be treated that way by Liliya. But you are wrong, I did know, and I ignored it, because I loved her more than I had ever loved another living being."

He looked down fondly at the pile of bones on the floor, which was both creepy and sweet, which in itself was a head fuck.

"I do not think she meant to be bad, or that she even saw herself that way, but she let her heart rule more than her head, she saw things that weren't there, right from the start. I watched her covert men that were not for her, though she thought they were. I watched as she came between lovers

284

and destroyed their happiness in pursuit of her own. But once she had the male, she quickly grew tired of him, not feeling the spark of a true Soul Mate, she no longer wanted him. She was in search of that perfect love and never found it." His voice was low and sad, as if it pained him to talk of it, but Sapphire and Avery kept quiet, simply letting him talk, unable to think of anything else to do.

Grigory bent and picked up the sharpened handle, tossing it in one hand almost absently, yet Avery tensed, pushing Sapphire behind him again in an effort to protect her.

"I couldn't let her actually come between real Soul Mates. That was too much. I couldn't let her ruin more lives in search of her imagined happy ever after. I had to act. Liliya left a diary for you, it is in her handbag in the living room above, it will explain everything to the council," he paused and looked thoughtfully at the stake in his hand.

"The council will, of course condemn me as much as they would her. I never killed any of those girls, but I lured them in, I contributed to their deaths, I helped to either dispose of the bodies or to lay them out as she wished and I didn't stop her. For that, I will be given the harshest of punishments, a stake and the sun. I do not want that."

He began to toss the stake again, watching the way their eyes followed his movements nervously.

"Don't worry, this is not for you." He tossed it again and caught it, sharp point in his hand, and offered it, handle first, to Avery.

"It is for me. I wish to die here, with my Liliya. Please." Tears gathered in his eyes again as he looked down at the floor, at all that was left of the woman he had loved and devoted himself to all of his Vampire life. He had done.

"I did everything I could to please her, everything I could to make her happy, but she never was, I was never enough for her. She used me when she had no one else, as someone that would love her when she had need and step back when she so desired. Yet, I love her still, and I always will. Please, I know I have no right to ask for mercy, but please, let me be with her. Give me release from the horrors in my head."

Avery felt Sapphire shaking behind him and turned his head to look, worried that she was scared, but instead he found her crying silent tears, tears for the man that had hurt her, attacked her and scared her. Yet, she still felt compassion, he could not deny her that.

Nodding, Avery carefully reached for the makeshift stake, not wanting to be within easy range if it had all been a ploy, yet Grigory handed it over almost gratefully, and without another word, laid down on the floor beside Liliya, his arm tucking itself under her skeletal remains as if to cradle her to his chest.

"Do it now, if you please."

Then the big man that had been the last face that Cassie and probably many others remembered seeing in their last minutes on earth, closed his eyes and lay still.

Sapphire glanced at Avery, wondering what he would do. She knew that Grigory had done bad things, but his story, it tugged at something deep inside her, making her feel so very sorry for him. She knew he deserved to die, he was right about that, but even thought they were Vampires, they were not monsters, it was only their humanity that kept them from straying down a very dark path, and part of that humanity was compassion and forgiveness towards those who had done wrong.

"Turn away, darling, you don't need to see this." Avery instructed her, but she shook her head, she didn't want to. She needed to see it. Now that Avery had the stake in his hand she felt safer, and she believed Grigory when he said that all he wanted was release.

She stepped away from the protection of Avery's body and walked over, kneeling down beside Grigory, she took his hand in hers.

The Vampire's eyes shot open in surprise.

"You honour me too much, but I am grateful for it. I must confess to being scared of what the next life will hold for me. But when I think of those poor girls, I feel I have no right to fear as they did. I go to my death willingly." Once again closed his eyes, squeezing her hand within his.

Avery couldn't believe that Sapphire had done that, but it only made him love her even more. His fingers flexed around the stake as he stood over Grigory. He watched the other man for a moment, assuring himself that she was in no danger before he knelt down beside her and grasping the stake firmly in both hands, brought the wood down firmly into the male's big chest, putting as much force behind it as he could, driving it clean through his flesh and into the ground below him.

Grigory barely twitched, but his lips parted in a sigh, one filled with regret, resignation but most importantly relief.

Sapphire held his hand as his body went limp, the last spark of life leaving his body, then she let go, because for some reason, at the back of her mind, she knew he wouldn't want her to see any more.

She laid his hand gently on top of the skeletal one of Liliya's even as his skin began to flake away, just as hers had. Amethyst had told her that the older the Vampire, the quicker they turned to dust. The rate of decomp and the amount they rotted was equal to the amount of years they had been dead, a very new Vampire wouldn't rot at all, one that was maybe five years old would make a rather nasty puddle, and so on. So, where a hundred year old body would be nothing but bones, so too would theirs, but in a very short space of time. It had taken less than two minutes for Liliya to fade away.

Sapphire couldn't look any more, she couldn't stand one more minute in this house, the dark, depressive, sadness that seemed to permeate the walls had grown more intense with the two recent deaths and she needed to get away, she also needed to feed, quite badly at this point, she felt like her stomach was beginning to eat itself.

"Let's go and find that diary then call the council, I need this day to end."

Chapter Thirty-One

Time and that evil, inconsiderate thing that they called the Sun, had both conspired against Avery and his determination to claim his Soul Mate before anything else could happen to stop him. No more exs, or even the specter of them in Sapphire's case, though he was still debating the wiseness of finding Tristian's address and paying the dickhead a little visit. No murders, no ghosts, no self doubts or misunderstandings, nothing was going to come between them again.

Apart from the fact that, despite his reputation, Avery was a gentleman through and through, and he believed in giving his female as much time and attention as possible, so that definitely didn't include rushing the most important moment of their lives. No, he would take his time worshipping her as she deserved, he wouldn't even push her to voice her desires, that could wait, they had the rest of their lives for that.

So, he waited. They got home with maybe quarter of an hour to spare before the sun rose and their death sleep hit. Just enough time to make Sapphire strip so he could check her over and put his mind to rest, seeing with his own eyes that she wasn't hurt more than a couple of bruises that would fade during the night.

He settled her in his arms and despite her protests that she was too tired, convinced her to feed before they slept, giving her body the fuel it needed to heal itself. He relaxed back against the pillows, her little fangs in his wrist as she sucked contentedly, his fingers playing with a strand of her hair, and he reminded himself, once again, that he was so incredibly lucky to have found her.

She was perfect for him, even if she didn't believe it. She saw their differences as obstacles, whereas he saw them as the thing that would make their lives even better. He knew now that he needed someone like her, someone that was a stabilizing influence on him, someone that could tame his wilder behavior, while still allowing him to be himself. He realised that if he had found the person he had been picturing all his life, someone just like him, wild, fearless and just that little bit crazy, they would have been a dangerous mix. They would have spent their days egging each other on to do more and more outrageous things, working against each other rather than clashing enough to rub off the sharp edges of their personalities until they were a perfect fit.

With Sapphire he had that. She was sensible enough to calm his more outlandish behavior, yet able to unbend enough-with a little persuading-to relax and have fun. She needed someone that would push her to enjoy herself, someone that was far enough apart from her previous partners that there was no way she could compare them. She needed someone that would, and could, prove to her that there was more to life than work and being normal. She needed someone that viewed normal as overrated and actually quite a bad thing. Someone that wouldn't be put off by her family or her rare and special gifts. And he was the one that could do all that and more.

He felt the sun begin to rise, felt it in the way his limbs grew heavy and his eyelids began to drift shut, knew that Sapphire felt it too, her draws on his wrist becoming more and more languid as her body relaxed. She withdrew her fangs and licked his skin delicately before curling closer to his side, her arm sliding around his waist, her head snuggling in against his shoulder as sleep took them.

Amethyst's fingers stroked the length of her Vampire's arm, his chest solid and warm under her cheek as they lay in bed, the excitement and worry of the night fading away as they relaxed, waiting for dawn.

It had been Tanzi that had noticed Sapphire and Avery were missing, having come in from keeping Nikos company outside. Regular patrons had been showing up all night and needed turning away, not liking the fact that their favourite bar was closed or that all Donors were under house arrest, ordered to stay inside and away from any Vampire until the killers were caught.

No one had a clue where they had gone, something Amethyst felt rather bad about. Unfortunately, she and Cassian were still in the honeymoon phase of their still relatively new relationship, at the stage where they were still discovering new things about each other every day and finding it endlessly fascinating. Cass had been telling her all about the 1666 Great Fire of London, explaining how the streets had been so different then, which buildings had been destroyed and which still stood, and because of this she had been so enthralled she had failed to notice her sister and their friend slip away. Cassian had promised her that they would be OK, that Avery would never let anything harm her, but that didn't make them any less worried as the Guild sent out an alert and they waited anxiously for news.

Cassian and Amethyst had gone with the Guild to the house where Sapphire and Avery waited, demanding to know what had happened the second the phone call had come in, one that had almost all the patrons of the club jumping up from their seats without bothering to finish their drinks. Cassian had wanted to make himself useful, but Amy had wanted to make sure that her sister was indeed alright.

It wasn't that she didn't trust Avery, but she had to see for herself. Her poor sister had gone through so much in the past few weeks that, honestly, Amy had expected her to crumble, to fold in on herself, retreating from the world into her work, something that she was known to do when experiencing an emotional upheaval that she couldn't deal with.

Yet her sister seemed to thrive. Yes, she had had a few wobbly moments, but that was to be expected for the sister that despised anything that wasn't one hundred percent normal and boring. It seemed that Avery really had been the perfect person to look after her and see her safely through her change. His fun loving, carefree attitude seemed to have rubbed off on her and led her to be more relaxed than Amy had seen her in years. And somewhere along the way they seemed to have fallen in love. Amy could relate to that, she herself had undergone such a transformation in the short time she had known her Cassian.

Nikos kept Tanzanite close all that night, feeling the anxiety and fear coming off her in waves. Someone had had to stay at the club while the others were gone, and that duty had fallen to them, though in truth it had been better for Tanzi to stay busy rather than dwell on what might be happening. She blamed herself for not looking after her sisters better, always taking the blame squarely on her shoulders even when things were out of her control.

Being the eldest of the three and having notoriously flighty parents, who, though they loved their girls unconditionally, were less likely to care about bedtimes, regular meals and clean teeth, Tanzi had become

292

something of a mother to Amy and Saph, becoming the one they always ran to with a problem and the one to protect them from the bad things in life and comforting them when they were hurt. But in the last few years she felt she had failed. First Amy had ended up in the clutches of that monster, her confidence and self belief battered so much she couldn't get away, and now that same monster had stolen Sapphire away from the life she had taken such pains to create for herself, and although Tanzi had been sure it was the wrong life, she had still let her sister choose for herself. No one should take away someone's free will.

So she had waited with Nikos, busying themselves with tidying the bar and trying very hard not to think the worst. She had almost cried with relief when they had received the call that all was well.

Nikos had packed her off home to his place, her own house nowhere near to being habitable, probably not for more than a year, though it was no hardship to have her share his home with him. He just had to make sure that no one found out, especially his parents.

Now he held her close in bed, her breathing already settled into that deep, even rhythm of sleep. His fingers stroked up and down the length of her spine as he lay there, wide awake, unable to drift off. He refused to admit to the feelings inside him that had been building steadily, growing stronger and stronger since the moment he had first laid eyes on her. He had tried to stay away but like a glutton for punishment, he couldn't help but keep going back to her. And when the dead bodies started showing up and the girls' house had caught on fire, he'd thought he had lost her forever, and the relief when he had her safe was indescribable. He hadn't thought about the consequences of having her stay, he just had to have her near. Even if that caused him a whole world of problems.

Miss Angelica and Roger were nowhere near to being able to go home and catch some much needed sleep. They had a whole heap of problems, most of them centered around the human authorities. The Detective, DCI Jacobson, who had unfortunately discovered Liliya's first victim, had not been easy to throw off the scent, even when the body had been 'misplaced' in the morgue, the wrong paperwork meaning the body of Miss Layla Jones had gone to the crematorium instead of a Mrs. Janet Howell, aged 55, cancer patient.

They had used their numerous contacts to shift evidence around various departments, had eye witnesses mysteriously forget most of what they had seen-a Vampire from nearby Hertfordshire whose talents included mind work had been very useful in that instance-still the human continued to dig.

They were just grateful that they had recovered the other victims before the human authorities had gotten wind of them. For now, they had done all they could, they would just have to keep an ear to the ground with regards to the investigation and hope that it was finally logged as a cold case and forgotten about.

They had put flags on the system to notify their informant inside Scotland Yard whenever someone looked at the files pertaining to the Layla Jones murder, and for good measure, ask him to notify them if anyone filed a missing person's report for Cassandra Ford, better known as Cassie, their ever helpful ghost friend, Melissa Evans the third victim found at the Guild's property and Gemma Bentley.

Their clean-up crew had done a stellar job in the house, taking away Gemma Bentley's body with as much dignity as possible while keeping their activities hidden from the neighbours, mind wipes having been performed on those that had noticed them. They had also taken away the remains of Liliya and Grigory, now nothing but a pile of bones, ash and accompanying clothes that was sitting in a lidded box on Vanessa's desk waiting for the Council to decide what to do with them. Vampires rarely, if ever had biological family, especially those as old as they had been. Family for Vampires usually consisted of turnees they had sired, and those 'siblings' whom shared a sire. Liliya and Grigory had none of those.

Yury, her sire hadn't been heard of in more than a hundred years and Liliya was Grigory's sire. And so, there was no one left to claim them. Their possessions would be auctioned off and split between the families of their known victims -normally in the form of some made up ancestor who had no heirs or a lottery win- and Sapphire and Avery for their part in apprehending them. There was no doubt in the Guild's mind that they would have continued killing had they not been caught.

Chapter Thirty-Two

From the memoirs of Liliya Khikov.

I am not a bad woman, I am simply one that is strong enough to fight for her rights, and my rights include keeping my male out of the clutches of certain females.

There is nothing I cannot stand more than a whore. Females that peddle their bodies to whomever pays them. Disgusting. And those that give their blood are just as bad. Donors they call themselves, bah, no matter what pretty name they give, they are still nothing but blood whores. And they are unworthy.

I never could stand a whore. The way they break up families and bewitch males into giving them what they want. Just like with my beloved Yury, the whores were taking you away from me. I will not lose another man to a Devil's

296

daughter, I will not lose another to a female of loose morals and smudged virtue, never.

I would not, could not stand for them thinking they were better than I, could not bear the thought of them touching you, their hands on your body, your fangs in their necks, it was simply too much. They had to be disposed of, it was for your own good and theirs too, for they would never find a good man of their own while they were whoring their bodies to the next available person. Such shameful behavior.

They were bewitching you with their feminine wiles, their beating hearts and warm blood, and that was wrong of them, you are a taken man, they should have more respect.

It was up to me to teach them a lesson, as no one else seemed to think that it was needed, I was the only one that was up to the task.

I'm not a bad person, I didn't enjoy ending their pathetic little lives, but they were a means to an end, they were in the way and they had to go. All is fair in love and war.

Now, there is nothing but that female to contend with. You, my poor, deluded love, are blind to her actions, to the treachery in her heart, to the way she has tried to steal you from me, I have tried to tell you, over and over, that we belong together, but you simply refuse to believe it.

I thought at first it would be simplest to drive a wedge between yourself and the female, that it would be in my best interest for her to refuse you, leaving you in need of comfort that I was only too happy to give. I tried to show her that you weren't really interested in her as you were me, that you didn't really love her. Really, I was doing her an enormous favour, letting her down gently so she would not have to suffer the pain of a broken heart like I myself had suffered so many times.

Yet she is stubborn, that little hussy that uses her lack of knowledge of our world to guilt you in to staying with her and helping her. She could not take a hint, and it was rather infuriating when, instead of dying in her home as our fire *consumed it, that Shifter saved both her and her Witch sister.*

But I will not be deterred, I can be just as stubborn and, even though my plans had not the desired result, I will not give up.

It is my job to save you from her, and from yourself.

I find that I must admit to myself that my impetuous nature is somewhat of a burden at times, one that has been known to cause me trouble in the past and has done so yet again.

This house is not the most pleasant of surroundings, in fact calling it a house is too kind, it is squalid to say the least, filthy and lacking all the comforts of the place we left behind. And yes, I know that this is my fault for being too hasty. If I had not publicly attacked the girl we would never have had to move, to hide, something Grigory is often telling me of. He does not like how I am, he does not like how I see humans and whores as disposable. They are nothing compared to us. Would anyone make such a fuss if a human killed a cow? No. Humans kill their food, I am simply doing the same.

Yet, I do regret my actions in allowing my anger to cloud my judgement at that time, something which allowed you, my dear love, to see me in a less than pleasant light. I know that it will take you a little while to understand the motivations behind my actions, but you will. You will, my love. Once I have you all to myself and you finally admit that our love is true.

Then you will understand and see that everything I have done has been for us, and that everything I will continue to do will be for the good of our love.

Cassian finished reading out loud the last entry in the diary that Avery and Sapphire had recovered from the house. They had called the Guild as soon as they found the slim leather book and within fifteen minutes, operatives were swarming the house, the next hour was a blur of activity as they sought to secure the scene and remove the bodies before dawn. It was an epic task, but they managed it.

It was the evening after the discovery of Liliya and Grigory's hide out and the subsequent deaths of the killers, and Cassian and Amethyst, along with Miss Angelica, Roger and Vanessa, had grown impatient waiting for Avery and Sapphire to appear.

Avery had given Cassian the diary the previous evening, stating that he didn't want anything that belonged to Liliya, especially not anything like that. Apparently they had flicked through it while waiting for the Guild and it had upset Sapphire a lot to read the crazy rantings within and to know just how close she had come to being truly dead. So, when Roger demanded to know what was in the diary, Cassian had taken it upon himself to read it aloud, knowing that Avery wouldn't want to hear any of it.

The Guild were impatient to talk to them about what had happened and their version of events, even though it seemed to be a pretty cut and dried case, taking into account the fact that the murderer had basically written and signed her own confession without even being alive to do it.

Amethyst couldn't believe the lengths that Liliya had gone to in her dogged pursuit of the perfect love, or her twisted version of it anyway. Amy understood doing anything for the ones you love, she would give her life for her sisters or Cassian, but she couldn't find it in her to understand just how Liliya thought she was doing the right thing by stalking men that she set her sights on and killing anyone that got in the way. It was crazy, and if there was one thing she knew, it was crazy.

She could only liken it to the way that Jason had sought to control her and everything she did, who she spoke to and how she acted. He'd claimed to love her and she actually believed it. Somehow in that twisted brain of his, he'd thought he was keeping her close, keeping her affections and love burning, when in fact he had been doing the opposite. He had been driving her away, and instead of loving her, he had been harming her, squashing the person that she was, taking away her individuality, her control of her own life. All in his own need to not lose her. You knew it wasn't true love when you thought more of your own desires than that of the other.

"So, what will happen now?" Cassian asked, conscious of the fact that the ones still very much in the middle of this were his best friend and his sister-in-law, which made for an anxious Soul Mate, something that he hated.

Miss Angelica looked at Roger, who in turn glanced at Vanessa. The Vampire simply shrugged, one of those expressive gestures that simultaneously meant everything and nothing.

Roger cleared his throat before speaking. "Well, from the Guild's point of view, now that the culprits have been eradicated, the girls are no longer in danger and so can return to their duties. We have no one to punish or bring up on charges, so once we have spoken to Mr. Avery Callow and Miss Sapphire Summerland, and arranged for the private funerals of the victims in accordance to their religious preferences, there is nothing more we need to do. Unfortunately, their bodies cannot be discovered as it would lead to questions from the human police, therefore their families cannot know anything in regards to their disappearance, although most Donors tend to be people without much in the way of close family. I believe the Council is on a similar page in that there is no punishment for them to enforce and once they have arranged for the internment of the killers remains and the distribution of their estates to the remaining families of their victims, there is little more to be done."

A quick glance at Vanessa's nodding head was enough of an answer.

"So, you'll be on your way then?" Cassian confirmed, his fingers already straying towards his laptop.

"Once we have spoken to Avery and Sapphire, yes," Miss Angelica repeated. "Though it might be in our best interests to arrange for them to call in on us at our offices rather than waiting here, I'm sure you have work to do just as we do and are anxious to get on."

Amethyst nodded as Cassian answered. "I think that would be the best idea. Sapphire especially, has been through a trying time and they might need a night to recover before they talk about it anymore."

This seemed to be taken in to consideration and after another few minutes of back and forth discussion, Cassian and Amethyst were blissfully alone.

"Do you think they're OK?" Amy asked, anxiously gnawing at her bottom lip even as Cassian drew her onto his lap and into his comforting embrace.

He laughed, a husky chuckle that never failed to raise goosebumps on her skin and send a shiver along her spine. She found herself leaning closer even though she bestowed upon him one of her best glares.

"What's so funny about me being concerned with my sister?"

He hastily held his hands up in a 'don't shoot' gesture. "Think about it, my heart."

Amy scowled, her nose wrinkling adorably as she thought about it.

"I don't know!"

He chuckled again, earning himself a half-hearted smack to his arm which he ignored in favour of pulling her closer, his nose nuzzling her neck.

"Isn't it obvious that Sapphire is to Avery what you are to me?"

"His Soul Mate you mean?"

Cassian nodded and unable to resist, he indulged in a little love nip to her throat before he continued.

"Yes, and they aren't bonded yet. Now, if Sapphire was mine, and I'd almost lost her, as I did with you, the first thing I'd be doing was making sure I never lost her again."

Her eyes widened as understanding dawned.

"Oh!, Oh, you mean they're…?"

Cass just grinned.

"Ewww."

Her response had him roaring with laughter even as he dipped his lips to claim hers. "How about I take your mind off the ewww?"

Amy smiled against his lips as she nodded,
"Yes please, I think I'm scarred for life with that vision in my head."

Chapter Thirty-Three

For once Avery awoke before Sapphire did and the first thing he did was pull her closer, even though they hadn't moved at all during their death sleep and she was still draped across his chest, he felt the need to squeeze her tight, as if making sure that she was real and whole.

His dreams had been haunted with visions of what could have been, how it could have turned out so differently if Cassie the ghost hadn't done her bit to help. In his dreams he saw Sapphire's body in place of Gemma's, saw her laying broken and bloodied, her beautiful green eyes staring sightlessly upwards. That image mixed in with one of her burnt body, surrounded by the remains of her bedroom, as dead as could be.

The thought of losing her was simply too much to bear. It would literally be like missing a piece of his heart, for that's what she was. She had quickly become his reason for living, his heart and soul. His life would be meaningless without her and he knew that he couldn't imagine even one day without her in it. He refused. He'd almost lost her too many times to count and that was going to have to stop. He wasn't sure that she felt the same way but he had to try.

Gently he shook her awake, stroking his fingers down her silky cheek until she stirred in his arms, blinking sleepily as she lifted her head to look at him.

"Evening, my love," he bent to give her a kiss, unable to resist the lure of her lips.

Sapphire smiled into his kiss, gladly accepting the affection.

"What did I do to deserve that?" she asked, only half joking.

"Just by being you." He smiled back, glad she had awoken in such a good mood. Maybe she wouldn't cut off his balls for what he was about to say next.

"I meant what I said last night, you know," his fingers slid into her hair to play with the silky strands that was almost the same exact shade as his, making it hard to tell where his hair ended and hers began when they mingled on the pillow and across his shoulder. He felt her stiffen against him and automatically began to massage her scalp with his fingertips, comforting, easing her.

"Meant what? You said a lot of things last night, we all did," her mind was racing. Did he mean that he really had loved Liliya more than he did her and that, if Grigory hadn't have killed her, he really would have gone off with her and left Sapphire behind? Much as she tried to squash them, her old doubts resurfaced, not knowing where she stood. She didn't want to be one of those clingy females that were constantly needing validation of their relationship, but with everything that had happened in the last few days, she needed reassurance more than ever.

He turned his head a little, his lips brushing her ear as he whispered the words she had been waiting a lifetime to hear.

"I meant it when I said that I loved you."

She couldn't help the tears that pooled in her eyes as she struggled out of his embrace and sat up.

"Do you really, truly, mean it?"

Avery nodded, taking her hand in his, entwining their fingers.

"More than I've ever meant anything in my life before. You are everything to me, my moon and stars. I love you more than I ever dreamed possible, and that won't ever change. I know you probably don't feel the same way but…" he was abruptly silenced with a kiss so sweet he actually sighed like some kind of girl.

"I do," she whispered against his lips. "Feel the same, I mean. I love you too." She leant back, squeezing his fingers. "I think I fell for you from the first moment you kissed me. You made me feel things that no one else ever had, and not just frustration," she gave a wry smile that he couldn't help but laugh at. "You really are the most frustrating man I have ever met, but also the most amazing. You're kind and sweet and loveable in this completely goofy way."

"Is this supposed to be making me believe that you love me?" he teased gently.

"Shut up," she whined, jostling their joined hands. "I was trying to tell you that my life is so much better with you in it, but now I take it back. You are annoying and argumentative, and you drive me crazy."

"Yet, you love me." A statement, not a question, one delivered with a smug smile so totally male that she had to laugh.

"Yeah, OK, I love you. Happy now?"

"Almost, but not quite.' He lifted their joined hands, brushing a tender kiss across her knuckles. "Bond with me. You're my Soul Mate, Saph, and I don't ever want to be without you again. I don't ever want to lose you again, to ever be without you. I want to eradicate any tiny trace of doubt that might linger between us. I want you to know, to feel, just what's in my heart."

Sapphire blinked. Then blinked again. His words sounded like they were coming from far away, like he was speaking from the end of a tunnel, yet she heard them perfectly all the same, she just wasn't sure she believed them.

"Avery the ladies man wants to commit?" she tried to lessen the tension by making a joke, yet the underlying sincerity in her question was all too clear.

She looked at him with those beautiful, forest green eyes, eyes that were begging him to not break her heart, a heart that he now knew she had given to him as fully as he had given his. He could never hurt her.

"That's exactly what it means. You and me, baby. Forever. Just us. Just as I promised before. Bond with me." He repeated his request and she was powerless to resist him.

"What does this bonding actually do? I mean, what does it consist of? What makes it so different from, for example, getting married?"

He lay back down against the pillows, taking her with him, pulling her down against his chest, waiting until she was settled, his fingers once again seeking her hair, wrapping a strand around his fingertip.

"Bonding is unbreakable. It's something that you can only do with your Soul Mate, your other half, the one that was made for you and you alone. When we bond, we connect ourselves to that person, so deeply that you will never truly be apart again. You can feel them inside you, not in some freaky way like an alien hitch hiker, but like an awareness of them and their moods. You can tell if they are sad, or happy, or hurting or feeling pleasure. You feel it like an echo. Soul Mates have no secrets from each other. They love unconditionally." His fingers strayed to the crown of her head, fisting her hair gently and lightly tugging until she looked up at him.

"Do you understand what I'm saying? The commitment this is? It's more than a simple vow that can be broken by a divorce, there is no divorce for us, you'll be mine forever, just as I'll be yours."

Sapphire understood this, had heard about it a little from Amethyst, but wasn't sure that she really believed it. The sceptic in her, the one that craved normality wasn't totally squashed and now it raised its ugly head, just to stir the doubt pot.

"What if it's wrong?"

Her voice was so quiet he barely made out her words.

"What if what's wrong?"

She really didn't want to be scared by this, and it wasn't the commitment that scared her, not at all, she knew that she loved him, and she knew that he loved her. But she had seen that love could fade, could transform into something else entirely. Something not so nice. And then they would be stuck together for eternity? That would be the worst thing she could imagine.

"What if I'm not really your Soul Mate, we bond and then, later, you don't want me anymore? You told me that vampires don't work together."

He shook his head, hating the fact that she had been so badly hurt by the male species that she could find doubt in herself even in this.

"There is never a mistake with bonding. If you aren't Soul Mates the bonding won't work. Only souls destined for each other can connect like that. Besides, you weren't a vampire when we met, and the Soul Mate magic would have known that."

Cute little wrinkles formed between her eyes as she frowned, pondering this new information.

"So, if we aren't really Soul Mates we can't bond?"

He shook his head again, "No."

"What if we're not?"

"There's no danger of that," he assured her, his fingers drifting up and down the back of her neck soothingly.

"But what if I'm not? Nothing in life is certain."

307

His fingers moved, grazing her cheek before curling under her chin and lifting her to look at him, hating the way she kept ducking her head to avoid his gaze.

"We are Soul Mates, I know this, I feel it. But, in the very *very* unlikely event that we aren't, nothing will change between us. I love you. I promise you that I'm not going anywhere."

Sapphire could hear the sincerity in his voice, the weight of the promise he made her.

"OK, we can try. But don't be all disappointed when it turns out that I'm not your Soul Mate as you think I am."

"Not gonna happen," Avery grinned. "You're mine, woman and soon the whole world will know it."

Now she was suspicious.

"Just what exactly does this involve?" For some reason she imagined him advancing on her with a big rubber stamper to mark her with the word 'mine' in big red letters across her forehead, but since her sister didn't sport such a blatant show of possession, she figured she was safe.

He shifted uncomfortably, another bad sign that he was about to say something she wasn't going to like.

"Just spit it out!" She had sat up again, not caring that she was naked, her arms crossed under her breasts, which had the unfortunate effect of lifting them up higher than they already where and thrusting them out for perusal, something Avery took full advantage of, his eyes locking on to them like a guided missile.

She snapped her fingers in front of his face, regaining his attention, thought he didn't look at all sorry to be caught openly staring.

"Talk, Callow."

"Ooh," he laughed, surprised she had used his last name like that. "Is teacher getting mad at me?"

This shocked a giggle out of her. "This isn't the time for roleplay."

"That isn't a no..." he wheedled, waggling his eyebrows in a suggestive leer. "You know it turns me on when you get all bossy, will you wear glasses?"

She shook her head, not knowing what the hell she was going to do with him. She must be losing her mind, knowing what she was getting into with him yet, wanting to run headlong in anyway. She guessed that love really did make you do crazy things, because she knew she didn't want to ever be without this man that made her laugh like no other had, someone she felt she could tell anything to and know that he would never judge her. Someone she could be herself with, totally and utterly. She sighed, yeah, he really was perfect. Not that she would ever tell him that, his head was big enough as it was.

"It wasn't a yes or a no. Though if you actually tell me about this bonding thing like I keep asking, I might make it an actual yes."

"So, to get sexual fantasies I just have to wait it out when you want to know things? I'm storing this information away for future reference, you know that, right?"

She smacked his leg where it lay under the covers, making him yelp even as he laughed at the expression on her face. Only his girl could look so fierce, glaring at him while she sat topless in bed, her hair mussed from sleep and her eyes smudged with last night's make-up. Yet, to him she looked like the most beautiful creature on earth. And she was all his. Because, despite her protests, he knew that she was his Soul Mate as surely as he knew the sun would rise. He stopped messing around, something that was hard to do, he was addicted to her laugh, to seeing her smile, something that she hadn't done enough of for most of her adult life, and something he was determined to change.

"The bonding is a multi-stage process, though it's slightly different between two Vampires, normally it's a human and a Vampire. One of the stages is recognition, that's when something inside you sits up and takes notice, this usually occurs in the form of an undeniable attraction for each other, I'm talking red hot passion. Everyone else pales in comparison to them, the most beautiful supermodel could be standing naked and you would still rather look at your Soul Mate, the other female wouldn't even register. It's thought to be so that the human can cope with the demands of Vampire sex, as we can be a little faster and stronger than a human, therefore our love making can be a little more vigorous at times."

She nodded, taking it all in as he spoke. She shifted, dropping her pissed off stance in favour of drawing her knees up to her chest and wrapping her arms around her legs, settling in like it was story time. What he didn't tell her was that this position, when naked as she was, gave him a fantastic view of one of his favourite parts of her body. He knew she would freak out if she knew she was giving him an unintended flash, so he forced himself to return his gaze to her face and not dive on her as he so badly wanted to.

"The second stage normally develops quicker with a human partner and after bonding with Vampires, and that's telepathy between couples. Not only do we share feelings but communicate without the need to speak out loud and over a far greater distance, some people might even share dreams and memories, it depends on what that couple needs really. Some are rather reluctant, some may come from a culture where Vampires are considered evil or monstrous, or they might simply not believe at all. They might have some mental or physical issues to work through and sharing memories of difficult times can help forge a closer connection and a deeper understanding of each other. This is sometimes called 'the knowing', not a brilliant name, I know, but it kinda explains it all. You just know, you know that this person is meant for you and you alone. This is the other half of your soul."

Sapphire let a little smile flirt with her lips, the idea of someone finding only her attractive, wanting only her for the rest of their lives was very appealing, as was them being her perfect match. And she actually understood what he was saying. Not understood in a 'you no speaky English' way but on an emotional level. Even as a human she had found him amazingly attractive, but her hard won control kept her safe, just by looking at him she had pegged him as a bit of a player and knew he wouldn't be good for her, so she had firmly told herself to stay away. But it seemed that fate had intervened after all, if you believed in that sort of thing, something Sapphire was finding harder and harder to deny.

"What's the other parts?"

He grinned, knowing that he had her now, she was interested, and he could practically see the cogs turning in her head as she thought things through, her logical mind was probably making a list of pros and cons and sorting things in to categories for future reference. But, just the mere fact that she was thinking about it showed that she believed that they might just be destined.

"The other stages can go in any order, usually all taking place at the same time. Both of us need to share blood, I know we've both fed from each other, but we'd need to do it at the same time. It's the sharing of our life blood that helps create the bond. It's a magical moment, literally. Sex is another part, and again, I know we've done that before but it's part of the bonding, bodies joined as we share blood, binding us inside and out. We make vows, promises to each other, kinda like wedding vows. And then, when it's the right moment, we mark each other. It's something mystical that happens, no one knows how, but wherever we touch a brand appears, signaling that this person is taken, the mark represents their partner and its different and unique to everyone, you don't know what it is until it appears."

Her eyes had grown wider the more he spoke, digesting the meaning of his words. But one thing stood out.

"Brand me? Like I'm cattle?"

She looked so indignant that he almost laughed, almost, it was more than his balls were worth to actually let it out.

He smothered it by biting his lip for a second before he felt able to continue.

"It looks more like a henna tattoo, love. Just a permanent one."

That didn't sound so bad.

"I don't know why I'm thinking about it, it probably won't work anyway," Sapphire sighed as he watched the light of excitement fade from her eyes. He'd had enough of this, time to prove to her that he knew what was in his heart, thank you very much, and that was that.

"I'll ask you again." He spoke slowly and calmly, catching her eyes. "Will you bond with me?"

Sapphire searched his face for any sign that he might be being untruthful with her, that he might not mean what he asked, but saw nothing other than the man she loved. Even if this didn't work, at least she would have tried for him. There was only one answer.

"Of course I will."

The joy on his face was wonderful to behold as he pounced on her, dragging her down to lay beside him, his lips finding hers in a bruising kiss.

Chapter Thirty-Four

Avery wanted so badly to make this perfect for her, he wanted it to be the most romantic moment of her life, something she could look back on in years to come and not feel an ounce of disappointment.

"Up," he commanded, sliding from the bed to stand beside it.

Sapphire looked confused but dutifully joined him.

"We dropped down in to bed this morning with barely a minute to spare, we spent the night in a filthy house. I thought a shower might be in order before we did anything else."

Huh, he actually had a point. Now that she thought about it her skin did feel a little grotty and a shower would be rather welcome.

"Do you want to go first?" She could be gracious when she wanted to be, even though she was now craving the feel of being clean more than anything, after all, it was his idea.

Avery looked at her like she had suddenly sprouted another head.

"I meant we should shower together."

"Oh…Oh!" She blushed, she couldn't help it. There was something so intimate about bathing together, even though they had had sex multiple times, and she wasn't sure how she felt about the idea. But, yet again, Avery didn't give her a chance to think too hard about it. He simply grabbed her hand and dragged her to the bathroom.

Sapphire was so cute. She was blushing like a nun at a Chippendales show. She kept trying to cover herself, oh she wouldn't admit it, but he knew she was, the way she stood, the way she held her hands, positioned her arms. He on the other hand was brazen with his actions, showing off his body to its best advantage.

He really had no shame. Not that she didn't admire the view, especially the way the water ran down his chest when he ducked his head under the spray…was that her hand? The one caressing his chest, following that water droplet as it snaked its way lower? Oh, look at that, it was. Now that she was touching him she found she couldn't stop.

She allowed him to tug her closer, his arms slipping around her waist as he drew her under the spray and closer to his body. His hands began their own exploration. He reached for the shower gel, getting a healthy dollop in his hands, he proceeded to make sure she was squeaky clean. And with a little encouragement she returned the favour, her hands delighting in the feel of his silky skin under them. He took his time shampooing and conditioning her hair, surprised to realise that he knew exactly how to take care of her wavy hair, though she supposed it was because his own hair was so similar to hers, just not as long.

They took their time, turning the shower into a form of foreplay, the sensual slide of their slick skin, the stroking hands that wandered to more interesting places, and the slow, languid kisses they indulged in until the water ran cold, leaving them shivering as the cooler air kissed their damp skin.

Without warning Avery scooped her up in his arms and carried her back to bed. She squealed like an idiot and begged him to at first put her down and then when he refused, please not to drop her. Like he would ever do that. He was holding the most precious thing in the world, that wasn't something you would let go of.

He laid her gently on the bed like she was made of glass and followed her down. He loved the way she immediately wrapped her arms around his neck, pulling him down for a kiss.

He went willingly, more than happy to let her dictate the pace for a while, even though he was naturally a dominant person in bed, usually moving the female exactly where he wanted them, taking the lead to make sure they both had a good time. He was content to let her tell him exactly what she wanted and how, he knew that she still wouldn't be that comfortable voicing her desires, but for now her body was doing a good enough job. He would push her another time, this time was for her. He wanted her to understand exactly what it meant to bond, to be Soul Mates, to know that she would never be alone again.

He let his hands leisurely explore her body while she took charge of their kiss. She had grown in confidence in just a few weeks, her kisses going from tentative and shy to deep and demanding. He deliberately kept his lips loose and pliant, allowing her to use her tongue to push them apart and explore his own. He didn't want to push her at this point, didn't want them to get so swept up that she didn't think about what she was doing, he wanted her to be fully aware when they bonded.

Sapphire let herself sink into their kiss, letting it overwhelm her senses until she felt drugged from the sensations. She loved the slowness of it and the unhurried

315

way that his hands stroked her skin, the tip of one finger tracing small circles on her breast, getting closer and closer to her overly sensitive nipple. He touched her like they had all the time in the world, like nothing else mattered but the two of them and she loved that, the knowledge that for the moment they were suspended in their own little bubble, the rest of the world fading away into nothing.

She felt her body slowly heating, arousal beginning to pulse through her like a steady drum beat and by the time his skilled fingers slid their way down her stomach to between her thighs she was aching and more than ready for him. He purred low in his throat to feel just how wet she was for him, his fingers easing inside slowly, seductively, making her arch closer, her hips rising in welcome.

"More?" he questioned gently, finally breaking their kiss. He wanted to make sure that she knew there was no going back from this, that this was forever.

She nodded, rolling her hips encouragingly but instead of moving to cover her as she had expected him to, he lay down, pulling her over him to straddle his waist, his hardness pressing against her damp flesh.

She blinked, surprised at the sudden position change, suddenly nervous again, she'd never made love like this, with her on top and she wasn't really sure what to do.

His hands settled on her hips, guiding her, encouraging her to lift up and take him inside. He wanted her to be in control this time, so that he knew for sure that she was understanding what they were doing, so that she had the ultimate say. He knew that the thought of a Soul Mate could be strange and even scary for someone who knew barely anything about their world and he wanted it to be her choice. But now that she was hovering above his twitching cock he had a sudden flash of fear. What if she didn't want him? What if she didn't love him as he did her?

He let out a sigh that was a mixture of relief and pleasure as she lowered herself down, her slick flesh parting to take him in deep.

"Oh!" she gasped, her mouth open in shock.

"Baby?" Was she hurt? Had she changed her mind?

Sapphire wiggled atop him, making him groan.

"You're so much deeper like this. I feel so full. Just…just give me a moment." She squirmed again, the action making his eyes cross as she ground his cock even deeper and herself against his pelvis.

Her moan, when it came out, was lust filled and deep, her pleasure obvious as she swivelled again, grinding her clit against the base of his cock. He grinned, loving the way she had quickly discovered the advantages of this position. His hands settled on her waist allowing him to lift her up a little, drawing his hips back, pulling out about half way, all he could manage in that position, and slam back in to her welcoming heat, making her cry out in pleasure.

"Ride me, baby," he whispered, not quite sure if it was an instruction or a plea.

Slowly, almost tentatively, she lifted her hips, up, up, so slowly, her slick flesh gripping him tightly as she glided up the length of his cock until he worried he would fall out, losing all contact, then even more slowly, she fed him back in, lowering. And oh, it felt so good. The exquisitely slow pace was almost torturous. She did it again, and again, and with each stroke he felt her growing confidence, the way her moves became less jerky, beginning to flow smoothly as she gradually sped up, finding a rhythm that pleased her.

Once he was sure she was comfortable, and more importantly, that she wasn't planning on stopping, he let his hands release their death grip on her hips, allowing them to glide up her sides to cup her luscious breasts. He revelled in the way they bounced in time to her movements, the perfect size for his hands, plump juicy little nipples, like pert red berries called to him, and he was only too happy to answer. He rolled them gently between finger and thumb, gauging her reaction, pleased when she arched her back, thrusting her breasts closer to his hands. He risked a light pinch, just enough to give a small, biting sting. She almost leapt off his cock, her body jerked so hard, her sharp yelp of pleasure music to his ears.

He did it again, a little harder, wringing a lusty moan from her throat. Oh, how he loved that sound, loved the way she tightened around his shaft. He gave a little bounce, urging her to move faster which she happily did. He didn't know about her, but he could feel his cock swelling, straining, heading to the point of no return and he didn't want to risk finishing before she was ready. He let one hand wander lower, using his thumb to seek out that little pleasurable nub, stroking her in slow circle. The second he touched her she reacted like she had been electrocuted, her whole body jerking, going stiff as she groaned, exactly the reaction he was looking for.

"Baby, look at me," he commanded in a low voice, taking not a small amount of pride in the fact that when she did look at him, her eyes took a moment to focus.

He gave her breast a little squeeze to get her attention.

"I love you. Are you listening?"

She nodded, her hips having slowed but not stopped, a leisurely pace that kept him just on the edge but not in immediate danger of spilling his seed.

"I vow to you, here and now, that I love you. There will never be another for me. You are my everything, heart and soul, my reason for being. I will never leave you, I will always be honest with you, even if it makes you angry, I will do my utmost to protect you and love you, for the rest of our time together. I claim you as my Soul Mate."

Sapphire's eyes prickled with tears as he spoke, the words that she knew came from his heart, and that he meant every word. Almost instinctively she answered.

"I vow to you, here and now, that I love you. I promise to always be here with you, to love you even when you are annoying the crap out of me, to not beat you over the head when you check out another girl's chest, to try to laugh with you and to always be your lover, your friend and your partner. For the rest of our time together. I claim you as my Soul Mate." She knew that the words meant a lot to him, even if she didn't fully understand the true meaning of Soul Mate, not yet, but she hoped like hell that she would get the chance to. Now that it was happening she knew she would be devastated if they turned out not to be Soul Mates.

Avery smiled, a big, wide grin that made her smile back. His one hand remained on her breast while the other left off its teasing and moved to cup the back of her neck, pulling her down for a brief kiss before he directed her mouth to his neck.

"Feed, my love."

She wasn't really feeling that hungry but distantly recalled him saying about the exchange of blood being part of the bonding process and so she didn't protest to find her mouth pushed against his throat. She let her fangs down, tracing them against his skin, then following with her tongue, encouraging his vein to rise. Then she bit down, moaning as his sweet, rich blood filled her mouth. She heard his groan, felt his hips buck as she bit, and she reacted in kind, grinding against him as he thrust. Then it was her turn to scream against his neck.

He nuzzled his nose against her skin, his own fangs lengthening. He could recall just what her blood tasted like, how it would feel to have her skin wrapped around his sensitive fangs, how she would react to his bite and now he was about to feed and make her his forever, he found himself hesitating for a second, wanting to prolong the experience. That was until she bit down and pleasure rocked through him, his cock seeming to grow even harder as he thrust, making her bounce on his lap. He let his fangs break her skin, slowly, eking out the sensations as he bit harder and sucked down his first draw.

Her blood was like none he'd tasted before, maybe because of their connection or maybe just because it was unique to her, but it was the most delicious thing he had ever had, and he'd sailed all over the world tasting every delicacy they had to offer. She was like a fruity wine, sweet and refreshing with undertones of red berries, with just a hint of vanilla somewhere in the mix, heady and decadent. He sucked eagerly, his hand sliding down her spine, nails grazing her skin, resulting in a delightful shiver, down to her ass, which he used for leverage, holding her still as he thrust hard and fast, increasing the pace.

He loved the way her gasps of pleasure were muffled against his skin, each pull of her mouth he felt echoed on his cock, like she was sucking that just as hard, couple that with the way she was squirming against him, her inner walls clenching and unclenching in the most delicious way as her whole body stiffened, her breath panting against his neck and he knew she was right there with him. He let himself go, feeling his balls tighten, drawing closer to his body as he continued to pump into her, never wanting this to end.

Pleasure, oh God, the pleasure. She had never felt anything like it. She knew that it was good with Avery, she knew that she loved feeding from him almost as much as he liked her doing it, but she thought it was more because he liked that she was eating, not because it felt like this. Now she knew why they seemed to always have a ready stream of Donors willing to open a vein and their legs. It was heaven. A quick pin prick of pain that melted into bone deep pleasure that stole her breath.

She had never felt so connected to someone. The second he bit down it was like a circuit had been completed, two wires touched together to trigger ignition. She could feel him, feel him everywhere, inside and out. She could feel the way his skin slid against hers but also on a deeper level than that, like they were connected in mind as well as body. She could feel echoes of his pleasure as well as her own and it was amazing. She knew he was about to climax and that knowledge pushed her own release to breaking point

Her whole body seized up, skin seeming too tight for her bones as she tingled all over, a great pressure building inside her like a pot about to boil over. Aching pleasure pooled low in her body as her muscles tightened around his cock as it pumped hard and fast, catching and rasping over that one spot inside her that made her see stars. It was like his lips had a direct line to her clit, making it pulse and her squirm with each draw on her throat, the sensations rolling through her were beyond description.

He gave one particularly hard pull on her throat, timed exactly with an extra deep thrust and she came hard, screaming against his flesh as she tried not to choke on his blood. She retracted her fangs and let her head fall back as she screamed again, this time from a mixture of the orgasm raging through her and the burning pain on the flesh of her breast under his hand. She tried to squirm away but he held her close, her own hand feeling warm where it rested on his chest, trapped between their bodies.

One last thrust and he exploded, holding her tight against his chest as he stilled his hips, his cock buried deep as it pumped jet after jet of seed inside her, a bellow of pure pleasure erupting from his throat as he pulled away from her neck. He felt the burning of her hand on his chest and that just intensified the power of his release, knowing that he had been right, she was his, heart and soul.

Chapter Thirty-Five

What felt like hours later Sapphire lifted her head from where she had collapsed across his chest, their bodies shuddering with aftershocks of their bonding. Avery grinned at her, his arm behind his head, looking for all the world like the most satisfied male on the planet.

"I told you so," he crowed before she even got a chance to say a word, his eyes unashamedly checking out her chest as she sat up.

She wanted to smack him, but she couldn't deny it, something had happened between them, something magical and unbreakable.

"OK, OK, so you were right. I'm your Soul Mate, happy now?"

He stretched like a cat, the action highlighting the muscles of his chest and drawing her eye to the area above his left pectoral. There, clearly marked on his skin, was the letter "S". It was beautiful, all soft lines and wispy vines with flowers around it, rather like the calligraphy letters of an old book, looking for all the world like a tattoo. And it hadn't been there before. She looked down at her palm, the hand that had been resting in that very spot but saw nothing there.

Avery looked down at his chest, his grin stretching even wider.

"Ah, now that's a beautiful mark, that is. One that I will wear proudly the rest of my days." He seemed so smug, the little shit. So confident in the fact that he had been right, and now she was stuck with him.

She was just about to ask why he was looking so pleased with himself, other than the fact that for once he had proved himself right, when the telephone began to ring from the living room.

"You should probably get that," she sighed, moving off his lap, causing him to groan as his cock slid from the comfortable warmth of her body and landed with an undignified splat on his stomach.

"I think I need to clean up again," she giggled as he heaved himself up from the bed and headed for the door.

He looked back at her, flopped out on the bed and started to laugh.

"What's so funny?" she demanded, her eyes narrowing into a glare.

"Nothing," he soothed as he took another few steps into the hall and safety before he yelled back. "Nice tits, love!" He cracked up laughing again as her scream of outrage floated after him. He was still chuckling to himself when he snatched up the still ringing phone.

"Nice what?" Sapphire puzzled, until his meaning sank in and she recalled the burning she had felt just at the crucial moment. She closed her eyes and groaned out loud, gathering her strength before she looked down and immediately screamed.

"You marked my bloody boob!" Hazy, wonderful afterglow? Forget that. She was going to kill him.

Avery chuckled to himself as he listened to everything Cassian was saying, barely hearing it over Sapphire's yelling, pleased that the Donors Guild had sorted out most of the loose ends and they could finally put Liliya and Grigory into the history box where they belonged. He agreed to go to see the Guild as soon as they were able to, then made his excuses and hung up quickly, wanting to get back to his new Soul Mate.

Sapphire glared at him from the bathroom where she was checking her chest in the mirror. He lounged against the door frame, not in the least bit troubled by her hysterics. She would get over it. Besides, he thought it was quite fetching.

"There is an anchor on my chest!" her tone was accusatory as she turned and swiped at him aiming for his shoulder.

He ducked her smack and snaked his arms around her waist, hauling her up against his chest. He dodged her flailing arms and planted a kiss on her lips, effectively cutting off any further protests before he dipped his head and nuzzled his mark that rested on the swell of her left breast, almost in the same place as his.

"You'll grow to love it," he promised, dropping a kiss on her skin. "Besides, this way everyone will know that not only are you mine, but that I'm yours." He slanted a grin her way, one that almost made her melt. He was so annoying but also so damned adorable that she couldn't stay mad at him.

"That's true," she allowed, turning in his arms to look in the mirror again, stroking the brownish red mark on her skin. "Besides, I'm always fancied getting a tattoo."

Epilogue

"Where will you go?"

Sapphire watched Cassie practically bounce around the living room like she had a fire cracker up her butt. The ghost had cheered up so much since Grigory and Liliya had died. She had apparently been hanging around in the basement, watching everything and now that they were gone she said she had seen the light. Literally. A door had opened up in front of her, appearing out of nowhere. And she had ignored it.

"Everywhere! I'm going to go everywhere. When I saw that door I knew it was the one that everyone always talks about, the light. I didn't want to go. It wasn't my time to die but I had no choice in that, this I have a choice with. I've never left England before, and now I can travel anywhere in the world. Anywhere I want to go, with no cost, no limits. Why wouldn't I want to take advantage of that?"

Sapphire nodded. "I guess that makes sense. We're going to miss you though, well, I will. Since no one else can see you or anything."

Cassie laughed, she hadn't liked not being acknowledged by anyone but Sapphire, but she had learnt to deal with it.

"I'll miss you too. But you have Avery now, you're happy, and there is a big, wide world out there that I can explore. All parts of it. Even men's locker rooms." She gave an overly exaggerated wink, making Sapphire laugh.

"It won't be forever, I'll be back to bug you before you know it."

"Promise?" Sapphire really would miss her, she had grown rather attached to the mouthy female in the short time they had known each other, she guessed that something like one dying and another finding their body helped the bonds of friendship along.

"I promise," Cassie vowed. "I had better go, long goodbyes aren't really my thing."

Sapphire nodded, at a bit of a loss what to do next, she couldn't hug a ghost, she couldn't give her a keepsake to take with her. All she could do was say her goodbyes and be there for her when she came back, if she came back, that was.

"Goodbye, Cassie."

"Goodbye, Sapphire."

The ghost faded before her eyes, growing fainter and fainter, but just before she vanished completely, Sapphire caught sight of Cassie lifting her arm, and casually flipping up her middle finger, a big grin on her face.

Sapphire laughed, she couldn't help it, that ghost was something else.